STAR WARS

MILLENNIUM
FALCON

By James Luceno

The ROBOTECH series
(as Jack McKinney, with Brian Daley)

The BLACK HOLE TRAVEL AGENCY series
(as Jack McKinney, with Brian Daley)
A Fearful Symmetry
Illegal Alien
The Big Empty
Kaduna Memories

THE YOUNG INDIANA JONES CHRONICLES
The Mata Hari Affair
The Shadow
The Mask of Zorro
Rio Pasion
Rainchaser
Rock Bottom

Star Wars: CLOAK OF DECEPTION
Star Wars: DARTH MAUL, SABOTEUR (*e-book*)
Star Wars: *The New Jedi Order: Agents of Chaos I: Hero's Trial*
Star Wars: *The New Jedi Order: Agents of Chaos II: Jedi Eclipse*
Star Wars: *The New Jedi Order: The Unifying Force*
Star Wars: LABYRINTH OF EVIL
Star Wars: DARK LORD—*the Rise of Darth Vader*
Star Wars: MILLENNIUM FALCON

MILLENNIUM FALCON

JAMES LUCENO

BALLANTINE BOOKS • NEW YORK

Star Wars: Millennium Falcon is a work of fiction. Names, places, and incidents either are products of the author's imagination or are used fictitiously.

2009 Del Rey Mass Market Edition

Published in the United States by Del Rey, an imprint of The Random House Publishing Group, a division of Random House, Inc., New York.

DEL REY is a registered trademark and the Del Rey colophon is a trademark of Random House, Inc.

Originally published in hardcover in the United States by Del Rey, an imprint of The Random House Publishing Group, a division of Random House, Inc., in 2008.

This book contains an excerpt from the forthcoming book *Star Wars: Darth Bane: Dynasty of Evil* by Drew Karpyshyn. This excerpt has been set for this edition only and may not reflect the final content of the forthcoming edition.

ISBN 978-0-345-51005-1

Printed in the United States of America

www.starwars.com
www.delreybooks.com

9 8 7 6 5 4 3 2 1

STAR
WARS®
MILLENNIUM
FALCON

THE STAR WARS NOVELS TIMELINE

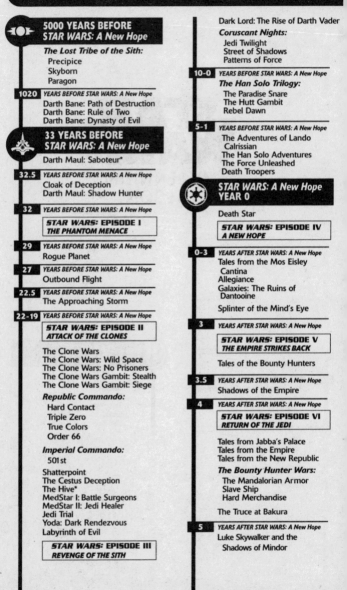

5000 YEARS BEFORE STAR WARS: A New Hope

The Lost Tribe of the Sith:
  Precipice
  Skyborn
  Paragon

1020 YEARS BEFORE STAR WARS: A New Hope
Darth Bane: Path of Destruction
Darth Bane: Rule of Two
Darth Bane: Dynasty of Evil

33 YEARS BEFORE STAR WARS: A New Hope

Darth Maul: Saboteur*

32.5 YEARS BEFORE STAR WARS: A New Hope
Cloak of Deception
Darth Maul: Shadow Hunter

32 YEARS BEFORE STAR WARS: A New Hope

STAR WARS: EPISODE I THE PHANTOM MENACE

29 YEARS BEFORE STAR WARS: A New Hope
Rogue Planet

27 YEARS BEFORE STAR WARS: A New Hope
Outbound Flight

22.5 YEARS BEFORE STAR WARS: A New Hope
The Approaching Storm

22-19 YEARS BEFORE STAR WARS: A New Hope

STAR WARS: EPISODE II ATTACK OF THE CLONES

The Clone Wars
The Clone Wars: Wild Space
The Clone Wars: No Prisoners
The Clone Wars Gambit: Stealth
The Clone Wars Gambit: Siege

Republic Commando:
  Hard Contact
  Triple Zero
  True Colors
  Order 66

Imperial Commando:
  501st

Shatterpoint
The Cestus Deception
The Hive*
MedStar I: Battle Surgeons
MedStar II: Jedi Healer
Jedi Trial
Yoda: Dark Rendezvous
Labyrinth of Evil

STAR WARS: EPISODE III REVENGE OF THE SITH

Dark Lord: The Rise of Darth Vader

Coruscant Nights:
  Jedi Twilight
  Street of Shadows
  Patterns of Force

10-0 YEARS BEFORE STAR WARS: A New Hope

The Han Solo Trilogy:
  The Paradise Snare
  The Hutt Gambit
  Rebel Dawn

5-1 YEARS BEFORE STAR WARS: A New Hope
The Adventures of Lando Calrissian
The Han Solo Adventures
The Force Unleashed
Death Troopers

STAR WARS: A New Hope YEAR 0

Death Star

STAR WARS: EPISODE IV A NEW HOPE

0-3 YEARS AFTER STAR WARS: A New Hope
Tales from the Mos Eisley Cantina
Allegiance
Galaxies: The Ruins of Dantooine

Splinter of the Mind's Eye

3 YEARS AFTER STAR WARS: A New Hope

STAR WARS: EPISODE V THE EMPIRE STRIKES BACK

Tales of the Bounty Hunters

3.5 YEARS AFTER STAR WARS: A New Hope
Shadows of the Empire

4 YEARS AFTER STAR WARS: A New Hope

STAR WARS: EPISODE VI RETURN OF THE JEDI

Tales from Jabba's Palace
Tales from the Empire
Tales from the New Republic

The Bounty Hunter Wars:
  The Mandalorian Armor
  Slave Ship
  Hard Merchandise

The Truce at Bakura

5 YEARS AFTER STAR WARS: A New Hope
Luke Skywalker and the Shadows of Mindor

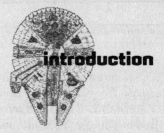

introduction

The first time Han laid eyes on her, standing with Lando on one of Nar Shaddaa's permacrete landing platforms a few short years before he had thrown in with the Rebel Alliance, he saw the battered old freighter not only for all she was but for all that she might one day become.

Staring at her like some lovesick cub. Eyes wide, mouth hanging open. Then quickly trying to get hold of himself so that Lando wouldn't know what he was thinking. Dismissing the ship as a hunk of junk. But Lando was no fool, and by then he knew all of Han's tells. One of the best gamblers that side of Coruscant, he knew when he was being bluffed. "She's fast," he had said, a twinkle in his eye.

Han didn't doubt it.

Even that far back it was easy to envy Lando all he already possessed, his extraordinary good fortune to begin with. But luck had little to do with it. Lando just didn't deserve this ship. He could barely handle a skimmer, let alone a light-fast freighter best flown by a pair of able pilots. He just wasn't worthy of her.

Han had never thought of himself as the covetous or acquisitive type, but suddenly he wanted the ship more than he had ever wanted anything in his life. After all the years of servitude and wandering, of close calls and failed partnerships, in and out of love, in and out of the

Academy, victim of as many tricks as he'd played on others . . . perhaps he saw the ship as a chance for permanence.

Circling her, fairly orbiting her, he nursed sinister designs. The old freighter drew him to her gravity, as she clearly had all who had piloted her and added their own touches to the YT's hull, mandibles, the varied technoterrain of her surface. He took the smell of the ship into his nostrils.

The closer he looked, the more evidence he found of attempts to preserve her from the ravages of time and of spaceflight. Dents hammered out, cracks filled with epoxatal, paint smeared over areas of carbon scoring. Aftermarket parts socked down with inappropriate fasteners or secured by less-than-professional welds. She was rashed with rust, bandaged with strips of durasteel, leaking grease and other lubricants, smudged with crud. She had seen action, this ship, long before Lando's luck at sabacc had made her his property. But in service to who or what, Han had no idea. Criminals, smugglers, pirates, mercenaries . . . certainly all of those and more.

When Lando fired her up for Han's inspection, his heart skipped a beat. And minutes later, seated at the controls, savoring the response of the sublight engines, taking her through the paces and nearly frightening Lando to death, he knew he was fated to own her. He would get the Hutts to buy her for him, or pirate her if he had to. He'd add a military-grade rectenna and swap out the light laser cannons for quads. He'd plant a retractable repeating blaster in her belly to provide cover fire for quick getaways. He'd install a couple of concussion missile launchers between the boxy forks of her prow . . .

Not once did it occur to him that he would win her from Lando. Much less that Lando would lose her on a bluff.

Piloting the modified SoroSuub he and Chewie leased from Lando had only added to his longing for the ship. He imagined her origins and the adventures she had been through. It struck him that he was so accepting of her from the start, he had never asked Lando how or when she had acquired the name Millennium Falcon.

chapter one

CORELLIAN ENGINEERING CORPORATION
ORBITAL ASSEMBLY FACILITY 7
60 YEARS BEFORE THE BATTLE OF YAVIN

WITH HIS SHIFT WINDING DOWN, SOLY KANTT'S GAZE drifted lazily between the chrono display mounted on the wall and a news feed running on the HoloNet. A tie score in last night's shock-ball match between Kuat and Commenor, and strife among some spacefaring folk known as Mandalorians. A lanky human with a family on Corellia and ten years on the job, Kantt had his soft hands clasped behind his head and his feet raised with ankles crossed on the console that constituted his private domain at CEC, Orbital 7. A holozine was opened in his lap, and a partially filled container of cold caf stood with two empties in the chair's cup holders. Beyond the transparisteel pane that crowned the gleaming monitoring deck moved a steady stream of YT-1300 freighters fresh off the assembly line, though not yet painted, and shepherded by a flock of guidance buoys slaved to the facility's cybernetic overseer.

Thirty-five meters long and capable of carrying a hundred metric tons of cargo, the YT had been in production for less than a standard year but had already proved to be an instant classic. Designed with help from Narro

Sienar, owner of one of CEC's chief competitors in the shipbuilding business, the freighter was being marketed as an inexpensive and easily modified alternative to the steadfast YG-series ships. Where most of CEC's starship line was regarded as uninspired, the YT-1300 had a certain utilitarian flair. What made the ship unique was its saucer-shaped core, to which a wide variety of components could be secured, including an outrigger cockpit and various sensor arrays. Stocked, it came loaded with a pair of front mandibles that elongated the hull design, and a new generation of droid brain that supervised the ship's powerful sublight and hyperspace engines.

Kantt had lost track of just how many YTs had drifted past him since he'd traded glances with Facility 7's security scanner eight hours earlier, but the number had to be twice what it was last month. Even so, the ship was selling so quickly that production couldn't keep pace with demand. Setting his feet on the floor, he stretched his arms over his head and was in the midst of a long yawn when the console loosed a strident alarm that jolted him fully awake. His bloodshot eyes were sweeping the deck's numerous display screens when a young tech wearing brightly colored coveralls and a comlink headset hurried in from the adjacent station.

"Control valve on one of the fuel droids!"

Kantt shot to his feet and leaned across the console for a better view of the line. Off to one side, bathed in the bright glow of a bank of illuminators, one of the YTs had a single fuel droid anchored to its port-side nozzle, where up and down the zero-g alley identical droids had already detached from the rest of the freighters. Kantt whirled around.

"Shut the droid down!"

Raised on his toes at a towering control panel, the tech gave his shaved head a shake. "It's not responding."

"Override the fuel program, Bon!"

"No luck."

Kantt swung back to the transparisteel pane. The droid hadn't moved and was probably continuing to pump fuel into YT 492727ZED. A form of liquid metal, the fuel that powered the freighters to sometimes dazzling speeds had ignited a controversy from the moment the concept ship had made its appearance. It had nearly been a reason for scuttling the entire line.

Kantt dropped his gaze to the console's monitor screens and gauges. "The YT's fuel cells are at redline. If we can't get that droid to detach before warm-up—"

"It should be detaching now!"

Kantt all but pressed his face to the cool pane. "It's away! But that YT's going to fire hot!" Turning, he ran for the door opposite the one Bon had come through. "Come with me."

Single-file, they raced through two observation stations. Third in line was the data-keeping department, and Kantt knew from the instant they burst in that things had gone from bad to worse. Clustered at the viewport, the Dralls who staffed the department were hopping up and down in agitation and chittering to one another without letup, despite efforts by the clan's Duchess to restore order. Kantt forced his way through the press of small furry bodies for a look outside. The situation was even worse than he feared. The YT had entered the test area for the braking thrusters and attitude jets. Superfueled, the ship had rocketed out of line, knocking aside and stunning a dozen or more gravitic droids responsible for keeping the line in check. As Kantt watched, three more freighters escaped the line. The YT responsible clipped one of them in the stern, sending it into a forward spin. The spinning ship did the same to the one in front of it, but in counterrotation, so that when the two ships came full circle they locked mandibles and pirouetted as a pair into the curved inner hull of the observation station on the far side of the alley.

As the test-firing sequence continued, the enlivened YT jinked to port, then starboard, leapt out of line, then dived below it. Kantt watched only long enough to know that all thoughts of returning to Corellia in time for dinner were up in smoke. He'd be lucky to get home by the weekend. Leaving the Dralls to bicker over how to balance the economic loss, Kantt and the technician stormed into the next station, where a mostly human group of midlevel executives was close to tearing their hair out. To a one, they looked to the newcomers for even a scrap of good news.

"A droid team is on the way," Bon said. "No problem."

Kantt gave the tech a quick glance and turned to the execs. "You heard him. No problem."

A red-faced man with shirtsleeves rolled to his elbows glared at him. "You don't think so?" His arm shot out, indicating the viewport. "See for yourself."

Kantt hadn't moved a muscle when two others grabbed hold of him and tugged him forward. The droid team had in fact arrived on the scene—a quartet of Cybot Galactica grapplers, angling for the bucking YT with clasping arms and waldoes extended. But the freighter was outwitting their every attempt at fastening to the engine access hatches. And though the line had been shut down, well behind 492727ZED a dozen identical units were heaped together where some of the displaced guidance buoys had ended their drift. Worse, the chain reaction of pileups had sent several fuel droids reeling from their respective freighters, and two of them were on a collision course.

Kantt squeezed his eyes shut, but the hellish flash that stabbed at his eyelids told him part of the story: one or perhaps both of the droids had exploded. His ears told him the rest, as gouts of molten metal and hunks of alloy began to pepper the transparisteel panel. Alarms blared throughout the monitoring stations, and streams of fire-suppression foam gushed into the alley from the semicircular structures that defined it. A collective moan of deep distress filled the room, and Kantt had a mental image of his bonus evaporating before his eyes. With it went the birthday earrings for his wife, his son's game deck, the vacation to Sacorria they'd been planning, and the case of Gizer ale he was expected to supply for the shock-ball finals party.

Kantt thought for a moment when he opened his eyes that the nightmare was over, or if not, that the explosion had reduced the unruly YT to blackened parts. But not only had the ship avoided the firestorm and flak, it had also managed to weave through the subsequent chaos and was closing fast on the sublight engine test-fire station.

Kantt gave his head a clearing shake and slammed his palm down on the console's communicator button. "We need a live crew at Alley Four sublight test fire—*now!*"

Sucking in his breath, he planted his other palm on the console and leaned forward in time to see an emergency sled nose from an up-alley vehicle bay. Little more than an engine surmounted by a cage of vertical and horizontal poles, the sled carried six wranglers outfitted in yellow EVA suits, helmets, and jetpacks. All carried assortments of cutting torches, hydrospanners, and shaped-charge detonators that hung from their belts like weapons. Kantt had a friend on the team, who like the rest lived for emergency situations. But a rogue ship was something entirely new.

Initially the sled pilot appeared to be having as much trouble matching the YT's maneuvers as the grappler droids had had. The freighter's sudden jukes and twists owed to nothing more than intermittent firings of the thrusters and attitude jets, but there were moments when the maneuvers struck Kantt as inspired. As if the ship were taking evasive action or in a race to reach the sublight engine test station ahead of its more-compliant ilk.

Dire thoughts edged into Kantt's mind of what might happen if the ship couldn't be reined in by then. Would the overfueled YT burn itself to a cinder? Detonate, taking the entire alley with it? Open a vacuum breach in the facility and launch for the stars?

Gradually, the sled pilot found the rhythm of the firings and was able to bring the skeletal vehicle alongside the YT. Rocketing from the sled, the wranglers alighted on the freighter, anchoring themselves to places on the hull with magclamps and suction holdfasts. Raised up on its stern like some unbroken acklay in a creature show, the YT refused to surrender any of its determination to shake them off. But slow and consistent effort allowed one of the wranglers to reach the dorsal hull access hatch and disappear into the ship. When he did, the execs hooted a cheer Kantt prayed wasn't premature.

Only when the ship quieted did he realize that he had been holding his breath, and he let it out with a long, plosive exhale, wiping sweat from his brow on the sleeve of his shirt. The cheering gave way to relieved backslapping and rapid exchanges as to how to get the line moving again. With waiting lists for the YT growing longer every day, production would have to be increased. Vacation leaves would have to be canceled. Overtime would become the norm.

Kantt and Bon didn't linger.

"Born of fire," the tech said as they were passing through the Dralls's station. "That YT," he added when

Kantt glanced at him. "A hero's birth if I ever witnessed one. When has that happened?"

Kantt made a face. "It's a freighter, Bon. One of a hundred million."

Bon grinned. "If you ask me, more like one *in* a hundred million."

chapter two

CORUSCANT
DURING THE BATTLE OF CORUSCANT,
19 YEARS BEFORE THE BATTLE OF YAVIN

"**Y**OU GOTTA LOVE THIS SHIP," REEZE SAID. "She knows her job, all right."

Jadak slipped the freighter in between a Corellian transport and a Santhe/Sienar passenger ship, then stood YT 492727ZED on her side to ease past the transport and continue to maneuver toward the front of the pack. Reeze muted the cockpit's enunciators so they wouldn't have to listen to the pilots and navigators who were cursing them out.

"Maybe they'll give us ownership after this run."

"We can hope," Jadak said.

"Ten years of sticking our necks out, Tobb. There should be a law."

"There should be, but there isn't. Besides, I'm just trying to help keep the galaxy on course. What's your excuse?"

"Like I told you, I want this ship to be ours."

Both pilots were human, Jadak a bit taller and twenty years younger, with a lighter complexion and a clipped beard that accented a square jaw. Reeze was graying at the temples but clear-eyed and as fit as an athlete. A traffic jam was the last thing they had expected to encounter at Coruscant, but the Separatists's attack on the galactic capital had come so unexpectedly that nearly everyone inbound had been caught up in it. Some had arrived in time to hear the HoloNet announcement of Chancellor Palpatine's abduction and witness the reversion to real-space of the Republic Cruisers that made up the Open Circle Fleet. Together with the Home Fleet crusiers, the huge *Venator*-class ships had succeeded in keeping the battle confined to the upper reaches of Coruscant's envelope. A few deft pilots had managed to spin their ships out of the fray and jump back into hyperspace. But tens of thousands of other vessels—ships of all sizes and makes and purposes—were still holding at the forward line, waiting for the battle to end one way or another, so that they could either continue on to Coruscant or flee for the Outer Rim.

"Even if they did," Jadak went on, "how could we afford to keep her running?"

"Same as we've been doing. But for the private sector."

"Gainful employment?"

"I'll settle for employment. I'm not as particular as you."

Jadak frowned. "I've known too many smugglers. That life's not what it's cracked up to be."

Reeze barked a laugh. "Neither's this one."

Jadak had brought the YT to a point where they had a panoramic view of the fighting. More slugfest than co-ordinated battle, the clash pitted the big ships against one another, crimson hyphens of annihilation pulsing among them while flights of ARC-170, droid tri-fighters, and vulture fighters buzzed about in seeming pandemo-nium. The melee's backdrop was perpetually lighted Cor-uscant itself, the planet's scintillating urban rings ravaged in places where defensive shields had been breached or ships had gone to ground. The Republic with everything on the line, and Count Dooku's Confederacy of Independent Systems with nothing more to lose than a cyborg general and an army of droids.

Reeze whistled in surprise. "Front seat on the fall of civilization as we know it."

"Not likely. But all the more reason to deliver our cargo."

"So you say." Reeze gazed out the YT's circular viewport. "I see a problem in our getting downside in one piece. A bunch of problems, actually, and the words *laser cannon* figure into all of them."

Jadak swiveled his chair. "We can't be late, Reeze. They said it's important."

Reeze returned a glum nod. "*Late* being the operative word. As in the late Reeze Duurmun."

"I'll tell everyone you died a hero."

"What—you'll survive?" Reeze stared at his friend, then laughed. "Yeah. You probably will."

Jadak swung forward. "See what you can pick up on the battle net."

Reeze tugged the headset over his ears and keyed a coded entry into the communications suite. He listened to the comm chatter for a moment, then craned his neck to study something off to starboard and brought a new view of the battle to one of the instrument panel display screens. He tapped his forefinger against the screen to indicate the icon profile of a large battle cruiser, with a stalked observation deck aft and a flyout bridge.

Jadak read the alphanumeric data beneath the icon. "What am I looking at?"

"The *Invisible Hand*."

"General Grievous's flagship."

"That's where they were holding Palpatine."

"Were?"

"The Jedi rescued him. Kenobi and Skywalker. But the three of them are still on board."

Jadak took the YT through a quick spin to improve the view. In the middle distance, a Republic Cruiser was hammering away at the *Invisible Hand*'s waist, where its elongated prow met a bulbous aft section. Maybe in retaliation for what the Republic ship had endured from the *Invisible Hand*'s flak arrays. Jadak glanced at the monitor.

"Looks like the captain of the *Guarlara* didn't get word that the Chancellor's on board."

"Could be because of signal jamming. Or maybe he just doesn't care."

Jadak scowled. "Palpatine's death would create as many problems as it would solve."

For several moments, the two men watched in silence as the *Guarlara* subjected the Separatist flagship to repeated laser cannon broadsides, blowing gaping holes in the hull and igniting fiery explosions that swept through the *Invisible Hand* stem to stern. Jadak couldn't imagine the cybernetic Grievous surviving the onslaught, let alone Palpatine and his saviors, the Force or no. When the flagship could endure no more, it listed, then fell victim to gravity and began a slow descent into Coruscant's atmosphere.

"She's dirt-bound," Jadak said.

"And already coming apart. Two to one she won't make it halfway."

"I'll take that bet."

With one hand clamped on the control yoke, Jadak tweaked the inertial compensator and shot the YT forward. No one tried to prevent them from plunging into the heart of the maelstrom. If they were hell-bent on becoming just another battle casualty, it was their business.

"We could at least try an end run, you know," Reeze said, one hand clamped to the chair's armrest.

Jadak countered it with a shake of his head. "The Seps have the rest of the planet blockaded. Our best shot's here, with the *Invisible Hand* breaking trail."

Reeze shot Jadak a look. "We're following her down?"

"Let's say, *in*."

Reeze nodded. "I'm good with *in*."

"Even if it means losing the bet?"

"Even if."

If they were to ride the *Invisible Hand*'s wake to the surface, first they had to reach her. That meant threading a path among the countless frigates and gunboats that stood in the way, dodging the fighters that continued to spill from the bellies of the KDY carriers and the curving arms of the Neimoidians' behemoth Lucrehulks, and avoiding the turbolaser fire that crosshatched near space. But they didn't doubt for a moment that the YT was up to the task. The ship had never let them down, and there was no reason to think she would fail them now.

An unknown quantity to the friend-or-foe interrogators of the warships they streaked past, the YT became a target of opportunity for one and all. Absent weapons of their own, Jadak and Reeze had to rely on the freighter's remarkable speed and near-preternatural agility. They pushed the ship for all she was worth, corkscrewing through churning clouds of fighter dogfights and executing twists and turns better left to Jedi Interceptors than forty-year-old light freighters—even one as upgraded and enhanced as the YT was. Power that wasn't being consumed by the YT's sublight engine was being gobbled up by the deflector shields, taxed by each glancing bolt the ship sustained.

Leaping out from behind one of Coruscant's crazed orbital mirrors, they raced to fall in behind the flaming deteriorating hulk the Separatist flagship had become, her blunt bow dipped toward Coruscant in a gesture of surrender, ablative shielding glowing red-hot, and sloughing pieces of armor like a monar serpent shedding scales.

"Cruiser's escape pods are away," Reeze said.

Jadak magnified the forward view of the ship. Hands vised on the yoke as the YT slalomed through a fragment cloud of parts and components, Jadak watched in awe as the warship altered vector for the planet's governmental district. The *Invisible Hand* was falling to be sure, but it was clear that someone still had the helm and was determined to guide the vessel in by deploying the drag fins and using the exterior hatches as needed to keep the ship from burning up in the atmosphere.

"Skywalker?" Reeze said.

"I doubt it's Palpatine—unless he's got talents he hasn't revealed."

Hundreds of warships too large to be annihilated by Coruscant's artillery and rocketry had penetrated the umbrella and cratered the urbanscape. But it was obvious that the standoff gunnery crews had been ordered to allow the *Invisible Hand* through, which in turn upped the YT's chances of making planetfall. All they had to do was remain close enough to the ship not to be spotted, but far enough from it not to be incinerated.

Jadak had his hand on the throttle when the entire aft portion of the *Invisible Hand* tumbled away in a mass of flaming wreckage. Only Reeze's last-moment evasive actions kept the YT from being atomized. Just as quickly, Jadak brought the freighter up on her side and barrel-rolling out of harm's way. But the hail of debris that slammed into the shields was worse than anything they had flown through earlier, and the deflectors might as well have yowled for all the alert tones the instrument panel issued.

Without warning, the YT veered sharply. Only the copilot chair's safety harness kept Reeze from landing in Jadak's lap. Status indicators flashed on the console, and another chorus of alarms filled the cockpit.

"Port braking thruster's taken a bad hit," Jadak said as he brought the YT back on course. "We'll check it out when we set down."

Reeze snugged the harness. "The eternal optimist."

"Someone in this cockpit's gotta be."

With half of the warship's mass lost to space, whoever had the controls was managing to keep the truncated forward portion on track for a controlled crash, probably on one of the old hardened landing strips in the governmental district. Repulsors howling, the YT continued to follow it down, shedding altitude and velocity. But with only twenty kilometers to go, icons began to paint the threat screen and proximity alarms wailed. Jadak saw flights of ships screaming up the well to render aid to the *Invisible Hand.*

"Fireships," Reeze said. "Couple of clone fighters, too."

"Time to make ourselves scarce."

"We've got that authorization code—"

"Better save it for when we really need it. Switch us over to terrain-following."

"Quick circumnavigation?"

"No time for that."

Jadak consulted the topographic display, then banked out of the warship's wake, main thrusters protesting and intense waves of heat assaulting them. Two of the clone fighters gave chase but ultimately peeled away to rejoin the *Invisible Hand,* which was fast approaching the landing strip.

The YT slewed west over the spaceport tower and the

Jedi Temple, then out over The Works, through columns of oily black smoke billowing from crash craters and fires that had spread into some of the outlying districts.

"Looks like the alien sectors took the brunt of it," Reeze said.

"A lot of folks have been trying to get rid of those slums for decades."

"Grievous in league with the urban renewal lobbyists?"

"Why not?"

Jadak had never seen the striated airlanes so empty. But in among the emergency vehicles and police cruisers were clone-piloted ARC-170s on the prowl for intruders until martial law was lifted. In the time it took to bring the YT about, several of the fighters had taken an interest in the freighter.

"About twenty gun emplacements have us in target lock," Reeze said.

"Open the comm."

"YT-Thirteen-hundred," someone said over the subspace comm. "Identify yourself and state your destination."

"*Stellar Envoy* out of Ralltiir," Jadak said toward the microphone. "Destination is the Senate Annex."

"The Senate is restricted airspace. If you've an authorization code, transmit it now, or turn about. Failure to comply will be met with lethal force."

Jadak nodded to Reeze. "Go ahead."

Reeze swiveled his chair and punched a code into the comm board.

"Transmitting authorization."

"*Stellar Envoy*," the same voice said a moment later, "you are cleared for the Senate Building."

chapter three

CLIMBING THROUGH THE LOW-LEVEL TRAFFIC LINES, the *Stellar Envoy* banked broadly as she approached the governmental district, which was delineated from the surrounding urban sprawl by a kilometers-deep canyon that encircled it like a moat. Some of Coruscant's most majestic towers ringed the area, rising like sandstone spires eroded over eons by wind and rain. Even deeper canyons radiated from the vaunted circle, and it was from one of these that the YT emerged, the dome of the Senate Annex dominating the foreground, the squat mushroom that housed the Senate Rotunda looming behind.

Just ahead of the *Stellar Envoy* and veering gently toward one of the annex's open-air upper-tier landing berths flew a blunt-nosed Senate speeder bus, trimmed in muted purple. The YT continued to ascend until she came even with the base of the annex, then leveled out and aimed for one of the minimal berths in the dome's lowest tier.

Jadak engaged the braking thrusters and repulsors, but the ship came down hard on her port-side landing gear despite his best efforts.

"We've gotta repair that jet," he said.

"I'll see to it."

Reeze shut down the engines, and the two of them unstrapped from their seats. Entering the narrow corridor that linked the outrigger cockpit to the freighter's circular core, Jadak palmed the control pad that lowered the starboard boarding ramp. Pinging and steaming sounds rose from the ship as they walked down the ramp, an alloy carry case dangling from Jadak's right hand. The *Stellar Envoy*'s whirring exhaust fans stirred the stale air.

The berth was dimly lit and empty of the load-lifter droids common to the upper tiers. Two beings in colorful Senatorial robes hurried forward to greet them. Des'sein was humanoid; Largetto, anything but. Both represented beleaguered worlds distant from the Core.

Off to one side stood a Kadas'sa'Nikto Jedi, whose long brown overcloak and tall boots made him appear even taller than his actual two meters. Clawed hands crossed in front of him; a lightsaber was clipped to his belt. He nodded gravely to Jadak. His gray-green face had the look of tanned leather. A toolbox of some sort rested at his feet.

Des'sein was the first to reach Jadak. "You have it?" he asked in a rushed voice, while Largetto glanced about nervously.

Jadak raised and proffered the carry case. "It's all in here. Everything you asked for."

Des'sein accepted the case and placed it atop a small table, his knobby fingers shaking as he worked the lock; Largetto leaned over him in anticipation. Opening the lid, the Senators activated a device inside the case and listened intently for a moment. Blinking lights reflected in Largetto's glossy black eyes.

Des'sein closed and locked the case and took a stuttering breath.

"This will prove of great value to our cause, Captain Jadak."

Largetto nodded in agreement. "Frankly, Captain, we feared that you wouldn't be able to land."

"You can thank the code you provided."

"You're being too humble. The code didn't pilot the ship."

Jadak inclined his head in a show of thanks.

A third Senator dashed into the landing bay from a doorway in the rear. A human with a bib of white beard and a topknot of dark hair, Fang Zar was breathless when he spoke.

"The Chancellor has been returned to us unharmed." He glanced at the Jedi. "Your confederates survived as well, Master Shé."

The small horns surrounding the Jedi's eyes twitched, but he said nothing.

"Chancellor Palpatine and his party arrived just ahead of Captain Jadak."

"The speeder bus," Reeze said from behind Jadak.

"Martial law has been rescinded," Zar went on. "And Count Dooku is dead."

Largetto grabbed hold of Des'sein's upper arm in excitement. "Then perhaps we won't have to act on the data Captains Jadak and Reeze have taken such pains to deliver."

"May the Force be with us," Fang Zar said.

"Yes. But we must carry on until such time that we can be sure of the Chancellor's intent." Des'sein looked at Jadak. "We have another assignment for your consideration."

Jadak and Reeze traded brief glances.

"We're all ears," Reeze said.

Des'sein lowered his voice. "We would ask you to deliver the *Stellar Envoy* to our allies on Toprawa."

Jadak's brow knitted. "Deliver?"

"Just so," Largetto said. "The Antarian Ranger who will take possession of the ship is called Folee. You will find her in Salik City, which is the capital of the western regions. Your code phrase is: *Restore Republic honor to the galaxy.* Will you repeat that for me, Captain?"

Jadak's mouth had fallen open. He closed it and swallowed hard. "Restore Republic honor to the galaxy. But . . . this Folee, she's taking the ship?"

Des'sein regarded him. "Is there a problem?"

"It's just that we've grown, you know, kind of fond of her," Reeze said. "I mean, couldn't we maybe buy the *Envoy* from you and find another ship to deliver to Toprawa?"

"Impossible," Fang Zar said. "The *Stellar Envoy* is crucial to this mission."

Jadak tightened his lips in restraint. "If we're leaving the *Envoy* . . . does that mean you're retiring us, too?"

"Not at all, Captain," Des'sein was quick to say. "Unless, of course, that is your wish."

"No," Jadak said. "But Toprawa's a long jump on the Hydian Way. I'm just wondering how we're supposed to return to the Core."

"We'll furnish you with sufficient funds for transport. More important, we'll have a better-behaved ship waiting for you when you return."

"Perhaps a faster one, as well," Largetto said.

"Not likely," Reeze muttered.

Jadak swallowed the lump that had formed in his throat. "I hope this mission's worthy of her."

"Oh, it is, Captain," Fang Zar said. "We assure you."

Jadak blew out his breath and nodded resignedly.

Des'sein studied him for a moment. "May I take your gesture to mean that you're willing to execute the mission?"

Jadak looked to Reeze. "We wouldn't want anyone else to do it."

Des'sein turned to Master Shé, who lifted the toolbox

and headed for the YT's boarding ramp, his brown over-cloak dusting the permacrete floor.

"Master Shé needs to modify the ship slightly," Fang Zar explained. "But his work won't affect your flight."

Jadak watched the Jedi disappear into the ship. Then he turned back to Des'sein. "What phrase will Folee use to identify herself?"

Des'sein blinked in short-lived confusion. "Oh, I see. No, you're mistaken, Captain. She is expecting you. The phrase we've provided you is a mnemonic aid she will need to carry out her part of the mission."

"Mnemonic," Jadak said.

"A memory shortcut," Largetto said. "Folee will understand. And the *Envoy* will handle the rest of it."

Jadak rarely asked questions about his assignments, but curiosity got the better of him. "The *Envoy* has been programmed—"

"Think of the ship as a key," Fang Zar said. "The key to a treasure."

Jadak waited.

"A treasure sufficient to restore Republic honor to the galaxy," Des'sein said finally.

Senate Intelligence Bureau Director Armand Isard was scanning the crowd that had welcomed Supreme Chancellor Palpatine when his comlink chimed. The speeder bus had berthed moments earlier, and the Chancellor and his handpicked party were moving down the red-carpeted colonnade toward the atrium turbolifts. In passing, Isard noted that Jedi Skywalker had lingered behind to speak privately with Senator Amidala.

A muscular man who had a talent for going unnoticed in a crowd despite his height, Isard was dressed in an unadorned gray uniform. His black hair matched the luster of his knee-high boots. Leaving the red carpet for the relative solitude of the tier's forest of ornate columns, he depressed the comlink's accept button and glanced down at the device, whose small screen displayed the face of the bureau's assistant director.

"I just wanted to alert you to a little confab that's transpiring in one of the lower-tier berths," the assistant director said.

Isard's dark eyes continued to track the movements of the welcome committee. "Go on."

"Senators Des'sein, Largetto, and Zar have taken possession of a carry case delivered by the pilots of an old YT freighter."

The three Senators were well-known members of the Delegation of Two Thousand, a loyalist coterie opposed to the strong measures Chancellor Palpatine had enacted since the start of the war.

"Jedi Master J'oopi Shé is also present."

"Technical division?"

"That's the one."

Isard walked while he spoke. "Interesting that they should be holding a private meeting while several of their cohorts are up here."

"Which ones?"

"Danu, Malé-Dee, Eekway . . . the usual bunch. Do you have audio of the meeting?"

"No. Countermeasures were taken. But we were able to snake a snoop-cam through the landing bay's intake vents, so we have acceptable video."

"The carry case . . ."

"Too soon to know what it contains. Our people are working on cleaning up the surveillance feeds."

"Do we have anything on the couriers?"

"Nothing yet. The freighter carries a Ralltiir registry, and is owned by a company called the Republic Group."

"That could be telling."

"I thought so, too. The pilots transmitted a valid authorization code to Senate Airlane Control."

Isard paused at the edge of the stark atrium, where the Chancellor and the others were awaiting a turbolift. The area was filling fast with Senators who had emerged from the shelters and wanted to offer their congratulations to Palpatine. Isard found the lack of security appalling. Fierce fighting had occurred in the vicinity of the annex while Palpatine had been held prisoner, and it was possible that the Separatists had infiltrated flesh-and-blood or droid assassins. Yet here Palpatine was, acting as if he'd only been out for a stroll, a pair of Republic guards his only protection. But that was typical of him, despite the strain it placed on the Intelligence Bureau. Typical of him, too, to admit only loyalist senators to the docking berth, in full knowledge of their growing impatience with the sweeping changes he had made, the liberties he had revoked. Palpatine had at least agreed with Isard's suggestion that the media be held at bay for a while longer.

Isard thought about the clandestine meeting. The Senators were harmless, but he didn't like the idea of a Jedi being present. Members of the Order had been doing more than their usual share of snooping about of late. Eavesdropping on Senate sessions, investigating old tunnels that ran beneath The Works and the subbasements of 500 Republica . . . It had to stop.

"Send a squad of shock troopers to disrupt the meeting," he said, "with orders to hold the Senators for questioning."

"What about Master Shé?"

"Supply a credible pretext for the intrusion. Senate security concerns, a bomb threat, whatever you need. Shé will keep out of it."

"And the couriers?"

"Charge them with possession of a stolen security code, impersonating emergency personnel, and violating restricted airspace." Isard paused, then said, "I'll see to their interrogation myself."

"It should hold," Jadak said into the mouthpiece of his headset from beneath the YT's port mandible. "But we might want to pick up a replacement on Kuat before heading to Toprawa."

Reeze was crouched inside an access bay at the tip of the mandible, evaluating the braking thruster from the inside. His response came through the earphones. "You don't have to twist my arm."

Jadak gave the damaged jet another look. Wiping lubricant from his hands, he walked around the bow of the ship and nearly collided with Master Shé as he was hurrying down the boarding ramp. The installation apparently completed, the Jedi had the toolbox in one hand, an activated comlink in the other.

"Shock troopers have been dispatched to arrest the Senators," he said, without slowing down. "I will lead them to safety. Raise the ship and be quick about it." He stopped a few meters from the ramp, then turned. "Good luck, Captain."

Halfway up the ramp, Jadak waved a casual salute. "Thanks for the heads-up." He brought the headset microphone to his mouth and commed Reeze. "Company's coming. Haul yourself out of there."

Reeze was climbing from a hatch in the main hold when Jadak entered.

"Clones?"

"Shock troopers."

Reeze scowled. "We're not being paid enough."

"Noted."

"Especially now that they're taking the ship."

"We knew this could happen."

"That doesn't soften the blow."

"How 'bout we have this conversation later?" Jadak

extended a hand and yanked Reeze up onto the deck plates. "Do a readiness check and get her warmed up. I'm going to see about delaying them." Moving to the engineering station, he pulled a small blaster from a compartment below the console.

Reeze planted his hands on his hips and laughed. "I'm sorry, Tobb, but that's the funniest sight I've seen in a long while. That toy against a couple of DC-fifteen blaster rifles?"

Jadak frowned at him. "I'm not planning on a stand-off. I just want to slow them down."

"I guess you can try." Reeze laughed again as he made for the cockpit.

Jadak raced down the ramp and hurried to the landing bay's rear door. Taking aim, he sent a bolt directly into the door controls, stepping back while sparks and tendrils of smoke erupted from the switch, and the smell of fried circuitry stung his nostrils. Broader and taller, the cargo door was a vertical hatch in the bay's west wall. Rearming the blaster, Jadak fired two bolts into the control, one of which sizzled past his right ear in sibilant ricochet. He was hastening back to the ship when gauntleted fists began to pound on the exterior of the frozen hatch. Amplified—though muffled by the durasteel door—the voice of a shock trooper rang out.

"Senate Security! Raise the hatch and move to the center of the bay with your hands above your head. Make no attempt to flee."

A smile of satisfaction was just taking shape on Jadak's face when he heard noise from above. A blade of white-hot light was tracing an arc through the ceiling. Taking the boarding ramp in long strides, he skidded into the connector, ducked into the cockpit, and threw himself into the pilot's chair.

"You tell them to go away?" Reeze asked, eyes on the status displays.

"I toasted the door locks, all right. But they're rappelling through the kriffing ceiling!"

Reeze glanced at him. "They want us that badly?"

"We're not waiting around to find out."

Jadak was strapping in when sounds of impact issued from the *Envoy*'s roof. Above the modulating whistle of the warming engines came the throaty rasp of a cutting torch.

In a rush Jadak enabled the repulsorlifts. The YT was a few meters off the floor when blaster rifle bolts began to sear into the hull.

"Bork them!" Reeze said.

Jadak grabbed the yoke and whipped the *Envoy* through a rapid about-face, trusting that centrifugal force would hurl the clone soldiers from the hull. A trooper in red-emblazoned armor flew past the cockpit viewport, arms and legs flailing.

Reeze winced. "That's not going to earn us any points with them."

Without a thought for approaching traffic, Jadak took the ship hurtling out of the landing bay.

chapter four

"I HAVE THEM," ISARD SAID INTO THE MIKE SECURED TO the short collar of his uniform. Standing at the rim of the speeder bus berth, he traversed the macrobinoculars to keep the fleeing YT centered in the visual field. Far below him, the freighter dived into the broad cleft opposite the Senate Annex.

"Captain Archer's ARC squadron will take up the pursuit," the assistant director said through the comlink.

"What about Fang Zar and the others?"

"Gone by the time the shock troopers entered the bay. Someone had to have tipped them off."

Isard lowered the macrobinoculars and hurried down the red carpet toward the atrium. "We'll see to them in due time. Right now that freighter is our priority."

"Disable or destroy?"

"Archer's call. Have a forensics team standing by to retrieve the bodies and pick through the wreckage if it comes to that."

Blaster bolts nipping at her stern, the YT dropped from the high ground, nearly colliding with a speeder bus that was making a stately approach to one of the upper-tier berths. Whizzing from around the east curve of the annex dome flew a pair of speeders with front-mounted repeating weapons. Jadak pushed the yoke forward, plunging the *Envoy* into one of the canyons that radiated from the Senate circle. Cutting through traffic lanes, he tilted the freighter up on her side, then completed a rollover and clawed for the sky. The speeders were soon a memory, but the *Envoy* hadn't ascended to the penthouse levels of 500 Republica when the threat-assessment board began to chime.

"V-wings and ARC-one-seventies," Reeze said. "Count five . . . six, seven. Closing from our four and nine."

Jadak nudged the throttle and pulled the yoke into his lap, fomenting chaos in several midlevel airlanes as the YT executed a vertical climb of several hundred meters, ahead of her own sonic boom, the threat board hollering all the while.

"More ARCs."

Jadak glanced at the instrument panel's main screen. Heat-shedding S-foils parting into attack position, the pursuit ships were flying full-out, laser weapons and proton missile launchers coming alive.

"Has the blockade been lifted?"

"Just," Reeze said, twisting the comm's selector dial and listening through the headset. "Ships are dispersing from the holding patterns. Most of the incoming traffic has been routed to Sectors Thirteen through Twenty."

Jadak changed vectors, slewing widely to the east and calling more power from the engines. The displays told him that the clone pilots had second-guessed him. The closest of the Advanced Recon fighters sent a flurry of warning bolts across the *Envoy*'s bow.

"Well, they mean business."

"Told you you were too rough on them back in the bay."

"Angle the front deflectors and keep an eye out."

Up ahead flew the vanguard vessels of a kilometers-wide swath of ships eager to reach their destinations at long last. Escorted by police vehicles and V-wing fighters, the ships were evenly placed and descending in measured speed. Jadak took the *Envoy* directly into their midst. Moving against the traffic flow and weaving his way through the pack, Jadak came close enough to some of the ships to see the startled expressions on the faces of the humans, humanoids, and aliens behind the canopies. And clearly the pilots didn't have as much trust in Jadak's ability as Jadak had in himself. Like a school of fish discombobulated by the sudden appearance of a predator, ships were suddenly diverting from their courses, doing what they could to avoid accidents but in many cases slamming against nearby vessels and initiating chain reactions of collisions. Trying in vain to match speeds with the *Envoy,* the ARC-170s kept to the perimeter, holding fire for fear of hitting innocent ships. But the pack was thinning before the *Envoy* had even reached the upper limits of the atmosphere, and the ARCs were climbing at high boost.

"Reallocate power to the rear shields," Jadak said as the *Envoy* parted company with Coruscant's gravitational field.

Local space was littered with debris—the smoking husks of Republic and Separatist warships, blackened pieces of annihilated fighter craft, shards of fragmented orbital mirrors. There was no sign of the Trade Federation and Commerce Guild ships that had survived the battle, but the cruisers of the Home and Open Circle fleets were still defensively deployed in the event the Separatists decided to have another go at Coruscant.

Reeze muttered to himself while he listened to the battle net. "Ships of the line have been alerted. We're designated an enemy target."

Jadak shoved the throttle home. But instead of trying to distance them from the giant, arrow-headed KDY ships, he brought the YT as close to the tightly arrayed Republic cruisers as he dared, running the hulls, darting from one clear space to the next, using the ships for cover in an effort to get far enough from Coruscant to make the jump to lightspeed. But the ARC-170 pilots hadn't given up the chase and were no longer worried about innocent parties. The deflector shields of the big ships were more than capable of warding off stray laser cannon bolts.

The *Envoy* was rocked by the first volley.

Jadak twisted the ship up on her starboard side, as if showing her belly to the pursuit ships. "We've gotta protect that port thruster—"

A deafening sound erased the rest of it, and a tangle of blue energy gamboled over the instrument panel. The cockpit lights and telltales blinked, then flickered back to life. Jadak slammed his hand against the ceiling to motivate the few systems that refused to come back online.

"Light turbo from the *Integrity*. They're coming about to tractor us in."

"You've got the yoke."

Jadak swiveled his chair to face the Rubicon navi-computer and entered a request for jump data.

"We can lose the V-wings," Reeze said, "but those ARCs have Class One-point-five hyperdrives. They'll follow us to Hell and back."

"Then Toprawa's out. We've got to throw them off the scent."

"Where, then?"

Jadak looked over his shoulder at Reeze. "Nar Shaddaa's our best option."

A follow-up bolt from the *Integrity* dazzled the *Envoy*.

"Any port in a storm."

Jadak waited for the Rubicon's go-to and reached for the hyperdrive lever. The stars had not yet become streaks when another powerful boom rattled the YT to her bones. The freighter didn't so much jump into hyperspace as get kicked into it.

*   *   *

They spent most of the hyperspace journey crawling through the ship's innards assessing the damage and effecting what repairs they could. The energy weapons that had caught them aft at the moment of the jump had dazzled the sublight engine. After conferring, they decided that they could nurse the ship into orbit around Nar Shaddaa by relying on the attitude and braking thrusters.

They returned to the cockpit for the remainder of the journey through the netherworld of hyperspace, neither of them speaking. Reeze broke the long silence.

"What do you think the Jedi installed?"

Jadak swiveled his chair, gazing around at the instruments. "No idea."

"You didn't think to ask?"

"Why would I?"

Reeze didn't respond immediately. "You know, we could just keep going. Repair the ship at Nar Shaddaa and light out for the Outer Rim."

"We could. But we're not going to."

Reeze snorted. "Mission always has to come first. Even when it involves surrendering the ship."

"The Senators are playing their part, we're playing ours. With any luck, it's all going to come out right in the end."

"But this thing's about over anyway, isn't it? With Count Dooku dead. You heard what they said. They might not even need us anymore."

Jadak mulled it over. "I'll tell you what, Reeze. If it does end by the time we reach Toprawa, I'll think hard about doing what you say."

Reeze sat up straight in the chair. "So you *are* mad at them—for giving the ship away, I mean."

Jadak finally looked at him. "Let's leave it at disappointment."

Reeze grinned. "Disappointment's good."

"You're ready to celebrate, huh?"

"Why not? It's been a lot of years, Tobb."

"It has. But don't go getting your hopes up."

"How could I with you around?"

Jadak smiled without showing his teeth. "So, Nar Shaddaa. Your old stomping ground."

"Ha! You mean the ground where I frequently got stomped."

The Rubicon navicomputer toned, and Jadak swung the chair around.

"Reversion coming up."

They fell into an uneasy silence while the ship emerged into realspace, stars and starfields taking shape after a moment of wake rotation, the *Envoy* shuddering and groaning, running on pure momentum now.

"That wasn't too bad," Jadak started to say—when the ship suddenly died.

Reeze began to toggle switches in the blackness. "No power of any sort. No lights, no communications. No response from the emergency systems."

Jadak watched Nar Shaddaa grow larger in the viewport. "That blast must have rattled the power core."

"Any way to bleed velocity manually?"

"There might be if we had time. As it stands, we're going to go wherever Nar Shaddaa dictates we go."

Back to toggling switches, Reeze cursed. "Any chance of inserting into orbit?"

"Hard to say." Jadak unstrapped from the seat and stood, leaning toward the viewport. "At this speed and vector . . . we could end up slingshot back into space. I'm more worried about traffic coming up the well."

"You should be," Reeze said. He had a pair of macrobinoculars pressed to his eyes. "I've got a visual on a ship." He fell silent, then said: "Oh, brother . . ."

Jadak peered at the enlarging ship. "What is it?"

Reeze lowered the binoculars. "Corellian bulk freighter—one of the big Action jobs. Large enough for a payload of Hutts with room enough for a herd of banthas."

Jadak grabbed the binoculars and raised them to his eyes. A rounded rectangle with a gargantuan V-shaped undercarriage, the freighter was driven by a trio of cylindrical engines. "She's climbing right into our path. Accruing speed for a jump. Their instruments will warn them."

"Warn them?" Reeze looked at Jadak in disbelief. "This is Nar Shaddaa. Who bigger, who better? We're like a mote in her eye. She won't yield."

Jadak watched the huge ship rise from the planet's envelope.

"Your call, Tobb," Reeze said after a long moment of silence.

Jadak gave the power toggles a final flick and blew out his breath. "Okay. We're outta here."

They hurried aft to one of the escape pods, which would be fired from the freighter's ventral surface, well below the hyperdrive and sublight engines. Reeze climbed in first and popped the cover that sealed the manual release switch. Jadak squeezed through the circular hatch and sealed it behind him. Reeze had just pulled the override lever when the *Envoy* gave a sudden start and the inside of the pod was bathed in red light.

"She's back online!"

Jadak's eyes were wide. "Now you wake up? *Now?*"

A whoosh issued from the sublight engine, and the YT veered abruptly, as if to avoid a collision, sending Jadak and Reeze slamming into the pod's curved wall.

An instant later they were spiraling through space.

chapter five

NAR SHADDAA
18 YEARS BEFORE THE BATTLE OF YAVIN

Viss and Heet came through the door to the waiting room and walked directly over to where Bammy was sitting.

"All right, mechanic. He'll see you now."

Bammy Decree knew Viss from school, before Viss had been expelled and taken a job as one of Rej Taunt's bodyguards. Bammy knew Heet, too. After Bammy's short stint at tech school, he'd worked on some of Heet's skimmers and sloops.

Bammy started for the door the two bodyguards had come through, but Viss stuck an arm out to hold him back and Heet threw him a bathrobe.

"He's taking a massage and a steam," Viss explained while Bammy stared blankly at the robe. He motioned with his chin to a small refresher off to one side of the waiting room. "You can change in there."

Bammy was a head shorter than Viss and Heet and fifty kilos lighter, and because most of the beings who came to visit Rej Taunt were closer to the size of the bodyguards, the robe fell off Bammy's narrow shoulders and trailed on the floor when he emerged from the 'fresher. He cinched it around his frame the best he could while two Klatooinians seated in the waiting room tried to keep from laughing.

Viss pointed to Bammy's balled-up clothing. "Leave those in the 'fresher and follow us."

Beyond the door, Rej Taunt's villa was even tackier than the waiting room, crammed with bric-a-brac of the sort that filled Nar Shaddaa's junk emporiums. But while only ten years older than Bammy, Taunt was an up-and-coming crime boss with a taste for the finer things. Bammy didn't doubt that Taunt would one day be living as lavishly as a Hutt.

Bammy followed his bulky former school acquaintances through several enormous though empty rooms, across a courtyard adorned with foliage imported from Ithor and columns from Coruscant, and down several broad stone stairways to a gaming room piled high with decades-old ovide wheels, sabacc tables, and dance cages. Half a dozen humans and aliens were busy at cleaning tasks. Bammy hadn't seen a droid since he showed himself to the front gate scanner two hours earlier.

Viss rapped his huge hand against the jamb of an old wooden door and someone opened it from the far side, clouds of steam wafting from the room beyond. The supersaturated heat struck Bammy like a ton of permablocks. The steam was so thick he couldn't see his pointed nose in front of him, and in seconds sweat was streaming into his eyes and dripping from his small chin. He was moving his hand in front of his face as if to part the steam when a deep voice boomed from somewhere in the mist.

"Over here, mechanic."

Bammy followed the sound to where Rej Taunt was lying supine on a table, rolls of water-storing fat avalanching off his naked torso, his thick arms being massaged by three comely human females. An Askajian,

Taunt was the eldest son of a family of tomuon cloth traders. He had come to Nar Shaddaa as a child and never left.

Taunt gestured to the adjacent massage table. "You want a rub?"

Bammy started to decline but the crime boss cut him off. "Of course you do. Doff the robe and set your skinny human body on the table. I've already instructed my fems not to make fun of you."

Bammy did as instructed. At twenty standard years old, he was already in poor shape, but he was certain the trio of masseuses had seen worse in their line of work. If nothing else, his body was absent the blaster scar tissue and elaborate tattoos common to most of Taunt's employees. Flat on his stomach, Bammy discreetly lowered the robe to the floor. The fem's slick hands felt good on his tense shoulders, he had to admit.

"The only reason I agreed to see you," Taunt said, "is because Viss and Heet recommended you. They say you've got talent."

"We were in school together," Bammy said. "For a while, anyway."

Taunt heaved himself over onto his massive belly. "They mentioned something about a ship."

"Word in the depths is that you're looking for one."

"For once the rumor is correct. What have you found me?"

"An old YT-Thirteen-hundred."

Taunt turned his head so he could look directly at Bammy. "Now what would I want with a freighter?"

"It's not just any freighter. It has a great pedigree."

"What year?"

"A 'twenty-five."

"Before Synch?"

Bammy nodded. "A classic."

Taunt did the mental calculations. "Now I've got to

ask: what would I want with a freighter forty standard years old?"

"You're looking for something low-profile but powerful, easy to maintain, and fuel-efficient."

"For the moment let's say I am. When could I see it?"

"It, uh, needs some work first."

Taunt's silence told him to continue.

"It was involved in a collision a month or so back."

Taunt's eyes narrowed. "You're not trying to sell me on that YT that slammed into the *Jendirian Valley Three*?"

Bammy swallowed audibly. "I am."

Taunt exhaled hard, steam swirling about. "What I heard, they had to scrape the pilots off the *Valley*'s hull."

"I heard the same. They ejected in a pod, but the YT spun at the last instant, and the pod was flattened."

"Ouch."

"That's probably half what the pilots said."

"And the YT?"

"It was hard hit. But the beauty of those ships is that they're pretty much made to come apart. Best of all, no other salvagers are interested in it. It's just drifting out there with all the other ships that haven't made it downside for one reason or another."

"Maybe that's what's best for it—and for Nar Shaddaa. Our own little asteroid field."

"It would have to be rebuilt bow-to-midships," Bammy went on, "but most of the core is sound. The sublight can be repaired, and the hyperdrive can easily be rebuilt or upgraded."

Taunt thought about it. "A freighter? I don't know. Can it be turned into more of a passenger ship?"

"Would you be piloting?"

Taunt laughed heartily. "Do I look like a pilot?"

"I was just thinking about seating and such."

Taunt raised himself up on one elbow. "I'd want a

couch and bunk suitable to my frame, and others for companions I might choose to bring along. I'd want to keep some areas for freight, but I want comfortable cabin spaces and secret compartments for whatever I may wish to conceal from the prying eyes of customs officials. I don't particularly care how the ship presents—it can look beat-up on the outside. In fact, the more dilapidated it looks, the better. But the interior has to be clean and tidy."

Bammy was nodding and grinning. "Again, that's the beauty. It can be configured just about however you want. For instance, if you want weapons—"

Taunt cut him off with a sharp wave of his hand. "Nothing like weapons to draw the attention of pirates. Maybe a couple of small repeaters tucked into the bow for emergencies. But I'll bring support craft if I anticipate major trouble." He thought for a moment. "The serial number, drive signature, and registry can be altered?"

"Can do. Of course I'd leave the name for you to choose. If you want, I can equip it with a transponder that will keep interested parties confused."

"Even those new Imperial ships?"

"Even those. So far we're managing to stay one step ahead of the Emperor's techs."

"How much is all of this going to cost me?"

"I don't have a final figure yet. I have to have it brought down the well. Then there's the parts . . . Assuming the power plant and sublights are reparable, the biggest cost will be the hyperdrive, if it needs one."

Taunt rolled over onto one side. "Get back to me when you have a firm price."

A recording droid keeping pace with him, Bammy took stock of YT-1300 492727ZED, which at some point during her forty-odd years had acquired the name *Stel-*

lar Envoy. His booted feet sloshing through lubricant puddled on the floor, he was practically yelling to be heard over the racket of servowelders and cutting torches, power hydrospanners, grinding wheels, and power washers. The more closely he inspected the wrecked ship, the more his distress mounted. The job that was supposed to be his first real break was instead in danger of becoming a catastrophe. How was he ever going to stick to the price he had quoted Rej Taunt? Where did he even begin?

Conveyed downside to his small garage in the Duros Sector, what remained of the Corellian-made ship hung in a cradle in the center of the bay. Bammy hoped that one day he'd be able to afford a repulsorlift, but until then he had to make do with cranes and gantries to support the vessels he repaired. He had hired a crew of salvagers to remove the twin mandibles, outrigger cockpit, and whatever else was loose or ruined. That left him with a crumpled saucer. The seven legs that formed the landing gear had fused to the carapace when the YT had skidded along the hull of the *Jendirian Valley III* before slamming into the underside of the bulk freighter's armored deck.

The ship was in much worse shape than he had been led to believe by the EVA team that had performed the initial zero-g assessment. Bammy had already filled a dozen oversized trash containers with hazmat debris, and he was just getting started. A YT-1300p that had collided with an asteroid near Nal Hutta would supply replacement mandibles, along with a more-spacious main hold, deflector shield generator, and a pair of six-being escape pods. But while the *Stellar Envoy*'s hyperdrive, Quadex power core, and still-state-of-the-art Rubicon astrogation computer were sound, the pair of Giordyne sublight engines would have to be rebuilt from top to bottom.

Worst of all, the ship needed a new droid brain.

"Boss, where do you want this?"

Bammy cupped a hand to his ear and whirled to one of his subordinates. "Shut that kriffing torch off!" Swinging back to the Iktotchi who had called to him, he asked, "What have you got?"

"Fuel drive pressure stabilizer."

"Serviceable?"

The horned alien rocked his head. "More or less."

"Which is it, more or less?"

"More."

Bammy indicated a pile of numbered and categorized parts near the stern of the suspended ship. "Stow it over there. And be sure to brand it."

The pile was one of many, the garage resembling an ongoing archaeological restoration project more than a ship rebuild.

While the Iktotchi was hauling the stabilizer across the bay, the voice of one of Bammy's pair of human employees rang out. "This flux compensator is shot. Same with the alluvial dampers."

"You can't fix them?"

"Not me."

Bammy's shoulders slumped. "Add them to the list."

He hoped one day he could afford to hire a Givin or a Verpine.

The situation was going from bad to beyond belief. But at least his full complement of mechanics was back on the job after a month of joining the rest of Nar Shaddaa in celebrating the end of the war. Nar Shaddaa had no special fondness for now-Emperor Palpatine, but many felt that Palpatine would be so consumed with consolidating power in the Core that worlds in the Mid and Outer Rims would once more become lucrative markets for spice and other proscribed goods. More important, smugglers would be able to travel without fear of interception or attack by Separatist droid ships or Republic cruisers.

There'd been no club or cantina partying for Bammy. Rej Taunt was expecting a ship, and it was best to avoid disappointing a crime boss by failing to deliver on time or superseding an estimate.

Bammy looked up at the saucer's singed stern. The blackened areas were carbon scoring—the result of a turbolaser hit from a big Republic ship. He couldn't be sure, but he'd stake credits that the hit had been indirectly responsible for the collision. The bolt could have overwhelmed the shields and left the guidance systems stunned. Once he tore apart the power core, he'd know for certain—but it was clear the freighter had gotten herself mixed up in trouble. It was clear, too, that Bammy wouldn't be the first mechanic to rebuild her. In all his years of tinkering with ships and landspeeders, he had never come across a vehicle hosting as many aftermarket parts. It was as if every owner of the YT had patched, upgraded, or retrofit the ship one way or another. And aftermarket parts weren't going to fly with someone like Rej Taunt—at least not those parts that would be plainly visible. Bammy was confident he could get away with using parts fabricated in Nar Shaddaa's shops for the comm and illumination systems, but he couldn't chance Taunt running independent checks on the life-support and computer systems. That's why the droid brain was problematic. Repairing the existing one was out of the question, and buying a new one would eat up what little profit he still hoped to make on the job.

He had tasked his newest employee—a young kid named Shug Ninx—with searching out someone with a line on a replacement brain, and it was the human–Theelin who entered the garage just then and hurried over to him.

"I might have found us a brain," Ninx said, flushed with excitement.

"Where?" Bammy started to say, but he stopped when he spotted a familiar figure saunter into the bay. Swinging back to Ninx, he shook his head in disappointment. "Kid, going to him was a bad idea."

The blue in Ninx's mottled complexion intensified. "I didn't know—"

Bammy put a hand on Ninx's shoulder. "Don't worry about it. Maybe it'll work out in our favor."

A Koorivar with a pronounced cranial horn, Masel was known on the Smugglers' Moon as a fence, an arms dealer, an opportunist who had worked for both sides during the war. A naturally sibilant tone complemented his deviousness.

"Your young half-breed tells me you're in need of a ship's brain."

Bammy steered the Koorivar to a cluttered table in a corner of the bay and motioned him to a chair. "Since when are you in the business of ship parts? I thought you only dealt in weaponry."

Masel's shoulders shrugged under his rich cloak. "Nothing's changed. Except in this instance, I may have something you can use."

Bammy compressed his lips. "I'll listen, anyway."

"I've contacts among the crews dismantling the Separatist fleet. I can get you a targeting and fire-control brain off a tri-fighter command ship."

Bammy scoffed at the idea. "Converting that to serve a YT freighter would take an expert slicer and way more credits than I can afford."

"I know that," Masel said. "But I have someone who will do the conversion for you. All you need to do is supply schematics of the ship."

Bammy thought about it. "I already have the schematics, direct from Corellian Engineering. But how much is this going to set me back?"

"Less than half of what a factory-warranteed Hanx-Wargel Superflow would run you—even at wholesale."

"You guarantee it?"

Masel smiled. "Of course I will. A full refund if there's any problem."

"A refund?" Bammy laughed. "You're gonna have to resurrect me if my client has any problems with it."

"Resurrection is the provenance of others. I'm only a simple profiteer."

Bammy thought some more. "How soon could I have it—assuming I decide to trust you?"

"A week after you hand over the schematics and a down payment of half the cost."

Bammy was still grappling with it when he returned to the YT. The Iktotchi was waiting for him under the starboard-side docking ring, a small module resting on his thick, grease-stained forearms.

Bammy's expression went from pensive to quizzical.

"I extracted it from the droid brain," the Iktotchi said. "It's the freighter's flight recorder."

Instead of returning to his apartment in Nar Shaddaa's Corellian Sector, Bammy remained at the shop, downloading data from the Hanx-Wargel Superflow IV computer. Registry information, ownership, and flight and service records. His interest piqued by what he discovered, he spent most of the night cross-referencing the data with HoloNet entries, and by morning had compiled what amounted to a brief history of the ship, which had been known by many names over the decades.

YT 492727ZED had come off Corellian Engineering's production lines at Orbital Facility 7, and for the first twelve years of her life had been one in a fleet of more than eight thousand ships owned by Corell Industries. CI Limited ferried goods to the so-called Five Brothers of the Corellian system, as well as to the enormous and enigmatic repulsor known as Centerpoint Station.

In numerous accounts by pilots who had flown the YT-1300, the freighter was alternately praised for her speed and maneuverability and condemned for her quirkiness and unreliability. Often the pilots employed terms more suited to describing the personality of a sentient being than to evaluating a ship's performance. As her several names suggested, the YT was obedient or willful, a joy to pilot or a demanding demon, a savior or a troublemaker. Where *Corell's Pride* had "heart," *Fickle Flyer* had "issues." *Meetyl's Misery* was a constant source of despair. Entry after entry detailed accounts of dazzling maneuvers, close calls, or unexpected and often baffling breakdowns. *"Made the run to Tralus in record time . . . ,"* one pilot recorded. Another said: *"Marooned five hundred k from Selonia with a load of defrosting plak fish . . ."* *"Beat the* Fusion Flame *hands down in a race around Drall . . ."* *"Unable to launch from Centerpoint . . ."*

So went the litany of testimonials and denunciations, with each instance of malfunction ending in makeshift repairs and retrofits, almost as if everyone had agreed to make the ship the subject of an ongoing experiment in improvised engineering.

To satisfy his curiosity, Bammy searched out the shoddy pulse generator a pilot had been forced to install; the place where a navigator had taken out his frustration on the Fabritech transceiver relay with a hydrospanner. He found dozens of areas where the ship had been similarly bruised and battered. A few pilots had gone so far as to scratch or torch epithets on the bulkheads or in the maintenance access crawl spaces.

The ship's history was equally eccentric.

For most of the dozen years that CI Limited had owned the YT, the company enjoyed continued growth and placed high on the list of the top investment opportunities in the Corellian system. Then business began to take a dive, thanks in part to actions by the monopolistic Trade Federation, which at the time had been devouring one small shipping concern after the next. Inaction by the complacent Republic Senate hadn't helped. In the years before Chancellor Valorum's first term of office, CI Limited's profits took a woeful slide. Eventually forced to sell its fleet of swift ships at rock-bottom prices, the company fell into bankruptcy and finally went belly-up.

YT 492727ZED was one of the last ships to go, sold to an enterprising pair of freelance traders named Kal and Dova Brigger. Siblings, the Briggers renamed the ship *Hardwired,* and for a brief period took over where CI had left off, moving whatever freight they could find between Corellia and other worlds. By Bammy's calculation, all their profits must have gone into upgrading the ship's hyperdrive, which had made for easier travel to Corellia's neighboring systems and, eventually, to the Core. The freight they carried began to change as well, from consumer goods to light arms, munitions, and similar contraband.

According to HoloNet entries, the Briggers's illicit dealings brought them to the attention of the Smugglers's Confederacy of the Cularin system, and ultimately to the attention of the organization's leader, Nirama, who loaned the siblings enough credits to have the YT further upgraded in exchange for their pledge to refrain from doing business with slavers. When after only a standard year the siblings reneged on the deal, Nirama put a price on their heads. Half the reward was collected by a celebrated bounty hunter who captured Dova and returned her to Nirama, who in turn had her executed.

Dova's surviving brother, Kal, renamed the YT *Wayward Son*, changed the registry to Fondor, and lit out for Thyferra, hoping to find work for Iaco Stark's Commercial Combine. A former smuggler himself, Stark headed a group of pirates, bounty hunters, and assassins working the Rimma Trade Route, but he'd allowed his ambitions to get the better of him and found himself in the midst of an armed conflict with the Republic over stolen shipments of bacta. Kal suffered an even worse fate for involving himself with Stark, having been eaten alive in an abandoned spice mine on Troiken by carnivorous insects loosed after an attack by Republic forces.

Fifteen or so years after the crisis on Troiken, the YT had become the property of the Republic Group, about which the HoloNet had very little to say, though the organization was linked in byzantine ways to holding companies on a host of important worlds, including Coruscant, Alderaan, and Corellia. Once more the registry had been changed—to Ralltiir—and the ship had been renamed *Stellar Envoy*. The flight recorder detailed frequent trips to far-flung worlds like Ansion and Yinchorr, and the Superflow IV recorded upgrades to the freighter's communications suite and hyperdrive.

For a short time, the ship may even have been piloted by a Jedi Master named Plo Koon. Pure speculation on Bammy's part, based on a holoimage he had uncovered completely by chance. Taken shortly after the debacle on Troiken, the holoimage showed Jedi Knights Plo Koon, Qui-Gon Jinn, and Adi Gallia standing in front of a YT-1300 that might have been the one Kal Brigger had flown.

The pilot who had flown the *Stellar Envoy* for the Republic Group was a human named Tobb Jadak.

It was close to sunrise when Bammy came across the entry, but the discovery gave him a second wind. He knew the name, and a HoloNet search confirmed his hazy recollection of the fact that half of Nar Shaddaa's gamblers had lost money on Tobb Jadak, as a result of his losing a swoop race he'd been favored twenty-to-one to win. Rumors abounded that the Hutts had forced him to throw the race, but also that Jadak, through intermediaries, had bet heavily on himself to lose. Whatever the truth, Jadak's ignominy hadn't prevented the Republic Group from hiring him to pilot their ship.

The flight recorder indicated that Jadak and his copilot had jumped the YT from Coruscant, where she had almost certainly been damaged during the battle there, only to collide with the *Jendirian Valley III* as the mammoth ship was departing Nar Shaddaa.

Only a kid at the time, Bammy wasn't one of those who had lost credits by wagering on Jadak. Still, death by collision seemed a cruel fate for a guy who had once been a prizewinning swoop racer and pilot. Then again, the universe rarely played fair with winners or losers.

chapter six

"REVERTING TO REALSPACE," THE PILOT SAID OVER the YT's intercom while Rej Taunt and the Gossam were sipping drinks in the main hold. "Entering the Tion Cluster."

"No need for undue concern," the long-necked alien said, taking note of Taunt's worried expression.

"I'm not comfortable with bugs—any of them. Not even Neimoidians, and they're almost humanoid."

"The Colicoids will be easily appeased by our cargo," the Gossam said in his most assuring voice.

Taunt said nothing in a definite way.

The Gossam's name was Lu San. A longtime Nar Shaddaa resident, he had spent two years in an internment camp on the Smugglers' Moon at the start of the war, but, like several other members of his species, he used the time to establish contacts among the criminal underworld, and was already reaping the benefits of that education.

"Your ship is a marvel," Lu San added after a moment, clearly hoping to put Taunt at ease.

Glancing around him, Taunt nodded. "A thing of beauty."

During the walk-through of the rebuilt freighter, Bammy Decree's enthusiasm was so contagious that Taunt hadn't even bothered to have the mechanic's work double-checked. Instead he'd relied on the word of his pilots, who had taken the ship on test flights to Nal Hutta and Ylesia, and pronounced her a wonder.

And she was.

Renamed *Second Chance* and bearing a Nar Shaddaa registry, the YT concealed enhanced sublight and hyperdrive engines and sophisticated sensor and communications suites. Refitted with new mandibles and cockpit, the saucer had been twisted back into shape and cleaned up but left to look its age, with fresh paint and duralloy only where needed, while the interior now sported a spacious main hold, a small galley, a refresher, and a private cabin for Taunt, with a bunk sized to his bulk and smaller versions for guests. It would take an expert eye to detect that the ship was now a composite of a 1300f and a 1300p. For a relative beginner, Decree had done a superb job and more important, had known better than to delay completing the work or add to the price he had quoted.

Taunt was so eager to try out the ship that he had accepted a job from a Black Sun Vigo he might otherwise have turned down. If only it hadn't involved dealing with bugs . . . But Taunt had long had his eye on furthering his reputation as an earner with the Black Sun leadership, and the chance to do that had offset some of his initial revulsion.

And fear.

Black Sun was finally recovering from an attack thirteen years earlier by an assassin who had executed the cartel's head honchos, including the flamboyant Alexi Garyn. During the war, several Vigos had attempted to assume leadership, but plans to align with the Hutts in controlling the flow of the specious healing agent bota had backfired and left Black Sun in shambles. Lately, though, there were signs of reorganization under the guidance of Dal Perhi and a Falleen crime lord named Xizor.

It was one of Perhi's lieutenants who had approached Taunt with the job and put him in contact with a Koorivar named Masel, who had recommended using Lu San as an intermediary with the Colicoids. Masel was one of a new breed of information brokers born out of the ashes of the war and the birth of the Empire. One day soon Palpatine's navy of Star Destroyers commanded by flesh-and-blood officers disgorged from the Imperial Academies would rule all space. But until then there were credits to be made by taking advantage of what the war had left in its wake. Many would miss the Jedi Order, but no one Taunt knew. The Empire was already better armed than Black Sun and other enterprises, but at the very least, Palpatine's proxies could be dealt with turbolaser for turbolaser rather than turbolaser against the force.

The *Second Chance* carried no major weapons, but the cargo holds were packed with what Taunt hoped would prove even more effective in dealing with the insectoid Colicoids: fifty metric tons of flash-frozen eopie meat.

The chitinous, carnivorous hive-minded designer-manufacturers of the tri-fighter, destroyer, and sabotage droids that the Separatist conspirators had purchased in mass quantities to hurl against the Republic had decamped from their native Colla IV at the end of the war and immigrated to worlds in the Tion Cluster, among other places. Most of their deadly inventions had been deactivated, but many of their self-modeled droidekas had been acquired by security companies operating in the Corporate Sector, and some of their other innovations had found their way onto the burgeoning black market. Among them were containerfuls of the melon-sized Pistoeka disassemblers known as buzz droids, which Black Sun had decided were perfectly suited for work in Nar Shaddaa's vehicle and vessel chop shops.

Taunt hadn't had personal dealings with the Colicoids, but he knew fellow criminals who had, back when the insectoids had attempted to assume control of Kessel's spice trade and had sought to take over a spice factory on Nar Shaddaa, only to learn the hard way that a former slaver would prove to be more deadly than they were.

"It's something about their posture," Taunt said, his anxiety triumphing over his pride in the *Second Chance*. "I can stomach Ruurians, Kamarians, even a Geonosian or two, but there's just something about their . . . *concavity* that makes them seem more aggressive." A shudder passed through him. "I'd feel safer sleeping with an Anzati."

"They *are* more aggressive," the Gossam said. "And your . . . how should I put it? Your healthy corpulence is bound to excite them to hunger."

Taunt's eyes widened. "Don't tell me that."

Lu San smiled pleasantly. "That's why the quadruped meat must be off-loaded before we make an appearance. Beyond its purpose as barter, the eopie will distract and placate them long enough for us to conduct and conclude our business. The tactic worked well for the Trade Federation when it placed its initial order for droidekas."

"But Neimoidians begin life as grubs. There's common ground."

Lu San waved his small hand in a dismissive gesture. "The Colicoids are well known to feast on even their own kind."

Taunt's ample mouth twitched. "Ever see one of them ball up—like the droidekas?"

"Once only," Lu San said. "In the presence of a hueche—their onetime predator on Colla Four."

"Couldn't we have gotten one of those, just in case?"

"The Colicoids are thought to have eradicated them. Perhaps from a cloner if there had been time."

Taunt stood up and paced across the main hold. "What else do I need to know?"

Lu San's bulging, saurian eyes tracked him. "Protocol dictates that you keep your chins down."

Taunt, who had almost as many rolls of fat under his mandible as the pregnant females of his species had breasts, pressed his chin against his upper chest. "Like this?" he managed to say.

"That will do. What's important is that you refrain under any circumstance from showing your neck."

Taunt shifted his gaze to Lu San's spindly, ring-encased neck. "You're not worried?"

The Gossam indicated himself. "Not nearly enough meat on my bones."

"You'd better hope."

Staggering through the ring corridor while the *Second Chance* raced away from the Tion planetoid at full speed, Taunt tried in vain to get control of himself. In his years on Nar Shaddaa, he had witnessed the brutal executions of collaborators and betrayers; he had seen would-be defectors fed to rancors, and traitors tortured at the hands of droids programmed for sadism. But he would be lucky to erase the Colicoids from his memory.

Emerging like a sudden plague from the burrows that hollowed the planetoid, slavering while the rapid-thawed and microwaved eopie meat was being off-loaded from the ship, tearing into it with such abandon that blood misted in the thin air and collected like dew on Taunt and Lu San, Viss and Heet as they deboarded the ship . . .

The Colicoids were so stimulated by the feeding frenzy, Taunt was certain that he and his entire party would be ripped limb from limb and consumed live before Lu San could close the deal for the buzz droids.

Somehow, though, the Gossam had made it happen, and the spherical droids had been moved with due haste into the same holds that had held the meat. But then poor Viss, lost in the effort of loading the cargo, had stretched out his neck to work kinks from his shoulders and the feeding frenzy had recommenced. Half a dozen of the barbarous insectoids pounced on him and stripped his bones of meat and flesh faster than Taunt could comprehend . . . Taunt tucking his chins against his chest the whole while, and Lu San, poor Lu San, ineffective in preventing the tragedy and paying dearly for it when he tried to intervene. Smelling the sudden fear coming off him, the Colicoids had sliced and diced the Gossam like raw filleted fish, indifferent to whether he constituted a meal or a snack, and not a scrap was left behind.

Taunt shuddered.

Two circuits through the ring corridor and he was still shaking uncontrollably. Two more and he finally began to calm down, the YT gaining speed and distance for the jump back to Nar Shaddaa.

That they had come away from the horror with their cargo intact was nothing short of a miracle. The sabotage droids were piled a meter high in the cargo holds—unsecured and rolling around like ball bearings in a duratin can—and a Colicoid Creation Nest computer sat in the number two hold, capable of tasking them for their eventual chop-shop duty.

Lumbering into the main hold, Taunt lowered himself onto the acceleration couch, waiting for the pilot to announce that the ship was ready to make the jump to lightspeed. But when after too long there was no word, he called forward.

"What's the delay in going to hyperspace?"

The response was a worrying moment in coming. "The navicomputer says that the hyperdrive isn't responding. I'm going aft to check it out."

Taunt cut his gaze to the cockpit connector in time to see the copilot hurry into the ring corridor. Before he could lift himself out of the couch, a cry of surprise echoed forward.

"The buzz droids are activated! They're disabling the entire ship!"

Bammy Decree's face filled the engineering station's main display, his expression a mix of confusion and deep concern.

"Pistoeka sabotage droids? But how—"

"I bartered for them," Taunt cut him off. From all directions came the sound of the droids chattering to one another and the *Second Chance* being taken apart. "I'll explain later, but right now we need to know how to deactivate them before they undo every system on the ship!"

"Did the deal include a control computer?"

"Yes, yes!"

"Then can't you just shut it down?"

"It is shut down! We never activated it."

"Then how—"

"And the navigator's telling me that the droids are mainly reversing all the work *you* performed! Like they're trying to return the YT to factory specs. How can that be?"

"The work I did?" Decree fell silent for a moment, his jaw unhinging slightly. "Did anyone help you broker this deal?"

"The Koorivar—Masel. But what's that have to do with anything?" Taunt didn't bother to wait for a reply. "Is this because of some component you installed? Some aftermarket part? I warned you, Decree, no aftermarket parts!"

Decree squeezed his eyes shut, then opened them wide. "You've got to bring the Pistoeka control computer online. Instruct your engineer to have the computer task the droids with reverting to their standard programming."

"Did you get that?" Taunt yelled over his shoulder.

"I'm on it," the engineer told him.

Taunt returned his gaze to the display. "What else, Decree?"

"Then you've got to jettison them—every last one of them. Can you do that?"

"Can we do that?" Taunt shouted to no one in particular.

"It'll take a while, but we can do it."

Taunt expelled his breath. "Decree, this had better work. If not, there won't be a planet remote enough for you to hide on."

Decree swallowed and nodded. "It'll work."

"What do we do about the damaged systems? The kriffing droids have torched their way into nearly everything!"

"Have your engineer inventory the damage. I'll get hold of the parts you need and find someone with a fast ship. I'll repair everything personally."

"Get started on gathering parts. I'll contact Nar Shaddaa and set you up with a ship."

Decree looked sheepish. "I, I—"

"Save it," Taunt said, and ended the communication.

Big hands shaking, he stood to his full height. He would have to come up with an explanation for the Vigo, as well as credits enough to pay for the eopie meat and the cost of the trip. The fiasco. He wasn't sure just how long he had been standing at the engineering station when Heet hurried into his peripheral view.

"The droids are shut down. Naath is below, getting ready to jettison them. But they did a lot of damage, boss. Comms up and running, but we've only got the sublight drive."

Taunt nodded absently. "Help is coming. Have a list prepared of everything needed to repair the hyperdrive."

"Will do."

Heet no sooner moved off than the voice of the pilot rang out from the cockpit. "Boss! You'd better get in here. We've got a serious problem on our hands."

Taunt whirled from the engineering station and thundered through the connector into the cockpit, nearly slamming his head on the hatch's low head jamb. The pilot indicated two glinting shapes in the center of the viewport.

"Imperial Navy. One of the older *Acclamator*-class assault ships, with a Destroyer escort." The pilot looked at him. "Do you think they've had their eye on the Colicoids? Could they have observed the deal go down?"

Taunt worked his jaw. "Even if they did, they're not going to find any evidence of it."

The pilot touched the earphones of his headset. "They're comming us. They want us to power down and submit to an inspection." He glanced at the viewport. "The escort's vectoring for intercept."

Heet squeezed into the cockpit behind Taunt. "The droids are jettisoned."

"Good," Taunt started to say, then stopped himself, all color draining from his face. "Decree had us retask the droids to their original programming."

Heet stared blankly.

"Their original programming is to disable Republic vessels!"

The three of them swung as one to the viewport.

A choice epithet flew from the pilot. "The escort's flying right into their midst!"

"Warn them away!" Taunt said. "Tell them we have a radiation leak!"

"*Overseer*, this is *Second Chance*," the pilot said into the mike. "It would be better if we came to you—But—But—No, that's not the case—It's—" Turning to Taunt, he said: "They suspect a trick. They're threatening to open fire."

For a moment, Taunt couldn't get his vocal cords to work. "How much time until the escort reaches the droids?"

The pilot brought a magnified view of the ship to one of the displays. You didn't have to be a technical whiz to grasp that the spherical sabotage droids were already maneuvering toward the escort.

"They're penetrating the deflector shield. Attaching!"

Taunt stumbled backward into the copilot's chair, which nearly collapsed beneath him.

The cockpit fell eerily silent, except for deliberate tones issuing from the communications suite. Then, without warning, an explosion blossomed in front of the YT and nova-bright light flooded through the viewport.

In the early days, there wasn't a sacrifice he wouldn't make for the Falcon—*even if that meant flying halfway across the galaxy risking his and Chewbacca's lives to rescue a man from prison in exchange for equipping the YT with an upgraded guidance system, a new rectenna, and a hyperdrive that would allow the ship to make 0.5 past lightspeed.*

The trip to the Corporate Sector was the first real voyage he and the Wookiee had made with the Falcon, shortly after he had won it from Lando at Cloud City. The first of their grand adventures. The idea had been to visit Klaus "Doc" Vandangante, an outlaw tech who knew better than just about anyone how to get the most out of a ship. The problem was that Doc had gone and gotten himself arrested and imprisoned in Stars' End on Orron III, and Doc's gorgeous blond daughter, Jessa, had made Doc's rescue part and parcel of the agreement to upgrade the Falcon.

Doing that had required having the Falcon masquerade as the brain of an ungainly barge, which had so slowed the jump to Orron III that he and Chewie were practically at each other's throats by the time the cumbersome vessel emerged from hyperspace. But the tedious journey had left him feeling proud of the fact that he was in some way responsible for having rescued the old freighter from a life of such duties. In the same way the Falcon had saved him from a life of having to pilot gaudy ships for the Hutts and other degenerates.

Over the years, as the sacrifices he made for the ship had mounted up, he came to think of himself as bound to the Falcon as surely as he was bound to Chewie and, later, to Leia. All the chances they had taken together, all the danger they had put themselves through, all the sacrifices they had made for each other.

chapter seven

ALLANA SOLO SAT ON THE RIM OF THE MAIN HOLD maintenance access, her thin legs dangling over the edge of the open hatch.

"Tell her to try it now," Han called from somewhere deep in the innards of the ship.

Allana cupped her hands to her mouth and turned toward the cockpit. "Grandma, he says to try it now."

A moment later the *Falcon*'s sublight engine loosed a whining groan but failed to come to life. In the compartment Han muttered a barely inaudible truncated curse.

"One hundred and eighteen," C-3PO said from behind Allana, who shifted slightly to look at him. "This is the one hundred and eighteenth time since it has been my privilege to serve aboard the *Millennium Falcon* that this very same event has occurred. Or events of a similar nature, I should say."

Allana smiled. "That's a good thing."

The protocol droid cocked his head to one side, as if he hadn't quite heard her. "I'm not certain I take your meaning, mistress."

" 'Cause Grandpa has always fixed it."

A pained yowl erupted from the compartment.

"Perhaps," C-3PO said. "Though not without requisite contributions of Captain Solo's flesh and blood."

Leia appeared from the cockpit connector, smiling at Allana, then stroking the seven-year-old's long red hair she settled down beside her on the rim of the hatch.

"Grandpa and his shortcuts."

"I heard that," Han said. "You're going to blame me for an uncharted gravity sink?"

"I can't very well blame the sink, Han."

"Yeah, well, it could be worse. We could have been drawn directly into it."

Leia had learned long ago that things could always be worse. Still, the sink had yanked the *Falcon* from hyperspace with such force that the power core had shut down, leaving the ship in danger of being drawn ineluctably into the sink, and certain catastrophe.

"That seems to be exactly what's happening, darling."

Han's head and shoulders emerged from the hatch, a lopsided, mirthless smile on his face. "Always looking on the bright side. That's why I've kept you around all these years."

She returned the look in kind. "I love you, too."

Han scowled and disappeared back into the compartment.

Sighing, Allana stood up and walked to the dejarik table's semicircular bench, humming to herself and gazing around. "Grandma, how long do you think we'll be here?" she said finally.

"Not long." Leia stood up and joined her at the hologame table. "What's a family outing without an unexpected twist or two?"

Allana nodded, mostly for Leia's sake, and Leia watched her go into self-entertainment mode, humming once more and touching this and that.

She was a remarkable child; precocious to be sure, but adventurous and infinitely patient, and Leia felt as close to her as she had to Anakin and Jacen, and continued to feel to her and Han's surviving child, Jaina. Allana was actually the daughter of Jacen and the Hapan Queen Mother, Tenel Ka, but that was a secret known only to a select few. Allana was known to most as Amelia, a Hapan foundling adopted by the Solos following the tragic death of Jacen, who by then had assumed the Sith title Darth Caedus. Or the tragedy that Jacen had become. Which was it? Leia frequently wondered. That he had died at the hand of his twin sister made it all the more unbearable. But try as she might, Leia could not purge her memory of those dreadful years.

I will always miss you, despite what you became.

As Tenel Ka's daughter, Allana was Chume'da—heir to the throne—of the Hapes Consortium. But after what Jacen had put the child through, and out of fear that her true paternity might one day be discovered, Tenel Ka wanted her removed from danger, as well as from political intrigue of the sort that was commonplace in the Consortium. And so Allana's death by a strain of targeted nanovirus had been faked, and Han and Leia had assumed custody of her. More, they had embraced her, and felt blessed by every moment she spent in their company.

The original plan had called for the Force-sensitive Allana to attend the Jedi academy, which had been relocated to Shedu Maad, near Terephon in the Transitory Mists, but thus far the plan wasn't working out. Tenel Ka felt Allana would be safer with the Solos than off at the academy. And Allana and the academy were hardly a perfect fit. Free-spirited and kinetic, Allana had trouble sitting still for lessons, and seemed less interested in honing her abilities in the Force than in following her instincts and investigating life's mysteries in her own fashion.

You were like that as a child. Sometimes it pains me to see so much of you in her. Pains me, and yet fills my heart to overflowing.

Allana rarely spoke of the father she had scarcely known. At the height of Jacen's misguided attempts to control the destiny of the galaxy, he had abducted her in an effort to force Tenel Ka to support his evil machinations, and Han and Leia had been instrumental in rescuing her, learning only then that Jacen was her father. The child had known danger all her life—from Hapan conspirators, members of a Killik nest, and hired assassins alike. But Jacen's treachery was the deepest cut, and his actions had put a premature end to her childhood. Gone was the button-nosed toddler who had once pronounced Jedi *Yedi* and who had named a stuffed tauntaun for the kind man who would later be revealed as her father.

Leia knew that Allana's silence about Jacen didn't mean that she had put him entirely from her mind, only that she had buried her dark memories of him where no one could find them. What worried Leia most was that those memories would fester and seep like a stain into Allana's psyche. It was all too close to what Leia had gone through on learning that Darth Vader had been her actual father, and for years carrying within her a fear that her children would inherit the same weakness for the dark side of the Force that Anakin Skywalker had evinced.

In Jacen, those fears had been realized.

Jacen, who for so long had represented a new hope for the Jedi Order. One who had ventured so profoundly into the Force and had traveled so widely in the galaxy. In the end only to fall victim to the same lust for power that had crippled Anakin Skywalker; to become so overwhelmed and mastered by power, he became unrecognizable to Han and Leia long before his necessary death.

His necessary death.

Leia supported Han whenever he said as much. But as a mother she was less efficient at distancing herself from Jacen. Yes, he had become a monster, but it was Leia who had given birth to him, nursed and nurtured and loved him unconditionally, and his death would haunt her for the rest of her life.

As you failed us, we failed you; failed to find a way to redeem you.

"Would a game of dejarik interest you, mistress?" C-3PO asked Allana.

"Not now, Threepio," she told him.

Leia watched. The two of them were still sorting out their relationship—but better 3PO than the angel-faced defender droid that had been Allana's companion and bodyguard for the early part of her life.

"Grandma, why does Grandpa keep this old ship?" Allana asked suddenly.

Leia's smile appeared almost as a reflex, in recollection of too many things to name.

"He's had this ship a long time, sweetheart. You know how some people keep albums of holoimages to refresh their memories of where they've been, what they've done, and who they've met along the way? The *Falcon* does that for Grandpa. It's filled with memories."

Allana mulled it over. "That's why he never changes anything in here? Because he wants to remember everything just as it was?"

"I think so." Leia lowered her voice to add: "He's also pretty tight with credits, in case you haven't noticed."

Her eyes sparkled. "Yep."

"All fixed," Han called, clambering like a much younger man from the engine compartment. "Threepio, get us going while I finish cleaning up down here."

C-3PO froze in place. "Must I, Captain Solo? You know how—"

"Don't give me any vocoder, Goldenrod. I'm going to make a pilot of you if it kills me."

"But, sir, what would be the point of that?"

"Just get the engines started and set her on autofunction. I won't be long." Han turned his attention to Leia and Allana while the droid was clattering toward the cockpit. "What have you two been chatting about?"

"Just girl talk," Leia said pleasantly.

Allana nodded. "Yep. Girl talk."

Leia took note of Han's suspicious look and glanced at Allana. "Actually, Allana asked me why you prefer traveling in the *Falcon,* and I was trying to come up with a reasonable explanation."

"Yeah, Grandpa, how come we never use our new ship—the one that my mother gave us?"

Han made a sour face. "That fully automatic marvel of modern technology that's supposed to take all the stress out of flying? Why don't we just hire a chauffeur to fly us around?"

Abruptly, the *Falcon* came to life and began to move.

"Good work, Threepio!" Han hollered toward the cockpit.

"What Grandpa means," Leia interjected, "is that he loves to flip switches and toggles and pull and push levers."

Allana studied him. "Is that the real reason? 'Cause you like to flip switches and . . . levers?"

"And let's not forget about pounding his hand against the navicomputer," Leia said, restraining a smile.

"Or banging his fist on the ceiling," Allana said, clearly enjoying herself.

Han planted his hands on his hips. "Hey, that's part of real piloting. Not voice-commanding some computer to do the work."

"Fixing things every time we travel. That's part of it, too?"

Han opened his mouth but no words emerged. The kid was right. Each trip lately had cost them something. Rust was taking hold, parts were wearing out; the superstructure itself was deteriorating. Han so identified with the ship, he lost sleep when she was ailing. But he wasn't about to try to explain that to a seven-year-old kid who'd grown up wearing an opalescent electrotex nanoweave flight suit.

"I'll bet you know every part of this ship by heart," Allana said, getting up from the dejarik table bench and wandering about the hold.

"Well, maybe not every part, but most of them."

While Allana moved to the engineering station, Han took a moment to direct a playful smirk at Leia. When he turned back to Allana, she had a small object in her hand.

"What's this part for?"

Han's eyebrows beetled. He accepted the object from her hand, stared at it, and began to scratch the back of his head in puzzlement. "Where did you find this?"

"Right here," Allana said, pointing to what was now a slight indentation on the curved bulkhead adjacent to the engineering station.

Han kneeled to inspect the divot. The object had been lodged at Allana's eye level into the chamfered edge of an old panel that abutted the station's vertical display board. The divot contained neither relays nor contacts, but Han knew from past repairs that that portion of the bulkhead contained circuitry connecting the engineering station to both the Rubicon navicomputer and the Isu-Sim hyperdrive engine.

"I've never seen this before," he said at last, laughing in disbelief.

Leia hurried over to peer at the object. "Allana, you've given your grandfather a puzzle."

"No, seriously," Han said. "I don't know what the heck this is."

As he was turning it about in his hand, C-3PO returned from the cockpit. "All systems are nominal. Thank the Maker." When no one responded, the crestfallen droid added: "Sometimes I wonder why I even bother."

"Threepio, what is this thing?" Han said, holding the device up to the droid's glowing photoreceptors.

C-3PO canted his head. "I'm sorry, Captain Solo, but I fail to recognize it. Although if I had to venture a guess, I would say that it resembles an antiquated transponder or transceiver of some sort."

Han regarded it. "You're right. It does."

"Maybe we should put it back, Grandpa," Allana said uncertainly.

He glanced down at her. "Oh, I doubt it still works or has anything to do with the ship."

"You never know, Han," Leia said.

"Come on, this little piece of tech? I know *that* much."

Leia extended her right hand. "Can I see it?"

Gently, Han placed it in her palm.

Leia tightened her fingers around the piece. "There's something about this . . . Did you feel anything special, Allana?"

She nodded. "I did. That's how come I found it."

Han looked from Leia to Allana and back again. "Don't you two start going Jedi on me."

"We're not," Leia said. "But you can't deny that objects can sometimes have a kind of inherent power."

"Like you can feel the other people who have touched it," Allana said.

Han blinked in stupefaction.

"We should find out," Allana prompted.

"We should, sweetie. It would be like a treasure hunt. Right, Han?"

He gazed at her. "Huh? Oh, yeah, sure. Next time we attend the galactic engineers' convention."

"I'm serious, Han. For all you know it could have been placed here by someone who owned the *Falcon* long before you got it."

"I suppose," Han said. "Or it could have been put there by any of the hundreds of beings who've been in the *Falcon* since. Some friend or foe, some spy. Like the Imps who tracked us to Yavin Four."

Leia laughed at the unexpected reference. "Was that really in this lifetime?"

"Last time I checked."

"Who owned the *Falcon* before you did, Grandpa?"

"Well, there were lots of owners. The *Falcon*'s over a hundred years old."

"Uncle Lando used to own her," Leia said.

"He did?"

Han nodded. "For a couple of years, anyway."

"Did you buy her from him?"

"Uh, not quite."

"Grandpa won her from Uncle Lando. In a game of cards."

Allana's eyes widened in delight. "Wow!"

Leia smiled. The tale of Han's winning hand was well worn—his pure sabacc besting Lando's near-idiot's array. When Han had confessed to having bought his way into the Cloud City tournament with stolen property— a golden palador figurine he had taken from a Ylesian high priest and a dragon pearl he had swiped from an Imperial general—Leia knew she had finally found the title for the second volume of the memoir she would someday write. It would be called *The Crook, the Wook, and Me.*

Han was laughing. "Here's something even better. Lando—Uncle Lando—he won her from someone else in a game of cards."

"So the *Falcon* is like a prize," Allana said.

Han threw Leia a look. "Exactly what I've been saying all these years."

"Who did Uncle Lando win it from?"

Han pinched his chin in thought. "What was that guy's name? The professional gambler . . ."

Leia shook her head. "I'm not sure you ever told me."

"Sure I did. The guy that lost to Lando at Cloud City?"

"Who owned it before the one Lando won it from?" Allana pressed.

Han blew out his breath. "I don't know."

Leia looked surprised. "You don't?"

"Nope. Every time Chewie and I set out to find out, something would interfere."

"I can imagine," Leia said drily.

Han shook his head. "You only think you can. 'Course, I've heard rumors through the years. I just don't know which ones are true."

"That would be really fun," Allana said.

"What?" Han and Leia replied in unison.

"Finding out all the people who owned the *Falcon* before Grandpa."

Han smiled tolerantly. "I don't think that's possible."

"Why not?"

"For one thing, because unless a lot of the owners were Bith or Muuns or some other species that lives longer than humans, most of them are probably dead."

Leia watched Allana's smile collapse. "Even if that turns out to be true, Han, it would be so much fun trying. And we haven't visited Lando and Tendra in ages. We could start there."

Allana showed Han an imploring look. "Please, please let's do it."

"I, uh . . ."

Leia cocked an eyebrow. "Some pressing engagement you haven't told me about, darling?"

"No."

"Well, then?"

Han blinked and exhaled through his nose. "Okay. Let's do it."

"Another escapade," C-3PO sighed while Allana was hugging Leia's legs.

Han gazed at the device that might be an archaic transponder. Putting it to his ear, he thought he could detect a faint humming sound, as if the device were awaiting a long-lost signal.

chapter eight

A T THE AURORA MEDICAL FACILITY ON OBROA-SKAI, life-support systems and bioscanning devices chirped and beeped to one another. Gathered around the patient's bed, a group of physicians and med droids evaluated the data and conferred.

"Brain waves indicate an elevation from phase three to hypnopompic," one of the droids reported. "Rapid eye movement has ceased."

"Carefully now," Sompa told the droid, his head tresses writhing in anticipation. "He is surfacing, but the transition must be managed delicately." The Ho'Din physician paused to study the readouts, then turned to another of the droids. "Increase the dosage by a factor of point-five."

The droid complied, widening the aperture of a petcock that regulated the flow of drugs into the patient's arm.

"Carefully," Sompa warned. He stole another glance at the monitors, finding encouragement in the neuroimaging displays. "I'm confident we will be able to bring him all the way back this time."

The human patient moaned, though not in pain; more as if awakening from a long afternoon nap.

In keeping with Aurora's reputation, the med droids included the best that money could buy: a humanoid Industrial Automaton 2-1B; a twenty-year-old Medtech FX series 10 assistant, upgraded with the latest in heuristic processors; two Chiewab GH-7s, whose repulsorlifts allowed them to remain overhead and out of the way; and two MD series 11 medical specialists programmed for neurological analysis. None of the members of the mixed-species team of physicians wore surgical gloves, gowns, or masks; all were dressed in the immaculate jackets, trousers, and skirts that were standard issue at Aurora.

The med droids were on hand to administer drugs and monitor and record the procedures. Chief neurologist Lial Sompa wasn't expecting any surprises. The patient's vitals were excellent, and the chances of his going into shock or cardiac arrest were nominal. He had the heart and lungs of a thirty-year-old—literally—and the kidneys, spleen, pancreas, and liver of someone half his chronological age. For weeks following the most recent nerve splicing and deep-neuron stimulation, he had been in and out of consciousness, experiencing sleep–wake cycles, tossing and turning, talking out loud, grinding his teeth, laughing and crying, perhaps in reaction to some of the lucid dreams Sompa had been feeding him for more than a decade now. In effect, the patient was surfacing like a deep-sea diver on a waterworld—slowly and methodically, to keep from going into decompression sickness. Assured of success, Sompa had ordered the feeding tube removed.

"You're too sure of yourself," Ril Bezant said. A Twi'lek, she was Aurora's most celebrated psychotherapist. "We've been at this same juncture more times than I can count."

"This time will be different," Sompa promised.

"I find it morally indefensible that you continue to devote half the resources of the facility to a pet project."

Sompa's head tresses took on sudden color. "Need I remind you that you are here only to observe?"

"I wouldn't want it any other way, Lial."

Sompa gazed at her. "Why is it you seem determined to see this man die?"

"No more determined than you are to keep him alive at any cost—if we concede to call this living."

"I want him more than alive."

"You're not omnipotent, no matter what they told you at the Rhinnal Academy."

"I'm profoundly aware of my limitations."

"Then you've done a fine job of fooling many of us all these years." Bezant gestured to one of the display screens. "Reticular formation damage remains extensive. Segregated corticothalamic networks show limited connectivity and only partial functional integrity . . . Even if he does emerge, the chances for viability are minimal."

Sompa directed his response to the entire team. "We have kept his body alive. His muscles have been stimulated and kept healthy. Failing organs have been replaced. His blood has been cleansed. Cerebral damage notwithstanding, I'm confident we have kept his mind as sound as we have kept his body."

"Meat can be kept frozen," Bezant countered. "Beings can be preserved in carbonite. But the sentient brain isn't a muscle."

"We have given him dreams and memories. His mind is healthy."

"Implanted memories," Bezant said more firmly. "Memories of a life he hasn't lived. Even if he does awaken, he'll be a psychological mess."

Sompa was dismissive. "Side effects we can treat with therapy. As easily dealt with as recurrent dreams."

"He'll be in therapy for the rest of his life."

"Many have who didn't sustain the neural damage he did."

Bezant exhaled in defeat, her lekku quivering. "I'll never understand this, Lial. You already have a shelfful of Faan'er awards."

"This isn't about prizes, Doctor."

"Then what? You can't possibly believe this approach has universal application. Most of the beings who receive treatments here could scarcely spend what it has cost to keep this one on ice."

"Dr. Sompa," the 2-1B interrupted.

Sompa turned in time to see the patient's eyes flutter, blink, then snap open, blue irises staring up into an assortment of human, alien, and droid faces.

"Some disconjugate motion of the optical orbs," the same droid said.

"Lower the lights," Sompa said, eyes fixed on the displays dedicated to heartbeat and respiration rates. Leaning slightly toward the patient, he said in a soft voice: "Captain Jadak."

Jadak's irises dilated, and his heartbeat increased.

"Lie still," Sompa continued. "Don't try to speak just yet." Sompa waited for Jadak's vital signs to stabilize. "You're in a medical facility, Captain. You've been here for some time—a very long time, in fact, but we'll speak of that later. As a result of suffering multifocal brain injuries, you lapsed into a persistent vegetative state. As your long recovery progressed, we saw fit to keep you in a coma until we could be certain that your injuries had healed. You've undergone a series of operations and treatments. Your muscles have received steady stimulation to prevent resorption and atrophy, and we've nourished your mind with dreams that may strike you more like memories. In time, however, you will begin to differentiate those from your actual memories."

Jadak blinked repeatedly, tears coursing from the corners of his eyes.

Sompa laid a calming hand on Jadak's shoulder. "I'm going to ask you a series of yes-or-no questions. I want you to respond with a single blink of your eyes for yes, a double blink for no. Do you understand?"

Jadak blinked once.

"We have attached a sensitive microphone to your throat. Later, should you feel up to it, I would like you to speak. Do you understand?"

Blink.

"Did you recognize your name when I spoke it?"

Blink.

"Do you have some recall of your life?"

Blink.

Sompa glanced briefly at Bezant, who had her arms folded across her chest.

"Here at Aurora Medical Facility, we specialize in keeping beings alive long past what would be their normal time spans," Sompa went on in the same soft, slow voice, "but you are a one-in-a-hundred-million case— what some might call a medical marvel. Few beings are fortunate enough to have a second chance. Do you understand?"

Blink.

Sompa straightened somewhat. "Do you have any memories of the accident that resulted in your coma?"

Jadak blinked twice.

Sompa glanced at the heartbeat display. "That's all right, Captain. Your memory will return in due course. Are you in any pain or discomfort?"

Blink, blink.

"Do you have a physical awareness of your body?"

Blink.

"Do you want to try to sit up?"

At Jadak's single blink, one of the med droids triggered a remote that raised the head of the bed. Another proffered a glass of water, from which Jadak sipped through a straw.

"Do you wish to speak?" Sompa asked after a moment.

"Yes." Jadak wheezed and cleared his throat. "Reeze?"

Sompa looked to one of the droids for explanation.

"The copilot."

"I'm sorry, Captain. Your copilot did not survive the accident."

Jadak lowered his head in grief, then raised it. "The ship."

Sompa allowed the same droid to respond.

"We have no information regarding the ship."

Jadak's forehead creased suddenly, and he glanced down at his body. "I can't feel my legs."

Sompa's head tresses swayed. "Yes, well, that's because we were unable to save your lower legs. We opted not to install prosthetics until we were certain you were going to be able to make use of them."

Jadak absorbed it in silence. "How long have I been in recovery?" he asked finally.

Sompa traded looks with Bezant, who beat the neurologist in responding.

"Sixty-two standard years."

Jadak's blue eyes all but bulged from his head.

chapter nine

N EW LEGS ATTACHED, JADAK FLOATED IN A ZALTIN PRE-
mier bacta tank, the translucent bluish gel warmed
to match his body temperature and formulated to mimic
the salinity of his own fluids. *A miracle mix for a miracle man,* a Bothan technician had joked on the day of the
first long session. Naked except for swim shorts, Jadak
wore a lightweight breathing apparatus and face mask
that was actually a holoscreen, on which was running
the tutorial Sompa and his team had prepared: a sum-
mation of the past sixty-two years of galactic history.

For the first two weeks following Jadak's emergence
from his coma, Sompa had kept him mildly sedated and
wouldn't permit him to view or use the HoloNet. He
wasn't allowed a mirrpanel, either, though he had managed to get a look at himself in the reflective surface of
one of the machines that monitored his vital signs. Aged,
but not nearly as aged as he should have been, and full-
bearded as well; his still-blond hair was parted in the
center and touched the tips of his shoulders.

Nurses and aides, some human, some not, would escort him through the facility's broad, gleaming corridors
or out onto the manicured grounds, which seemed to extend all the way to the distant skyline of Obroa-skai's
capital city. He would encounter other beings on these
outings, many of whom were recuperating from rejuve-

nation procedures, but all of whom had been briefed to confine their comments and conversations to the moment. Nothing about the past, nothing about the news. *Isn't it a lovely day? Don't the gardens look marvelous? This evening's dinner promises to be a pure joy . . .* With his mind slowed by drugs, the daily routine and nightly dreams were almost enough to convince him that all was well, and that he was merely recovering from a swoop race crash, like the one he'd been involved in on Fondor before the war.

That a mere week had passed rather than sixty-two years.

But the truth would stalk and pounce on him in the middle of the night, in between peaks of whatever time-release drugs they had him on, and he would wake up screaming.

Sixty-two years!

Added to his actual age he would only have been ninety-three, but he didn't look or feel nearly a century old. To Hutts, Wookiees, Muuns, and a handful of other species, ninety-three years barely put one past adolescence, but humans were still in the habit of dying in their early hundreds. Unless they were wealthy enough to afford rejuvenation procedures of the sort available at Aurora. Then 125, even 150 years wasn't uncommon. More important, Jadak hadn't simply been blessed with longevity; he had skipped ahead in what seemed to him an instant.

He had jumped.

No matter the time of day or night, Sompa or Bezant was always on hand to ease him through episodes of despair, reminding him that he needed to take things slowly, one step at a time, and to help him differentiate between false and real memories. He didn't really have a wife and kids or own a home on Brentaal IV. He hadn't actually done half the things he half recalled doing.

Despite the support he received, he kept thinking he would simply wake up from the longest, most dream-filled night of his life and find himself in a bunk aboard the *Stellar Envoy,* with Reeze whipping up breakfast in the galley. Sompa and Bezant refused to tell him anything about the accident that had landed him at Aurora. They conceded that his mind could be compelled to give up the memory, but they insisted that his long-term psychic health would be better served if the memory surfaced of its own accord. The last memory he recalled with any clarity was of sitting at the controls of the old YT-1300 as it skimmed through hyperspace. But he couldn't place the event in time, didn't know where he and Reeze had come from or where they were headed and why. So how could he be sure he wasn't still in a coma, and that all he was experiencing wasn't simply another programmed dream?

Every day for the first two weeks, Sompa had told him that he was going to be moved to the tank, holding it out like a panacea for everything, not just his replacement legs. Then one morning, without warning, he was inside the tank with the holoscreen mask adhered to his face and the tutorial running, and all doubts about the reality of his situation were laid to rest.

Because no one could have made up the catastrophic events the tutorial led him through.

The war between the Republic and the Confederacy of Independent Systems—the one in which Jadak and countless others had tried so hard to serve the cause of peace and justice—was revealed to have been nothing more than an elaborate ploy to eliminate the Jedi Order and place the galaxy in the hands of a Sith Lord. The Force had triumphed in the end, however, with Emperor Palpatine brought down by the son of a Jedi everyone had once looked to as a hero. But it had taken years of fighting with the remnants of the Empire before a New

Republic rose from the ashes of the Old. And even then peace hadn't endured for long. Already beset with problems, the New Republic had been invaded by an extragalactic species known as the Yuuzhan Vong, who brought an unprecedented level of barbarity to the galaxy. Planets had been destroyed or transformed; entire species exterminated. Worlds like Coruscant and Obroa-skai were still recovering from the alien mantle the Yuuzhan Vong had seeded. Even more recently, the Galactic Alliance had suffered a threat from a young Jedi Knight who, like Anakin Skywalker before him, had embraced the teachings and tactics of the Sith in an attempt to foment a new order. And now, irony of ironies, guidance of the Galactic Alliance rested in the hands of a former Imperial officer named Natasi Daala.

The crushing revelations, the entries recounting the brutal deaths of so many of his friends and family members, the utter devastation of cities, worlds, and species he had come to cherish, were enough to make Jadak's own problems seem insignificant. Though his legs were healing, he came to dread the approach of each immersion session, not because of the sickly sweet aftertaste of the bacta treatments themselves, but for what the tutorials continued to reveal about the tortured state of the galaxy.

For a week Jadak had resisted doing a HoloNet search on himself, and he was sorry when he finally gave in to the urge. The entries were accurate up to a point, but history hadn't been entirely kind to the memory of Tobb Jadak. Initially regarded as one of the finest competitive swoop and starship racers to appear on the scene in a hundred years—he'd set a speed record of 655 kilometers per hour on the Grandine Swoop Loop—he was, following the Balmorra Invitational, reduced to a might-have-been in the kinder entries, a discredit to the sport in others. Even those entries that told of Jadak's having been forced to throw the race as part of a point-shaving scheme controlled by Hutts aligned with the Rigorra/Groodo Family held him in contempt for having bet widely on himself to lose the race. The fact that not a single entry told the full story weighed on him. But how could it have been otherwise when the HoloNet was all but devoid of references to the Republic Group, let alone mentions of Jadak's service, despite all that had come to light about the so-called Clone Wars and Palpatine's evil plottings?

It was true that the Hutts had ordered him to throw the race. They had promised to engineer a comeback for Jadak, but he knew that a comeback, if it happened at all, would come too late to rescue his reputation or his self-respect. So he could either comply and accept the credits the Hutts were offering as compensation, or be killed along with the rest of his family. But betting on himself to lose had not been Jadak's idea; that was the Republic Group's doing. Having somehow learned of the Hutts's directive, representatives of the group had approached him shortly before the race, saying that they had a fast ship that needed a skilled pilot who was as distrustful of Palpatine as the members of the group were, and from what they knew of Jadak, he fit the bill perfectly. He wasn't surprised. He had never known when to keep his political opinions to himself, especially when some pretty reporter was pushing a microphone toward him. But the Republic Group wasn't looking for an ally so much as a being with a tarnished reputation who could mix and mingle with the galaxy's information brokers without suspicions being aroused. They needed him to play the part of a down-on-his-luck mercenary who would do anything for a credit, but in fact serve the interests of the Republic Group as a spy and courier.

Initially Jadak had refused the offer. Just because he

was finished on the swoop-and-starship race circuit
didn't mean he couldn't find piloting work with a police
force, a security organization, or a private investigation
firm. But as Palpatine's power increased and war began
to seem inevitable, he had a change of heart. If nothing
else, he could at least put his piloting abilities to some
good use.

And then there was that faster-than-all-get-out YT-1300
freighter the group had picked up somewhere . . .

He remembered the prewar and war years, infiltrating
the Metatheran Cartel and other crime organizations,
the hundreds of trips to far-flung worlds, the encounters
with arms merchants, spice dealers, CIS sympathizers . . .
more often than not he didn't know what he was carrying or what he was delivering. He simply did as instructed, trusting that he was furthering the causes of
the Senate Delegation of Two Thousand and the Jedi
Order, fighting the war in his own fashion and taking
care of his scattered family at the same time. With
Reeze, also recruited by the group, Jadak had piloted the
Stellar Envoy through the thick of some of the fiercest
battles of the war—on Muunilist, Cato Neimoidia, and
other worlds.

With each session in the bacta tank, his actual memories began to resume chronological order. But he still
couldn't recall events leading up to the accident. Some
HoloNet entries listed his death as having occurred
shortly before the official end of the Clone Wars. There
were no facts about where his death was supposed to
have occurred, but it was undeniable that in some sense
he had died then.

A few of the Republic Group Senators to whom he
answered had survived to see the Alliance to Restore the
Republic—the so-called Rebel Alliance—defeat the Empire, but all of them were now dead. Several had died as
early as the Ghorman Massacre, and others were lost on

Alderaan when it was destroyed by the Death Star. Many more died during the extended conflict with the Imperial warlords. Only a handful had died of natural causes.

By his final sessions in the tank, Jadak was questioning the importance of recalling the details of the accident—especially now that a bigger question had begun to gnaw at him. With all the members of the Republic Group dead, who had been keeping him alive all these years . . . and why?

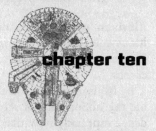

chapter ten

Han and Lando exchanged vigorous handshakes and a warm back-clapping embrace. When it came to greeting Leia, Lando held her in his arms for a long moment, smiling roguishly when she finally pushed him away, shaking her head in amused disapproval.

"The galaxy's one constant," Tendra said, indicating her husband with a toss of her head and hugging Leia hello.

"No," Leia said, "I've got one of those, too."

The Calrissians were dressed casually, in loose-fitting pants, simple pullovers, and sandals, and for perhaps the first time in her life Leia felt overdressed in their presence.

"And who is this gorgeous little creature?" Lando was saying, dropping down on one knee in front of Allana. "It can't be Amelia. Surely she hasn't grown up this much in only one year."

"Someone has to," Allana said while Lando hugged her.

"Hey," he said with theatrical surprise. "Learning your dad's bad habits already?"

"No, I come by them naturally."

Leia laughed with everyone else, relieved that the mere mention of the word *dad* didn't throw Allana into conflict. The Calrissians knew nothing about her secret paternity, and assumed, as most did, that Han and Leia had adopted her in part to offset their grief over the death of their second son. For a time, Allana had found it difficult to refer to Han and Leia as her parents, but she had since grown accustomed to doing so in mixed company.

"Amelia, do you remember little Lando?" Three years old and all but a clone of his father, he was holding a toy dragon and dressed in the same outfit worn by Lando Senior.

"Hi, Lando," she said, going over to him. "Is that the dragon from *Castle Creep*?"

The toddler nodded shyly. "Perystal."

"I watch that show, too! Is Perystal your favorite toy?"

"I have a Prince Gothik."

"Wow. I used to have a stuffed tauntaun."

The boy ran to Lando and wrapped his arms around his father's legs. Lando bent down and scooped him up, beaming. "His nickname's Chance." He tousled his son's curly hair. "He's my lucky star."

Han smiled, and Lando caught it. "Don't say it."

Han shrugged. "Hey, even Boba Fett's a grandfather."

Lando set Chance back on his feet, and the boy ran to Tendra. "Hello, Threepio," Lando said, straightening. "Good to see you."

"And you, sir," C-3PO said. "If you don't mind my saying so, sir, your home is quite exquisite."

"This home," Han corrected. "They got six of them. Or is it seven?"

"Actually it's eight since we bought a small place on Kuat," Lando said. "But this is becoming our favorite."

Leia could see why. Lujo was a gem of a world, the equatorial regions especially, where the climate was balmy year-round and the aqua ocean glinted under a golden sun. A cluster of beautifully appointed interconnected pavilions, the Calrissians's place was only a hundred meters from the sea and open to the cooling breeze.

Outside of a brief get-together a year back, the last

time Leia and Han had spent extended time with Lando was during the Alliance–Confederation War. Leia's Noghri protectors, Cakhmaim and Meewalh, had just lost their lives, and the *Falcon*, fired on by the Star Destroyer *Anakin Solo*, had lost both gun turrets and large sections of armor. At Tendrando Refueling and Repair Station in the Gyndine system—and at his own expense—Lando had had the *Falcon* rebuilt and had joined Han and Leia in executing a mission in Corellia, bowing out only when he'd received word that Tendra was pregnant.

"What happened to the cane?" Han asked.

Lando threw Tendra a look. "Someone convinced me it was an affectation. Made me look older than my years."

"At least she allowed you to keep the mustache," Han said.

Everyone laughed again. Last time, on Coruscant, Jacen had been the white bantha in the room, his actions during the war and his death too painful to discuss. The four of them had talked around those events, talked about anything but what had happened only two years earlier. It was different now. They had all moved on, a fact that was as disconcerting as it was comforting.

"So what brings you to Lujo?" Lando asked.

"We're on an adventure," Allana announced.

"Really? What sort of adventure?"

"We're going to find all the people who ever owned the *Millennium Falcon*."

Lando turned to Han. "Is that right?"

He nodded. "It's something I promised myself I would do one day, and there's time to do it now."

"Well, that's a grand adventure," Lando said, turning back to Allana. "Did your dad tell you that I once owned the *Falcon*?"

"Yep. He said he won it from you in a game of cards."

Lando put his tongue in his cheek. "More or less. But

what's important is that I knew how much your dad loved the *Falcon,* and I had so many other ships, I decided to let him keep her."

Han cocked an eyebrow.

"I can't even imagine where we'd all be now if it weren't for your dad and the *Falcon,*" Lando continued. "But I doubt he would have ended up marrying a princess and becoming a galactic hero."

Han had his mouth open to reply when a silver protocol droid stepped down onto the veranda. "Everything is prepared, Captain Calrissian."

"Captain?" Han said.

"Of the good ship *Windchaser,*" Lando told him.

"What d'you do, sell the *Love Commander?*"

"She's not a starship, old buddy." Lando pulled a billed cap from his pants pocket and slapped it down over his graying hair, tipping it at a jaunty angle. "We're all going sailing."

Han and Lando sat side by side on the catamaran's bridge, Lando with the old-fashioned wheel in hand, the main sails fluffed, iced drinks in the cup holders. The ship was doing a good speed through pellucid water, the sun brilliant gold and easing toward the horizon. To all sides rose steep-sided islands lush with foliage and rimmed with beaches of white sand.

"I notice you've got an auxiliary motor," Han said.

"Solar. Imagine me becalmed."

"I can't." Han peeled his shirt off and luxuriated in the warmth of the sun. "Nature's not so bad when you get used to it." He gazed into the sky. "Amazing to think that people used to live like this."

"A lot still do. You could if you wanted to."

Han dismissed the idea. "You know me. I can't sit still."

Lando fell silent for a moment. "You two doing all right?"

Han understood. "We're beginning to. I try not to think about it. Having Amelia's made a big difference."

"And Jaina?"

"Doing well."

"Back in the fold?"

"With one foot, anyway."

Lando didn't pursue the point. "You're on the level about tracing the history of the *Falcon*?"

Han nodded. "It started out as Amelia's idea, but I'm all in now. It's something we can all do together, and while there's still a chance of locating some of the old owners. The guy you won her from, for instance—"

"Cix Trouvee," Lando said.

"That's the name I've been trying to remember!"

Lando snorted a laugh. "He had the wildest swings in luck. One year he'd be flush, the next he'd be pawning his chrono for a hot meal. Card players used to call him Glass Eye because once he began to lose you could practically read his mind. I don't have to tell you that that doesn't always mean much with sabacc, not with the randomizer, but when he was cornered you knew what his hole cards were. He was desperate when he used the *Falcon* as a marker. I actually felt bad about winning it—for about two heartbeats. Just the way I'm sure you felt when you took the *Falcon* from me."

Han loosed a plosive laugh. "I know you still believe I outplayed you, but I was as surprised as anyone that you were bluffing. You're just sorry about losing her."

Lando compressed his lips. "How many times do we have to go over this before you're willing to concede that you didn't *win* the *Falcon*, because I never bet her? I don't begrudge you winning the hand. I begrudge your claiming that you won her when my marker was simply for one of the ships on my lot. I could have reneged, you know. Anyone on Nar Shaddaa would have understood my side of it."

"There were plenty of witnesses who heard you say *any* ship on your lot."

Lando shook his head in irritation. "My biggest mistake was leaving the *Falcon* behind and trying to make an impression by arriving at Bespin on the *Queen of Empire*."

The glower they traded evaporated into laughter.

"It's official," Han said, wiping a tear from his eye. "We've both become a couple of old coots."

Lando nodded. "We'd better drop the subject before I capsize us."

"Good idea. But at least we can remember that far back." Han paused. "You have any idea where Cix Trouvee is now?"

"I actually heard from him when I was operating the *Belt-Runner*. I've no idea where he is now, but I'm sure we can find out."

"Lando," Tendra called from the boat's spacious deck. "We want to go swimming." She gestured to one of the islands.

Lando saluted and turned the big wheel through his hands, making for an isolated cove.

Han took a long pull from his drink glass and relaxed back into the padded chair. "I'm guessing business has been great."

"Not as good as you might think." Lando sipped at an orange-colored concoction his protocol droid had whipped up. "Tendrando's facing a lot of competition all of a sudden. The Verpines, Mandalorians, even Baktoid and the Colicoid Nest are trying to get back in the droid market."

"The Colicoids." Han shuddered. "I thought that bunch was forced to disband."

"They were, but Colla-Arphocc Automata has reformed and petitioned the courts under some new fairtrade agreement. They claim to have documentation signed by Palpatine that they were only required to disarm for a certain period of time."

"The courts are willing to hear them out?"

"If Daala had her way I think she'd eradicate all the insectoid species, but her hands are tied."

"Have you had any dealings with her?"

"Some."

"And?"

"She seems determined not to repeat past mistakes. She's not a dictator, and she doesn't appear to nurse any aspirations of becoming one. Star systems are putting aside their differences in the interest of forging an enduring peace. But that has less to do with Daala than the simple fact that there's nothing to be gained by isolationism. We've had fifty years of war and wobbling. The time's come to understand that what happens in the Core affects the outer systems, and what happens there affects the Core."

"So you're optimistic."

Lando wagged his head from side to side. "I've been fooled before. Daala's still an unknown quantity, and I'm not all that comfortable with her alliances with the Remnant and the Mandalorians." He turned to look at Han. "A lot of folks are still wondering what possessed you to install Daala in the first place."

"Me, personally?"

"We can start with you."

Han sniffed. "My daughter had just killed my surviving son, Lando. At that point nothing seemed insane."

"Even after what Daala did to you and Chewie way back when?"

Han held his gaze. "We got even with her. Besides, if I'm going to list all the beings who've tortured me over the years I've got to include Leia's father in the mix, so what's the use? It is what it is."

"Not to the Mon Calamari. They'd sooner see a Yuuzhan Vong on Coruscant than a former war criminal. And from what I hear, the Jedi aren't too thrilled with her, either."

"Daala's feeling is that a just system doesn't need overseers, so Luke's not sure just where the Jedi stand anymore." Han gazed out at the sea and inhaled deeply. "I try to stay out of it."

Lando spun the wheel. "I guess we're all looking for answers of a sort."

"That reminds me." Han prised from his pocket the device Allana had discovered aboard the *Falcon* and held it up for Lando's inspection. "Ever seen anything like this?"

Lando squinted. "Looks like some kind of comlink. Where'd you come by it?"

"Amelia found it—aboard the *Falcon*."

Surprise shone in Lando's eyes. "I would have figured you knew every rivet by now."

"It was cached in the bulkhead behind the engineering station. I think the alloy has some mimetic properties, which is probably why I missed it."

"Couldn't be your eyes, huh?" Lando grinned.

"Not likely, pal."

"Well, I sure didn't install it, so unless it got installed under your watch, it must have already been there when Cix owned the *Falcon*. Stands to reason that no one in the past fifty years would use something that old."

"That's what I'm thinking."

"Some of my techs are staying in the guest house. You could see what they have to say."

Han pocketed the device. "I'll do that."

Lando glanced at him. "You want to take the wheel for a while before we drop anchor?"

"I'm game," Han said.

chapter eleven

"THE ALLIANCE FOR THE RESTORATION OF THE Republic."

Jadak woke from tumultuous dreams with the words on his lips and a 2-1B med droid gazing at him from where it was standing at the monitoring device Sompa had yet to remove from the room.

"Sir?" the droid said.

Jadak stared.

"You said, 'The Alliance for the Restoration of the Republic.' Is there more you wish to add?"

Jadak ran a hand over his bearded chin and shook his head. "Did I say anything else in my sleep?"

"Nothing intelligible, sir."

"Business as usual," Jadak muttered.

He swung off the bed and shuffled to a bedside mirr-panel the nurses had finally provided. Each morning he expected to see the reflection of a man who had climbed from a grave. Instead it was the same blond stranger who greeted him. He used the 'fresher and dressed and downed some of the breakfast a different droid deliv-ered. Sompa had lifted the moratorium regarding the HoloNet, but Jadak found he had no stomach for it and left the room. Still growing accustomed to his new legs, he moved carefully through the hallways, exchanging greetings with other patients when he couldn't avoid them, but mostly wrapped up in his own thoughts and growing more agitated by the moment.

Sompa had warned him to expect periods of frustration as his mind sought to reconstruct the chronology of his memories. But Jadak hadn't anticipated a physical response that sometimes made him want to put his fist through the nearest wall. He couldn't escape the feeling that he had left something important undone. He accepted that the feeling was probably linked to what had turned out to be his final mission for the Republic Group, but his frustration over not being able to retrieve the memory ran deep. As if recalling the mission and concluding it would somehow complete his recuperation and restore him fully to life.

The Alliance for the Restoration of the Republic.

It had its beginning with the Delegation of Two Thousand, to some extent with the Republic Group, and by the Battle of Yavin was known as the Rebel Alliance. But what did any of that have to do with him when he had been comatose for most of it? When he shut his eyes, images of Reeze and the *Stellar Envoy* would strobe in his mind. Reeze had hoped that the YT freighter would one day be theirs. He had imagined a life of profitable and rollicking adventures; of women and wealth and the freedom to travel wherever they wished.

Jadak ground his replacement teeth. What had they left undone that seemed so urgent now? Why did he have to wait for his memory of the accident to kick in? Why couldn't Sompa just give him the details so he could move on?

Jadak stepped into sunshine beaming down onto Aurora's verdant grounds through scudding clouds. In the distance, luxury yachts were descending gently toward the facility's private landing field. Aurora even had its own fleet of ships. Patients—clients of many species— were emerging from airspeeders with tinted windows and being welcomed by security personnel, staff members, and droids. Some arrived with entourages of aides and servants. If there were celebrated or familiar faces among them, Jadak didn't recognize any. But how could he be expected to when most of the famous beings of his time were either dead or rejuvenated beyond all recognition? And what was a once-disgraced swoop racer turned surreptitious starship captain doing among them, convalescing in a private room in one of Aurora's most exclusive wings?

The comlink Sompa insisted he wear on his belt chimed.

"Captain Jadak," a droid voice said, "you are requested to return to Building One and report directly to Dr. Sompa's office. If you need assistance, simply state your present location and transport will be arranged."

"I'll get there on my own two feet," Jadak said.

He wasn't scheduled to meet with Sompa until later in the day, but the neurologist had an annoying habit of altering appointments, and the last-minute change in plans did little to improve Jadak's mood. By the time he reached the office he was wound up, but Sompa wasn't there waiting for him. In the reception area sat the most attractive female Jadak had ever seen, human or humanoid, and for a moment he wasn't entirely sure whether she was one or the other. Dr. Bezant, the Twi'lek psychotherapist, was a vision, but this woman—

"Captain Jadak," she said, standing up and extending her hand. "I'm Koi Quire. With CH and L."

In high-heeled shoes she was almost his height; she wore a long skirt and a short jacket that hugged her torso. Her skin was tinged with gold; her eyes pale lavender, with a nictitating membrane. A rainbow of colors, her hair fell below her shoulders in curls and ringlets.

"CH and L?" Jadak said.

"Core Health and Life Insurance Consortium. I'm here to discuss your policy."

Jadak shook his head in confusion. "I don't recall having any kind of policy with Core Life or any other company."

Quire frowned and consulted a handheld data device. "I see the reason for your confusion." She smiled, revealing snow-white teeth. "Let's find somewhere to chat, shall we?"

He followed her down the corridor to an unoccupied conference room, and they sat at right angles to each other at the end of a long table. Quire opened her carry case and set a computer between them, angling the display so that they could both see it. She called data to the screen and used the lacquered nail of her forefinger to enlarge one of the lines of text.

"The policy was taken out for you by a company called the Republic Group."

Jadak stared at the text, then at Quire. "When?"

"Um, let's see." She touched the screen and ran her finger under a few lines of text. "But that's impossible."

"What?"

"The policy was taken out sixty-two years ago. But you . . ."

"I'm a lot older than I look," Jadak said.

Her brows formed a V under curly bangs. "By perhaps fifty years!" She sat back in the chair. "I know what they do here at Aurora, but I had no idea—"

"Let's get back to the policy. Was it taken out on my health or my life?"

She laughed. "You're obviously quite alive, Captain. It was a health policy with a rider covering accidents."

"You know about the accident I had?"

"Not the details. That's handled by a different department. When Aurora contacted CH and L to report that you had—" she glanced at the screen "—emerged from a coma, I was dispatched to deliver the indemnity."

Jadak turned the screen toward him. "Can't you find the details of the accident in my file?"

She swung the computer back toward her. "No, Captain. And even if I could, I'm not permitted to divulge any information beyond what I've been instructed to provide."

Jadak narrowed his eyes. "So you're what, a claims adjuster?"

"That's a rather old-fashioned term, but, yes, you're essentially correct."

"Exactly how much does this accident clause entitle me to?"

She cleared her throat in a meaningful way. "You should understand, Captain, that CH and L has been covering your quite substantial health-care costs all these years."

"How much?" Jadak said.

"Ten thousand credits."

"Is that a lot? By current standards, I mean?"

"It would barely pay for a month of treatments in this place. But if you're sensible in your spending you could probably stretch it to cover a year on a world like Obroa-skai."

"I'm not about to stay on Obroa-skai."

"Well, then it would all depend, Captain, on how much travel you do and which world you eventually settle on."

Jadak considered it briefly. "Forgive my asking, but what world are you from?"

She looked at him out of the corner of one eye. "Is that a polite way of asking my species?"

"I suppose."

"I'm Firrerreo."

"If everyone on Firrerre is as attractive as you, maybe I'll just settle there."

"I don't think so," she said flatly.

"Too expensive?"

She shook her head. "No."

"Your people don't take kindly to strangers?"

Her skin took on a silver hue. "Firrerre was dosed with a virus. It's a dead world. Quarantined."

Jadak winced slightly. "The Yuuzhan Vong?"

"Killed by one of our own," Quire said, "who aligned himself with the Emperor. Many of my people were placed in stasis and sold to slavers. Some of us were lucky enough to be rescued and find a new life on Belderone."

Jadak frowned. "I know Belderone. I don't want to live there."

"Neither did I," Quire said. She fell silent for a moment, then asked: "Choosing a place to live is that simple for you? You've no job, no unfinished business?"

Jadak appraised her. "What kind of question is that?"

Quire averted her gaze. "I apologize, Captain. I was simply curious."

Jadak reeled in his anger. "I don't have a job, but I've got skills."

"I'm certain you do, Captain."

A smile formed on his lips. "How about I show you around Aurora before you leave?"

Quire laughed. "I don't think I've ever been asked to tour a hospital."

"Medical facility," Jadak said. "The food is great."

"Are you flirting with me, Captain?"

"Trying to."

Her skin resumed its golden color. "I'm flattered. But I'm afraid I'll have to decline your offer."

"You don't date older men?"

She laughed warmly. "Yes, it's because of your age. Suppose we leave it at that."

Jadak shrugged. "Then how about one small favor?"

"What?" she said warily.

Jadak motioned to the computer. "You bend the regs just enough to tell me what my file has to say about the accident."

Her smile collapsed. "I told you, I'm not at liberty to say."

"It's my life we're talking about," Jadak said more firmly than he had intended.

She started. "I'm sorry—"

"Why would the Republic Group take out an accident policy on me? And why would your company keep paying for my treatments here when I was a brainwave shy of dying?"

"A vegetative state is not the same as being brain-dead."

Jadak's nostrils flared. "It doesn't add up. Did the Republic Group take out a policy on Reeze, too? Was someone liable for the accident?"

"I have—"

"My copilot. Did Core Health cover the cost of his funeral?"

Quire was stone-faced. "And here I thought we were beginning to get along."

Jadak balled his fists. "I'd like you a whole lot more in trade for some private time with your computer!"

Closing the computer, Quire slid it into her carry case and stood up. "Do I need to call security, Captain?"

Jadak closed his eyes and blew out his breath. "No."

"Then I'll leave the indemnity voucher with Aurora's treasurer."

chapter twelve

A HOLOIMAGE OF THE T-SHAPED COMMUNICATIONS DE-vice spun and turned above the analyzer's projec-tor. Lando's towering chief technician, a Cerean named Tal-lik-Tal, paused the image and gestured to it.

"You can see the amplification relay here, just at the upper juncture."

"Then it *is* a transponder?" Leia asked from the far side of the projector. The glow emanating from the pro-jector's base enhanced the slight sunburns she and Han had sustained from two days of swimming and taking long beach walks with Allana.

"Pre-Imperial in design, and I suspect rarely encoun-tered even in its day." Tal-lik-Tal moved to the analyzer and called onscreen a similar but far-from-identical piece of hardware. "This is an image from the database library. Manufactured by Chedak Communications dur-ing the Clone Wars. But I've no way of determining whether yours was made by the same company."

"There's no manufacturer's symbol?" Han asked.

"Or model or serial numbers."

"Could they have been deliberately removed?"

"There's no indication that any existed."

Tal-lik-Tal put the holoimage in motion, and Han cir-cled it, his hand rubbing the stubble on his chin.

"You were correct regarding the device's mimetic properties," the Cerean said. "In that, it is not unlike comlinks and transceivers developed for use by intelligence organizations. As I say, this one does not match any known Republic or Imperial-era designs, but the use of mimetic alloy at least suggests the possibility that the device was installed covertly, or for covert purposes. Have you detected any changes in the performance of your vessel since the device was removed?"

"No, nothing like that."

"With the *Falcon*, how would we even know?" Leia asked, smiling.

Tal-lik-Tal laughed. "The reason I ask is that the transponder is still active."

"I told you I wasn't hearing things," Han said to Leia.

She turned to Tal-lik-Tal. "Isn't there some way to prompt it?"

"I made several attempts at interrogating the device using codes common during the latter Republic and early Imperial eras, but to no effect. It appears that it will only transmit its encoded message in response to a predefined received signal."

Leia frowned, then brightened. "Amelia will be thrilled to learn that we failed to solve the mystery."

"I would vouchsafe one suggestion," Tal-lik-Tal said. "Do not reinstall it."

A holoimage of Jadak's brain was revolving on a display screen when he entered Ril Bezant's office and lowered himself into an armchair.

The Twi'lek psychotherapist smiled and came around the desk to take a seat opposite him. "How are your legs?"

"Getting me around."

She took note of his sullen tone of voice and nodded. "And, in general, how are you?"

"Well, let's see, my memory's still shot full of holes,

and I feel like I'm imprisoned in someone else's body. I'm sleeping an hour a night if I'm lucky, and my hands shake." Jadak showed them to her. "Other than that everything's fine."

"Go on," she said.

"My body seems to know that a lot of time has passed but my mind hasn't caught up."

"It will."

"So you keep telling me. But sixty-two years ago feels like yesterday to me."

"The past is nothing but yesterdays, Captain, whether years or decades have elapsed."

"I'll try to keep that in mind next time I watch some HoloNet documentary about Emperor Palpatine and think to myself that I caught a glimpse of him last week on Coruscant." Jadak looked her in the eye. "I've got this phrase stuck in my head. *Alliance for the Restoration of the Republic.* I can't get past it. Like my mind's waiting for some kind of prompt that'll bring back the rest of my memory."

"And you feel that your agitation has something to do with the phrase, with the words themselves?"

"Restoration . . . Republic . . . like they're on a loop."

"You said yourself that you're waiting for your memory to be restored."

Jadak considered it. "What about the rest of it?" He worked his jaw. "It's beginning to get to me."

Bezant moved her head-tails behind her shoulders. "I warned Sompa this might happen."

"What might happen?"

"That posttraumatic stress might engender a form of dissociative disorder—feelings of depersonalization, accompanied by severe anxiety and depression. It's likely there are underlying organic factors as well." She gestured to the display screen. "Your brain imaging shows damage to key areas of the cortex."

Jadak glanced at the display. "I know starship engines, Doc, not brains. And I don't really care about the cause, I just need to know if I can be fixed."

"There are drugs, but I'd caution against using them."

"What do you suggest—twice-weekly sessions with you?"

"Even if that were possible, I'm not sure how much help I could be."

"You're booked that far in advance, huh?"

"No, Captain. The fact is, you're being released."

Jadak sat up straight in the chair. "When?"

"Soon. Your body is healthy, your legs are healed. Aurora specializes in rejuvenation, not rehabilitation. There's really nothing more we can do for you."

"Then why was I brought here to begin with?"

Her eyes shifted slightly. "You'd have to direct that question to Dr. Sompa."

"Sompa's too busy to see me." Jadak rested his forearms on his thighs and leaned toward Bezant. "Just tell me about the accident and who's really been paying for my care. Obroa-skai stores data on just about everything in the galaxy, but nobody at Aurora can tell me a single thing about what landed me here."

Bezant regarded him, her expression softening. "One moment." Rising, she went to her desk and tapped a code into the control pad. "I've turned off the security cams," she said when she returned to the chair. "Captain, believe it or not, I'm as curious as you are to learn what landed you at Aurora. Dr. Sompa has treated you like a special project for the past forty years—ever since he joined Aurora's staff."

"Forty years? Where was I for the first twenty-two?"

"I don't know. None of us knows."

"Except Sompa."

She nodded. "Except Sompa."

*   *   *

Insomnia had allowed Jadak to familiarize himself with the routines of the night-shift nurses, droids, and security personnel. He had a window of opportunity to make his move while the staff was getting the rundown on newly admitted patients and receiving updates on existing ones. The beauty of Building One was that most of the security details were posted outside. Once inside, clients were allowed to roam about freely—to the entertainment rooms, the dining areas, the libraries and workout centers—and the med and maintenance droids were programmed to keep a low profile and refrain from speaking unless spoken to.

Sompa's office was on the fourteenth floor and overlooked the rear gardens. The broad corridors leading to it were dimly illuminated and empty, except for floor-polishing droids. Using the same code he had seen Bezant enter into the desk pad, Jadak deactivated the surveillance cams and tricked Sompa's office door into opening with a device he had cobbled together from parts liberated from the bank of monitoring machines in his own room. Once he had deactivated the waiting room cams, he entered Sompa's personal office and did the same. Raising the lighting a bit, he took a long look around. Holoscreens niched into the walls showed Sompa in the company of rejuvenated beings Jadak could only assume were wealthy, important, or both. Politicians, celebrities, lawyers, the executive officers of major corporations. In nearly every holo, Sompa looked the same age.

The neurologist's huge desk was cluttered with data cards, flimses, and durasheet documents. Jadak activated a shaded illuminator and began to rummage around. He got lucky almost immediately, discovering his name and patient identification number on a durasheet listing clients who were slated for discharge. The desk drawers were locked, and the private files on

Sompa's stylish computer were password-protected. Digging deeper into the strata of documents, Jadak found a data card marked with his identification number and slotted the card into a reader. Most of the terabytes of technical data were devoted to the convoluted procedures he had undergone while in a vegetative state and subsequent progress reports, but there was a history subfolder, as well. In anticipation of what he might find, Jadak took a deep breath and tried to ignore the pounding of his heart.

His eyes scanned the scrolling text, seizing on every appearance of the word *accident,* and in every instance he was left disappointed by the absence of details. The accident resulted in damage to this or that part of him, interfered with the functioning of one organ or another, required a procedure time-tested or experimental. But in a subfolder labeled PREVIOUS HISTORY Jadak struck pure aurodium. He had been transferred to Aurora after languishing in a coma for twenty-two years at a public medical center. There was no mention of cost covering by Core Health and Life.

The medical center was on Nar Shaddaa.

The images that ignited in his mind drove him back into Sompa's ample chair.

He and Reeze had jumped the *Stellar Envoy* to Nar Shaddaa! The YT had sustained damage. All systems were down. The ship was streaking into the planet's envelope on a collision course with a bulk freighter. They had hurried aft into the escape pod. The YT had suddenly powered up and veered. But too late: they had jettisoned the pod—almost directly into the mammoth ship's V-shaped hull—

Fresh as yesterday, the images assaulted his mind and body, accelerating the beat of his heart and drenching him in sweat. When he finally could, he began to pick the images apart.

They had jumped into hyperspace at Coruscant, on the heels of the battle in which Palpatine had been held hostage. But preceding a chase to the stars and a hasty jump to hyperspace, they had been a downside . . . at the Senate Annex.

Meeting with members of the Republic Group.

Senators Des'sein, Largetto, and Fang Zar.

Jadak pivoted to Sompa's computer. State-of-the-art, it would have outwitted Jadak's best attempts to slice into the files it contained, but he knew enough to gain access to the HoloNet. Conjuring an image of the white-bearded Senator from Sern Prime, he used it as one would a meditation aid, to prompt recollection.

A Jedi was present at the meeting.

A Kadas'sa'Nikto Jedi who had installed something in the *Envoy* . . .

"Right!" Jadak said aloud.

The Senators had wanted him to deliver the *Envoy* to one of their allies on Toprawa!

Jadak recalled his disappointment. After all his years of service, he had been asked to surrender the ship he loved to a stranger. But there had been something of great importance at stake . . . something that had to do with *restoring the Republic*.

No.

With *restoring Republic honor* . . .

He had asked the Senators about the phrase. And they had provided an answer.

Jadak stared at the 3-D image of Fang Zar.

And slowly the Senators' words bubbled to the surface:

Think of the ship as a key—the key to a treasure. A treasure sufficient to restore Republic honor to the galaxy.

He pulled the computer toward him, practically into his lap.

A search on the name *Stellar Envoy* returned hundreds of hits, but none of the entries coincided with a YT-1300 freighter. Navigating his way into Nar Shaddaa's subnet, he requested data on air and space collisions that had occurred in the year of his accident.

Suddenly there it was, staring him in the face in green holotext: a brief report of a collision between two Corellian ships—one, a bulk freighter named the *Jendirian Valley III*; the other, a '25 YT-1300 freighter. Both pilots were presumed to have died in the crash, but the ship had survived and been claimed by salvagers.

The ship that was now a key to the puzzle his life had become had survived.

There was no telling for how long, but Jadak had a starting point—and pursuing the ship was worth whatever risks he would be forced to take.

chapter thirteen

"ONE HUNDRED AND TEN THOUSAND."

"Lord Oxic bid'sa hundred ten thoussand. Do'sa we hear ten-five?"

"One hundred ten thousand five hundred," someone in the back of the room said.

Lestra Oxic turned in his seat and looked over his shoulder. The rival bidder was a Bith sporting a stylishly embroidered headcloth, his handheld identity screen displaying nothing more than a number.

"Eleven thousand," Oxic said, displaying his screen while he swung to face the auctioneer's podium.

"We'sa have'a bid'o one hundred eleven thousand. Do'sa we hear twelve?"

The guest auctioneer was a Gungan clothed in a long embroidered robe and celebrated for his rapid-fire delivery; the item up for bid, a small statue that had once graced the northwest atrium of Coruscant's Galactic Courts of Justice. A rare and valuable piece, as all examples of Republicana had become since the Yuuzhan Vong had devastated half the galaxy almost twenty years earlier.

"One hundred and twelve," the same Bith said, drawing excited inhales from the mixed-species audience of one hundred or so bidders.

Oxic immediately raised his screen above his head. "One hundred twelve-five."

Hydians, as the auction house was known, was itself a prime example of Republicana, studded with elegant columns and floored in the finest polished stone. Originally it had sat at the center of Sah'ot on Chandrila, but two years into the Yuuzhan Vong invasion a team of architects and construction engineers supervising an army of flesh-and-blood and droid laborers had worked feverishly to disassemble the building piece by piece and ship it to Epica, which, as hoped by those who had funded the undertaking and despite its natural beauty, had proved too remote and insignificant to attract the attention of the invaders. Many of the beings responsible for the building's relocation and tedious reassembly had remained onworld after the conclusion of the war, and had since raised opulent palaces and mansions in the forested hills that embraced the spaceport, in the process transforming Epica's once-nondescript principal city into a place of privilege and sophistication. Transformed, too, was the native population of humans, Bothans, Duros, and Bimms, who now served to satisfy the increasing needs of the wealthy who had co-opted their planet.

"We'sa stil'la waitin' for a bid'o one hundred thirteen thoussand," the auctioneer was saying.

Oxic pivoted in his chair to regard the Bith, this time through a pair of compact alumabronze macrobinoculars. In his free hand, the being from the Clak'dor system was holding an expensive comlink.

"One hundred thirteen thousand," the Bith said.

"One hundred fourteen," a woman seated a few rows in front of the Bith countered. Oxic recognized her from past auctions as an employee of the Trouvee family, which owned a gambling complex on Oseon VII.

"One fourteen-five," the Bith responded.

Oxic squirmed in his seat. Unusually tall for a human, he had a flawless, clean-shaven face that belied his advanced age. His narrow frame bordered on the skeletal, and his hands and feet were unnaturally long, yet his custom wardrobe was cut in a way that emphasized his delicate thinness and contributed to an overall impression of his being larger than life. A force of nature.

He knew just the spot for the small figurine: atop the fluted pedestal from 500 Republica that stood alongside his office desk. But he hadn't planned on paying more than 114,000 for it—the piece was somewhat overvalued even at 113,000—and certainly not when other items on the block would suffice. Still, the statue was hard to resist.

"One hundred and fifteen thousand," he said, taking himself by surprise.

When he turned, he saw the Bith whispering into his comlink, then listening to whoever was at the other end of the link.

"One hundred and seventeen."

The crowd gasped and Oxic's shoulders sagged. He resisted an urge to look at the Bith.

"We'sa have'a bid'o one hundred seventeen thousand," the Gungan said in excitement. "Will'sa any'say eighteen? How'sa 'bout seventeen-five?" He waited a moment. "One hundred seventeen'sa goin' once . . . 'sa goin' twice . . ." His mallet struck the podium with a resounding *thock!* "Sold to bidder six-three-seven!"

Nearly everyone applauded.

A Falleen stepped to the podium. "The next item up for auction is number seventy-one-dash-zero-zero in the catalog—a chandelier from the principal dining room of Ralltiir's Darpa Hotel. Made of electrum, the piece has undergone substantial restoration but is fully provenanced. The piece has a suggested opening bid of . . ."

Oxic stopped listening and turned his attention to the

exquisitely designed holocatalog. Items from Ralltiir were of no interest to him, Republicana or no. Some beings were fascinated by items from Alderaan or Naboo; others with Hutt artifacts. But Coruscant was and would remain the focus of his collection, and his obsession. He was advancing through the catalog when Koi Quire slid effortlessly into the adjacent seat he had held for her.

"How was the trip?" he asked.

"Uneventful. A pity you lost the statue."

Oxic cut his eyes to the Bith. "I'd like to know who he's representing."

"We can find out."

"Yes, by all means, let's do that."

With Firrerreos on the brink of extinction, Koi Quire was herself a collectible, rare as any of the pieces up for auction. She had come to Oxic's law firm fifteen years earlier, following the Yuuzhan Vong's success in turning Belderone's native population against the displaced Firrerreos it had once welcomed, and had instantly become an invaluable asset. Her innate powers of intuition were unmatched, and often her mere presence in a courtroom was enough to sway a jury. Aware of the peculiarities of Firrerreon culture, Oxic had never asked to know her real name and Koi had never volunteered it, though he believed she trusted he would never have made use of the knowledge to secure her allegiance.

"Standing room only," she said, taking in the room.

"More and more with every auction." Oxic sighed. "We have Chief of State Daala to thank for it. Her leadership of the GA has resulted in a resurgence of interest in late Republicana and early Imperial artifacts. As a speculator, one can't go wrong. But the serious collector suffers for it."

"Then I have news that may cheer you up," she said softly. "Your investment is on the move."

Oxic tensed in excitement but managed to keep his voice conspiratorial. "Where is he?"

"Headed to Nar Shaddaa—on the new legs you paid for, and using Core Life's indemnity payment."

"His memory has returned?"

"Presumably, since he didn't bother to check out of Aurora or wait for an official discharge. Sompa followed instructions and allowed him to pay a midnight visit to his office. He managed to deactivate surveillance using a code we think he picked up from Ril Bezant."

"The psychotherapist?"

"During a session in her office, she briefly turned off the cams, either in the interest of earning Jadak's trust or to provide him with the code in the belief he would take matters into his own hands. He has a way, in any case."

Oxic inclined his head in interest. "Don't tell me—"

"He wanted to show me around Aurora."

"Why did you decline?"

"He was already suspicious about the insurance policy. I decided there might be some benefit to keeping him agitated. By the time I left he was ready to bite my head off."

"Your insight appears to have served us well."

"He didn't bother checking Sompa's office for redundant cams. Or maybe at that point he didn't care about being watched. He used Sompa's computer to execute a number of searches and requests, and discovered a Nar Shaddaa Holonet reference to the collision."

"Clever. But why would he opt to go to Nar Shaddaa? Surely Palpatine's opponents wouldn't have cached the treasure there."

Quire shrugged. "It could be that he's looking for additional information regarding the death of his copilot, Reeze."

Oxic shook his head. "Jadak wouldn't need to go all the way to Nar Shaddaa for that."

"Then perhaps he's hoping to pick up his life where it left off."

Oxic considered it. "I suggest we collect him."

"So soon?"

"I don't want to risk involving others in this matter."

"There's always a chance of that."

"Direct Cynner to attend to it."

Quire frowned. "Are you certain he's the one for this? My inclination would be to use someone more judicious. Gomman, perhaps."

"He is safeguarding our star witness for the trade case."

"The Colicoid? What did Gomman do to warrant that assignment?"

"It's simply a matter of his having a high tolerance for bugs."

Quire nodded. "I'll let Cynner know."

Oxic reclined in his seat. The next round of bidding was about to begin.

It was soon after he and Chewbacca returned from the Corporate Sector and began running spice for Jabba the Hutt that the *Millennium Falcon* started behaving erratically. One moment the ship would outperform herself and complete the Kessel Run in record time; the next, she would develop glitches in the worst possible situations, almost as if she were intent on drawing Imperial attention or involving him and Chewie in the Rebellion. He wondered if the *Falcon's* unpredictability owed to the fact that—part by necessity, part by design—he had transformed the onetime freighter into a well-armed warship.

The lost barrels of glitterstim spice that had earned them the enmity of Jabba wasn't the first cargo they had been forced to jettison in those days leading to the trip to Tatooine. For a time it appeared that Imperial tariff vessels were lurking on the dark side of every planet they passed or approached. It got so that they had had to affix trackers to the loads before a run, just to ensure being able to recover them after dumping them and submitting to a search. But he always thought the *Falcon* had seemed peeved at having to partake in those missions.

Even the return to the Death Star after leaving Yavin 4 had seemed as much the *Falcon's* idea as Chewbacca's.

Of course, it was sheer lunacy to think that a ship could think for herself or know right from wrong— even one equipped with a trio of droid brains that rarely agreed on anything. But the Falcon *could be willful in that way, stubborn about going where he pointed her. And look what the about-face had led to. Aside from saving Luke's hide and thus being indirectly responsible for the destruction of the Emperor's super-weapon, the* Falcon *had effectively enrolled him and Chewie in the Rebel Alliance.*

But the Falcon *had saved her finest act for later in the game, breaking down shortly before the forced evacuation of Hoth and seeing to it that he and Leia were thrown together for the slow trip to Bespin. True, he had been falling in love with Leia since their first encounter in a Death Star cell block, but their private time in sublight cinched it for him.*

His own high opinion of himself wouldn't let him credit the Falcon *with actually bringing them together, or with playing any real role in their courtship and eventual marriage. But he always thought that the ship deserved the equivalent of a Corellian Bloodstripe, not only for her actions during the Rebellion, but also for helping steer him into Leia's life and heart.*

chapter fourteen

Han, Leia, Allana, and C-3PO gaped at the crowd of beings and droids assembled near the foot of the *Falcon*'s boarding ramp.

"Lando," Han said out of the corner of his mouth.

Leia nodded. "He must have commed ahead."

"So much for trying to blend in."

"It never would have worked anyway." She sighed. "I just wish I had dressed more appropriately."

"You look great."

She smiled at him. "Then I wish you'd worn something more appropriate."

A male Lutrillian dressed like a Republic-era opera extra separated himself from the welcome committee. "Oseon Seven extends a heartfelt welcome to the esteemed Solo family," he announced with a courtly bow.

"Thank you," Leia said, speaking for everyone. "This is completely unexpected."

"And unnecessary," Han muttered.

"I am See-Threepio," the droid said, descending the *Falcon*'s ramp.

The Lutrillian inclined his large head. "Welcome, See-Threepio." He turned to Han. "Is this your first visit, sir?"

"First time."

"Then we hope Oseon Seven will live up to its reputation."

Han laughed shortly. "It already has."

The planet's sprawling and frenetic spaceport swarmed with ships of all sizes and descriptions, from the most expensive yachts to shuttles crammed with tourists from worlds along the Perlemian Trade Route, ferried downside from the cruise ships in synchronous orbits. But spaceport control had directed the *Falcon* to put down in a spotless and spacious docking bay far from the principal terminals and customs areas. Inbound, Han had noted that a skyhook was under construction.

"Is there luggage, Captain Solo?" the Lutrillian said.

Han indicated the *Falcon* with a nod of his head. "In the ship."

"May I instruct our droids to fetch your bags?"

"Uh, our droid will do it." Han glanced at C-3PO, who turned and climbed the ramp without comment.

An absurdly long repulsor limo floated into the docking bay.

"Is that for us?" Allana asked Leia.

"I'm afraid so, sweetie."

She whispered: "That's even bigger than my mom's!"

"We have already had you cleared through immigration and customs," the Lutrillian said. "The pilot will convey you directly to the resort by way of tunnels reserved for our special guests. Is there any service you wish done to your ship while you're onworld—washing, refueling, or routine maintenance?"

"No," Han said firmly. "The ship is off-limits."

"Of course, sir."

The rear doors of the limo began to elevate. When C-3PO emerged from the ship toting three small bags, Han raised the ramp and enabled the *Falcon*'s security system.

"There is space in the cargo compartment for your droid, as well," the Lutrillian said.

"In the cargo compartment?" C-3PO said in distress.

Han grinned. "That's all right, he can ride with us."

"Thank you, Captain Solo."

Han shoved C-3PO gently into the rear of the limo. "Don't say I never do anything for you."

Smoothly and quietly, the repulsor limo exited the docking bay and disappeared into a broad tunnel.

Allana slumped in the seat, disappointed. "I wanted to see the Ribbon."

"We will," Leia said, patting her on the knee. "After we check into our room."

Han decided he was fine with going straight to the hotel. Normally he and Leia traveled incognito, but what sense did it make to pretend to be someone else when they'd come to Oseon VII to peel back a layer of the *Falcon*'s history? What's more, it would only be a matter of time before tourists on the Ribbon recognized them. Although on Oseon VII they could probably claim to be celebrity impersonators and get away with it.

One of several dozen systems that made up a region of space known as the Centrality, the Oseon—much like the Corporate Sector—had been left to develop in its own fashion. Some of the galaxy's most unusual planets were located in the Centrality, but what set the Oseon system apart and made it a hub for tourism was an annual stellar event known as the Flamewind—a radiation storm of shifting colors that lasted three weeks and was said to provoke emotional reactions in spectators. Almost fifty years earlier, Lando and his droid-that-would-be-a-spacecraft, Vuffi Raa, had been forced to negotiate the Oseon system during a Flamewind without the aid of the *Falcon*'s navicomputer.

Over the centuries, Oseon VII had become not only a base for exploring the Centrality but a gambling center as well, with elaborate casinos modeled after other wonders of the galaxy—both natural and artificial, past and present—strung out along a fifty-kilometer-long strip known as the Ribbon. The former Ithor and Vortex's Cathedral of Winds, present-day Kashyyyk, and even Republic-era Coruscant were among the planet's richly detailed facsimiles, lovingly re-created by an entertainment consortium known as PlanetDreams, Inc., whose current vice president was none other than the onetime owner of the *Millennium Falcon*, Cix Trouvee.

Attendants were on hand to see to the Solos' every whim when the repulsor limo came to a halt at the Oseon Resort's majestic entrance. First to exit, Leia said, "Oh, no."

Han saw why. A lavish runner had been rolled out for them, lined on both sides with uniformed Centran species staff members and servant droids. Accustomed to pomp and circumstance, Allana took all of it in stride, and C-3PO in undisguised delight, but it had been a long while since Han had allowed himself to be subjected to such deferential treatment. The lobby had been cleared of guests, and a small army of managers, assistant managers, concierges, event planners, and hospitality specialists was arrayed before the front desk. Off to one side stood a group of A-list celebrities and entertainers, some of them making discreet use of their comlinks to capture holoimages.

"Captain Solo, Princess Leia, and Mistress Amelia," a thin-faced, spotlessly attired human began, "if only we had been notified sooner of your arrival, we would have been better prepared. It's a pity you were not here last month for the Flamewind, which was spectacular this year. Regardless, we have moved guests from the penthouse suite to accommodate you. Naturally, the suite and all services will be complimentary, and a personal staff will be placed at your disposal. You will enjoy unlimited credit in the casino, and, of course, should you prefer private games—"

"Actually, we're not here to gamble," Han said.

"Oh, I see. Well, in that case, private performances can be arranged. At the moment the Oseon is proud to present the Saffin Omlick Group, Moosh Kole, and the Kinetic Krew of the Molpol Circus, among a host of others." The manager gestured to his subordinates. "The Oseon would also be happy to arrange sightseeing visits to Rafa Four, Trammis Three, the ThonBoka Star Cave Nebula, or other destinations in the Centrality."

"That won't be necessary," Leia said pleasantly.

The manager bowed slightly. "Of course. If you've come simply for privacy—"

"We were hoping for a chance to speak privately with Cix Trouvee," Han said quietly.

The manager stared at him.

Han returned a blank look. "Isn't he still the owner?"

"Captain Solo, I'm sorry to have to report that Cix Trouvee passed on some weeks ago."

Han lowered his head, but before his full disappointment could show, the manager added: "But the Oseon is now owned by his children, and I'm certain they would be more than happy to speak with you about whatever matter has brought you here. In fact, they had hoped to fête you privately once you were settled in."

Han, Leia, and Allana traded smiles.

"That would be great," Han said.

The office occupied the summit of the Oseon Tower. A round room decorated with exceptional examples of sculpture and statuary, it enjoyed a kilometer-high view of the planet, from the Ribbon clear to the spaceport and nascent skyhook. A ridge of arid mountains stood sentinel on the horizon, and the lavender sky, cross-hatched by contrails, was filled with ascending and descending ships. Leia sat on a cushioned bench at one of the transparisteel windows, Allana on her knee, pointing to different resorts along the Ribbon.

"That hotel with the giant wings is a replica of a building on a world called Thyferra," Leia said.

"Where bacta comes from."

"Exactly. And those gardens are similar to ones on Ossus. And look, do you recognize that one?"

Allana followed Leia's finger down to the crenellated turrets of a fanciful castle fronted by a gargantuan fountain.

"Is that supposed to be Hapes?"

Leia nodded. "It's called the Seven Moons Casino. We can go there tomorrow if you'd like."

"That'll be weird."

"You're right, it will be weird. But it will also be fun."

Allana reached up to wrap her arms around Leia's neck and hugged her. "I love you, Grandma," she whispered into her ear.

Leia shut her eyes and tightened her embrace. "I love you, too."

Allana pulled away and Leia smiled. "Mistress Amelia."

Allana twittered a laugh and hurried to one of the adjacent window panels. Leia stood and moved toward Han, who was speaking with the three siblings from Cix Trouvee's first marriage. As with many long-term residents of Oseon VII, they were holding on to their natural good looks with the help of surgical procedures and other rejuvenation techniques. Leia stopped to regard a wondrous sculpture of a double helix.

"Is this piece from Alderaan?"

"It was made there," Doon said, the oldest of the three, tan, slim, and fit. "But it spent many years in the presidential suite of the Hotel Manarai on Coruscant.

We were fortunate enough to acquire it at a recent auction."

Leia turned to take in the other sculptures. "Are these others genuine?"

"How we wish—since it is our goal to make the Oseon Resort as authentic as possible. Unfortunately, most Coruscant Republicana now resides in the hands of private collectors. But they are museum-quality reproductions."

They ambled over to where Han was seated with the daughter and younger son. A droid had delivered a small feast of snacks and drinks.

"What is it you wished to speak with my father about, Captain Solo?" Doon said.

Han set his drink down. "The *Millennium Falcon*."

The daughter grinned. "The galaxy's most famous vessel. Or is that infamous?"

"A bit of both," Leia said.

Doon shook his head in amusement. "Our father was so proud to have once owned the *Falcon*." He turned to Han. "He followed all of your exploits as though some small part of the ship still belonged to him. In fact, we have images of our father with the *Falcon*, if you'd care—"

"Yes!" Allana said, hurrying over to them.

Everyone adjusted their chairs to face a small holoprojector. Doon activated it with a remote and navigated through a menu of options. All at once there was the *Falcon*, in one-meter 3-D, almost as Han remembered the ship from the day Lando showed it to him.

"Here's one of Dad in the cockpit," Doon said.

Han leaned forward, a big smile plastered on his face. "Look at that. Only one pair of chairs." He squinted. "The instrument panel was so simple. And the same Rubicon navicomputer."

"No dice hanging in the viewport," Leia said.

Han made a face at her.

"Here's another, with Dad fixing something or other."

"The port-side braking thruster," Han said. "I can't tell you the number of times I've had to repair that jet."

"Here, he's inside the ship . . ."

"The main hold," Han said. "And a dejarik table was already there! Your father must have removed it at some point, because it wasn't onboard when Lando won the *Falcon*. I installed a new one to appease my copilot, Chewbacca."

"The celebrated Wookiee," Doon said.

Han gazed at the floor and nodded.

Leia spoke up. "Lando said that he won the ship from your father in a sabacc tournament at Bespin."

"That's true," Doon's brother said.

Han looked up. "Did he ever explain why he offered the *Falcon* as a marker?"

The siblings burst out laughing.

"He most certainly did," Doon said finally. "And it's quite an interesting tale, if you have time."

Han relaxed into his chair. "We have nothing but."

chapter fifteen

IN WHAT HE OFTEN CLAIMED WAS AN HOMAGE TO HIS
father, Cix Trouvee was a confirmed and incorrigible
gambler. He had learned to play the odds at an early age,
and by eighteen had left prosperous Corulag to embark
on a career as a professional player. Where his father
had bet on swoop races exclusively, Cix was all over the
board, and as he approached midlife he would bet on
just about anything: Podraces, Chin-Bret matches,
rounds of laro, pazaak, Point 5 and sabacc, the roll of a
jubilee wheel ball or a cupful of dice, the weather, the
population curve, or the fluctuating value of salthia
beans. Fortunes passed through his hands, slipped
through his fingers. As fast as the credits rolled in he
would spend them—on wine, women, luxury hotel
suites, suits of shimmersilk and chromasheath. More
often his spending outpaced his winnings, and in his
wake he left a string of bad debts, splintered friendships,
and broken hearts.

For a brief period the one constant in his life was a
quirky YT-1300 freighter someone had named the *Millennium Falcon* and others had seen fit to equip with a
Class One hyperdrive, a dejarik hologame table, and a
dorsal-mounted laser cannon. But when you're the
owner of a fifty-five-year-old starship hosting as many
retrofits as original parts, you had better be good with

your hands, and Cix simply wasn't, except when it came to dealing cards, gathering winnings, or scrawling his name on markers. Cix loved the *Falcon,* but she was slowly bleeding him dry. The hyperdrive one day, the droid brain the next, a hundred little parts that needed to be tightened, torqued, repaired, or replaced. Even so, he'd never once given serious thought to selling the freighter or trading it in on a more customary vessel, at least until the *Falcon* broke down unexpectedly, causing him to miss out on a high-stakes Outlander match on Coruscant. Cix realized he was in desperate need of a big score—one that would continue to finance not only the lifestyle to which he had grown accustomed, but also a complete overhaul of the credit pit the *Millennium Falcon* had become. So when a Rodian told him that the Hutts were taking action on a one-of-a-kind contest, Cix knew he wanted in even before he knew the details.

"What's the game?" he finally got around to asking the Rodian.

"The *contest,*" the Rodian had emphasized. "Between Imperial forces and a band of would-be insurgents. At Yag'Dhul, a standard month from now."

Just how the Hutts had gotten wind of the imminent showdown, Cix would never learn. But according to the Rodian and other gamblers in the know, the Empire had learned that the insurgents were constructing a space station at Yag'Dhul, and had decided to make the installation the first target of a newly inaugurated Star Destroyer called the *Desolator.* The insurgents, however, had learned of the Empire's plans and were hoping to add the *Desolator* to their short list of victories.

The Battle of Yavin wouldn't be fought for another five years, and the Empire thought of the insurgents as more of a nuisance than a real threat. Most actions by disaffected militia groups had been limited to harassment widely scattered bands, and runs against supply convoys and Imperial installations. If the Rebels had scored any significant victories, the news had been suppressed by the Empire-controlled HoloNet, though word on Nar Shaddaa was that a nascent insurgent alliance was growing in numbers and in strength. The underground was rife with rumors of impending action at Ylesia, and of successful militia raids in a cluster of black holes known as the Maw, where the Empire was thought to be completing work on a massive warship fifteen years in the making.

The terms of the wager couldn't have been more straightforward.

Clearly the Hutts had no faith in the insurgents' ability to destroy the *Desolator;* but neither would they allow themselves to be drawn into murky definitions of victory. They were offering action based solely on the number of Imperial and insurgent fighters that would be destroyed during the engagement.

Impartial but intent on taking a percentage from both winners and losers, the Hutts had fixed the line at forty-five fighters. How that cumulative number was reached— whether mostly at the cost of Imperial fighters or insurgent fighters, or the outcome of a close-to-even split—was unimportant. At identical odds bettors had the option of wagering whether the combined total would exceed forty-five or come in at fewer. Ideally, the Hutts would get an equal number of bets on both sides. If not, they were likely to adjust the line up or down to be certain of clearing a profit.

Cix wrestled with the ethics of betting on a battle, but that didn't stop him from doing his research. In the process he hoped he would discover a way to rationalize getting in on the action. He went to ground, talking to as many contacts as possible. Smugglers, arms dealers, information brokers. Beings he suspected were militia members or sympathizers. Bartenders, musicians, and waitresses in sleazy cantinas and tapcafs, and Imperial officers who had had one too many drinks in those same places. If the Yag'Dhul wager was going to be the score of his lifetime, he wanted to go into it with as much solid information as possible, because the Hutts wouldn't have set the odds as they did unless they had already done their homework.

The *Desolator* was typical of the new ships of the line: a sixteen-hundred-meter-long Dreadnaught bristling with laser cannons and carrying a complement of ground assault troops, war machines, and TIE fighters. A successor to the old V-wing fighters, TIEs didn't so much maneuver as swarm. Frequently their victories owed to superior odds. Outfitted with a pair of powerful laser cannons, the sinister black-and-gray fighters lacked hyperdrives, life-support systems, and defensive shielding. Mention a TIE to a seasoned combat pilot and nine out of ten times you'd get a sneer in response. Many asserted that TIEs were as easy to eradicate as bugs if you knew how to target them.

The insurgents, on the other hand, were making do with Z-95 Headhunters retrofitted with better weaponry and hyperdrive units. If lightly armored and difficult to maneuver, the Headhunter was dependable. More important, the majority of insurgent pilots had spent time in the Imperial Academies or the navy itself before jumping ship, and the rest were said to have heart, whereas a lot of the Imp fliers had been drafted into service and saw no way out.

Notwithstanding the rumors of militia victories in the Maw, Cix took the fact that the Empire kept spitting out ships as a sign that these groups were being taken seriously. And at Yag'Dhul the insurgents had the equivalent of a home-field advantage. Finally, the insurgents knew an attack was forthcoming.

As word of the wager spread, Cix learned that Coruscant's notorious Baath Brothers had opted to take a stand on the outcome of the contest. Convinced that the Imperials would win, they were offering a spread of ten fighters, regardless of the Hutts' combined total of forty-five. Cix's inclination was to give the points and bet on the favorite. By doing so he was essentially counting on the fact that the tally of destroyed insurgent fighters minus ten would be greater than the number of destroyed Imperial fighters. Still, he wanted to be sure.

With enough facts and stats to fill a data card, he hired an outlaw slicer to load everything into a protocol droid that had been programmed to serve as a handicapper and had a good record of predicting the outcome of swoop races.

"There are many variables you have neglected to include," the droid told Cix in an officious way.

"Such as?"

"The commander of the Imperial Star Destroyer."

"I tried."

"The commander of the insurgent forces at Yag'Dhul."

"No luck there, either."

"It helps that you saw fit to provide me with a date for the engagement, as I was then able to calculate the possible effects of tidal forces from Yag'Dhul's trio of moons. But you failed to provide data on the hyperspace origin coordinates of the Star Destroyer."

"You can't expect me to have contacts in Imperial central command."

"And you can't expect me to return an assured prediction."

"Then I'll settle for your best estimate."

"Be forewarned that I refuse to be held accountable."

"All right, I'm forewarned. Now just tell me the odds!"

The droid did.

His own hunches reinforced, Cix next went about the business of borrowing enough credits to lay down a wager that would leave him sitting pretty—even after paying the juri juice commissions the Baath Brothers would add to the bet and the lenders had added to the loans. He never even considered that he might lose.

Yag'Dhul was the homeworld of an exoskeletoned species of humanoids known as Givin, who had contributed their mathematical skills to the Confederacy of Independent Systems during the Clone Wars. Located near the intersection of the Rimma Trade Route and Corellian Trade Spine, the planet was a major reversion point and the site of skirmishes going back millennia. At certain times of the year especially, the same three moons that wreaked havoc with Yag'Dhul's seas and atmosphere conspired to extend the time required for ships to revert from hyperspace and navigate to new coordinates before returning to lightspeed. The perilous tidal conditions left the ships vulnerable to attacks from pirates that operated from a base on the outermost of Yag'Dhul's moons. Shortly after the conclusion of the Clone Wars, the pirates had been killed or driven away, but the base had become a way station for travelers, then a sports resort catering to gamblers and spectators who attended Yag'Dhul's starship races. The local militia put an end to the races when construction of the space station began, but the Givin-owned and -operated sports resort had remained open and ultimately served as the gathering place for many of the high rollers involved in the Yag'Dhul wager.

A droid-piloted vessel in stationary orbit between the planet's two inner moons transmitted live feeds of the battle to an enormous holoscreen in the resort's gaming room, around which a mixed-species crowd of rowdy bettors had gathered for near-continuous drinking and impromptu wagering on whether the space station itself would survive. The remote vessel captured the moment of the *Desolator*'s reversion from hyperspace in what was to have been a sneak attack on anti-Imperial forces, as well as the insurgents' swift counterstrike, which not only caught the Imperials off-guard but drove the TIE fighter kill count to twenty in a matter of minutes. Cix was relieved that he hadn't wagered on the over–under of forty-five, but suddenly found himself having to root for a rally by the Imperials lest the insurgents ruin the spread by destroying too many TIEs.

Gnawing at a fingernail, he studied the updates on the screen, shutting his ears to the game room's caterwaul of energized voices. The insurgents had scored thirteen kills; the Imperials, five. But TIEs were still buzzing from the *Desolator*'s launch bays, and the Star Destroyer itself, safe within its combat shields, was beginning to bring its turbolaser arrays to bear on the flights of Headhunters and ARC-170s.

Cix kept his eyes riveted to the scoreboard. The Imperials were beginning to score, driving the number of insurgent kills into the teens. But the Imps were going to have to do a whole lot better in order for Cix to collect on his bet.

Evading individual engagements with the TIEs, the foolhardy militia pilots were actually going after the big ship, flinging at it everything they had in their limited arsenal, and disappearing one after another in short-lived blossoms of roiling fire.

The crowd was in an uproar, clearly split down the middle in terms of those who had bet the spread and others who had wagered with the Hutts—the over–under number already closing on forty-five with a lot of fight left in both sides.

All at once the holoimages grew noisy with static then vanished altogether, with the score standing at insurgents with nineteen kills; Imperials with twenty-eight. A deafening shout rose from the bettors, many of whom were clambering onto the tables and waving balled fists at the club's Givin proprietors.

"The remote has been destroyed!" one of the owners finally announced. Receiving an update from somewhere, he added: "The *Desolator* intercepted the coded feed from the remote. The Imperials believe that we're furnishing intelligence to the militia. The Star Destroyer is coming around . . . *We're being targeted!*"

"To the ships!" someone in the crowd yelled, and twenty beings leapt from their seats and raced for the corridors that led to the moon's small spaceport. Chaos gripped the room as bettors began to scurry every which way, colliding into one another, tripping, slipping on sloshed drinks and going head over heels. Wading into the turmoil, Cix located his copilot and the two of them managed to squeeze into one of the crammed corridors and run for where the *Falcon* was docked—all the while Cix asking everyone he passed for an update on the score.

The Imperials were still leading the kill count, a Rodian said; the insurgents had evened the score, said another; the Hutts' over–under number had already been superseded.

The first ground-shaking volley from the *Desolator* struck the moon base as the *Falcon* was warming for launch. Half of the docking bay collapsed, and the ceiling aperture froze a few meters short of fully opened. Cix nosed the YT up through rampaging flames and clouds of black smoke and shot for space even while packets of scarlet energy continued to rain down on the hapless moon. Ships to both sides of the *Falcon* disappeared in fiery explosions.

"Get the deflector shields up!" Cix told his copilot. "Then plot us a way out of this mess!" He pulled the comm headset on with one hand and enabled it with the other. "I gotta find out the score!"

The ship shook and nearly flipped over onto its back.

"Laser cannon," the copilot said when he could. "The Givins' resort is history. The Imps are targeting departing ships!"

Cix took his eyes off the communications suite to glance out the viewport. The *Desolator* was a few degrees to starboard and employing all its forward batteries to make mincemeat of the moon and everything close to it. He threw the ship through a barrel roll and accelerated to port, narrowly evading a stream of destruction.

"We can't jump to lightspeed from this side of the second moon," the copilot said. "We need to find a way around the battle."

"Or through it," Cix said. He whipped the headset off and locked his hands on the control yoke. "Listen for a score!"

A globe of explosive light flared in the distance and washed into the cockpit.

"The space station," the copilot said. "That'll set the insurgents back some."

Cix muttered a curse. "I knew I should have taken that bet."

"Comm from the *Hole Card* outbound from Yag'Dhul. The militia have destroyed twenty-one Imperial fighters and lost thirty of their own. The remaining Headhunters are jumping to lightspeed."

Cix turned to him wide-eyed. Subtracting ten from the number of Imperial kills would put the score at twenty to twenty-one, and mean that he had won the bet. "Is that a final?"

"He didn't say. But with insurgent fighters out of play—"

Cix hooted in celebration. With ten deducted to the Imperials, the spread was a guarantee. "Now we just have to survive this." Nudging the throttle, he sent the *Falcon* on a corkscrewing course for the second moon;

the *Desolator* was far off to starboard now but several TIEs were taking a keen interest and dropping into the YT's wake.

The copilot gripped the instrument panel as bolts hammered against the rear deflectors. "What are you trying to do, add us to the tally?"

"That's exactly what I don't want to do," Cix said through clenched teeth. "Just keep your finger away from the laser cannon trigger."

"Shields are down to sixty percent. Don't take another hit."

"Easy for you to say."

Cix changed course, slipping between two inbound TIEs and rolling into a course change.

"*Desolator* is coming around, aft batteries traversing." The copilot swallowed hard. "We're not going to make it!" The light-side crescent of the second moon expanded in the viewport. "Even the *Falcon*'s not that fast."

"You want to bet?"

Cix leveled the ship and maxed the throttle. Energy bolts streaming across the bow and whizzing past both mandibles, the *Falcon* hurtled forward at bone-jarring speed. Something rattled loose from the bulkhead and crashed on the deck.

"*Desolator*'s got a lock on us. Firing—"

Cix twisted the control yoke, following the cratered sweep of the moon into blazing starlight.

Off the fantail, just to port, two fireballs flashed.

"What was that?"

"Two TIE fighters. Friendly fire from the *Desolator*."

Cix blew out his breath. "Close, too close." He was swiveling toward the navicomputer when the copilot launched a curse at the ceiling.

"The TIEs count!"

Cix whipped around, slack-jawed. "That's impossible! The battle was over!"

The copilot listened for a long moment, his eyes growing dull. "One Headhunter hadn't jumped to hyperspace when the TIEs got hit. The officials are ruling that the battle didn't end until the final insurgent Rebel fighter jumped."

Cix continued to stare at him. "The TIEs were in play? The TIEs were *in play?*"

The copilot nodded. "The first TIE kill made for a push, but the second puts us one fighter under the spread!" He blinked. "We lost."

"Big-time," Cix said softly. "Big-time."

"After Yag'Dhul, everyone he had borrowed from was out looking for him," Doon was telling Han, Leia, and Allana. "Dad saw only one way out: the annual Cloud City Sabacc Tournament. He showed up at the Yarith Bespin Hotel with just enough to cover the ten-thousand-credit buy-in and the ante for the few hands he figured he would need to win to remain in the tournament to its end."

"Obviously that didn't happen," Han said.

Doon's sister nodded. "More than half of the players bombed out by the second day. Dad made it to the third, but he was hanging on by his teeth. On one round the pot grew to ninety thousand credits. He didn't have anything near the amount needed to remain in the game, but he had a hand he didn't think anyone could beat."

"Except for Lando," Han said.

Doon nodded. "An idiot's array. And of course, by then Dad had thrown the *Falcon* into the pot. Not all that different from the way you won the ship, if the stories are true."

"In our match, Lando was one card short of an array," Han said.

"What happened with all the credits your dad owed?" Allana asked.

Doon smiled at her. "You know, it's the strangest thing, but as soon as Dad lost the *Millennium Falcon* his luck changed completely. He convinced some folks to stake him to one game or another, and he had a lucky streak that continued for the rest of his life."

"He used to joke that losing the *Falcon* might have been the best thing that ever happened to him."

"The two happiest days in a starship owner's life," Doon's sister said. "The day he buys the ship and the day he gets rid of it."

Han could feel Leia's eyes on him, but he refused to look at her.

"The result of that streak is what you see here," Doon said, gesturing broadly to the finely appointed office. "PlanetDreams was only too glad to bring him aboard as a partner."

Han absorbed it. "So it wasn't Cix who named her *Millennium Falcon*."

"No," the younger brother said. "He certainly would have taken credit for that if he had."

"Did he ever mention how or where he got the *Falcon*?" Leia asked.

"Yeah," Allana said. "That's what we want to know."

Doon thought for a moment. "I'm sure he did, but I don't remember anything specific." He looked to his siblings, both of whom shook their heads. "There *is* someone who would know," he added finally. He touched a button on a comlink set into the top of the table. "Is Waglin around?" he asked of the voice that responded.

"He is, sir."

"Tell him I need him in the office."

"Who's Waglin?" Allana asked.

Doon grinned. "He was my dad's copilot."

Lando's face was onscreen in the main hold when the *Falcon* blasted away from Oseon VII two standard days later. "Cix never told me the full story," he said to Han and Leia. "Now I'm back to feeling sorry about having taken the *Falcon* from him."

"Yeah, well, don't," Han said. "He ended up doing pretty well for himself without her. Anyway, if you hadn't taken her from him, I couldn't have taken her from you." He grinned for the cam.

Lando forced an elaborate frown. "Did you learn anything about where the *Falcon* was before Cix?"

"Yeah," Han said uncertainly. "From his copilot. A Weequay. Must be at least a hundred and fifty years old. As wrinkled as the Lava Labyrinth."

"What's he doing on Oseon Seven of all places?"

"Cix kept him employed all these years," Leia said. "He's not much more than a fixture now, but Cix's children treat him like family."

"He was with Cix when he got the *Falcon*?"

"No, they hooked up much later," Han said. "But he knew the story."

"He bought the *Falcon* from a circus," Leia said.

"The Molpol Circus."

Lando touched his mustache. "You know, I think I remember hearing that the *Falcon* had been part of a circus."

Han nodded. "The story sounded familiar to me, too."

"You have the name of the being who owned her?"

"Vistal Purn," Han said.

"He's no longer with the circus," Leia said. "Now he organizes creature shows."

Lando laughed. "That's a short leap. Any idea where he is?"

"Running a show on Taris."

"Really," Lando said slowly. "Tendra, Chance, and I were just there—well, two months ago, at any rate."

"Business or pleasure?" Han said.

"A bit of both. We were finalizing a deal with the

Taris government for a shipment of YVH droids, and doing some shopping."

"What's Taris need with Hunters?" Leia asked.

"A well-armed criminal element has moved in. The deal was sanctioned by Chief of State Daala herself. But the point I was trying to make is that we had what you might say was a strange encounter while we were there." Lando paused briefly. "With Seff Hellin."

Leia blinked in surprise. "We know Seff." She turned to Han. "Seff was the oldest of the Jedi group that was moved from Yavin Four to the Shelter station. Maybe fourteen years old at the time."

Han scratched his head. "Tall kid with curly hair?"

Leia nodded. "His mother is Corellian."

"Okay, now I remember him."

Leia positioned herself for the cam. "What happened, Lando?"

"He came to visit me at the hotel where we were staying. He wanted to know the details of the YVH deal."

"Did you tell him?"

"I told him it was none of his business. Then he wanted to know what I thought about the fact that Daala is employing Mandalorians as a kind of royal guard."

"Why would it matter to Seff what you think?" Han said.

"Beats me. But I finally figured out what he was getting at."

"Which was what?"

"Whether Tendrando had given thought to manufacturing a Mandalorian Hunter droid."

Leia and Han traded glances. "Are you certain, Lando?"

Lando shrugged. "Not a hundred percent. But that's what it sounded like."

Han turned to Leia. "You think he's still on Taris?"

"I don't know. This new crime syndicate could be the reason Luke sent him there in the first place."

"Anyway," Lando interrupted. "Just thought I'd let you know. And make sure to fill me in on what you find out about the *Falcon*, buddy."

"Will do," Han said.

From a room high in the Oseon Tower, Waglin watched the *Millennium Falcon* emerge from a private docking bay and launch for the sky. Merging with outbound traffic, the century-old freighter rose on a column of blue energy and disappeared from view.

"They're on their way to Taris right now," the Weequay was saying into a comlink. "I'm watching them with my own eyes." He paused to listen. "You're right, who'd want to tangle with Han Solo and a Jedi? But Solo has a lot of influential friends, and I thought he might be a way for you to get what you're after. Besides, Solo's a far cry from the hotshot he was. Slower on the draw."

He listened some more.

"That's up to you, of course. But I agree, you'd have to give him a good reason for helping you. I'm just being neighborly by letting you know he's headed your way. There is one more thing: they're traveling with a young girl. Some war orphan they adopted a few years back." Waglin waited, then said: "I don't have any permacrete ideas to offer along those lines. I'm just saying that the Solos would probably do anything for her."

Waglin listened. "I appreciate that. You didn't hear about her from me, though. Old-timers like us have to stick together. Plus, I've got a job and a reputation to protect."

The being at the other end of the communication spoke for a while.

"That could work. Good luck with it, then. And let me know how it ends."

chapter sixteen

As a much younger man, Jadak had done his fair share of planet-hopping. But few of the trips he had logged could match the two days it took him to travel from Obroa-skai to the Smugglers' Moon, going by way of Balmorra and Onderon in an effort to foil possible pursuers. To his eyes, the galaxy had changed that much.

There was a time, for instance, when Nar Shaddaa's spaceport officials couldn't have cared less who arrived on the moon, or for what purpose. Sixty-two years later, human visitors had to submit to retinal and body scans.

Basic was still the prevalent language of trade and exchange, but Outer Rim accents were now heard as often as Core dialects. And perhaps as a result of what the Yuuzhan Vong had wrought during their push for Coruscant, you encountered fewer beings from Perlemian Trade Route worlds and more from the outlying systems. Putting their war reparations to work, Corellians and Wookiees were scarce, busy rebuilding their worlds and putting out fires. The only place a traveler might rub elbows with a Kuati was in premier class. Jedi had never been a common sight even when they were twenty thousand strong. Now they were said to be as rare as mynock teeth. What you saw instead, and in unsettling numbers, were members of various militaries, security personnel, and surveillance droids of all description.

The sight that had widened his eyes the most was a band of Mandalorians strapped into their cumbersome trademark armor and marching down a spaceport concourse like they owned the place. A near-mythic group when Jadak was piloting for the Republic Group.

In many ways, the galaxy seemed as wide open as it had been in the years preceding the Trade Federation's embargo of tiny Naboo. Human travelers no longer had to wonder every time they dealt with a Gossam or a Koorivar or a Muun, or watched a pack of Geonosians hurrying into one of their organic-looking starships, if they had just crossed paths with an enemy agent. But if even distant star systems were more accessible, beings of all species seemed more self-absorbed, quieter about who they were and whatever business they were up to. There was something purposeful in the way they spoke and moved; something about them that struck Jadak as driven. Maybe that was the reason for all the tight security. The current regime wanted everyone marching in step. Disturbances to the hard-won peace, by accident or design, would not be tolerated. The cams and scanners that tracked everyone's movements seemed to say: *Your actions are being monitored, and we don't care that you know.*

Jadak hadn't liked running out on Aurora the way he did. He owed Sompa and the rest for at least prolonging his life, if not precisely saving it. But he couldn't forgive the fact that they had tried to toy with him. Tracing him wouldn't likely pose a problem for anyone with a speck of know-how, but Jadak thought there might be some advantage to getting a running start. With any luck he'd be able to hold on to the lead until he could be fitted with a new identity, which on Nar Shaddaa used to mean only a couple of hours. Now he wasn't so sure.

At Balmorra Spaceport, feigning interest in seeing how his new legs looked on the display screen, he had bribed a Bothan security agent to allow him a peek at his scanner image. The everyday identity chip Aurora had implanted in his wrist showed clear as day, but nothing else leapt off the screen. If the Smugglers' Moon was still the criminal paradise he remembered, he would have himself scanned for locator chips, as well.

Provided that his credits held out.

The galactic jump had eaten deeply into the ten thousand he had received from Core Life. If he kept spending at the same rate, he'd be looking for a job long before he caught up with the *Stellar Envoy*—assuming it was still in one piece somewhere, under someone's command.

In Aurora's library he had read that Nar Shaddaa, much like Obroa-skai, had suffered greatly during the war with Yuuzhan Vong. Obroa-skai had even hosted a war coordinator. But Jadak was encouraged by what he saw and heard on passing from customs into Nar Shaddaa Spaceport's main terminal. Beyond the terminal's floor-to-ceiling window panes rose the ancient, kilometers-high refueling spires and loading docks he remembered from a lifetime ago. The reek of widespread pollution was beyond the capacity of the terminal's air scrubbers. And if nothing else, Vertical City was still the loudest place in the galaxy. The moon's residents were so accustomed to outyelling the decibel racket of construction droids, deliberately loud skimmers, blasting radios, and blasterfire that whenever or wherever a Nar Shaddaan was encountered, you could be assured of a high-volume conversation.

Angling for the exits, Jadak waded deeper into the mixed-species crowd. Short of the automatic doors, he stopped to gaze at a bewildering splash of advertising holodata that crowned them—images of hotels and restaurants, come-ons for transport to different sectors of the ecumenopolis, and other local services. Only weeks into his new life and he was already wondering if he would ever be able to keep in step with those around him. Or if he wanted to. But his sense of having unfinished business compelled him to forge ahead. Something needed to be put to rest before he could even hope to move on.

Flitcher Poste spotted his mark on the arrivals level of the spaceport: a lanky human of forty-five or fifty years, blond hair worn long, a short beard and mustache. He was gazing out on Nar Shaddaa's skyline like he'd just arrived from some backrocket world in the Cron drift. Studying the holoadverts above the exit doors, trying to figure out if he should ride a hovercab, a mag-lev, or a shuttle, or maybe risk renting an airspeeder.

Just a rube from a faraway planet.

Poste kept him in his sights as he rode a turbolift down to the arrivals level. He walked out the tall doors and moved toward the hovercab stations, carrying a small black attaché case. That struck Poste as curious. Only beings who had business on Nar Shaddaa arrived with attaché cases. Tourists, gamblers, players, visiting dignitaries, and criminals usually arrived with luggage, sometimes a full pallet of bags. Clearly the guy wasn't a resident—not with that lost look on his face. So maybe he had arrived from a low-tech world and was carrying all his worldly possessions in that one case. But then why would anyone with so little come to Nar Shaddaa? Well, okay, the moon was often a final stop for folks who had nothing more to lose, but this human didn't give that impression. Maybe he had family or friends here. But friends or family wouldn't leave someone to the mercy of people like Poste, who made a living prowling the spaceport for innocent travelers, getting to them before they could be fleeced or set upon by the currency changers, holdup artists, and scammers who worked the rest of the urban sprawl.

Hurrying after the human, Poste noted that he walked like someone who was still getting used to his legs, like someone who had had ill-fitting prosthetics installed. That meant he could be a veteran who had lost his legs to blasterfire in one war or another. Though the human didn't meet anyone's gaze, Poste could tell that he was taking stock of his surroundings, aware of everything that was going on around him. How else would he be able to steer through the spaceport throng with such an easy grace?

That was it.

New legs or no, there was something inherently nimble about his movements. Something capable, one might say. Self-possessed.

Poste drew nearer. The stranger didn't appear to be armed. No weapon strapped to his ankle or wedged into the rear of his trousers that might create a telltale bulge beneath the thin material of his jacket. Poste began to wonder if the lost look and awkward gait might be for show. Maybe the newcomer was looking for marks. Worse, maybe he was trying to lure petty criminals like Poste by baiting, then entrapping them. But the idea of a plainclothes cop on Nar Shaddaa was even crazier than the idea of arriving onworld with no more than an attaché case.

Poste was intrigued. He made up his mind not to pick-pocket the mark or entice him into buying a bogus nightlife tour, but he hadn't given up on the idea of seeing what that attaché contained. Perhaps the newcomer would set it down carelessly, or become distracted just long enough for Poste to move in and move on. It was simply a matter of waiting for the right place and the right moment . . .

Poste studied the newcomer's clothing more closely as

the two of them edged into the public transport area. The wrinkled jacket and drab trousers had the look of clothes you might be given if you'd just been released from stir, or from a psychiatric ward. Even the lower-level panhandlers and canyon kids dressed better. So there went the cop theory. Or did it reinforce it?

Poste came to a halt and turned to one side, pretending sudden interest in the display window items of a tech store. In the window's reflection, he could see the newcomer standing in a HoloNet booth, running a search of some sort. If he was looking for a hotel, it meant he wasn't sure where he wanted to go. If he was looking for a name, it meant he didn't know where the being was. Whichever, he was focused on what he was doing. On the hunt. The newcomer pulled a disposable comlink from the upper pocket of his cheap jacket and sent something to it from the HoloNet. Then he set off in the direction of the mag-lev express to the Corellian sector.

Poste sighed in disappointment. That ended it for him. He wasn't about to follow the guy all the way into Vertical City—not with his airspeeder parked in the lot across from the hovercab station and already costing him credits. Reluctantly he fell back, and he was on the brink of heading for the pedestrian walkway that accessed the lot when his trained eye settled on two beings who were plainly up to no good and beginning to converge on the newcomer as he stepped from the people mover onto the mag-lev platform. One was human, the other Nautolan, and both were heavyweights.

The interesting thing was that the newcomer had also spotted them. In what could have been interpreted as an abrupt change of mind, he made a sharp turn. Infiltrating the crowd waiting for the mag-lev, he slipped effortlessly into and out of spaces beings often claimed as their own, then hastened for one of the platforms accessed by hovercabs and air shuttles.

The two goons had also picked up speed, the human touching his left ear in a way that suggested he was in communication with his partner, or others as yet unseen. Without displaying any of the finesse the newcomer had shown, the pair circled the edge of the crowd using their bulk to shoulder or shove stragglers aside. Instead of making for free space, the newcomer was staying well inside the crowd. If his pursuers were going to get to him, they were going to have to plow their way through.

Ultimately, that was exactly what they did, prompting Poste to do something anyone who knew him would have described as uncharacteristic.

Fast as his legs could carry him he ran for the pedestrian walkway, then for his roofless airspeeder, which was parked only a level up and close to the lot exit. Hurling himself over the vehicle's door—which didn't work in any case—he settled at the controls and hit the ignition button. A short line of similar repulsorlifts was queued at the exit, so he shot for the entrance, ignoring the synthvoices of two security droids and the strobing flashes of recording cams. The speeder's virttags were counterfeit, so who cared?

By the time he had sped around the lot and maneuvered into the restricted air traffic lanes that accessed the hovercab platform, it was obvious that a melee was in progress. Beings were scattering in all directions, security droids were rolling in, and the sirens of police vehicles were wailing in the distance. When the crowd parted briefly, Poste caught a glimpse of the newcomer leaping over the spread-eagled body of one of the goons, the other one down on all fours and scrambling for a blaster he had apparently lost hold of, blood streaming from his nose. But the newcomer's handiwork or footwork or whatever he had used to incapacitate his assailants hadn't left him in the clear. A showy SoroSuub airspeeder whipped past Poste, then cut him off and came to a sudden stop at the edge of the platform. Two humanoids—one an Iktotchi—clambered out of the passenger nacelle, gleaming weapons in hand. Spotting them, the newcomer whirled and dashed for the far side of the hovercab payment booth. The black attaché case was gone.

Poste saw his chance and made the most of it. Swerving around the idling SoroSuub, he pulled up past the booth just as the newcomer was emerging from the crowd, scarcely winded and professionally alert.

"Get in!" Poste shouted. He jerked a thumb over his shoulder. "You've got more coming!"

The newcomer hesitated, but only for a moment. Hurdling the door, he landed adroitly on the speeder's bench seat. "You have a blaster?"

Poste lifted the front of his shirt to reveal a Frohard Galactic F-7 tucked into the waistband of his trousers. In a lightning-fast motion the newcomer snatched and activated the small weapon and raised it to Poste's temple.

"You'd better not be part of this!"

"I'm your way out!" Poste said, wide-eyed.

The newcomer squinted. "What's this, your good-deed day?"

Behind them, three of the assailants were hurrying toward the landspeeder, leaving their unconscious comrade to fend for himself. Farther away, two police vehicles were attempting to maneuver through a logjam of skimmers and hovercabs.

"What are you waiting for?"

Still trying to get past the newcomer's initial remarks, Poste froze for an instant. But it didn't matter. The newcomer shoved the throttle forward, snapping Poste's head back against the rest and almost yanking his hands from the steering yoke. Rebounding, Poste saw that the newcomer had his bloody-knuckled left hand clamped on the yoke and that he was already steering them into the thick of traffic.

Speeders to both sides veered and collided. Air traffic on Nar Shaddaa was often compared to that on Coruscant, but with one major difference: where on the capital world rude driving earned you a few curses or filthy gestures, on the Smugglers' Moon drivers frequently replied with blaster bolts and joined the chase.

Berating himself for having gotten involved, Poste tried to wrestle the controls back. "I'm still making payments on this thing!"

The newcomer refused to remove his hand. "Whatever you're paying's too much."

"Who's rescuing who?"

"That remains to be seen."

The first of the pursuers' blaster bolts crackled past Poste's head, and he slumped deeper into the seat.

"Drive!" the newcomer said, hauling him upright. "Don't let yourself get distracted."

Poste glanced at him in disbelief. "They're firing at us, in case you didn't notice!"

"If they wanted me dead they would have killed me on the platform."

"Then maybe you should talk to them."

"Only on my own terms."

The newcomer pivoted on the seat and took aim on the SoroSuub. The vehicle swung out of the line of fire, slammed into a smaller airspeeder, and bounced back into the traffic lane.

"Turn here!" the newcomer said, motioning with his free hand.

"It's one-way."

The newcomer laughed. "You've already broken ten laws and you're worried about a traffic violation?"

Poste threw the speeder into the turn, weaving

through approaching traffic five hundred meters above the floor of the city canyon.

"That's it. Stay focused."

"Like I have a choice."

"You had a choice about inviting me in."

"I still don't know what I was thinking."

"Yes, you do," the newcomer said. "You're a chiseler."

Poste's eyebrows arched. "Chiseler?"

"You're hoping there'll be something in this for you."

Poste swallowed what he had in mind to say and began again. "Who'd you cross?"

The newcomer shook his head. "I'm not sure yet."

"What was in the attaché case?"

"Nothing."

"Nothing important, you mean?"

"No, I mean it was empty." The newcomer raised himself up over the retractable windscreen. "Turn into the second chasm."

"You know your way around?"

"Not like I used to." He used his hand to shield his eyes from Y'Toub's harsh light. "Pull up in front of that truck and switch places with me."

Poste gaped at him. "My first impression of you was right. You did escape from a psych ward."

"I've piloted swoops, speeders, skyhoppers, and just about everything else that flies." The newcomer gestured with the blaster. "Now shove over."

Poste clenched his jaw and traded places on the bench seat. The newcomer slammed the speeder back into motion and shot into traffic, finding space between vehicles where there shouldn't have been any, and creating spaces when he had to. Fifty meters behind them the pilot of the SoroSuub was trying hard to narrow the lead, or at least line up a shot.

The newcomer glanced at Poste. "You actually know how to use a blaster or you just carry it for adornment?"

"Adornment?" Poste laughed at the word. "Where've you been hiding for the past fifty years?"

"Can you use it or not?"

"I can use it."

The newcomer slapped the weapon into Poste's hand. "I'm going to put us behind the SoroSuub. When I do, you put a bolt into the ride side of the repulsorlift compartment. That'll end this little chase."

Poste looked over his left shoulder at the SoroSuub. "You're going to have to increase our lead."

"What are you talking about?"

"To get behind them. Cut around the TransBormea Building. If you can get them to follow us—"

Hitting the booster, the newcomer threw the speeder vertical, then into a loop perfectly timed to drop them almost directly behind the pursuit vehicle.

"Fire!"

Poste tried to swallow his stomach and force his eyes to focus.

"Fire!"

Taking unsteady aim, Poste triggered three bolts, the last of which connected, burning through the repulsorlift compartment and conjuring flames from within. Black smoke puffed from the blunt rear end and the SoroSuub began to veer wildly, then lose altitude. Poste leaned over the passenger's-side door to watch the speeder spiral down into Nar Shaddaa's lower depths.

"Nice move," he said when he could. "Fripping brilliant."

The newcomer pulled up to a crowded landing platform, shut down the speeder, and hopped out. Sliding behind the controls, Poste looked up to find a wad of credit bills centimeters from his face.

"Will this do?"

Poste thought about accepting it, then shook his head. "Keep it. You taught me a valuable lesson about picking up strangers."

The newcomer almost grinned. "Suit yourself." Shoving the wad into his jacket pocket, he stepped away from the speeder to regard it front to back. "Who's responsible for the paint job?"

Poste touched himself in the chest. "Me."

The newcomer laughed through his nose. "Looks like a piece of candy."

Poste exhaled wearily. "First you're a swoop pilot, now you're an art critic?"

"Expunge the flames."

"Ex—"

"And it needs a tune-up."

"I'm sure it does after your showboating."

"Have the turbine overdrive relay replaced."

Poste put his tongue in his cheek. "Okay, so maybe you're not a total psych case." He hit the ignition button. "Still, I hope I don't see you around."

"Hold on," the newcomer said.

Poste turned slightly in the seat.

"I need some information."

"Yeah, what a surprise."

"I'll compensate you well."

Poste laughed. "What world are you from where they use words like *compensate* and *expunge*?"

The newcomer ignored the question. "I'm looking for ship salvagers who would have been working Nar Shaddaa's envelope sixty or so standard years ago."

"Sixty . . ." Poste gestured dismissively. "Go to the library."

"I plan to. But I need someone to ask around in the depths while I'm doing that. Do you know of any starship mechanics or engineers who might have been working back then?"

"Old-timers."

"They'd have to be."

Poste considered it. "There are a couple of beings . . ." He tilted his head to the side. "In the event I'm sick enough to be interested, how do I find you?"

"You've got a comlink?"

Poste dug into the pouch pocket of his pants and set the comlink down on the bench seat. The newcomer set his comlink down alongside it.

"Mate them."

Poste enabled his comlink's pairing function. "You want to tell me your name?" he said, handing back the newcomer's comlink.

"Not yet."

The blond man turned and disappeared into the crowd.

Jadak showed up at the Slag Pit II half an hour before he was due to meet with the scammer his comlink had identified as Flitcher Poste. Nar Shaddaa's short night had just fallen, with Nal Hutta shielding the moon from the light of Y'Toub. He waited outside, across the street from the flashing front entrance, until he recognized Poste making his way through the mixed-species crowd. A thickset kid of twenty-five or so, Poste had a pleasant face with symmetrical features and bushy eyebrows. His hair was several shades of blond and brown, and swept straight back from his forehead. If Poste had grown up on Nar Shaddaa and was still fleecing tourists at his age, then he must have had a pretty lousy low-level childhood. Jadak watched him approach the tapcaf, exchanging greetings with a few beings. He had come alone, as Jadak had instructed, and was taking all the right precautions. Jadak waited awhile longer to make certain no one else showed up, then entered the Slag Pit II by way of the side entrance.

He had spent two days making info forays from a cubicle hotel in the heart of what was once known as the Red District. His research had returned a couple of promising leads, but he was hoping that Poste would have something substantial for him. Waiting for his eyes to adjust to the tapcaf's dim lighting, Jadak made a complete circuit of the large main room before heading for the table Poste was holding, a bottle of brew in front of him. Jadak got the attention of a waitress and told her to bring him a Meranzane on ice. He came up behind Poste, startling him, and slipped into the opposite seat.

"I wasn't sure you'd show," Poste said in genuine surprise.

"Why wouldn't I?"

"I figured you might have found what you were looking for."

"I haven't," Jadak said. The waitress delivered the drink, and he took a sip, letting the liquor linger in his mouth. "This guy you mentioned . . ."

"He'll be here. But he's had to come a long way. I promised him you'd make it worth his while, no matter what."

Jadak nodded. "I already told you I would. What do you know about him?"

"Not much, except that he had a reputation as being one of the best mechanics onworld until something went down that drove him into hiding for a couple of years. When he returned, he worked exclusively for Black Sun, keeping their cargo freighters shipshape. If he doesn't know whoever you're looking for, he'll probably know someone who does."

Poste paused for a moment. "What's this all about, anyway?"

"That can wait till the mechanic gets here."

"You know, I'm still not sure I want anything to do with you. The way you handled those goons. What are you, an undercover cop? Alliance agent?" He sniffed elaborately. "You've got that . . . aura about you. Who were they, anyway—rivals? Enemies?"

"Keep your voice down," Jadak said.

"I'm just telling you, I don't have any big dreams. I'm content making a small living here."

Jadak sat back into the chair. "Picking pockets? Making off with bags at the spaceport? Doing a bit of breaking and entering on the side? Some petty theft during power failures or while folks are attending funerals?"

Poste nodded knowingly. "See? You even talk like a cop." He started to rise from the table, but Jadak grabbed hold of his sleeve.

"Sit down. I'll explain everything after we talk to the mechanic."

"Bammy."

Jadak looked up from his drink.

"Bammy Decree. That's his name." Poste nodded with his chin toward the circular bar. "And I think this might be him."

Jadak followed Poste's gaze to an elderly human, nicely dressed but somewhat stoop-shouldered and hobbling on perhaps century-old legs. "Are you Poste?" he asked as he approached the table.

"That's me."

Poste stood, as if to offer to help him into a chair, but Decree waved him off and sat down unassisted, glancing uncertainly at Jadak.

"I've come all the way from the Duros Sector."

"We know," Poste said sympathetically, "and we appreciate it."

Decree glanced at Jadak again. "Then let's get on with this."

Jadak interlocked his fingers and leaned forward. "Bammy, I'm looking for information about a YT-

Thirteen-hundred freighter that collided with a Corellian ship sixty-two years ago."

Decree's jaw slackened and he stared at Jadak in astonishment. "Are you talking about the *Stellar Envoy*?"

Jadak practically came out of his chair, and had to force himself to speak softly. "That's the ship, Bammy. How do you know about it?"

Decree smiled, revealing gaps in his yellowing teeth. "How do I know? I rebuilt that freighter top to bottom after the collision. Added parts to it from an old YT-Thirteen-hundred-pea, retooled the engines and power core, beefed up the plating and the hyperdrive, redid the entire interior, even installed a new droid brain."

Jadak put his hand gently on Decree's upper arm. "Who bought it, Bammy?"

Decree gazed at Jadak's hand until he removed it. "A crime boss by the name of Rej Taunt."

Jadak logged the name. "Is this Taunt still alive?"

"Oh, yeah."

"Does he still have the *Envoy*?"

"He renamed it *Second Chance*. But, no, he doesn't have it." Decree smiled lightly. "He ran into a bit of trouble with that ship because of something I did without meaning to. You see, the computer I installed was built by the Colicoids, and it wound up activating a cargo of black-market buzz droids Rej was hauling for a Black Sun Vigo. Rej managed to jettison the droids before they could dismantle the *Second Chance*, but they went and attached themselves to an Imperial cruiser that was vectoring in to intercept the freighter." He looked from Jadak to Poste and back again. "The cruiser blew to pieces, killing more than seventy-five men and a lot more stormtroopers."

Poste whistled. "What happened to Taunt?"

Instead of answering, Decree turned to Jadak. "I didn't catch your name."

"Jadak."

Decree blinked in confusion. "Any relation to Tobb Jadak?"

Jadak stiffened. "You could say that."

Decree wet his lips. "You're his son."

"Whose son?" Poste asked.

"The son of the pilot who died in the collision," Decree said without taking his eyes off Jadak.

"No, I'm him," Jadak said finally.

Decree went white. "But . . . but that can't be."

"I survived the crash."

"You survived the crash." Decree tried to make sense of it. "Even so—"

"I know I don't look my age." Jadak motioned to himself. "Believe me, Bammy, underneath all this I'm older than you are. But how do you know my name?"

"From the YT's flight recorder," Decree said when he could. "I pieced together a whole history of that ship." He ran one hand down his face. "And now you're looking for it?"

"I am."

Decree's eyes narrowed. "Rej would know where it ended up. I can tell you where to find him."

"Where, Bammy?"

"Well, he was on Oovo Four for a time. Now he's in Carcel."

"The prison?" Poste said.

Decree grinned. "He's sure not there for the waters."

When Bammy Decree finally left the Slag Pit II three hours later, he was wobbling far more than when he had arrived. He had recounted all he had uncovered about the *Stellar Envoy*'s checkered past, and Jadak had told him about the sixty-two years he had lost to a coma. Jadak underplayed his interest in finding the ship and dismissed the Republic Group as nothing more than a courier service. He made no mention of the *Envoy* being the key to locating a hidden treasure, although he knew he would have to play up that fact if he hoped to enlist Poste in the search. The kid wasn't much with a blaster or an airspeeder, but he had talents Jadak lacked, and he knew the ins and outs of modern life. More important, he was a keen observer, and a second pair of eyes would be crucial to steering clear of whatever parties were after him, especially now that they had made a move.

Jadak paid Bammy more than Poste imagined the information about the old ship could possibly be worth, and sent him back to the Duros Sector in a private hover limo just as Nar Shaddaa's short, global night was waning.

"You're a lot more than I bargained for," Poste said when Jadak returned to the table.

"And you remind me of a former friend of mine," Jadak said. "His name was Reeze, and he was my copilot when we crashed into that bulk freighter. He died here."

Poste frowned. "Is Reeze part of the reason you're so keen on tracking down the ship?"

"Yeah, he is. But that's not the half of it." Jadak leaned forward in a conspiratorial way. "Poste, what would you say if I told you that the *Stellar Envoy* is the key to finding a treasure of maybe unimaginable wealth?"

Poste regarded him over the neck of the bottle of ale. "As in you have no idea, or you can't even calculate it?"

"Both."

Poste took a sip of brew, set the bottle down, and wiped his mouth on the back of one hand. "First I'd ask you how you know."

"I was told so by the folks who were paying me to pilot the YT. Reeze and I were on our way to delivering it to someone when we crashed."

"And the YT is the key to finding this treasure?"

Jadak nodded.

"Then you don't know where the treasure is."

"I know enough. And what I don't know the ship does."

A look of revelation dawned on Poste's face. "Are you asking me to join you on this treasure hunt?"

"Chance of a lifetime, kid."

Poste threw his head back and laughed. "You must be space-happy."

Jadak snorted. "You ever been off this rock?"

"No, but—"

"I'm offering you an opportunity you don't want to pass up."

Poste shook his head back and forth. "Jadak, sorry to have to remind you, but folks with blasters are after you. I appreciate the opportunity to see the galaxy, but I'm not interested in returning to Nar Shaddaa in a body bag."

Jadak waved his hand. "We can handle them."

"We can . . ." Poste took another pull from the bottle. "What do they want with you, anyway?"

"I figure they expect me to lead them to the treasure."

"Maybe you could cut a deal—"

"Forget it." Jadak downed the contents of his drink. "I'm not lying about the ship, Poste. And the only thing Nar Shaddaa has in store for you is jail time. You know it as well as I do."

Poste crossed his arms and leaned back in the chair. "Even if that ship of yours isn't scrap by now, it could be on the far side of the galaxy going to rust."

"You're not telling me anything I haven't thought through a hundred different ways. Maybe it is scrap. Maybe it got vaped during the Rebellion or swallowed whole during the war with the Yuuzhan Vong. Maybe it was dismantled for parts. If any of those possibilities turns out to be the case, then I pay you for your services as a guide to modern life and we shake hands and walk away." He paused to let it sink in. "But if we find it . . ."

Now Poste leaned forward. "This is where it gets interesting, huh?"

"If we find the ship, we split down the middle everything it leads us to."

Poste pinched his lower lip between his thumb and forefinger. "And just who's going to finance this quest?"

"I have a small stash."

"How much?"

"Close to eight thousand credits."

Poste's eyebrows arched in surprise. "That amount could carry us for a while—depending on just where the ship ended up. I mean, if we wind up having to travel all the way to Ord Mantell or somewhere . . ."

"Suppose we start with Carcel and see where that leads us."

Poste smiled. "Rej Taunt probably hasn't had a visitor in decades."

chapter seventeen

"A LITTLE TO THE LEFT," LESTRA OXIC TOLD THE droid. "Make certain it's centered before lowering it into place."

The loadlifter droid made a series of adjustments and slowly set the marble plinth on the floor alongside the study's large hearth. Oxic motioned for the droid to move aside, and stepped back to regard the result. A slender metal rod half a meter high extended from the pedestal's square top. The rod terminated in a cup-shaped holder not much wider than Oxic's thumb and into which he placed a crystal sphere. The smallest but most costly of the items he had purchased at the auction, the star map sphere was thought to have been one of a vast assortment of similar devices housed in the Jedi Temple. Found shortly after the end of the Yuuzhan Vong War by a member of a reconstruction crew, the crystal had been smuggled offworld to a warehouse on Bilbringi. Discovered accidently by a cleaning droid, the piece was sold by unknown parties to a private collector, who ultimately put it up for auction at Hydians. In the time of the Old Republic Jedi, the sphere's map function would have been activated by a cup-shaped reader similar to the facsimile Oxic had had fabricated to serve as a holder. Now the sphere could be initiated by a small remote that had come with the piece.

Moving to the center of the study, Oxic depressed a button on the remote. Instantly the crystal sphere glowed with brilliant light that expanded nova-like to fill the entire room with tiny illuminated globes. Face uplifted and spotted with light, Oxic was revolving in place when the study's wooden doors parted and Koi Quire entered.

"Impressive," she said, gazing at the display.

"The star systems of the Bright Jewel Oversector." Oxic switched off the remote and looked at her.

"They're here."

He glanced at his wrist chrono. "I shouldn't have to devote time to this. Discovery on the Colicoid case has to be completed by tomorrow. A judgment in our favor will mean a windfall for us, but success hinges on having our star witness properly prepared."

"I can handle Cynner and the others, if you wish."

Oxic gave it thought. "No, they need to hear from me if we're to avoid future mistakes. Send them in."

Quire nodded and turned, leaving Oxic to pace before the bank of windows that lined the study's west-facing wall, long-fingered hands clasped behind his back and rail-thin legs propelling him a meter with each step. The view took in all of Epica City, which had grown in recent years to fill the bowl formed by the surrounding mountains. Where at one time Hydians Auction House was the city's cynosure, a number of Republic-era structures had sprung up around it, rich in period detail. The cold waters of the nearby sea created fog that obscured the city for part of the year, but Oxic's mansion was well above the fog line, beneath an azure sky even when you couldn't see your hand in front of your face down below.

The star map crystal was one of many examples of authentic Coruscant Republicana that Oxic had spent a fortune acquiring in more than twenty years of collecting. But he collected for love rather than investment. Some of his fondest memories were of the years he had spent on the galactic capital before the Clone Wars, living the high life with the Senators, dignitaries, and celebrities represented by his law firm. During the war, Oxic had frequently served as a defense lawyer for beings accused of sedition by Chancellor Palpatine and his cadre of sinister minions, all of whom Oxic had loathed.

In the long years since, the firm had dwindled in size if not importance and was largely a one-man show, though Oxic employed close to one hundred beings in various capacities. Escorted by the stunning Quire, four of them entered the room now, two—Oxic noted peripherally—still badged with bacta patches as a consequence of the mess on Nar Shaddaa.

Long accustomed to performing before juries or judges, Oxic was suddenly in a position of being both, and unhappy about it. While celebrated for his ability to synthesize information and speak with a facility envied by lawyers of many species, words failed him. Even when he swung away from the windows to glance at Quire, the woman who knew him better than anyone could only return what amounted to a sympathetic shrug.

Oxic came to a halt and whirled on his employees. "Do you have any idea how much I've invested in this man?"

His anger caught him by surprise, and he regretted having led with a question. Though it hardly mattered; they got the point. That was the reason for Koi's rueful expression. She had warned against allowing the Nautolan to organize the pickup. And now all four of them were behaving just as they expected he would want them to behave, keeping their heads down, studying their hands.

"Look at me."

They raised their heads in unison.

"He's not a criminal. He's not someone who skipped bail. Why did you feel it necessary to treat him like one?"

"We don't know any other way?" Cynner said, speaking for all of them.

Oxic stood over him, using his towering height to maximum advantage. "Is that a question or an explanation? Because if it's the latter," he added while they were trading uncertain looks, "then I can't have you in my employ."

"It's not that we don't know how, it's just that we didn't expect the reaction we got."

"Which was what?"

Cynner's half a dozen head-tentacles twitched, and he gestured to the quartet's sole human. "Remata's nose. My ribs."

"My airspeeder," Oxic thought to point out.

Cynner nodded. "The airspeeder."

"He knew he was being tailed," Remata said. "And he sure reacted like someone who had jumped bail."

"Did it occur to you to wait until he was somewhere less public than the spaceport? Somewhere with fewer cams to record your every action?"

"His reaction would have been the same," Cynner said.

Oxic looked at Koi, and she nodded in an understated way.

Oxic loosed a long exhale and folded his arms across his narrow chest. "Next time my instructions will be more explicit."

Their signal to leave. They rose and filed out. Koi had already moved to the bar and was preparing Oxic a drink.

"Anger will only sabotage the fine work Dr. Sompa has been doing all these years," she said.

Oxic hurried to the mirrpanel behind the bar to inspect his face for signs of reappearing age lines. "Not all species are blessed with your natural flawlessness, Koi."

"And few have the longevity you've purchased. What does it matter how you look?"

He glanced at her reflection in the mirrpanel. "I'm not a Hutt. I've a public face to uphold. I can't be expected to win cases against young lawyers if I look like a crippled old human."

She handed him the drink, and he carried it to the couch.

"Sompa is a fool. I shouldn't have agreed to his plan. If he had told Jadak the truth about the accident or forced Jadak's memories to surface, we could have simply taken him into custody at Aurora. Instead we've given him a mystery to unravel, another mission to execute." He looked at Quire. "Is he still on Nar Shaddaa?"

"We don't know."

Oxic swung to her. "Don't tell me we've lost him."

She motioned in a calming way. "Nar Shaddaa isn't what it used to be. He won't be able to get offworld without our knowing it."

Oxic stood up and paced away from the couch. "Do we know anything at all?"

"Spaceport security cams captured images of the airspeeder in which he escaped, along with images of the speeder's owner. The vehicle's virttags are forged, but we were able to match the owner's face. His name is Flitcher Poste, a canyon orphan. He has a record of committing minor offenses and has spent time in various detention centers on Nar Shaddaa." Quire dug a data device from her purse. "Want to see him?"

"Why would I?"

"Because I have a suspicion that Poste and Jadak are now partners."

Oxic took a moment to respond. "Is there some prior connection?"

"Nothing has emerged. But I thought there might be, so I ordered Cynner to find Poste on the off chance he could lead us to Jadak. Poste wasn't hard to find or to follow—for a time, at any rate."

"You lost him, too?"

"Poste spent a day or so visiting different starship garages, asking questions about mechanics who would have been in business sixty years ago."

Oxic absorbed it. "When Jadak had his accident."

"I think he's looking for his old ship—the *Stellar Envoy*." Quire waited for Oxic to sit down. "We were unsuccessful at eavesdropping on Poste's comms, but we picked up enough to know that a meeting took place in a tapcaf in the Corellian Sector."

"With Jadak?"

Quire nodded. "But we only learned that after the fact, by visiting cantinas and showing their images around. Jadak and Poste met with an old human someone identified as a mechanic who works for Black Sun."

Oxic stared at her. "Black Sun?"

"I don't think there's a connection. This is all about finding the *Envoy*." She held his nervous gaze. "Did Senator Des'sein say anything that led you to believe the ship would play a pivotal role in this?"

Oxic thought back to the deathbed exchange he had had with his old friend and client. One of the more vocal of the two thousand Senators who had banded together to oppose the strong measures Palpatine had taken before and during the Clone Wars, Des'sein was also a member of a clandestine organization that called itself the Republic Group. The group had unmasked traitors in the Senate by following the credits that flowed from Coruscant to weapons manufacturers and starship-building companies throughout the galaxy. Following

Palpatine's proclamation of his Empire, many members of the Republic Group had disappeared or been killed. Des'sein had survived, though not as a politician but a business consultant, during which time his friendship with Oxic had flourished. Privy to all his dealings, Oxic had drawn up Des'sein's will and had been present at the marriage of Des'sein's daughter. When the ravages of a congenital disease had finally caught up with his old friend, Oxic had journeyed to Coruscant from Epica to be at his bedside.

That was when Des'sein had whispered the secret.

Fearing that Palpatine would one day proclaim himself Emperor, the Republic Group had hidden a treasure on a remote world—a treasure they hoped would be sufficient to restore the Republic. And the key to locating that treasure was a former pilot for the Republic Group named Tobb Jadak, who had disappeared just days before the end of the war in a '25 YT-1300 freighter called the *Stellar Envoy.*

Others knew of the hidden treasure and had been actively seeking it, but only Oxic had Jadak's name. Even so, the name hadn't amounted to much of a lead until shortly after the Battle of Endor, when documents belonging to onetime Imperial Intelligence Director Armand Isard had come into Oxic's possession. Kept from Isard's daughter, who wound up being Armand's successor and executioner, the documents contained a brief mention of the *Stellar Envoy,* which had been pursued from Coruscant by clone pilots following the battle there. The clones had been unable to keep up with the *Envoy,* but had logged the coordinates of the freighter's jump to hyperspace. After a year of investigating possible destinations, Oxic had discovered not only that the *Stellar Envoy* had jumped to Nar Shaddaa, but also that Tobb Jadak had survived a collision there—though in a coma that had already endured for more than twenty years.

At great personal expense, Oxic had had Jadak moved to the Aurora Medical Facility and had installed a young neurosurgeon named Sompa to oversee his care and possible recovery, which had required another forty years.

"Des'sein told me that Jadak was the key," Oxic said finally.

"Could he have hidden something aboard the *Envoy*?" Quire said. "Or could the ship actually know something about the location of the treasure that Jadak doesn't know?"

Oxic shot to his feet once more. "We should have put a locator on him."

"Sompa wouldn't hear of it."

"Sompa, Sompa," Oxic said, whirling. "I'm sick of hearing that name."

She smiled tolerantly. "Only until your next visit to Aurora for treatments."

He sighed. "Perhaps you know me better than I know myself."

"Sometimes it takes two imperfect beings to make one perfect one."

As if unaware that he was still holding the star map crystal's small remote, Oxic began to thumb the activating button on and off, on and off, on and off.

chapter eighteen

A S HAD BECOME A HABIT DURING MOMENTS OF TEDIUM or preoccupation, Han, wearing a fake beard and wig, reached absently into his pants pocket for the archaic transponder and began to turn it about in his hand, sliding his thumb along the T-shaped device's seamless surface, hefting it as though in an attempt to ascertain its weight in lieu of being able to divine its enigmatic purpose.

If they had bothered to time their arrival on Taris, they would have been able to meet with Vistal Purn the previous day. But now the onetime owner of the *Millennium Falcon* and former manager of the Molpol Circus was engaged in overseeing the judging of creatures vying for titles in Sok Brok's Fiftieth Annual Pet Show.

Any meeting with Purn would have to wait until after the prizes had been handed out.

A dozen rows forward of where he sat with Leia, Allana, and C-3PO, hundreds of pets accompanied by their owners or handlers were parading around the arena floor, strutting their stuff for groups of judges in the hope of being crowned most ferocious in species or ugliest in show. As far as Han could determine, the contests had little to do with talent or skill, other than whatever ability it took to prance with poise, grovel with grace, or stalk with style. In a galaxy where so many species had evolved to sentience, the very notion of keeping a pet struck Han as absurd, and yet in even the most far-flung star systems you'd find beings who doted on their miniature nagaths and toy moings more than they did their own offspring. Sometimes it was merely pathetic, and often it was downright comical. Especially at Sok Brok's, where it wasn't unusual to encounter an arachnoid Critokian walking a leashed bipedal ornuk, or a sanus feline leashed to a canine-faced Dug half its size. Sometimes the owner was more exotic looking than his or her pet; and sometimes the pets made the owners look as if they had yet to reach an evolutionary stage where sentience was a guarantee.

In one of the arena's many competition areas stood a Shistavanen who looked far more ferocious than the fanged-and-clawed anooba he was showing. Closer still was a Sauvax who would have looked better as the main course on a waterworld than the bred-for-food beast with whom she was partnered. The bushy-maned Calibop behind the Sauvax looked better suited for flight than the scantily feathered reptavian perched on his shoulder.

Han had sat patiently through the awards for ugliest in rodent, marsupial, and reptilian, but he knew he had reached his limit the moment Gands and other insectoid owners began appearing on the arena floor with their bandara beetles and scorplans. The sheer repulsiveness of the pets they walked raised every hair on the back of his neck.

Allana, on the other hand, was mostly fascinated. From the start she had evinced a great empathy for animals and other creatures, even the ones Han considered repulsive. She had that in common with her father.

C-3PO used to entertain you with tales from The Little Lost Bantha Cub. *He took you and Jaina on outings to zoos and game habitats. You escaped him once, ventured deep into one of Coruscant's murkiest and most dangerous canyons—*

Han tried to derail his train of thought, but failed.

You were kidnapped by Hethrir. You rescued your mother from captivity by Warmaster Tsavong Lah. You watched your brother die, and were tortured by Vergere. You killed Onimi. You spent five years learning from Force-users throughout the galaxy and returned a changed person.

How could you have grown into what you became? Once my dear son, later so unrecognizable it hurt to admit that I'd fathered you, let alone raised you. How did I allow you to grow away from me, so far out of reach, so distant, so bound up in your own beliefs of what constituted right and wrong you drove even the Jedi against you? Did your ambition pass to your daughter? Did she inherit your susceptibility along with your curiosity, your weaknesses along with your strengths? Will she, too, be lured by false promises and unattainable goals? How closely do we need to watch her, Jacen? Or is she a benign alternative to the future you once represented?

Han clenched his hands and inhaled a stuttering breath.

I want to be able to forgive you . . .

Han felt a tug on his sleeve and turned to Allana. "What's up, Short Cake?"

"Can we get a treat?"

Han smiled. "I thought you'd never ask."

"Captain Solo," C-3PO said, "I would be only too happy to escort—"

"Uh-uh. You stay here and keep Leia company." Han gestured broadly to the arena floor. "Pick out the breed you like and I'll think about buying one for you." He looked past C-3PO to Leia, whose eyes were hidden behind tinted glasses and whose long hair was concealed under a short-haired wig. "We're going to the concession stand."

"Bring me a Bama Bar."

"Will do." Han took Allana by the hand and led her to the aisle. "Shoulder ride?"

"Yes!"

He threw her gently up onto his shoulders, her legs dangling around his neck. She had extraordinary balance. He liked that she was a real kid. He and Leia had promised each other that their next kid wouldn't be a Jedi, and Han had been thrilled to learn that Allana would not be attending the Jedi academy.

The lobby swarmed with customers. He set her down on the tiled floor.

"What do you want?"

"Whipped treat."

"Single or double?"

"Double?" she said shyly.

Han grinned. "Does Leia want a regular Bama Bar or one with blumfruit?"

Allana closed her eyes. "Um . . . with blumfruit."

"Coming right up."

In line ahead of Han were two interesting-looking beings. A Yinchorri and a . . . Tintinna, Allana decided, proud of herself.

As Han was ordering at the counter, Allana caught sight of an even more peculiar creature all the way on the other side of the lobby. Just about her height, the animal had long, floppy ears and two big feet and was wearing a vest like Han sometimes wore and carrying a small cane like Uncle Lando used to carry. The curious thing was that the creature seemed to be staring at her, like it wanted her to follow it. When it started to launch itself from the lobby on those two big feet, Allana couldn't help herself: she had to see where it was going, or at least get a closer look at it.

It could almost have been a character on *Castle Creep*.

Without so much as a backward glance she hurried off in pursuit of the creature, trailing it into a large room filled with suspended ceiling lights and long tables covered with chairs that had been turned upside down. The creature bounded to the far side of the room and disappeared into what Allana first thought was some kind of hole in the wall, but it wasn't. It was a small turbolift like the ones in the palace on Hapes that were used to move plates and food between the royal dining room and the lower-level kitchens. She wondered for a moment if the turbolift was big enough for her to fit into.

It was.

So down she went.

Han's mounting confusion reverberated like a scream in Leia's mind.

Mentally scanning for Allana, she dashed for the lobby, C-3PO hurrying behind her.

"I turned around and she was gone," Han said, eyes darting about. Melted whipped treat was running down his left hand.

Leia looked inward. "I don't sense her in any danger . . ."

"Good, but where is she?"

Leia turned to the broad, curving staircase that led to the arena's upper tiers, then looked across the lobby toward the entrance doors. "She wouldn't have gone outdoors."

"I'll take the stairs," Han said, already in motion. "We meet back here in five."

Leia nodded.

C-3PO came to a halt in front of her. "What should I do, Princess Leia?"

"Alert security, Threepio. Tell them that our child has gone missing."

"Yes, mistress, I will."

Leia put her emotions on hold and calmed herself. Reaching out, she began to feel a lingering trace of Allana. She walked across the lobby and stood still, her gaze fixed on the wide doorway to an adjacent room—a conference room, by the look of it. Removing the tinted glasses, she continued to move, allowing the Force to guide her. Again she stopped and stood still, waiting for her eyes to alight. She hurried forward and dropped down on one knee in front of a service turbolift.

It would be a tight fit, but, yes, it would accommodate a small, seven-year-old girl.

Without bothering to puzzle out why Allana would have squeezed into it, what she might have been chasing, or what might have been chasing her, Leia rushed to the turbolifts she had noticed in the lobby. In her mind, she called to the child, but received no response.

Was she hurt? No.

Preoccupied. Fascinated. Intrigued . . . Playing.

Exiting the turbolift, she followed the same path she had taken on the floor above, this time through a maze of corridors into a kitchen filled with appliances and floor-to-ceiling shelf units stocked with pots and pans and a vast assortment of serving trays and bowls. Her path led her into another corridor—closing on Allana, she was certain—and into a huge underground space housing hundreds of pets in cages. But not just ordinary pets, Leia realized. What the pet show industry referred to as novelties—bioengineered creatures of all description. And Allana was somewhere among them.

Leia gave voice to sudden and overwhelming concern.

"All—Amelia!"

Han had just arrived at the top of the sweeping staircase when he realized he was on the right track. The revelation came in the form of an alumabronze ashtray stand that swung down seemingly out of nowhere, narrowly missing his head but striking the floor with such force that it loosed a thick cloud of gray ash causing him to sneeze, dislodging the wig that was part of his disguise. Head flung forward from the force of the sneeze, he inadvertently dodged the first pass of a nonhumanoid foot that whizzed over the top of his doubled-over torso. As he straightened, the foot caught him as it was coming full circle, but the spindly being the booted foot was attached to had been thrown off-balance, so that when Han's hands absorbed the force of the blow—saving his nose at the same time—assailant and victim both tumbled to the floor.

False beard and mustache askew, Han rolled out from under another attempt by the Rodian wielder of the ashtray stand and tried to scramble to his feet, only to be tripped by the second assailant—a Duros wearing the uniform of a security guard. Landing on his back, Han began to slide down the steep ramp that led to the balcony seats and private viewing platforms, his head thumping the floor as it passed over the ramp's widely spaced shallow steps and the wig sliding down over his eyes. On both sides of the ramp, spectators were rising from their seats, shouting, screaming, and clutching their children to them. Han had enough sense to know that he was sliding headfirst for the low retaining wall at the foot of the ramp. Forcing his feet from the floor, he managed to complete a backward somersault and come to his feet just short of the wall, but with his arms extended straight out to the sides and flailing desperately in an effort to keep him from plunging over the wall to the arena floor. At the same time, the Duros and the Rodian were hurrying down the ramp straight for him.

Han waited until they were two meters away and ready to lunge; then he let himself roll backward over the wall, hands poised to fasten themselves to the top as the rest of his body fell and the wig slipped off. The Duros went sailing out into space over his head and a few heartbeats later slammed down onto the arena floor, prompting a stampede among the pets and handlers amid whom he had landed. Though the Rodian came to a skidding stop, momentum carried him face-first over the wall. At the last instant the green biped secured a grip on the wall and wound up hanging alongside Han, but gazing out over the arena floor where Han's face was pressed to the wall.

Han felt the Rodian's fist slam into the back of his head and responded by slamming his right hand into the Rodian's snout. Above them, spectators angered by the turmoil the brawl had caused were making for the retaining wall with clear intent. Before a blow could land on his white-knuckled fingers, Han seized hold of the Rodian and began to work his way down to the Rodian's skinny legs, which began to swing side to side. At the height of one of the swings, Han threw himself into the nearest of the private booths, even as the Rodian was plummeting feetfirst to the arena floor.

Saucer-shaped, the booths were similar in design and function to the hover platforms of the old Senate Rotunda. The Bimm occupants of the private booth Han had chosen as a destination shrieked as he came crashing into their midst, his feet striking the booth's autopilot control panel. With a suddenness that spilled the Bimms into the private seating platform below theirs, the booth undocked from the balcony and went soaring out over the arena floor, inciting greater chaos among the pets, owners, judges, and everyone else unfortunate enough to be nearby. Hands fidgeting with the controls, Han attempted to land the booth, but it refused to obey any commands outside its programming. The programming was already returning it to the balcony docking station, where two stout human security guards were waiting with drawn blasters. Instinctively Han reached for his BlasTech, remembering even as he did that he had surrendered it to security on entering the arena. Diving once more for the controls, he began to fumble beneath the panel for the relays that would disable the repulsorlift.

Instead, his hands found the hover's limiter relays.

The booth shot forward, dumping Han onto his backside before barreling into the docking station with enough force to shatter the magnetic connectors. The pair of armed humans beat a hasty retreat to the balcony, but now Han was facing a new problem. Refusing to take no for an answer, the booth began to slam repeatedly into the retracting arm clamps in an attempt to dock. Time and again it tried, as if growing increasingly frustrated at being rebuffed. Before long, smoke was wisping from both the magnetic field generators and the booth's repulsorlift. Han considered making a running leap for the balcony, but the security guards, satisfied that he was effectively trapped, were returning. He thought about hanging over the side of the booth and dropping to the floor, but knew he would be lucky to escape with two broken legs.

The decision was made for him when the booth suddenly short-circuited and fell sputtering and spinning toward a swarm of scurrying pets.

The floppy-eared creature in the vest was directly in front of her at the end of the aisle. Confined in cages to all sides were dozens of other animals that were strange and sometimes scary combinations of many of the pets that were performing in the show. Some of them had too many limbs or more than one head, and others looked like they couldn't decide whether to be insects or lizards, birds or fish. Just about all of them were barking or coughing or howling. But the fact that some of the cage doors were open eased her wariness somewhat.

Even so, Allana slowed down, not wanting to scare away the creature she had followed from the lobby. Then a big man suddenly stepped into her view and she stopped completely. He was smiling, but not in a way that seemed friendly or comforting. When the creature leapt up into the man's arms without being afraid, she told herself that she might be wrong about the man, but she didn't think so. Especially when a second man appeared from behind one of the larger cages and started walking toward her.

Allana backed away.

"Don't you want to see our prize pet up close?" the man said. "He's a Chandrilan squall, and he likes children a lot. He might even let you pet him."

Allana didn't like any of what she was hearing or how the words were being said. She continued to back away.

"I don't think you'll be able to find your way back without my help."

"I don't need your help," she said, even though she wasn't supposed to talk to strangers.

The man sort of laughed. "Maybe you don't. But we need *yours*." His left hand disappeared behind his back and reappeared holding a military-style blaster.

Emptying her mind of thought and emotion, Allana made herself a vessel for the Force, and felt the Force flow in to fill her up. Then she made her intentions as clear as the purest water.

The Chandrilan squall bared fangs and sank them into the nose of the man in whose arms it was sitting. And from some of the cages leapt the creatures that frightened her most, attacking the other man before he could take a step in any direction.

Allana spun around and began to run as fast as she could. But she hadn't even reached the other side of the kennel room when a humanoid carrying a blaster raced in to block her way. Raising it without saying a word, he fired straight at her.

Concentric rings of blue energy dazzled her eyes.

Then everything went black.

Leia was weaving her way through the rows of cages when she felt Allana cry out and lose consciousness. Homing in on her granddaughter, she hurried forward with Jedi speed, racing into a center aisle in time to see three beings running toward a doorway on the far side of the room, Allana's legs dangling over the forearms of one of the men. Leia caught a glimpse of Allana's silken red hair.

Leia fairly flew across the room, arriving at the duranium door as it shut in her face. She motioned for it to open, but it didn't budge. She tried again, then resorted to pounding her fists against it. She stepped back, wiping her hair from her face and wishing she had the strength to flatten it or the Force talent to unravel the lock's security code.

Stepping away from the door, she listened through and to the Force. Then she turned and raced back the way she had come.

The hover booth was still a few meters from grinding down onto the floor when Han saw the same two guards maneuvering toward him through a crowd of panicked spectators, determined to place themselves as far from the descending booth as possible. Still others, hands and claws pressed to their heads in alarm, were hurrying toward the booth's probable landing spot, calling desperately to frantic pets that were circling directly beneath the out-of-control booth, barking and snapping at it in confusion. Han didn't wait for touchdown. As soon as the guards broke free of the throng he launched himself over the edge, as much to incapacitate them as cushion his fall.

Han's velocity and weight brought the guards straight to the floor, where the three of them tussled for a moment before Han succeeded in wrenching a blaster from one of them and jumped to his feet.

"He has a blaster!" a Twi'lek female shouted.

Han swung to her, aiming a finger at the guard. "No, *he* had the blaster."

"They have blasters!" someone else yelled.

A panicked pet sank its little teeth into Han's ankle and he yelled. Hopping on one foot, he sent the Kowakian monkey-lizard flying with the other.

"Beast!" someone shouted.

Han turned his head and caught a glancing left hook on the jaw. A starfield burst into being before his eyes, but he managed to hold on to the blaster. Twisting away from a follow-up punch, he leveled the weapon at the guard on the floor.

"We've got your kid, Solo," the guard said.

Han's finger froze on the trigger.

The guard gestured with his thumb. "Take a gander."

Han's attention was drawn to a booth twice the size of the one he had ridden almost to the floor, docked to the balcony farther along the curve of the arena wall and accessed by a private entrance. In the doorway, wedged between a human and a Barabel, Allana stood swaying on her feet.

Drugged, Han wondered, or stunned. Instantly he lowered the blaster, which was whipped from his hand.

"I told them you could be reasoned with." Grunting as he came to his feet, the guard pressed a blaster against the small of Han's back. "Head for the lobby."

"What's this about?"

"We won't keep you in suspense for long. Do what you're told and no one gets hurt."

"No one else, you mean."

"Have it your way."

"Everything is under control," the other guard was telling the crowd. "Return to your seats and the show will resume as soon as possible."

"Madman!" someone yelled at Han.

Someone else pelted him with candy.

The guards escorted him to one of the lobby turbolifts. They descended a couple of levels, emerging in a security area equipped with a holding cell. A human officer was seated at the desk.

Han peeled away the false mustache and beard. "Where's my daughter?" he demanded.

"Your daughter?" The officer appraised Han. "A man of your age. I'm impressed."

"Cut the flattery. Where is she?"

The man stood. He was nerfy, with big hands and a pale scar over his right eyebrow. "Safe and sound. You get her back in one piece after you've done something for us." He pushed a comlink across the desk toward Han. "Contact Lando Calrissian."

Han's brows beetled in genuine surprise.

"Tell him we want twenty YVH droids delivered to Ord Mantell no later than tomorrow noon, local."

Playing for time and trusting that Leia was on top of the situation, Han said: "You never heard of the black market?"

The officer smiled faintly. "Not a YVH to be had, thanks to our new chief of state. We're forced to go directly to the manufacturer."

Han shook his head and pushed the comlink forward. "Lando won't do it. He's immune to blackmail."

"He'll do it for you," the officer said, shoving the comlink toward Han. "You're his pal."

Han shoved the comlink back. "Don't believe everything you read. He's held a grudge against me for years."

The officer's smile vanished. "What is it with you, Solo? You've already lost two kids, so you don't care about losing another one?"

Han propelled himself across the desk with such force that he drove the officer halfway across the room, his hands so tight on the man's throat it took three guards to tear him away.

Stroking his neck, the officer rasped, "That's not going to change things—"

A familiar *snap-hiss!* issued from a room adjacent to the holding cell, followed by agonized screams. Han was as surprised as anyone to learn that Leia had smuggled her lightsaber past arena security. But he had to admire her foresight.

"That'll be my wife," he said, grinning.

Moving silently and locked in on Allana's Force presence, Leia approached the lower-level detention rooms. A sudden chill raced through her and she came to an abrupt halt. The child of two powerful Jedi, Allana was innately strong in the Force, but her abilities were limited by age and experience. What Leia was sensing made no sense—

An unmistakable thrumming sound infiltrated her thoughts. Intense light radiated from the center of the room, and two beings screamed in pain. Before Leia could react, Allana was racing through the doorway straight to her.

"Jacen!" she said, encircling Leia's legs with her arms.

"What?"

"Jacen!"

Abruptly Allana whirled out from under Leia's comforting hold, glaring at something in the room beyond.

Leia felt a small storm of negative energy swirl in the Force and quickly reached for her, spinning her around.

"No, Allana, no! You mustn't do that."

Fury had turned Allana's face as red as her hair. Her eyes were narrowed in hatred.

"I won't let him hurt me!"

"No one's going to hurt you," Leia said firmly. "I'll protect you. Nothing bad is going to happen."

Despite the words, the storm began to build once more. Leia took Allana by the shoulders and gently shook her. "Come back to yourself!"

Allana went rigid, tears streaming from her eyes. "Mom gave me a needle to use! Where is it? I want the needle!" Sobbing and shaking uncontrollably, she buried her face in Leia's shoulder.

Leia held her tight, stroking her hair and using the Force to calm her. Picking her up, she stepped back from the doorway in apprehension. The thrumming returned, and with it blaster bolts and yet more screams. Leia saw movement inside the room and caught a glimpse of Jedi Knight Seff Hellin moving stalwartly toward a different doorway, his lightsaber raised in front of him.

The sight of two armless Barabels staggering from the room behind the desk made Han's jaw drop. Even a grandmother's anger wouldn't prompt Leia to be that brutal. Two of the beings who had escorted Han to the detention center were directing blasterfire through the doorway, but the bolts were being deflected back into the front room. Han threw himself to the floor in front of the desk, evading a bolt that nearly decapitated him. One of the guards fell backward, his chest on fire; the other took a deflected bolt to the left thigh and dropped to the opposite knee. The officer made a dash for the turbolifts, but a detonation in the hall sent him flying backward.

Blaster rifles raised at high port, five soldiers of a

swift-response team burst into the room from the direction Han had come.

"Everyone down! Down! Down!"

Considering that everyone was already on the floor, the amplified commands didn't mean much. The security officer was unharmed, but the rest of them—those Han could see, at any rate—were either unconscious or dead. The floor was flecked with blood and scraps of burned clothing. Han heard a sound behind him and realized that someone was standing in the doorway. A tall twentysomething Jedi with curly hair . . .

All but ignoring the soldiers' blaster rifles, Seff Hellin walked calmly into the room, deactivating his lightsaber when two men in suits and C-3PO appeared behind the members of the swift-response team.

"Galactic Alliance Intelligence," the shorter agent said, flashing a badge at Seff, then hurrying over to Han to help him to his feet. "Are you all right, Captain Solo?"

Eyes on Seff, Han dusted himself off. "Ask me later."

The agent waved for the soldiers to lower their rifles. The other agent held a comlink to his mouth.

"Get a medical team down here on the double."

"My daughter—"

"She's fine," Leia said, emerging from the doorway behind the now blaster-bolt-scarred desk, Allana clinging to her neck, visibly upset and—it seemed to Han—refusing to look at Seff Hellin.

The shorter agent, however, was looking directly at the Jedi. "I take it you're responsible for this mess."

"They should have known better," Seff said. "They were attempting to blackmail Captain Solo into procuring weapons for them."

The agent stared at him. "Who are you?" Getting no answer, he turned to Leia for help. "Who is he?"

"Seff Hellin."

Seff inclined his head. "Master Organa."

The second agent made note of it.

"We've been watching this bunch for a couple of standard months," the short one said for Han's benefit. "They're part of an illegal arms syndicate based on Denon. How did they know you were here?"

Han scratched his head. "Let me know when you find out." He glanced at Allana. "They took our daughter hoping to force me into contacting Tendrando Arms about delivering twenty YVH droids."

The agent nodded. "That figures. Of course, we were hoping to round everyone up at the same time, but your Jedi here has ruined that plan."

"He's not my Jedi," Han said.

"You have no law-enforcement jurisdiction on Taris," the other agent told Hellin. "I order you to surrender your lightsaber. We're placing you under arrest."

"Do as he says," Leia said. "I'll contact Master Skywalker—"

"I'm not surrendering my lightsaber to anyone," Hellin said. "And you're not taking me into custody."

"Seff!" Leia said sharply as the soldiers raised their rifles.

"Master Skywalker doesn't understand."

Hellin took a sudden step backward and waved his free hand at the soldiers. Torn loose, the rifles flew to the far side of the room, hit the wall, and clattered to the floor. When the two intelligence agents moved on him, Hellin waved a second time, and the men froze as if paralyzed.

Then, moving with blinding speed, the Jedi was gone.

Han went to Leia and Allana, whose eyes were squeezed shut.

"He shouldn't have been able to do that," Leia said in quiet astonishment.

chapter nineteen

"MOVE TO THE CENTER OF THE ROOM WITH ALL your belongings and prepare to be scanned," Carcel's Codru-Ji security officer ordered over the loudspeaker.

Jadak and Poste and a mixed-species group of two dozen other visitors moved deeper into the room. Positioning marks on the metal floor indicated where each of them should stand.

"You with the leg implants," the Codru-Ji said. "Take two steps forward and raise your arms out to your sides."

"Hope they don't find the laserfile you hid in the birthday cake," Poste said as Jadak and a Gran separated themselves from the group.

"Just the human male," the Codru-Ji said. "All right, you can rejoin the others," he added a moment later.

Everyone waited while a quartet of archaic gatekeeper droids performed the scanning.

"Gather your belongings and report to visitor registration," the guard said finally.

Having left their small packs in the prison's small hotel, Jadak and Poste were alone in being empty-handed; the rest of the visitors were bringing foodstuff, clothing, holozines, smokes of a wide assortment, and refresher flimsi to friends, family members, and former accomplices.

Carcel was the most miserable piece of rock Jadak had ever put down on, and perhaps the worst possible place for Poste to begin his galactic travels. Regardless, he was like a kid at an amusement park, soaking in every experience and elated to be away from Nar Shaddaa. Jadak had had himself fitted for a new identity and thoroughly scanned for locator implants. As a further precaution, they had booked passage on a merchant ship to Saleucami before hopping a passenger vessel to Roche and transferring to the dedicated shuttles that ferried visitors to and from Carcel. In their short time together, Poste had already shown himself to be a quick-thinking and amiable companion. Jadak had been mostly correct about the kid's criminal activities, but there was more to him than met the eye. Born in one of the Smugglers' Moon's deepest chasms, Poste had all but raised himself, learning the ropes of foraging, theft, and scamming early on. He had been jailed numerous times, and maintained a soft spot for kids growing up as he did, often to the point of sharing his meager pickings with them. Naturally inquisitive, he was full of questions, only some of which Jadak was able to answer, having spent the past six decades in dreamland.

The questions he couldn't answer for reasons that had nothing to do with the coma were where the treasure was hidden and precisely what part the *Envoy* would play in finding it. In the years he had flown for the Republic Group, Jadak had insisted on never being given the details of his missions. The less he knew, the less he could reveal if exposed as a spy and captured. But in the Senate Annex on that fateful day, the Senators had provided more than the usual information, and the phrase *restore Republic honor to the galaxy* was somehow a thread to unraveling their revelations.

Arrived at the visitor registration station, Jadak submitted their request.

"Rej Taunt," the Falleen guard said. "Do you have an appointment?"

"Just visiting."

"You're visitors."

Jadak swapped looks with Poste. "What, as opposed to guests?"

The Falleen regarded them for a moment, then pointed to a bench and said: "Take a seat and I'll let you know."

"Maybe they're holding him in solitary," Poste ventured.

Jadak shook his head. "Not by the sound of it."

For more than a standard hour they watched a HoloNet screen and sipped at sweet drinks purchased from a machine. Finally, the guard summoned them to the station.

"Taunt will see you now." He slid two electronic passes forward. "Hook these to your belts. Follow the floor-routing lines to the west building, then follow the red line to its end. Someone there will tell you what to do next."

"Taunt will see us now?" Poste said as they set out.

Jadak shrugged. "Maybe he was busy knocking out illuminator covers."

The walk took a solid quarter hour. The doors they passed through slid every which way—up, down, and to both sides. Some were barred and some were a meter thick. The guards and few prisoners moving through the sterile corridors looked as miserable as Carcel itself. Even the droids looked unhappy.

Ultimately a human guard led them to Taunt's cell, which, oddly, was sealed by a greel wood door that had to be two hundred years old. The door concealed a palatial suite of rooms covered with fine carpets and filled with furniture and antiques dating back to the late Old Republic era. An assortment of beings was busy at tasks while several human and humanoid females lounged languidly on divans and sofas. Well over a century old, Taunt was sitting like a Hutt on a huge pillow in the center of the least-occupied room.

"I'm Sorrel, and this is Mag Frant," Jadak said, using their new identities.

The Askajian gave them the once-over. "Do I know you gentlemen from somewhere?"

"We've come from Nar Shaddaa."

Taunt glanced at Poste. "You're from Nar Shaddaa." His gaze flicked to Jadak. "You . . . you're from . . ."

"All over."

"That would have been my first guess." Taunt's tone remained conversational. "So what brings you here all the way from Nar Shaddaa? Business?"

"Information," Jadak said.

Taunt smiled faintly. "That's business, isn't it?"

"This is old business. It concerns a YT-Thirteen-hundred freighter called the *Stellar Envoy*."

Taunt's expression changed, and he took a long moment to reply. "The *Second Chance*," he amended.

"That's what I meant."

Taunt studied Jadak. "Who did you say sent you?"

"No one sent us. But it was Bammy Decree who told us where to find you."

"The mechanic. How is he?"

"Still hobbling around."

"He was a young man when I first met him."

"He told us he rebuilt the *Envoy* for you."

"That he did." Taunt smiled with his eyes. "Did he tell you what happened?"

"Some of it."

Taunt motioned for them to grab pillows and make themselves comfortable.

"At first, the Imperials wanted to execute me for the deaths of the cruiser's crew members and clones. Instead a military court sentenced me to life. For the next couple of years, I was transferred from one penitentiary to the next—Agon Nine, Fodurant, Delrian, I saw the inside of all of them. Meanwhile, Bammy Decree learned that I'd taken a contract out on him and fled Nar Shaddaa for the stars. A bounty hunter found him hiding in Nomad City at Nkllon, and I had him turned over to the Black Sun Vigo who had paid for the cargo of buzz droids I jettisoned. Long story short, the Vigo was so impressed by my honoring the debt, he suggested a business partnership whereby he would furnish me with information I could feed to prison authorities in exchange for my being allowed to conduct illegal business while incarcerated—and in surroundings suited to my tastes. A kind of Black Sun franchise, you might say. All through the Imperial years, the New Republic years, and all the wars since, I've been sitting pretty while the rest of the galaxy has gone to rot. But in all that time, I've never forgotten that first run I made, jinxed as it was. I had high hopes for that ship."

"Maybe you should have named her *High Hopes* instead of *Second Chance*," Jadak said.

Taunt gazed at him. "Have we met before? Because you seem familiar. Ever been in lockup?"

Jadak shook his head. "I would remember."

"What's your interest in the *Second Chance*? You don't look like the historian type."

"My uncle was one of the pilots who died in the collision at Nar Shaddaa. His name was Reeze Duurmun."

Taunt flicked his big head in a nod of recognition. "You get to be my age, you forget faces. But I never forget a name. I knew Reeze when he was flying contraband for the Ilk family. He and I ran into some problems on Nar Shaddaa, but we managed to work them out."

He paused briefly. "Fancy that, Reeze dying in the ship I wound up with. I never knew . . . but Reeze being your uncle still doesn't explain why you'd come all the way to Carcel looking for the freighter."

"If she still exists, I want to own her."

"That's an if of major magnitude considering how much time has passed."

"We know that."

Taunt appraised them. "Kind of a fling, is that it, your looking for the ship? You don't have jobs? You're independently wealthy?"

"I lost my legs in an industrial accident. I'm blowing the insurance settlement pursuing a lifelong dream."

"And I'm supposed to help you make your dream come true?"

"We just want to know what became of the freighter after your arrest."

Taunt considered it. "I could tell you straight-out, I suppose. But I have to ask what you're bringing to the table."

"I won't insult you by saying credits, since it doesn't look like you lack for anything."

"Nice of you to notice."

"How about we reframe the question by asking if there's something we can do for you in exchange for the information we're after?"

Taunt rubbed his chins. "I do have something in the works. My employees are already on it, but they could use a couple of human hands. You'd have to be willing to jump your way to Holess. Are you flush enough to do that?"

"Providing you don't mind us taking the local."

"Even the local will get you there in time for the job."

"What's involved?" Jadak asked cautiously.

"Revenge."

"We're not muscle."

"Clearly. But this job isn't revenge of that sort."

"Who's the target?" Poste asked.

"The Colicoids."

Jadak was caught by surprise. "I didn't know they were still around."

Taunt sneered. "Like any pest, they're hard to eradicate."

"Revenge on an individual Colicoid or the entire species?"

"I don't overreach," Taunt said. "Here's the way it lays out. Though things turned out well enough for me, I've never forgiven them for what they did to some of the members of my crew, and for what those karking buzz droids did to my future. I've waited a long time to even the score, and the chance is finally at hand."

"What part do we play in this?" Jadak said.

Taunt leaned forward on the pillow. "Ever hear of a creature called a hueche?"

"An extraordinary creature," Vistal Purn was telling Han, Leia, Allana, and C-3PO in his office on the upper tier of the arena. "Certainly the finest example of a marsupial ever entered into competition. His name is Tamac's Zantay Aura. The radiance of the orange stripes is what won him the prize. And so well behaved. You know, the female produces a salubrious milk called kista."

"I didn't know," Leia said politely.

After the previous day's events it was difficult to care much about the pet who had won most placid in show, and she and Han might have postponed the meeting with Vistal Purn had Allana not insisted on honoring the appointment they had made. She gave all appearances of having put the brief abduction behind her; but Leia knew that wasn't the case. She had the ability to compartmentalize experiences and lock the painful ones away, a knack she had inherited from Tenel Ka rather than Jacen.

"What will happen to Tamac's Zantay Aura?" Allana asked.

Purn was only too happy to answer. Ten years or so younger than Han, he was tall and elegantly dressed and charming in a way Leia guessed would be required to deal with the sort of beings who entered pets into competition.

"He will father many chitliks that will be sold for obscene amounts of credits. Also, chitliks will become the must-have pets until some other species wins next year's competition. There's always a bit of politics involved," Purn added, almost as an aside to Han and Leia. "An adviser to Chief of State Daala is said to have a pair of chitliks. Still, the shows can be fun. I'm so sorry that your introduction to them had to be spoiled . . ."

"Sorry about the pets that got flattened," Han said.

"No need to apologize," Purn said. "From what I understand, the group that attempted to force your hand was smuggling weapons onto Taris inside false-bottomed cages. Galactic Alliance agents discovered a recent shipment of arms cached in the arena's subbasement. Between us, I think this conspiracy may go all the way to the top. My hope is that it doesn't completely tarnish the reputation of the show. Next year is shaping up to be an extraordinary year for insectoids and avians. If you have time I can show you some of the holoimages we've received." Purn fell silent for a moment, then said to Leia: "Captain Solo's eyes look as if they're glazing over."

"They have closed completely on three occasions in the past four cycles," C-3PO said.

Playfully, Leia patted Han on the hand. "He missed his afternoon nap. He might wake up if you'd tell us about the years you flew the *Millennium Falcon*. We know you sold it to Cix Trouvee, but Cix's children weren't able to shed any light on where you acquired the ship, or what it was being used for."

Purn sat back in his chair and grinned. "The *Falcon*. Just thinking about it brings me back . . ." He sat forward. "You see, I was young and in love . . ."

chapter twenty

"I WAS YOUNG AND IN LOVE AND THE MANAGER OF
Molpol's Traveling Circus.

But perhaps I should start at the beginning.

I grew up on Generis, where my parents owned and
operated a wilderness ranch on a white-water stretch of
the Atrivis River. The ranch was a four-day walk from
the closest population center, but most guests opted to
pay extra to be delivered by airspeeder, which could
make the trip in a little under a standard hour. My parents eventually purchased an airspeeder of their own
and taught me to pilot it. By the time I was twelve, it was
my job to ferry guests in and out of the ranch and to
oversee all routine maintenance and upkeep of the
speeder. When I wasn't flying I did whatever needed
doing at the ranch, where life was pleasant if somewhat
boring for a young man who had his sights set on seeing
the stars.

The place attracted wealthy travelers who wanted to
experience the wilderness in comfort. For my siblings
and me, that meant catering to their needs all hours of
the day and night. As more and more guests began to arrive with their children in tow, it became my responsi-
bility to entertain them while their parents were out
fishing, hunting, hiking, or running the rapids. This
might sound like the worst of all possible tasks, but in

fact I love to laugh, and I was born with a gift for making others laugh—frequently at my own expense. I never minded playing the fool, and my popularity with the kids brought me to the attention of the adults, who rarely said good-bye without inviting me to visit them on their homeworlds, which were like imaginary places for me. From them I heard wonderful stories about Mid and Outer Rim worlds, which only reinforced my desire to escape Generis as soon as I could.

Generis was far removed from the effects of Imperial rule, but guests at the ranch kept my family well informed of galactic developments. I knew that the quickest route to earning a starship pilot's license was through one of the Imperial Academies, but I didn't want to spend years of compulsory service in the navy and had no interest in learning to fly TIE fighters. So I took a civilian approach, apprenticing with several shipping companies and commercial enterprises before striking out on my own as a freelance pilot. Ultimately I was hired by the Molpol Circus to pilot one of their light freighters.

By then Molpol had been in existence for about one hundred standard years. It wasn't a big operation, but it was a profitable and popular one, especially on the remote worlds on which the arrival of the circus became an annual reason for celebration. On civilized worlds, we would lampoon everyone. HoloNet celebrities, sports figures, politicians—even Palpatine, until we received a warning from the Imperial Palace to remove him from our repertoire or face the consequences. On remote worlds, we would research local myths and legends beforehand and tailor our acts accordingly. And by remote I mean planets where the indigenes were still burning fossil fuels for energy, suffering through spells of unpredictable weather, and dying of diseases that had been eradicated on the Core Worlds millennia earlier.

Planets on which the mere act of defying gravity was still thought of as magical. To most of the populations, the fact that we had arrived from the far side of the galaxy meant next to nothing; we could just as easily have arrived from the far side of their own planet. The important thing was that we brought with us everything one could wish for in a circus: exotic animals, live music, and a host of skilled performers, from sideshow oddities to Ryn acrobats to master illusionists on the order of the Great Xaverri.

Molpol liked to think of itself as the antithesis of Circus Horrificus, with its ferocious arqets, akk dogs, and gladiatorial contests. As an alternative to inciting the kind of chaos Horrificus once did on Nar Shaddaa, Molpol delivered wonder and pure entertainment. Although, like Horrificus, we had a rancor—an albino mutant named Snowmass—and the usual assortment of carnivorous felines, herd animals, cameloids, and simians. Our beastmasters and handlers had scoured the galaxy to find the most interesting creatures—dianoga, nexu, mynock, and lava flea—but for the younglings in the audience we also had taurill, hawk-bats, energy spiders, and kyntix. Molpol's owner at the time, an Ortolan named Dax Doogun, dreamed of adding a sarlacc to the menagerie, but could never come up with an efficient way to transport it.

To move the animals we relied on an old Haor Chall C-9979 landing ship, reconfigured to be piloted by a flesh-and-blood crew—since Molpol owned few droids— and retrofitted with a bulky, Class Six hyperdrive. The cargo areas, racks, and massive turntables the Neimoidians had created to deploy their tanks and battle droid transports were redesigned to carry and reposition our banthas, acklays, and gundarks—and, of course, Snowmass.

The *Millennium Falcon* was already a part of

Molpol's fleet when I joined. It struck me as odd that such a powerful ship should be the property of a circus. Earlier owners had equipped the freighter with a military-grade hyperdrive and a dorsal turbolaser turret. But the more time I spent at the controls of the *Falcon,* the more I came to appreciate what a perfect fit she was for Molpol, being as agile as our acrobats and as motley as our sideshow performers. She was also long past her glory days as a ship of any sort—battle-scarred, held together with spit and wire, in sore need of bodywork, and about as capricious a vessel as I'd ever piloted.

In time I grew very fond of the *Falcon,* but for me Molpol's chief attraction was a young aerialist who was known by the stage name Sari Danzer. She was beautiful and graceful, and she could perform repulsorlift stunts that would amaze and astound even the most jaded members of the audience. Unlike me, the circus was in her blood, and the performances she gave had been honed over several generations by family members who guarded their secrets as closely as the Jedi once guarded theirs. Through the clever use of lasers and other aids, Sari could make herself appear to vanish, shrink, grow larger than a bantha, or streak through the sky like a meteor. Even when she wasn't performing, she moved in a way that seemed almost weightless.

She was Molpol's star, and unfortunately she knew that.

Her demands knew no bounds, and she insisted on bringing meticulous attention to everything she did. Never an eyelash out of place; never a piece of clothing that didn't fit perfectly; never a misstep. If she executed one of her routines less than perfectly, she would be angry for days. And if you were a member of the crew, you definitely didn't want to be the one responsible for spoiling the lighting or the music. Sari wouldn't scream at you, but her cold silence could be deafening.

None of that, however, stopped me from falling in love with her.

I was a mere pilot and she had little time for me, but I managed to bridge that gap. Since everyone involved with Molpol did double duty of some sort, I decided to join the clown squad—if for no other reason than to be able to exchange a few words with Sari between acts. Fifteen other clowns and I would have just emerged from a landspeeder meant for four, or I would have just worn myself out doing pratfalls, and there she'd be, waiting in the wings to go on, and I'd wish her luck or compliment her on her choice of costume. I don't think she was physically attracted to me in the slightest, but she loved that I could make the audience laugh and leave everyone in the best possible mood to appreciate her performance.

Normally the performers traveled together from world to world in an old passenger vessel, aboard which privacy was difficult to come by, gossip was rampant, and arguments were a constant. The *Falcon* was reserved for transporting the owner and the ringmaster, their occasional guests, and whatever cash proceeds emerged from the performances. Still, Sari would frequently ask me how I could stand to travel in "that junk heap of a ship." At such moments I would try to sing the *Falcon*'s praises, but my best efforts fell on deaf ears. Finally, however, I summoned the nerve to ask if she would consider trading her somewhat cramped quarters aboard the passenger ship for the relative luxury of a private cabin aboard the *Falcon*. The schedule called for us to perform on two backrocket planets in the Anoat Sector, for both of which Dax Doogun and the ringmaster would be traveling on a ship owned by the governor of the star system. Even I couldn't have dreamed up a more perfect situation: no hyperspace travel—as a means of conserving fuel and lowering expenses—simply three long days and nights of realspace transit from the third planet in the system to the seventh. I was careful to make the invitation sound casual, but I was certain she knew what I was up to, and that I knew she knew. Her response was that her decision would depend on the outcome of a thorough inspection tour of the ship she would undertake without prior warning. She made it sound like a joke, but I grasped that she was deadly serious.

I spent days cleaning and detailing the ship inside and out. I vacuumed the holds and the ring corridor, polished the cockpit instrument panel, and had the copilot's chair reupholstered. I was so obsessed with making the ship as spotless as possible, I wouldn't even entrust Molpol's labor droids with the task. The *Falcon* had two cabins, but I focused on the larger of the pair—the one normally reserved for Dax Doogun—laundering the linens, installing new illuminators, scrubbing the 'fresher, and recalibrating the sonic shower. I covered the tables that flanked the largest bunk with candles and I created a selection of music that could be pumped through the ship's intercom. I stocked the galley with food and wines and asked Molpol's cook to prepare a special meal I could reheat and serve. Performers and crew alike were entertained by the lengths to which I was willing to go to win Sari over, and most were more than happy to enroll in the conspiracy. I even managed to persuade Dax Doogun to finance the installation of a dejarik hologame table in the *Falcon*'s main hold. I knew that Doogun was a fan of the game, but more important I knew that Sari was, and I devoted every spare moment to brushing up on moves and the rules of play. I knew, too, that she had a strong distaste for violence, so I made certain that the accessway to the turbolaser battery was sealed.

While I toiled, I imagined the entire scenario: the meals and wines we would share, the mood music we would listen to, the competitive but flirtatious dejarik contests in which we would engage—my Kintan strider besting her Mantellian savrip . . .

The day finally arrived when Sari sprang the surprise inspection tour. We had just given the second of three performances on Delphon, where the planet's more primitive cultures had a legend of an ancient asteroid bombardment and a starship that had left carrying genome samples of all the native flora and fauna. The primitives weren't fooled by our attempts to make use of the legend—nor were they meant to be—but they played along just the same. As a result we performed one of our most successful shows, in which Sari was a standout, as ever.

Her tour of the *Falcon* began with the boarding ramp, which she went down on one knee to inspect. Once inside the ship she went directly into the cockpit, where she ran a white-gloved hand along the instrument panel, the steering yoke, and several of the control levers and toggle switches. She sat in the copilot's chair and swiveled through a full circle. Then she returned to the main body of the ship and made two circuits through the ring corridor before entering any of the secondary cabin spaces and holds, peeking into dark recesses, on the lookout for dust or cobwebs, smiling when she was impressed, or at least satisfied by the efforts I'd made. Once she had returned to the main hold, I swept aside the tarpaulin under which the dejarik hologame table was concealed, and knew by her bright-eyed gaze that I had passed the test.

In the end, all she said was, "Yes."

We struck camp on Delphon, collapsing the tents and cleaning up after ourselves. The handlers and beastmasters herded the animals into the Haor Chall lander; the crew went to their ship, the performers to theirs, and Sari and I boarded the *Millennium Falcon*. I had the freighter's navicomputer plot the most straightforward course to Delphon 7, because I planned to task the autopilot with most of the flying. In those days, in the years before the Rebel Alliance began building hidden bases on worlds in the Greater Javin, the only risk posed by sublight travel was pirates. But from everything I had heard, Imperial forces had the pirates on the run. What's more, pirates were not known to attack circuses.

While Sari showered and rid herself of makeup and glitter, I set the table in the main hold, opened the wine to let it breathe, got the meal warming, lighted the candles I'd strewn about, and started the music running through the intercom. When she emerged from the ring corridor into the main hold she had changed into something more comfortable, and the sight of her changed me forever.

We sat across from each other at the table, and I filled our glasses with wine.

"To an eventful journey," I said, raising my glass.

Smiling, she raised hers.

The glasses were millimeters from clinking when the voice of the lander captain howled from the enunciators in the engineering station.

"Pirates!"

I leapt up, flinging wine in every direction, and rushed to don the comm headset.

"Are you certain?" I asked.

"They're flying the Blazing Claw," the captain told me.

"Do they know we're a circus?" I said.

"They do, and they don't care," he shot back.

"Have you commed for help?" I asked, fully expecting the answer I received.

"They're jamming us," the captain said.

Sari and I hurried into the cockpit and strapped into the chairs in time to see warning bolts whizz across the bows of the big double-winged lander and the passenger ship. The fire had come from a light cruiser that was every bit as old as the Haor Chall C-9979, emblazoned with the pirate emblem of the Blazing Claw, and escorted by a dozen modified fighter craft.

"Who are they?" I asked the captain.

"Black Hole," was his answer.

I swore under my breath. Perhaps the least creative in terms of naming themselves, Black Hole was one of the most feared bands along the spaceways that side of the Core.

"Have they issued any demands?" I asked.

He said: "Only that they want us to put down on Regosh."

The primary moon of Delphon IV, Regosh was a low-g orb lacking population centers and as heavily forested as my homeworld. There was oxygen enough for the humans and humanoids among us, but I suspected that some of the sideshow performers would be forced to wear breathers—assuming the pirates weren't planning to kill us outright.

I considered bringing the *Falcon*'s turbolaser to bear on the cruiser, but rejected the idea almost immediately. As dexterous as the ship was, I wasn't talented enough to engage simultaneously in combat and evasive flying. Sari seemed to have read my thoughts, in any case.

"Let's wait and see what they want," she said.

"They could be slavers," I posited.

She nodded. "Then we'll just have to deal with that."

Changing course, I followed the lander and the other ships into Regosh's thin atmosphere. The Black Hole vessels led us to a large clearing in the northern hemisphere, where a group of their cohorts was waiting, some armed with repeating blasters. A miscellany of some of the most cutthroat species the Outer Rim had to offer, the pirates didn't look like the type that could be reasoned with. I doubted that even my finest pratfalls would elicit so much as a grin. When all of Molpol's ships had set down, the leader of the pirate band, speaking butchered Basic, ordered the crew of the C-9979 to deboard. The rest of us were to remain aboard our separate ships.

Black Hole's intentions were suddenly clear, and were at once a relief and a worst-case scenario: They were hijacking the lander.

For three standard hours we watched as the animals were herded from the big ship and left to mill about in the clearing, as well behaved as they would have been prior to a performance. Unaccustomed to being unrestrained, many of them meandered to the edges of the clearing, where they began to nibble at Regosh's abundant foliage. Some of the felines and gundarks skulked away and disappeared into the forest. Confused, the smaller animals—the snow lizards, eopies, nerfs, and others—clustered together in the center of the landing zone as if awaiting instructions.

No sooner was the off-loading completed than several pirates hurried into the lander and lifted off. The rest of the Black Hole ships launched, and in the blink of an eye the pirates were gone.

Sari and I raced out of the *Falcon* to join Molpol's crew and performers, who were also hurrying out of their ships. A few steps from the foot of the boarding ramp, I stopped to have a look around. Regosh's pale sky was darkening, and the surrounding forest was now raucous with the calls of indigenous animals. I had a bad feeling about the situation, which worsened as I saw hundreds of pairs of eyes begin to glow in the tree line.

With astounding speed something emerged from the trees and raced across the clearing, disappearing into the forest with one of the small animals clamped in its mouth. Seconds later, another creature emerged, carrying off another of the animals. Then a third, and a fourth . . .

Molpol's armaments consisted mostly of ceremonial weapons used by our sharpshooters during their portion of the show. Some of the crew members had actual blasters, but too few to fend off attacks that were likely to continue throughout the night. I was giving thought to using the *Falcon*'s turbolaser to lay waste to the trees when several of the handlers hurried over to me.

"We've got to get these animals into the *Falcon*," someone shouted in my face.

I must have returned a confused look, because he repeated the statement at even higher volume.

I shook my head to clear it and tried to point out that the *Falcon* wasn't large enough to accommodate even a third of the animals—and that would include using the living quarters of the ship as well as the cargo areas.

"Then you'll just have to make three trips," said the Ryn who often served as my copilot.

"Three trips to where?" I asked in a voice that sounded too high-pitched to be my own.

"Back to Delphon," I was told.

Everyone began shouting at once, filling my ears with statements I already knew.

We had to do this for the sake of the animals. We couldn't abandon them on Regosh to become prey. The large animals could fend for themselves, but the small ones had to be rescued. Only the *Falcon* was fast enough to accomplish the task. Only I had the skill to plot and execute the microjumps that would be necessary. Meanwhile, the rest of them would remain on the moon and hold the predators at bay.

With that I stepped aside to make room for the handlers, who immediately set themselves to the task of herding animals into the *Falcon*. How I wished the pirates had left us with at least enough Taanabian straw to cover the ship's deck plates, but all the feed and grain had disappeared with the Haor Chall lander. When I could finally move, I raced into the ship to enable the oxygen generators and inertial dampers belowdecks and set the air scrubbers on maximum. But my nose already told me that there was simply no way the scrubbers were going to overcome the stench produced by nervous snow lizards and other cameloids. In fact, I began to doubt that the *Falcon* would ever smell the same again.

Then, just when it seemed that matters couldn't get any worse, Snowmass somehow got it into his flat-faced head that the *Falcon* was actually *ingesting* the small animals and decided to come to their rescue. I don't know that there's ever been another instance of an albino rancor attacking a YT-1300 freighter, but that was exactly what happened, and the only way I could prevent the ship from being pummeled flat and pitted by corrosive drool was to engage the repulsorlifts and dance the *Falcon* out of Snowmass's considerable reach while his handlers tried to calm him down. I don't know precisely how long the dance went on, but by the end of it many of the animals were shipsick and adding to the mounting miasma by retching and emitting other noxious odors.

In all the confusion I had completely lost sight of Sari, though I suspected she had fled to her confined cabin in the passenger ship. So perhaps you can imagine my surprise when I exited the *Falcon*'s cockpit connector to find her seated cross-legged on the now-filthy deck of the main hold, her evening dress torn beyond repair, face smudged with unidentifiable substances, and makeup in disarray. When I saw that she was crying softly I hastened to her side, babbling apologies for everything I could think of, including the pirate attack.

She gazed up at me for a long moment before wiping the tears from under her eyes and laughing. "You are a fool," she told me, "even when you're not acting the part."

I started to stammer a reply, but she cut me off.

"Why do you think I'm with the circus—for the applause? For the few credits we earn?" She gestured broadly to the stinking snow lizards and eopies crowded around her. "I love animals, Purn. And I think that after we get all of them back to Delphon, I'm going to be in love with you."

"It actually took my Ryn copilot and me four trips to transport all the animals back to Delphon," Purn continued. "But thanks to the *Falcon*, we made the microjump round trips in what had to be record time, and in the end we lost only twelve animals to Regosh's predators."

"What about the big animals?" Allana asked, on the edge of her chair.

"Well, they made new lives for themselves on Regosh."

"Even Snowmass?"

"Even Snowmass." Purn smiled. "He seemed very happy the last time I saw him."

"Because he didn't have to perform any more circus tricks?"

"Maybe that had something to do with it. But I think Regosh reminded him a little bit of his native Dathomir."

"My mom—" Allana started to say, then stopped herself and began again. "What happened to the small animals?"

Lament crept into Purn's smile. He turned slightly to face Han and Leia. "Ultimately the pirate attack proved so costly that Dax Doogun was forced to sell everything—even the name *Molpol* itself."

"Black Hole was never apprehended?" Leia said.

"Some members were caught. The rest joined forces with the Zann Consortium."

"I take it that *everything* included the *Falcon*," Han said.

"Unfortunately. If I'd had the credits, I would have purchased the ship, but wealth was long in coming to me."

A gentle rap sounded from the door and a striking Twi'lek female poked her head into the room. "Sorry to interrupt, but you're scheduled to distribute the final prizes."

Purn beckoned her into the room. "I won't be a moment." He looked at Han. "Where was I?"

"You would have bought the *Falcon* . . ."

Purn nodded. "It's true. The *Falcon* was one of the first things to go, and, as manager, I personally arranged for the sale to Cix Trouvee."

"Then what?" Allana asked.

"After Molpol's I returned to piloting, only to discover that I had lost my taste for it, and in its place I had developed a fondness for animals. I worked as a ringmaster for several other outfits and eventually found my way into judging pet shows. Which is what I've been doing ever since."

Han rubbed his chin. "You said the *Falcon* already belonged to Molpol when you signed on."

"Yes. Dax Doogun had acquired the ship several years earlier."

"Do you know where Dax got it?"

Purn thought for a moment. "I recall that the *Falcon* was a medical vessel of some sort."

"Really," Leia said in surprise.

"But I'm afraid that's all I remember about it."

"Doogun would remember, wouldn't he?" Han said.

"I'm certain he would. But I haven't had any contact with Dax in, oh, twenty years at least."

Allana's face fell. "Do you know where he is?"

"I'm sorry, young lady, but I don't know where he is."

"We'll find him," Han said confidently, and mostly for Allana's sake.

"You never mentioned what became of Sari," Leia said.

Purn laughed out loud. "Shame on me. I married her." He gestured to the Twi'lek waiting patiently by the door. "Sari, allow me to introduce Han, Leia, and Amelia Solo, and their droid See-Threepio."

"A pleasure," Sari said.

"On the contrary," Leia said, smiling broadly.

"You could say the circus brought us together," Purn said, "but I like to credit the *Millennium Falcon*."

chapter twenty-one

"I LOOK RIDICULOUS," POSTE SAID. WHEN HE EX-tended his arms straight out in front of him, the sleeves of the ocher-colored suit rode up almost to his elbows.

"Of course you do. But you're supposed to be an advertising exec, so who's going to notice?"

Dressed in a magenta jumpsuit and knee-high soft boots, Jadak guessed he didn't look much better. But he was certain that he and Poste could pull off the charade long enough to hold up their end of the job.

Wearing only underwear, the two actual owners of the suits were slumped in the hotel room's spacious and opulent refresher, ankles and wrists bound with electrocuffs and mouths covered with adhesive tape. Poste and Jadak had arrived on Holess only a local hour earlier. At the spaceport they had rented a luxury airspeeder and had flown directly to their posh hotel in the center of the city. In their thirty-sixth-floor room, which enjoyed an unobstructed view of the Mount of Justice, Jadak, Poste, and two of Rej Taunt's hoodlums were lying in wait. The executives scarcely had a chance to open their luggage when they were rendered unconscious by the pair of Weequays. The larger man's suit was simply a loose fit on Jadak, but the smaller man's made Poste look like he'd been shrink-wrapped in lineneen. Still, the two of them looked a whole lot better than the topknotted Weequays would have.

"You ready?" the Weequay named Erf asked in slurred Basic.

Jadak gave the suit jacket a downward tug. "Good to go." He nodded to Poste, who scowled but managed to pull himself away from the refresher's full-length mirrpanel.

Erf pulled two blasters from the roomy pockets of his longcoat. "Safety engaged. Already set on stun." He flicked the selector switches to make sure, then handed the blasters to Jadak.

Jadak hefted them, then passed the more powerful one to Poste, who rechecked the selector switches, checked the battery charge and gas levels, and slipped the weapon into a shoulder holster.

"Here the case," the other humanoid said. "Inside is data card."

Jadak took hold of the small alloy case and experienced what he initially took to be a déjà vu moment. In fact, memory transported him to the docking berth in the lowest tier of the Senate Annex on Coruscant, where he had delivered a similar case to Senators Des'sein, Largetto, and Zar. In Jadak's mind, the memory felt no more than a month old.

"The Antarian Ranger who will take possession of the ship is called Folee. You will find her in Salik City, which is the capital city of the western regions. She is expecting you. The phrase we've provided—"

"You all right?" Poste said.

The memory receded and was gone.

"Lost you there for a moment."

Jadak looked away. "Just running through the plan."

"Second thoughts?"

Jadak shook his head. "Thoughts."

They grabbed their small rucksacks, located the rented

airspeeder in the hotel garage, and folded themselves into the bucket seats. A forty-year-old Incom T-11 with a stylish body and sloping prow, it was fully tricked out with a powerful repulsorlift and wide thruster nozzles. Jadak's hands went instinctively to the proper controls, and within moments they had lifted off and were slicing through the planet's thick air, merging with traffic in the thirty-meter lane.

A world of varied terrain, Holess was home to a species of portly humanoids thought to be related to the long-eared Lannik. The native population was clustered in towering cities built on wealth derived from the planet's rich deposits of duranium, which had been mined and exported for thousands of years. With more disposable income and free time on their hands than most species would know what to do with, the Holessians had elevated their innate reverence for law to what amounted to a religion. As a result Holess had more petty laws than just about anywhere in the galaxy, and the native population was litigious to a fault. Laws were enacted simply for their sake, in the surety that someone would break them and be forced to mount a legal defense. Judges were revered as god-like figures, and lawyers—prosecutors and defense attorneys alike— were treated as celebrities. To be selected to serve on a jury was tantamount to being chosen to partake in a sacred ritual. Holessians followed cases as fervently as other species followed sports seasons. Betting on a verdict was viewed as sacrilege, but decisions were endlessly discussed, debated, and analyzed, often for years after the cases were concluded.

The center of all the legal activity was the Mount of Justice, a cathedral-like structure built atop a natural prominence in the center of the capital city and reserved for the highest-profile cases, frequently those of galactic import. Though often compared to the Tower of Law on pacific Bimmisaari, the mount was the focal point of Holessian life, and a destination for pilgrimages all natives had to undertake at least once during their lifetime. The mount was accessed by a broad ramp that spiraled from the tor's monolithic base to the massive, gaping front doors of the structure itself. Above the entrance loomed an enormous holoscreen that could be seen for kilometers distant, and on which ran live coverage of cases being tried, along with advertisements for a host of products and services.

The stately spires of the mount filled the forward view from the airspeeder as Jadak maneuvered effortlessly through traffic. Far below, the boulevards that surrounded the mount were lined with spectators, who were cheering on judges, lawyers, and jury members as they made their way to the base of the ramp. Makeshift stands erected along the processional route supplied food, drink, facsimile legal briefs, and souvenirs, including replicas of the chief participants.

The fastest-selling item at the moment was a scale model of the star witness in a case that had consumed the Holessians' attention for the past several months. The case had been brought by Colla-Arphocc Automata against the Galactic Alliance government for the right to resume production of the battle droids that had earned the carnivorous Colicoids a reputation for barbarity in the years preceding the Clone Wars. Forced to disarm at the conclusion of the war, and in fear of violent reprisals by Imperial forces, the Colicoid Creation Nest had gone into hiding. They had recently emerged, represented by a celebrity attorney from Epica, claiming to be in possession of documents that bore the personal seal of Emperor Palpatine. The alleged documents stated that the ban placed on production of their war droids had expired a year earlier, and the Colicoids were arguing that they should now be free to compete with Roche, the Givin Cartel, Tendrando Arms, and others suppliers of armament and munitions.

The fact that the star witness for Colla-Arphocc Automata was a former member of the think tank known as Colla Designs had given Holessian souvenir makers a real chance to shine. The facsimiles sold in the stands not only looked like a miniature destroyer droid—save for the twin blasters and distinctive defensive bubble—but could also be balled into a near-solid sphere. A seldom-witnessed, uncontrollable startle reflex triggered by encounters with an ancient predator known as a hueche, the transformation owed to the overlapping epidermal scales of horn that were the foundation of the Colicoids' bony shell. Some xenobiologists believed that the Colicoids' commitment to wiping out the hueche was the impetus for their eventual success in the field of weaponry design.

Even from thirty meters up, Jadak and Poste could see that many spectators were having fun with the toy Colicoids, playing catch, juggling them, rolling them along the broad sidewalks, and using the foamite models in mock battles with one another.

Closing on the controlled airspace around the Mount, Poste transmitted the entry code they had taken off the advertising execs. Landing on or anywhere near the helical ramp was prohibited, as most participants and all pilgrims made the climb on foot—some on hands and knees. Bordered on both sides by low fences made of duranium, the ramp offered numerous resting areas for the weary, most of which were accessed by gates and decorated with duranium tablets elaborately engraved with laws and edicts.

Granted clearance, Jadak banked for the hover platform that housed the control booth for the mound's colossal holoscreen.

A Holessian sporting a blue tunic was waiting at the

platform docking area. "You're the representatives from Desicare Deodorant?"

"Fresh from Coruscant," Jadak said, climbing from the pilot's seat.

"Bone-dry and fragrant."

Poste showed the Holessian a blank stare, then grinned. "Hey, you know our slogan."

"I use your product every day."

"Our favorite kind of customer," Jadak said.

"We have laws that govern perspiration," the Holessian said solemnly.

"Raise your hands," Poste said.

The Holessian swung to him. "I assure you I'm quite dry—"

At the sight of Poste's blaster he reached for the sky.

"No reason to break a sweat," Jadak said, drawing his blaster. "Just lead us into the control booth and follow our instructions like they're law."

Everyone but a lone security guard had their backs to them as they were led into the oval-shaped booth. Sensing that something wasn't right, the guard went for his blaster, but Poste was ready for him. Disarming the guard, Poste repeated the warning Jadak had given their greeter moments earlier. The commotion got the attention of some of the technicians, who swung around from their individual display screens to find the human executives from Desicare Deodorant leveling blasters in a general way.

"If you want your product to have more screen time, you need only ask," one of them said.

That brought the rest of them around.

"You are in violation of provision one-three-three-three-six-slash-two-slash-B of the penal code regarding unlawful entry. Be advised that we have the right to bring suit against you, notwithstanding your—"

The bolt Poste fired into the acoustic tile ceiling put an end to the gabbing.

Jadak popped open the carry case and raised a data card above his head. "A new spot we want you to run."

The Holessian in charge objected. "All advertisements are required to be submitted to the Ministry of Media for prior viewing to ascertain whether the content is fit for public consumption or should be rated according to the guidelines hithertofore established by the Board of Decency."

"So sue us if it doesn't meet your standards," Jadak said.

"We most certainly will."

"Do you have a permit to carry those blasters?" a technician asked.

Poste triggered another bolt. "I'm going to stun the next one of you who speaks."

Jadak marched down a carpeted stairway that led to the booth's curving observation window. The mount and that part of the spiral ramp that ended at the front doors seemed close enough to touch. The huge screen was displaying live video of the jury being seated in the courtroom. Jadak swung around to face the production technicians.

"We're going to wait until the star witness reaches the top of the ramp. When he does, and on my word, you're going to run our spot on the holoscreen." He slapped the data card into the hand of the chief Holessian, who regarded it with revulsion.

"If you are attempting to impress the Colicoid species," the chief said, "I suggest you consider that, being insectoids, they do not perspire in the same fashion as humanoids. Toxins and waste are excreted by means other than sweat glands. What glands they do possess are for generating defensive odors and pheromones."

"We're hoping to market a special product just for them," Jadak said.

"Why not do that on their world?"

"Because most of the nest is probably accessing your live feed."

"In that case, we reserve the right to claim a participatory share in all revenues generated by the sale of . . . whatever your new product is."

Jadak nodded. "Sure, and if it fails, Desicare reserves the right to bill you for a portion of the research-and-development costs."

A dozen separate conversations broke out.

Jadak turned back to the window. He studied the patrol patterns of the Holessian security speeders and appraised the turbolaser battery installed at the summit of the mount's tallest spire, a holdover from the Yuuzhan Vong War. Lowering his gaze to the ramp, he spied the Colicoid nearing the top, under escort by a powerfully built Nautolan and a slim woman most likely in the employ of the attorney representing Colla-Arphocc Automata.

Jadak moved quickly to the closest display screen. "Give me a close-up on the star witness and its escorts," he told the technician at the controls. The Holessian selected one of the live feeds and brought it onscreen while Jadak watched over the tech's shoulder. The Nautolan was one of the thugs who had jumped him on Nar Shaddaa. The woman—the female, at any rate—was Koi Quire, of Core Health and Life.

"Who's the attorney representing the Colicoids?" Jadak asked when his thoughts had stopped whirling.

"Lord Lestra Oxic," the technician said.

The name didn't ring a bell, but Jadak tucked it away.

"Get ready," he said loud enough to be heard over the ongoing arguments.

"You do realize that your spot is going to interrupt our interview with Chief Justice Margo?"

"Run a breaking-news announcement."

"We could do that," the chief Holessian said to his assistant. "If nothing else, we will have protected ourselves from possible action by—"

"Do it," Jadak said, brandishing his blaster.

Peripherally he saw the giant holoscreen go blank for a moment, then display a news bulletin icon. Below, the Colicoid, the Nautolan, and Koi Quire were completing the final curve in the ramp and ascending straight for the front doors.

"Run the spot—*now*!"

A 3-D image of a snarling feline with two rows of razor-sharp teeth all but leapt from the mount, baffling some of the nearby spectators, surprising others, and frightening the rest. But only in the Colicoid did the twenty-meter-high visage inspire panic. Leaping straight up from the ramp, the star witness for the plaintiffs curled its body into an armored ball two meters in diameter and went rolling down the ramp at incredible speed.

The chief Holessian hurried to the observation window. "What sort of advertisement is this? What is that creature?"

"It's called a hueche," Jadak said, without taking his eyes from the rolling alien.

Spectators still climbing the ramp were leaping for cover as the ball flew into their midst, kept on track by the duranium fences that lined the ramp. At one point it looked like the Colicoid had gathered enough momentum to leap the fence entirely, but Rej Taunt's henchmen were on hand to see that that didn't happen. Throwing open one of the rest-area fences, they effectively flipped the balled Colicoid back onto the ramp, where its spiraling descent continued. Farther down, a second team of henchmen did the same, directing the fleeing alien toward the base of the mount where a speeder truck was waiting. In its bed sat a huge containment sphere, its hemispherical lid open wide.

Jadak signaled Poste to head for the airspeeder. He thought about putting a couple of blaster bolts into the control booth's communications suite, but decided that they had already done enough damage. Chances were that security patrols had already been notified, and that he and Poste were going to have to do some evasive flying.

The Holessians were too busy restoring normalcy to the broadcast to attempt to slow or prevent their retreat. Hurling themselves into the airspeeder, Jadak and Poste launched from the platform just in time to see the balled Colicoid swish into the speeder truck's gaping container, which slammed shut, trapping the insectoid inside.

"Case closed," Poste said from the passenger's bucket seat.

At the same time, security vehicles circling above the truck broke from their holding patterns and began to race for the control booth.

"Here we go," Jadak said.

They already had a good lead on the patrols and with any luck would arrive at the spaceport long before the speeder truck. Twisting the yoke, Jadak swerved the T-11 away from the mount, just in case anyone got reckless and decided to bring the turbolaser battery to bear. The throttle maxed, Jadak was angling for a cluster of tall buildings in the southern part of the city when he heard Poste loose a string of epithets.

"What?" Jadak shouted.

Poste was leaning out of the speeder, looking at something behind them. "They lost it! The sphere, the Colicoid—they dropped it."

"*Dropped* it?"

"I didn't see exactly what happened but the kriffing thing is rolling down the street!"

A dozen possibilities fought it out in Jadak's mind: the truck had taken fire from one of the security vehicles; the tractor system that anchored the containment sphere had failed; the Colicoid had somehow decompressed itself just enough to rock the sphere from the bed of the truck . . .

"Is it still rolling?"

"And picking up speed," Poste said, looking over his shoulder. "It's downhill all the way to the river."

"Where's the truck?"

"Chasing it."

"How many patrol craft on our tail?"

Poste pivoted in the seat. "I make it three, but they're way behind us."

Jadak settled himself at the controls and blew out his breath. "Buckle up."

Poste had no sooner fastened the seat straps than Jadak threw the speeder through a twisting half loop and sped back toward the Mount of Justice.

"You promised no more stunt flying!" Poste said after he had reswallowed his breakfast.

"Old habits die hard."

Jadak had the rolling containment sphere in sight, but the security vehicles now had the T-11 in sight and were darting in from both sides, with sirens howling and lights flashing. SoroSuub Police Specials, they were as fleet as the Incom, but only in the right hands, and the repeating blasters they carried were light-duty and of limited range. Text crawled across their rooftop-mounted display screens, showing the number of laws Jadak and Poste had broken.

Less than a hundred meters ahead and twenty meters below, the containment sphere was zipping toward the river, going airborne at each shallow hill. Flying five meters above the street, the speeder truck was still in pursuit, but short of cutting the Colicoid off there wasn't much it could do. Jadak took a moment to study the stretch of roadway ahead, then pushed the yoke forward and dropped the airspeeder almost to ground level and so close to the front of the truck that it was forced to veer off. Seeing what was coming, Poste extended his legs and arms to brace himself against the floor and passenger's-side door.

Jadak waited for the next dip in the roadway; then, just when the containment sphere took to the air, he called all speed from the T-11 and dived beneath the sphere.

The airspeeder's forward motion drove the ball up onto the slanted prow, over the low windscreen and the lowered heads of Jadak and Poste, and down into the rear nacelle, where it wobbled for a moment before nesting into the bucket seats. The extra weight sent the T-11 onto the street, sparks fountaining from the undercarriage, until Jadak managed to regain control of the repulsorlifts and get the speeder back into the air. By then, though, the police SoroSuubs had caught up and were attempting to keep the Incom from gaining additional altitude.

A sudden hail of blasterfire from the truck turned the situation on its ear. Holed by bolts, two of the patrol speeders slewed to opposite sides and plummeted to the ground, leaking smoke and fire as they screeched along the street, then plowed through two fences, furrowed an area of lawn, and splashed into the river.

The containment sphere prevented Jadak from seeing behind him, but the abrupt disappearance of the other SoroSuubs suggested that they were now chasing the speeder truck. Accelerating, the T-11 streaked out over the river, twenty meters above the choppy water, banking into morning sun and on course for the spaceport.

The freighter that was to have accepted delivery of the sphere from the speeder truck was warming in a docking bay. As Jadak lowered the Incom alongside, several humanoids and two Gamorreans hurried to roll the containment sphere out of the Incom and up the freighter's boarding ramp.

Eyeing their clothes, the ship's captain asked: "What are you two dressed for?"

Poste smiled without amusement. "We have parts in the school play."

"What happened to the truck?"

"The pilots dropped the ball," Poste said.

"Last we saw," Jadak added, "police units were after them."

The captain nodded once. "That's their problem." He cocked his head toward the freighter. "The Colicoid's got an appointment on a world a long way from anywhere." He began to ascend the ramp, then stopped and turned around. "Can we drop you two somewhere?"

"Yeah," Jadak said, tapping Poste into motion. "But the where's going to depend on whether Rej Taunt honors his part of our arrangement."

"He will. Find yourselves a couple of bunks in the common cabin."

They went directly there. After testing all the bunks, Poste set his knapsack on one and began pulling items from it while singing to himself, exactly as Jadak had seen him do on Nar Shaddaa in his hole-in-the-wall crypt the day before they left.

"What's with the song?"

"It's to make sure I have everything." Poste pointed to items while he sang. "Socks and shirts and pants and comb, and boots and hat, and—"

"All right, I get it," Jadak interrupted.

"I was taught to do it by one of the old-timers who lived in the canyon my tribe haunted. In the beginning I only owned a few things, but every one of them was important to me, and it hurt when something went missing, either through theft or my own carelessness. I was only five or six at the time. But as I got more things I was able to add more lines to the song, and on the day I added a second verse I decided I was rich."

Jadak nodded and smiled. "If things work out, kid, that song of yours is going to take a week to sing."

Poste grinned. "The old-timer who taught it to me called it a mnemonic."

"Your code phrase is 'Restore Republic honor to the galaxy.' *Our ally is expecting you. The phrase we've provided you is a mnemonic aid she will need to carry out her part of the mission. The* Envoy *will handle the rest of it."*

Jadak extended his trembling hands to Poste. "You have a datapad in there?"

chapter twenty-two

"I'LL MAKE A DEAL WITH YOU," LEIA SAID. "YOU AND Muzzle can stay in here for the entire trip to Coruscant. But you have to promise that when we get there you won't shut yourself inside your room."

"Muzzle, too?" Allana said, holding the simian hand puppet up to her shoulder.

Leia nodded. "Muzzle also has to promise."

Allana frowned and turned aside to confer quietly with the toy.

The *Millennium Falcon* was in hyperspace, and Allana was in low spirits. She had been distant ever since Taris, sitting on her bunk in the principal cabin with the puppet, perhaps telling Muzzle all she wouldn't say to Leia or Han.

Leia eased into the cabin and sat down opposite her, putting an arm around Allana's shoulders. "What do you say?"

"Muzzle says he doesn't want to stay in here for the whole trip."

"What about you?"

"I don't want to, either."

Leia smiled. "That's good, because Grandpa and I miss having your company." She took a moment. "You seem a little sad. Is anything wrong?"

Allana shook her head.

"We still haven't talked about what happened during the pet show."

She averted Leia's gaze. "It's not that."

"What, then?"

"I'm just sad our adventure is over."

"You mean because we haven't learned who owned the *Falcon* before Vistal Purn?"

Allana nodded. "Grandpa said it's a dead end."

"He said that he was pretty sure we'd be able to learn something from the Ortolan who owned the circus— Dax Doogun."

Allana looked at her. "That's what he told me. But I heard him tell you it was a dead end."

Leia kept a straight face. Han had said as much. It concerned her that Allana would eavesdrop on a private conversation, but she decided not to make an issue of it.

"It's been a great adventure so far, hasn't it?"

"Sort of."

"You haven't had any fun?"

"I guess."

Leia moved closer to her. "Allana, can we talk a little bit about what happened on Taris? If you don't feel like talking now we can do it some other time, but I think it would help if we discussed it."

"What do you want to talk about?"

"Well, let's start with those beings who tricked you into following the squall."

"I hate them."

Leia fell silent for a moment. "They tricked you and took you because they wanted to force Grandpa to do something."

"What?"

"They wanted him to make Uncle Lando send them some war droids."

"Why?"

"I guess they had some bad plans."

Allana's brows beetled and she lowered her chin.

"Do you remember what you said when you ran away from Seff?" When Allana didn't respond, Leia said: "You said 'Jacen.'"

"I know what I said."

"Why do think you said your father's name?"

Allana gave her head a firm shake.

Leia thought for a moment. Could she get to the bottom of this without leading her too much? Should she drop the matter for the time being?

I can't, she told herself.

"When those bad beings took you, did it make you think of when Jacen took you from your mom?"

"No," she snapped. "*Seff* made me think of Jacen."

Leia had already guessed as much. Still, she said: "Jacen didn't look like Seff, or even sound like him."

"Not like that, Grandma. I felt him in the Force like I felt Jacen."

Leia recalled the storm she felt in the Force before she spied Seff. It troubled her that Allana had picked up on Seff's raw power.

"Jacen made me afraid," Allana said suddenly. "And then Seff made me afraid in the same way."

Leia took hold of Allana's hands. "In what way, honey?"

"That he was going to hurt me."

Leia blinked in consternation. "Jacen would never have hurt you, Allana. He loved you so very much. He would have changed the galaxy for you if he could."

"Why?"

"To protect you from harm—from any evil."

Allana seemed to consider it.

"Do you miss him, Allana?"

Allana looked away. "A little. Sometimes." She turned to face Leia. "Do you wish he was still alive, Grandma?"

A lump formed in Leia's throat. "I'm sorry he had to die."

So very sorry.

"Was he sick?"

Leia nodded. "He was sick. But not like when your stomach hurts. He was . . . he had a kind of sickness in the Force." Someday Allana would have to be told the full story, in all its gruesome and tragic details, but now wasn't the time.

"Can the Force get sick?"

"No. But beings can use the Force in a way that endangers others."

"Is that the dark side?"

"Perhaps. And one path to the dark side is anger. Another is hate. That's why I scolded you when you ran from the room and you wanted to hurl the Force at Seff."

Allana fidgeted. "Was Jacen angry?"

"Jacen was very angry."

"What was he mad at?"

"He was mad at not being able to have his way."

"I get mad sometimes when you tell me to stop doing something," Allana said quietly.

"We all get mad sometimes," Leia said. "But getting mad in that way, getting frustrated or feeling like you should be able to do something, is not the same as filling yourself up with anger and hatred and letting those emotions take control of your thoughts and actions."

"It makes you see red," Allana said, brightening somewhat.

"When anger fills you up enough, you can see red, and that's not good for you or for the Force."

Allana linked her arms about Leia's neck. "I'm not mad now. Just a little sad. That's what I was telling Muzzle when you came in."

"What did Muzzle say back?"

"That being sad is stupid."

Leia hugged her. "Muzzle is wrong. It's not stupid. Sometimes we can't help feeling sad."

Han rapped on the jam of the open hatch. "Okay to come in?"

Leia whispered: "Is it okay?"

"Come in, Grandpa," Allana said.

He stepped into the cabin. "I've reached Luke."

Leia let go of Allana and stood up in a rush. She started for the doorway, then stopped. "Do you want to speak to Uncle Luke after I finish speaking with him?"

"Uh-uh."

Han grinned at Allana. "I sure could use some help piloting the ship."

Allana smiled and jumped up.

"What should I do, Captain Solo?" C-3PO asked from the ring corridor.

"I want you to keep searching the comlink nets for Dax Doogun."

"The odds of my locating him—"

"Threepio—*please*?" Allana said.

"We'll even let you connect to the cockpit comm suite," Han said.

C-3PO straightened. "In that case, I'll continue the search."

Holding hands, Allana and the droid set off for the main hold.

"How does Luke seem?" Leia said when Allana was out of earshot.

"Melancholy."

"When are you two going to break down and install a holoprojector aboard the *Falcon*?" Luke asked when Leia had settled herself at the engineering console in the main hold.

"We don't have enough problems with the ship already?"

"Point taken," Luke said.

To Leia's eyes he looked not just melancholy but haunted. The comm showed him to be communicating from Coruscant.

"Han says that the search has been interesting."

Small talk, Leia thought, but what was the harm?

"We traced the *Falcon* to two men who owned it before Lando," she told him. "But we may have reached a dead end."

"You're returning to the Core?"

"Assuming something doesn't come up."

Luke stirred. "You wanted to let me know about Seff."

Leia smiled faintly. "You can read my mind from that distance?"

"If you wanted me to. But there was no need. Galactic Alliance Intelligence gave me the full story."

"Luke, Allana told me that Seff reminded her of Jacen. She couldn't articulate the reason. But she felt that he posed a danger to her."

Luke withdrew for a moment. Leia could almost feel him absorbing the news. Did his face pale, or was it simply the comm connection?

"Seff has given Daala another reason to distrust us," Luke said.

"Because a single Jedi behaves recklessly?"

"A young Jedi who reminds Allana of Jacen."

Leia was lost for words. "Luke, Allana is a child."

"Is it true that Seff disarmed half a dozen soldiers?"

"It was the way he did it that concerned me."

Luke nodded. "I was certain that ability was the sole province of Jacen, taught to him by Force-users he visited during his travels."

"Could Jacen have instructed some of the Jedi?"

"I don't see how he could have done that. Not without one of the Masters knowing." Luke shook his head. "This is something new."

"And Daala thinks what?" Leia said. "That Jacen was the beginning of a trend? That all of us are going to the dark side?"

"I think she'd like to be persuaded that that was the case—as frightening as it would be."

"I don't care what she thinks. Do you believe there's some connection between Jacen's turn and Seff's actions?" Leia paused to let Luke think it over. "Has Seff contacted you?"

"Seff is at large. Galactic Alliance Intelligence has several groups of Mandalorian troops looking for him."

"Luke," Leia said.

"I know. In the meantime, I'm recalling everyone."

"Including Jaina?"

"Yes."

"How is she?"

Luke was silent for a long moment. "If you'd had a chance to kill our father, would you have done it?"

"I don't understand what you're asking me."

"Our father stood by while Alderaan was destroyed. If he had done that knowing that you were his daughter, would you have killed him if you'd had a chance?"

"I might have tried, yes."

"Imagine if you had been a Jedi at that point. Would you have tried to kill him?"

"How can I know? I might have made the same choice you made at Endor."

"It's long been rumored that the Jedi Masters who went to arrest Supreme Chancellor Palpatine at the end of the Clone Wars were intent on killing him if he didn't surrender. They were convinced that he was too dangerous to be allowed to live."

"That was Palpatine's claim," Leia countered. "We don't know what the Jedi were intending to do." After a long moment, she said, "Han has set a course for the Core. We'll join you on Coruscant."

"No, not yet," Luke said sharply. "Not until I've spoken with Daala. She needs to be persuaded that using Mandalorians to hunt down Seff is a mistake. And she needs to be reassured that the Jedi police themselves."

"Are you certain we can't help?"

"I want to assess the situation before drawing you into it."

Leia nodded in a resigned way. "We'll wait to hear from you."

She was still sitting at the engineering station when Allana hurried into the hold from the cockpit connector.

"Grandma, we found him! Threepio found him!"

Leia caught her in her arms. "Slow down, sweetie. Threepio found who?"

"The circus owner."

"Dax Doogun," Han said as he and C-3PO entered the hold. "Apparently he lives on Agora."

"Naturally, Orto was first on the list of the worlds I searched," C-3PO said. "But in my haste I neglected to consider that he might reside on a neighboring world in the Sluis sector."

"You did great, Threepio," Allana said.

Han nodded in agreement. "Good job, Goldenrod. I'm bringing us out of hyperspace so we can send him a message."

"The case of Colla-Arphocc Automata versus the Galactic Alliance is dismissed," the chief justice of Holess proclaimed. His gavel struck the bench with resounding finality. "The court rules that the plaintiff is responsible for all costs incurred . . ."

Lestra Oxic all but put his fingers in his ears. The gavel blow might as well have been the sound of a stake being driven through his heart. The Colicoids had paid well for his services from the start, but a decision in their favor would have netted him five times what he had already earned. More important, the Colicoids had promised to reward him with something special if he won the case: a tall, impressionistic statue that had once graced Senate Plaza on Coruscant. Just how the insectoids had come by the prime piece of Republicana was anyone's guess. And now Oxic would have to purchase the statue from them, at what would surely be an exorbitant price.

On learning of the abduction of his star witness, he had asked for and been granted a stay of one local day. But he doubted that even a local year would have been sufficient to locate the witness. Not if his suspicions were accurate, and the Galactic Alliance itself had been responsible for the holoscreen image of the hueche and the subsequent disappearance of the Colicoid witness. Chief of State Daala's anti-Colicoid stance was a matter of public record, and it must have become clear to her that the ruling of the Holess court was going to favor the insectoids. While the justices accepted that an act of subterfuge had been perpetrated, Oxic was compelled to make his appeal before a criminal court. But Holess's prosecutors were already grumbling about the absence of evidence of Galactic Alliance involvement.

Nothing to do but take the criminal complaint to Coruscant, he told himself.

Across the face of Holess, bells were tolling the decision to dismiss and spectators were exiting the courtroom as if a bomb threat had been announced. The judges, members of the jury, and the trio of lawyers representing the Galactic Alliance were preparing to meet the media. Ignored by all but his assistant litigators and aides, Oxic was locking the last of the document cases when he spied Koi Quire moving against the tide in an effort to reach him. Rarely ruffled, she seemed agitated as she maneuvered between the rows of seats. Perhaps she feared she would be held accountable for the Colicoid's abduction, when in fact she had only been an escort.

"Am I right?" Oxic said when she was still a few meters away.

She shook her head. "Dead wrong."

Oxic locked the final case.

"The pilots of the speeder truck were captured and identified as associates of Rej Taunt."

Oxic knew the name well. Convicted of mass murder sixty or so years earlier, Taunt was serving a life sentence on Carcel. But Taunt's criminal past was of little interest. What mattered was that the former crime boss was a noted collector of Republicana and had outbid Oxic on several occasions for noteworthy pieces. The Bith agent at the recent auction on Epica was now known to have been in Taunt's employ.

"What does Taunt have to gain by sabotaging my case?"

"We're working on it," Quire said with a note of impatience.

"Is there any word on the witness?"

"A ship launched soon after the abduction. We have evidence that links it to Taunt. We're trying to determine where it was headed when it jumped to hyperspace."

"Can't we—"

"Stop for a moment," Quire said, holding up a hand, then pulling a holoimage from her satchel and showing it to Oxic. "Recognize him?"

"I don't think much of the outfit, but of course I do." He cut his eyes to her. "You found him?"

"You might say that he found us. The image was captured yesterday—on Holess."

Oxic looked as if she were speaking an unknown language.

Quire laughed. "It's not often I get to see you speechless."

"How . . . ," Oxic stuttered.

"Jadak and Poste—the kid he partnered with on Nar Shaddaa—were the two who infiltrated the media platform and put the hueche image onscreen. There's every reason to believe that they also had something to do with transporting the Colicoid to the spaceport. And perhaps worse for you, I suspect that Jadak may have recognized me."

Oxic felt behind him for a seat and dropped into it. "Jadak is in league with Rej Taunt? How would they even know each other?" He looked numb. "Didn't you tell me that Jadak was busy searching for his old ship?"

"I continue to believe that," Quire said.

Oxic waited.

"Suppose for a moment that Taunt knows where the *Stellar Envoy* can be found."

Oxic frowned. "If we're going to deal in theories, then suppose for a moment that Taunt is trying to send me the message that he knows the location of the treasure." The veins in Oxic's temples bulged. "If he beats me to the prize after all these years—"

"We've managed to reach out to someone inside Carcel," Quire said. "Taunt practically runs the show, but our man has promised to keep an eye out for Jadak and Poste."

Oxic shook his head in disbelief. "We're looking for Jadak and he comes to us . . . Stranger things have happened, I'm sure, though none occur to me."

"It is an unexpected and unparalleled honor to speak to you, Captain Han Solo," Dax Doogun said through the engineering station's enunciators. Onscreen the pachydermoid's velvety blue face was spotted and his snout was shriveled. "I've followed your heroic exploits for forty years."

"Another adoring fan," Leia sighed. Allana laughed quietly alongside her.

Han shot them a glance, then returned his attention to the comm. "Thanks, Dax. Sorry I never got to see your circus. Vistal Purn made it sound like a real barrel of taurill."

"More fun I never had," the Ortolan said. "But the best things in life come with an expiration date, is it not so?"

"No arguing with it, Dax," Han said with sudden seriousness. "Like we said in our message, we're wondering if you can tell us anything about how Molpol acquired the *Millennium Falcon*."

"I most certainly can, Han Solo. I purchased her myself from an itinerant doctor named Parlay Thorp. Visited many a remote world, enacting many a medical miracle, Parlay Thorp did. An 'unshod physician,' as they're known here on Agora."

"Thorp's still alive?"

"Oh, yes, and probably will be for some time to come."

Han traded big grins with Leia and Allana. Even C-3PO was visibly thrilled by the news.

"Do you know where we can find him, Dax?"

"*Her,*" Doogun corrected. "Dr. Thorp is a human female."

"Wow!" Leia and Allana said in unison.

"She did quite well for herself with the credits I paid for the *Millennium Falcon*. Opened a research facility on Hijado, then a clinic on Enferm. Subsequent to that, Dr. Thorp became a noted expert in aging, rejuvenation, and longevity."

"And nowadays?"

"Currently she heads up research at the Aurora Medical Facility on Obroa-skai."

During the long years of struggles to defeat the last of the Imperial warlords, the Falcon spent as much time grounded as she did in flight, and Han was spending as much to repair her as it might have cost him to purchase a newer ship. On those rare occasions when Han and Chewbacca turned to outside help, some old-hand mechanic would invariably remark that the Falcon's parts were in fine working order but that she was unhappy being a military ship and needed to get back to her roots.

Even if Han had no such desire.

He'd been a pauper, a pirate, a pilot, a smuggler, an Imp, and a thief, and had achieved a contentment he never would have thought possible. Leia completed him, and the twins, then Anakin brought him immense joy.

And just what were the Falcon's roots, in any case? Serving the needs of smugglers and traders by carrying cargo to remote areas of the galaxy?

Twice Han had started out on journeys to discover the ship's ancestry, and twice he had allowed himself to become sidetracked. The first time was shortly before he and Leia had embarked on a trip to Tatooine, which had ended up filling in many of the most important blanks in Leia's past. The second time was shortly *before his trip to the Koornacht Cluster, from which he had returned with physical scars that had never entirely healed.*

After that he asked himself how much he really wanted to know about the ship's past. Already she had been stolen on Dathomir, drafted into serving in a Kessel mercenary fleet, repaired by R2-D2, and rebuilt and upgraded by a New Republic tech team. She'd answered to the aliases Sunfighter Franchise, Sweet Surprise, and Shadow Bird, among others . . . Maybe he wanted to convince himself that the Falcon's real life had begun and would end with him. Suppose he should learn that the ship had been used for evil purposes—by the Empire or by a Jedi Knight who had strayed from the light side of the Force? Unconditional love had never been his strong suit, and sometimes history and love just weren't enough to warrant forgiveness.

He drew a hard line, Leia always said.

Over the years, he had armored himself in the same way that he had added alloy to the Falcon. He was as suspicious of outsiders as the Falcon's sensors were, and sometimes as conflicted as were the ship's trio of droid brains. He was every bit as jumpy and restless as the YT, if not as prone to enigmatic breakdowns.

So maybe his uneasiness about learning the full truth of the Falcon's ancestry had owed to apprehension regarding what he might discover about himself.

chapter twenty-three

"WE'RE LOOKING FOR A HAIRSTYLIST."

"Guess you've been looking for your entire life."

Keeping a straight face, the Balosar planted his hands on his hips and rocked back and forth on his feet, as if awaiting Jadak's comeback.

"I think he wants to be helpful," Poste said, appraising the humanoid. "Just try not to feed him another straight line."

Jadak nodded dubiously. "This being's a specialist—"

"You don't need a specialist, you need an expert."

Antenepalps quivering slightly, the Balosar took stock of Jadak's mood. Sensing frustration rather than anger, he grinned.

"Once more," Poste said. "Skip to the gist."

"Her name is Zenn Bien."

The Balosar's grin blossomed into a smile. "You should have said so to begin with." He gestured for them to turn left at the corner. "Four blocks down from there."

Jadak watched the colorfully dressed humanoid saunter off. As ungoverned as Holess was law-abiding, New Balosar seemed to have attracted every joker in the galaxy. A holosign at the spaceport welcoming new ar-

rivals read: NATASI DAALA IS CHIEF OF STATE, SO WHY
GIVE A POODOO?

It was the last place Jadak would have expected to
find a former owner of the *Stellar Envoy*—or the *Second
Chance*—but Rej Taunt had assured him and Poste that
Zenn Bien was here. Taunt's underlings had dropped
them off on the way to wherever it was they were delivering their Colicoid cargo. Taunt had made a point of
saying that while Zenn Bien had never actually owned
the ship, she could probably tell them where it had
ended up. Jadak took in stride the fact that the YT had
had a female pilot, but he had been surprised to learn
that Bien was Sullustan.

"Someone must've installed a smaller pilot's chair,"
Poste had remarked.

Jadak had also been surprised to learn that his opponent in the race for whatever treasure the Republic
Group had buried was a high-powered human attorney
named Lestra Oxic. The HoloNet listed millions of references to Oxic, but Jadak had found as much as he
needed in the first entry he'd called up. Oxic's face had
been among the distinguished dozens of holoimages on
display in Sompa's office at Aurora Medical. The lawyer
had been celebrated even as far back as the Clone Wars,
and had associated with some of the same members of
the Republic Group whom Jadak had answered to. One
of those members had to have told Oxic about the treasure and about Jadak as well, since it was likely that
Oxic, hiding behind Core Health and Life, had been
covering the costs of Jadak's prolonged reawakening.
What Oxic didn't seem to realize was that the genuine
key to finding the treasure was the YT-1300.

Regrettably, Jadak was no closer to solving the ship's
place in the puzzle than he had been before recalling that
the code phrase the Senators had given him was a
mnemonic device. He had spent most of the jump from

Holess with Poste's wand and notepad in hand in a futile effort to decipher the phrase. He had run the words *restore Republic honor to the galaxy* through the few simple decryption methods he knew, and dozens more he was able to access through the HoloNet. He dismissed that the phrase was an anagram, but he had toyed with possibilities nevertheless.

Senators Zar, Des'sein, and Largetto had said that the Antarian Ranger on Toprawa who was to accept delivery of the YT was *expecting* Jadak, and that the phrase had been designed as a memory aid for her. So she must have known in advance what was expected of her, if and when a time should arrive to retrieve the treasure.

The mnemonic phrase told her *how* to do it.

Then there was the modification the Jedi had made to the *Stellar Envoy*. Were the modification and the mnemonic phrase linked in some way, or did the modification assure that the *Envoy* would be able to execute her task? Was that what Senator Largetto meant when she said that the *Envoy* would handle the rest of it?

Perhaps the answer would have to wait until he found the ship.

Closing on The Kindest Cut, as Zenn Bien's salon was called, they passed half a dozen café-emporiums stocked with balo mushrooms, ryll spice, and a host of other mind-altering organics outlawed on other worlds. The sidewalks were crowded with tourists dressed as vibrantly as the indigenous humanoids, and many of them were sporting earbeads that allowed them to hear in the Balosars' natural subsonic range.

The planet's polluted namesake world in the Core had by the end of the Republic era become a haven for criminals and death-stick addicts, but the new iteration was unspoiled and arguably the most tolerant and crime-free planet in its sector of the galaxy. Some of that was due to the soporific substances that drew visitors from across the galaxy. But the planet's youth culture was equally responsible. Many of the young who came were artists, whose dreams of success often wound up taking a backseat to languor. Why strive to create when New Balosar's pleasant climate, toothsome inexpensive cuisine, plethora of sensual entertainments, and continuous pulse of subsonic music were more than just about anyone could ask for from life?

"There's a story on Nar Shaddaa about a Hutt crime lord who wanted to open a death-stick processing plant on New Balosar," Poste said as they walked. "The Hutt figured that the Balosars' immunity to toxins would make them ideal workers. What happened, though, was that the Balosars kept consuming all the balo mushrooms he delivered without turning a single batch into death stick extract."

If the planet was a veritable melting pot for sentients, then The Kindest Cut was a kind of saucepan for the galaxy's most diminutive species. Scarcely through the door Jadak spied several Chadra-Fan, a pair of Ugnaughts, three Squibs, and an entire warren-clan of Sullustans. In chairs of varying sizes, hirsute beings of larger stature were having their coats combed, their fur oiled, their claws filed and lacquered, their beards and mustaches waxed, and their manes cut and styled. In one chair sat the first Wookiee whom Jadak had seen in, well, sixty-two years. New Balosar's most industrious enterprise, The Kindest Cut was tonsorial beautification on a grand scale, with fuzz and fleece as thick in the air as spring pollen on Taanab.

Jadak asked to see Zenn Bien, and he and Poste sat down to wait. A Bimm served them steaming cups of herbal tea, and a Jawa set a basket of cookies on the table they shared. The salon's Sullustan owner wasn't long in arriving. Judging by the droop in her dewflaps, Jadak put her age at seventy-five standard years. But she was otherwise spry, clear-eyed, and pink-skinned, with a tattooed forehead and lustrous plaits that spilled from the back of a stylish bonnet.

"You must be the ones Rej Taunt told me to expect," she said in staccato Basic.

Jadak supplied the same aliases they had given the crime boss on Carcel.

"He told you that I never actually owned the *Second Chance*?"

"He told us."

"He said you're seeking the ship for nostalgic reasons."

Jadak nodded. "That's a good way to put it. My uncle owned it before Taunt."

Her round ears twitched, and she sighed. She took a seat opposite Poste, her feet dangling in the air. "Perhaps I should tell you the full story first."

"I hope it has a good ending," Poste said.

She glanced at him. "Let's just say that it ends."

Zenn Bien, whose name meant "tranquil breeze," didn't realize until she left Sullust that beings had not been created entirely equal. As a member of a bipedal near-human species, she was afforded a bit more respect than insectoids and saurians, but as a member of a *diminutive* near-human species she was both literally and figuratively looked down on by countless varieties of humanoids, from Falleen and Bith to Duros and Gotals. Despite the fact that each species was blessed with unique talents and abilities, size seemed to matter most. And yet the discrimination she experienced was never enough to send her scurrying back to the safe inclusiveness of Sullust. Not when there were so many worlds to explore and adventures to be had, whether you were 1.3 meters tall or 2.5.

Tuerto was a world that had attracted intrepid Sullustans before her, although even on Tuerto short beings received short shrift. Jobs were hard to come by, and anonymity was a constant companion. However, when you're a being of natural technical expertise who can see in the dark and memorize a map at a glance, opportunities of an illegal sort present themselves, and it wasn't long before Zenn Bien found her way into one of them.

Ship theft, she convinced herself after committing the first of many such acts, was not in the same league as shipjacking, in which violence almost always played a part and victims were often injured while trying to hold on to their property. Also, victims of ship theft were usually reimbursed for their loss by insurance companies; so sometimes you were actually doing beings a favor by separating them from vessels they couldn't really afford to own or operate.

None of the vessels Zenn Bien stole in her first couple of years in business were for her personal use. Nine times out of ten she worked for crime families that filled orders for beings in need of a certain class of ship, or obsessed with one ship in particular. Rarely did she see a ship after she had done her part—overriding security, disabling a wide array of tracking and anti-theft devices, hot-scrambling it. Most stolen vessels were piloted to far-flung worlds where registries were altered and telesponders swapped, and the ships began new lives under new ownership.

Quip Fargil was one of the few humans on Tuerto she counted as both employer and friend. A notorious joyrider, Quip had learned much of what he knew from Zenn Bien, and on two occasions only had hired her to steal a ship for resale. When he approached her about adding a third to the list, she had to suppress a strong urge to talk him out of it. But Quip was nothing if not persuasive.

"A fifty-year-old YT-Thirteen-hundred," he told her.

"It's been in Imperial impound for so long, no one will even know it's gone."

"What do you want with a fifty-year-old freighter?"

"We're going to jump it to the Tungra sector, strip it, and sell it for parts."

"Freighter parts?"

"It's a YT-Thirteen-hundred, fem. Parts for those ships sell for a small fortune in the Outer Rim."

She laughed at the foolhardiness of the idea. "You know how much fuel a trip like that will require?"

He had an answer for that as well. "We're going to put in at Sriluur on the way. I've got a contact there who can get us fuel at wholesale—without the Imperial tax. He'll ride with us to the Tungra and supervise the dismantling himself. He already has a slew of junkyard owners lined up."

"How much are you planning to pay me?"

"Ten for helping get the ship out of impound, another fifteen for piloting it to Sriluur and the Tungra, plus fifteen percent of what we make on the parts after costs are met." He paused, then added: "More than enough to pay for that operation on your eyes."

As with many Sullustans, her corneas were already showing signs of deterioration. Corrective surgery was certainly preferable to having to wear spectral goggles for the rest of her life.

"Where's the impound facility?"

"Practically next door. The Nilash system. I've also got a contact there who's going to make things easy for us."

"An Imperial contact?"

"You know what enlisted-ratings make? You might as well be a stormtrooper the way you're forced to live."

"So paying him falls under the category of costs."

"Right."

"And your friend on Sriluur?"

"He's satisfied to take a split of the profits."

Zenn Bien took a day to decide, and told Quip she'd do it.

Guarded by a contingent of aging stormtroopers overseen by a cadre of bored human officers and enlisted-ratings, the Nilash Imperial Impound Facility opened its hangar door every so often to prospective buyers of ships that were being put up for auction—a wide assortment of vessels confiscated from pirates, spicerunners, smugglers, and slavers. Good bargains could be had but you had to be careful, because the Imperials were known to substitute worn-out parts for what they stripped from the captured vessels. Ferrying to the Nilash system, Zenn Bien, Quip, and a mixed-species couple of dozen others traveled from Nilash III to the immense orbital pen aboard an Imperial picket.

Zenn Bien couldn't imagine a more dreary duty than Nilash Impound.

Questioned, patted down, and scanned, they had just been admitted to the inspection area when Quip's inside man, a young raven-haired warrant officer, separated them from the pack, ostensibly to double-check their identity documents. In the act of examining their travel permits, the Imperial slipped Zenn Bien a flimsiplast map.

Zenn Bien glanced at it, committing it to memory, and slid it back.

"That fast?" the Imperial said.

"Want to test me?"

He sniggered. "We could sure use some of you folk."

"Sullustans don't clone as easily as humans."

"I'm sure that's true." The Imperial returned the documents. "Make as if you're inspecting the auction ships. In exactly half an hour local I'll be on the other side of the starboard hatch." He gestured with his chin. "The security cams will be disabled. I'll dim the illuminator once; that's your signal to come through. The only way to reach the YT is by patrol boat. Have you ever piloted one?"

"How hard can it be?" Zenn Bien said.

"Maneuver the patrol boat to the YT's port-side docking ring and secure to it. The ship's life-support systems will be on standby, so all you'll have to do is wait for the air lock to cycle and you're in."

"Anything we need to know about anti-theft or anti-intrusion devices?" Zenn Bien said.

"No anti-intrusion. That's the best I can tell you."

"What about fuel? Quip says the ship has been gathering rust and micrometeors for years."

"There's enough fuel and power to complete a jump to Sriluur."

"How'd you accomplish that?"

"It took me six months to see to it."

Zenn Bien looked from the Imperial to Quip and back again. "You two have been planning this heist that long?"

Both of them nodded.

"Guess the Empire doesn't pay very well."

"That's the least of it," the warrant officer said.

Half an hour passed in no time. Ambling to the hatch, Zenn Bien and Quip waited for the illuminator to dim, then hurried through. The Imperial directed them down a dark corridor to the waiting patrol boat and wished them luck.

The YT-1300 that Quip was after was corralled with several dozen other vessels—many of them CIS warships—in a zero-g docking station adjacent to the inspection hangar. The perimeter of the impound facility was patrolled by roving illuminators and clone pilots flying old V-wing fighters, but the patrols were so widely spaced they were able to reach the YT undetected, thanks in large measure to Zenn Bien's ability to see in the dark.

As they made their approach, she regarded the freighter through the boat's small viewport.

"This isn't a stock YT-Thirteen-hundred. It's more of a Thirteen-hundred-pea hybrid."

"Is that a problem?"

"Just the opposite. We'll have more parts to sell."

Fastening the boat to the docking ring, they enabled the lock and waited for it to cycle. Then they scurried into the ship's pitch-black ring corridor, Quip holding on to the back of Zenn Bien's flight jacket. Glancing around, she shook her head in astonishment.

"Wait till you get a load of this ship."

Stepping out from behind her, Quip stubbed his foot against a large round object and fell back against the bulkhead, shining a handheld glow rod along the deck.

"Is that what I think it is?" he said while he nursed his foot.

Zenn Bien bent down to inspect the sphere. "Buzz droid," she said, clearly baffled. Moving to the bulkhead, she palmed the actuator that brought up the emergency lights and headed aft down the ring corridor.

Quip planted his sore foot on the deck and began to hobble after her. "Where are you going? The cockpit's the other way."

"I want see what other surprises this ship has in store for us."

Poking her head into the main cabin, she marveled at the huge double bunk and luxurious appointments. Aft, she gazed in awe at the sublight and hyperdrive engines. Moving forward through the starboard ring corridor, she peeked into the secondary cabin and chuckled in amazement at the galley's fixtures and devices.

"Who owned this ship?" she asked Quip over her shoulder as they headed into the cockpit connector.

"What I heard, the Imps took it off a criminal from Nar Shaddaa."

Zenn Bien nodded. "That would explain it. It'll be a shame to chop this one."

"Like you said, more parts equals more credits for us."

In the cockpit, Zenn Bien climbed up into the pilot's chair, adjusting its position to suit her size. Strapped into the copilot's chair, Quip adjusted it to place himself on an even height with her.

Humanity needs more like him, she told herself.

They waited an hour for the clone-piloted V-wings to complete their patrol of the corral; then, disabling the magnetics that kept the YT from drifting, they maneuvered out of the press of CIS warships, firing the attitude thrusters briefly to drop the ship out of the corral.

"The port-side jet has a problem," Zenn Bien said as momentum began to carry the YT away from the impound facility.

"We can have it looked at on Sriluur."

Zenn Bien centered herself at the controls. "Ready?" She grabbed hold of the throttle and sent the YT hurtling into space.

"Dial up the compensator!" Quip said, struggling to remain in the chair.

Catching her breath, she eased up on the throttle and reached for the inertial compensator, dialing it up to 99 percent. "I had no idea this thing would be so fast!"

The Nilash Impound Facility was already a distant memory. Zenn Bien swiveled to the Rubicon navicomputer and tasked it with plotting a course for the Sisar Run. A moment later the stars elongated into lines and the ship leapt into hyperspace.

Zenn Bien blew out her breath and extended a hand toward Quip. "Look at this—I'm actually shaking."

"I told you it would be a breeze."

She laughed. "Not from stealing her. From *flying* her."

They put in at a remote desert spaceport on Sriluur,

where they paid a couple of Weequays to watch the ship while they went looking for Quip's contact. A Verpine more than twice Zenn Bien's height, Luufkin was waiting for them in the spaceport's small tapcaf. The four-limbed hermaphroditic insectoid greeted Quip like a long-lost friend.

"Everything is prepared," Luufkin said, struggling with Basic. "I have computer documentation for new registry and name for freighter—*Gone to Pieces*. Fuel is waiting, full recharge of power systems. A cargo of fine brandy and tabac sticks on hand."

Noting Zenn Bien's puzzlement, Quip said: "Good for bribing officials in the Tungra sector."

"And for celebrate with junkyard owners who purchase parts," Luufkin added.

Quip smiled. "May as well celebrate our luck so far."

While Quip hurried to the bar to order drinks, Luufkin turned to Zenn Bien. "You leave Sullust long time back?"

She nodded. "Long time back."

"Quip tells us much technical ability you have. Why not working for SoroSuub Corporation?"

Zenn Bien scowled. "SoroSuub is part of the reason I left Sullust. They were wrong to support the Confederacy during the Clone Wars, and they're wrong to support the Empire now. But most Sullustans know better. Things will change."

No slouches when it came to technical wizardry, the Verpine species had their own version of SoroSuub in the form of the Roche Hive Mechanical Apparatus Design And Construction Activity For Those Who Need The Hive's Machines. Among other ships, Roche had manufactured the predecessor of the V-wing fighter used by the Republic during the Clone Wars, and still in use at remote Imperial facilities like Nilash Impound. Luufkin had the manner of someone who had worked for the hive.

"Support Rebels you do?"

She laughed. "I can barely support myself."

"Understand that. No time for political affinity when belly empty."

It took the better part of a local day to see to the refueling, load the cargo of brandy and tabac, and install the computer programs that would provide the YT with its new identity. All Zenn Bien could think about was getting back behind the freighter's controls. Most of the journey to the Tungra sector would be in hyperspace, but opportunities to put *Gone to Pieces* through her paces were bound to arise.

"Task the Rubicon with plotting us a course through the Yarith," Quip said when the three of them had settled into the cockpit chairs.

Zenn Bien swiveled to face him. "Why do that when we can just jump the Trade Spine?"

"Make certain registry telesponder and authenticators working properly at Yarith before continuing to Tungra," Luufkin said.

She didn't question it. Being caught with a ship stolen from Imperial impound would get them ten to twenty at Carcel or somewhere worse. Better to be safe than sorry.

A few hours short of Lutrillia, they were going over plans for dismantling the YT when the proximity alert system issued an earsplitting howl and the ship began to shudder as if she were in the grip of a powerful gravitational field.

"Can't be a mass shadow!" Zenn Bien said, eyeing the star map even as she fought to control the ship. "We're dead on course!"

But the heavens were telling her something different. Stars began to appear in the neutral folds of hyperspace, only to elongate and resume form.

"Something's pulling us into realspace!" The yoke rattled in her hands, and every system added a harsh new sound to the chorus of alarms.

"Power down or ship will break apart!" Luufkin advised.

Quip nodded in agreement, and Zenn Bien's hands flew across the console, zeroing one system after the next. Beyond the curved viewport the starfield rotated madly, then stabilized, and she found herself staring at a large Imperial ship in stationary orbit above a desolate-looking planet. The ship had the dagger shape of a Star Destroyer but was considerably smaller, more lightly armed, and distinguished by a quartet of globes that bulged from the stern.

Zenn Bien watched the YT's IFF transponder cycle in a futile attempt to identify the vessel.

"Interdictor cruiser," Luufkin said finally. "Prototype from Sienar Fleet Systems. Globes are gravity-well projectors."

"Yes, the Imps have added something new to their arsenal," Quip said.

Zenn Bien was speechless.

The cockpits enunciators crackled to life.

"YT freighter. Maintain your present course and identify yourself."

Luufkin nodded. "Now we see if registry functions."

"Imperial cruiser control," Quip said into the headset, "we are *Gone to Pieces* out of Sriluur. Transiting to the Corellian Trade Spine."

A moment passed before the voice said: "*Gone to Pieces*, no one apprised you when you filed your jump plan that the Yarith system is restricted space?"

"Sriluur spaceport control failed to advise us."

"What is your cargo?"

"We're empty, control. Pilot, copilot, and navigator."

"Hold at coordinates three-seven-dash-seven and prepare for inspection."

Zenn Bien commenced reenabling the systems, then stopped. "The maneuvering thrusters are down. They must have failed when we were yanked into realspace."

"Inform cruiser control," Luufkin said, leaning forward in what seemed expectation.

The reply from the cruiser was slow in coming.

"*Gone to Pieces,* scans confirm that you are empty and unarmed. Our tractor beam will bring you in."

Zenn Bien sat back in the chair. "Well, this is a first for me."

Luufkin sat back as well. "No worries. Imperials are only human."

And some of them were grown rather than born, Zenn Bien thought as a squad of stormtroopers formed up in the main hangar once the Interdictor's pincer cranes had the YT in electromagnetic lock. No sooner had she, Quip, and Luufkin been marched out than several of the stormtroopers marched in to perform a routine inspection. When the troopers reappeared, signaling an all clear, a human executive officer in a gray uniform approached, eyeing Zenn Bien and Luufkin in disdain while he closed on Quip.

"We're allowing you to continue on your way, Captain Fargil. Next time you may not be as fortunate."

"I'll keep that in mind, sir. But we've a slight problem. Your gravity-well projectors have made it impossible for us to maneuver. We need to effect repairs."

"Here? You can't be serious."

Quip dropped his voice a notch. "Sir, when I said we were empty I neglected to mention that we are carrying several crates of fine brandy and superior tabac. As a way of thanking you for your hospitality we would very much like to donate the cargo to the commander and yourself."

The officer lifted an eyebrow. "Just how long will it take you to effect repairs?"

"Not more than a local day."

"You have twelve hours. Then I want you and your . . . crew on your way." He motioned for the stormtroopers to break formation and beckoned four of them to his side. "Captain Fargil will be off-loading some cargo. Have it conveyed to my cabin immediately."

He spun on his heel and marched off, the rest of the stormtroopers falling in behind him.

Zenn Bien watched him go and swung to Quip. "I don't know whether that was bold or just plain insane, but nice going, either way."

Usually quick to smile, Quip was all business. "Show these troopers to the cargo. We have work to do."

The troopers wasted no time loading six crates of brandy and tabac onto a repulsorsled and escorting it into the innards of the ship. Zenn Bien had located a cache of power tools in one of the cabins and was preparing to haul them into the main hold maintenance bay when she heard Quip call from the starboard ring corridor. "First things first. Give us a hand with these things." He and Luufkin had their hands gripped on the corridor deck plates when Zenn Bien joined them.

"The access bays are in the main hold," Zenn Bien started to say when Luufkin interrupted.

"Help lift out."

Without further word, she put her back into it. The alloy plates had well-concealed handholds and were not nearly as heavy as Zenn Bien had anticipated. The surprise came when three Jawas, two Chadra-Fan, and a quartet of Squibs emerged from secret compartments beneath the plates. Each of the rodent-like beings wore a utility belt and breather mask, and carried toolboxes, work-arounds, and an assortment of canisters of a type that typically housed knockout gas.

"They boarded at Sriluur," Quip said by way of explanation.

Zenn Bien regarded the beings, all of whom approximated her height. "Something tells me you didn't bring them along in case of breakdowns."

"No," Luufkin said. "They come to steal parts from cruiser's hyperdrive."

Angry, insulted, *hurt* that she had been manipulated, Zenn Bien returned to the tools she had found and disappeared into the maintenance bay to repair the thruster system. It didn't take long for her to realize that the YT's contingent of little folk had engineered the system to fail on the ship's being pulled into realspace. Repairs, such as they were, wouldn't take more than a couple of hours. She was laying out the tools when Quip wriggled down into the bay.

"I'm sorry I couldn't let you in on it."

"What, you were under orders?" she said without looking at him.

"It's true."

She lowered the hydrospanner and turned to him. "This isn't just another heist?"

He shook his head. "The hyperdrive parts are for upgrading this ship."

"I don't understand. We're not chopping it? That was never part of the plan?"

"Afraid not."

"Then why do you need . . ." Zenn Bien allowed her words to trail off as it came to her. "You've joined the insurgency."

"For over a year now."

"The warrant officer at Nilash? Luufkin?"

"They're the ones who conscripted me."

"The Jawas and the rest?"

"They're being paid. Just like you'll be paid." He paused. "Plus a bonus if you help us."

"Help how?"

Quip prized a flimsiplast from his shirt pocket and unfolded it. "A schematic of the Interdictor."

Initially Zenn Bien refused to look, then thought better of it. "Got it," she said.

Quip grinned. "You know, we could sure use people like you."

"Just this once," she warned.

Wearing a breather mask, Zenn Bien guided the team of Jawas, Squibs, and Chadra-Fan through a labyrinth of narrow, long-ceilinged corridors that coursed between the Interdictor's armored hull and habitable core, Luufkin belly-crawling behind them to execute a mission of his own.

Being small had its advantages, after all.

Exiting the interstitial network in the stern of the ship, they made their way into the hyperdrive housing, which was tended to by maintenance droids but absent security of any sort. Leave it to the Empire to overlook a design flaw, Zenn Bien thought as the scavenger team went to work, conversing quietly in squeaks and squawks.

They used the same corridors to transport parts back to the YT, stowing them in the ship's innermost freight room. Once Zenn Bien was satisfied that the team had learned the route, she remained behind with Quip to patch up the thruster system. Over the course of three hours, the stolen parts began to mount up: an Isu-Sim SSPO5 hyperdrive motivator, Rendili transpacitors, paralight relays, a null quantum field stabilizer . . .

"Just so you know," Quip said. "All of this is for a good cause."

"I'm not enlisting, Quip."

"We're in your debt either way."

"Save the thank-yous for when we get to wherever it is we're actually going."

With the repair work completed, they returned to the

main hold to find Luufkin replacing the final deck plate that concealed the hidden compartments.

"All accounted for," the Verpine said.

The three of them were walking down the YT's boarding ramp when the Imperial commander and an escort of stormtroopers returned.

"Captain Fargil, whatever repairs remain to be effected will have to be done in space or downside."

"What happened to our having twelve local hours?"

"Be grateful for those I gave you," the commander snarled.

"That I am," Quip said. "We're just about done anyway."

"Then ready your ship for launch. We're under way at six hundred hours."

Surprise tugged at Quip's features. "You're moving?"

"I don't see that our orders are any of your concern, Captain." The officer's eyes narrowed in sudden distrust. "I begin to wonder if I haven't misjudged you."

"It's just that I thought you were in holding orbit."

Hoots began to issue from deep in the ship.

"*Now,* Captain," the Imperial told Quip. "And take your Verpine and your Sullustan with you."

They hurried back up the ramp, Quip stopping to rap his knuckles against the deck plates. "Strap in! We're raising ship!"

Zenn Bien went directly to the cockpit and cold-started the repulsorlifts.

Quip threw himself into the copilot's chair. "If they discover—"

The distant hoots gave way to screeching alarms. The Interdictor rumbled beneath the YT, and rending sounds could be heard echoing from the stern of the ship. A voice blared through the comm.

"*Gone to Pieces,* hold your position!"

"We're under orders to launch immediately," Quip said into the headset.

"That order is rescinded. Resume your previous position—"

Quip silenced the speakers. "Punch it, Zenn! Get us out of here!"

Zenn whirled the YT around and sent her streaking through the hangar's containment field. Behind her, Luufkin staggered into the cockpit, extending his quartet of arms for balance.

"Gravity-well projectors disabled, but we have to avoid tractor beam."

Zenn Bien glanced out the viewport at the Interdictor. "I'm more worried about those turbolasers."

The words had just left her mouth when half the starboard batteries opened with a fusillade of crimson fire. Dialing the inertial compensator to full, Zenn Bien threw the freighter into a descending tumble, rolled her beneath the Interdictor, and brought her bubbling up on the port side at high boost.

"Tractors are trying to get us in lock!" Quip said.

Zenn Bien could feel the fingers of the beam grasping for the YT.

Inverting the freighter, she rolled her over the top of the Interdictor, nearly becoming ensnared in a strobing tangle of blue energy that was frolicking among the gravity-well globes. A jagged fissure had formed in one of the globes, and an instant later the projector cracked open like an egg, spewing flames that leapt into space like a stellar flare. The Interdictor listed, then rolled completely over, as if showing its vulnerable belly to the YT, as *Gone to Pieces* spiraled out of reach and disappeared.

"A day later we were in the Tungra system, and our run-in with the Interdictor felt like ancient history," Zenn

Bien told Jadak and Poste. "Deliberate run-in, I should say, since the Verpine resistance was determined to incapacitate the prototype almost from the moment they learned of it. Quip, Luufkin, and the rest of us spent a couple of standard weeks outfitting the YT with the stolen parts, replacing the central computer, and upgrading her hyperdrive to the equivalent of a Class One. At the time, *Gone to Pieces* had to have been one of the fastest civilian ships in the galaxy."

"Did the Jawas and the rest join the Rebel Alliance?" Poste asked.

"Not straightaway. In fact, I ended up a member of their team." Zenn Bien laughed and gestured broadly to the salon. "Some of them are around here somewhere."

"You worked as freelance scavengers?" Jadak said.

Zenn Bien nodded. "In the beginning, we were single-minded in our pledge to remain neutral. Our intent was to hire ourselves out to anyone who needed our unique services—smugglers, pirates, crime syndicates, it wasn't supposed to matter. We even did some work for Rej Taunt. But of course that didn't last long. The Empire was becoming more brutal by the day. SoroSuub gained full control of Sullust. The Zann Consortium pirates were using Sullustans as slave soldiers . . . When I learned that some of my people were rising up against Chairman Siin Suub, I persuaded the team to help out, and soon enough we found ourselves carrying out special missions for Sian Tevv and *Nien Nunb*. And soon after that—just before the Battle of Yavin—we became full-fledged members of the Rebel Alliance, taking part in the destruction of the *Invincible* and a host of other Imperial ships in the years that followed."

"So how does one go from being a demolitions expert to a beautician?" Jadak asked.

Zenn Bien took a moment. "After all the destruction we had wrought, it seemed only fitting that we devote ourselves to the beautification of the galaxy. When the war ended we came to New Balosar as a team, and most of us never left. I received a tonsorial degree from the Barbers of Sullust, took several husbands, and began populating my warren-clan. Life has been good ever since."

Jadak mulled it over. "Did Quip keep the YT?"

"He did."

"Did you ever learn why the Rebels needed a ship of that caliber?"

Zenn Bien shook her head, then said: "Boys, I hate to be the bearer of bad news . . ."

"We can take it," Poste said.

She looked at Jadak. "I never learned why the Alliance needed the ship, but I do know that you won't be able to find her."

"Why's that?" Jadak said.

"Because she was blown to pieces at Bilbringi nine years after the Battle of Yavin."

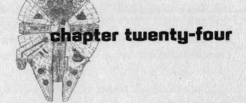

chapter twenty-four

"IS THAT YOUR NEW BEST FRIEND?" LEIA ASKED HAN while they were waiting for Dr. Parlay Thorp.

Han realized that he was absently toying with the archaic transponder and shoved it back into the pouch pocket of his cargo pants. "Habit forming."

"Maybe we should buy you a strand of worry beads."

"Ha ha."

Leia hadn't smiled when she made the suggestion, and Han's laugh was equally flat. Clearly, the brief communication with Luke had troubled her. She had barely said a word during the entire trip to Obroa-skai.

"We don't have to do this, you know," Han said quietly. "We'll explain to Thorp that something's come up and go directly to Coruscant. We can pick up the search right here when everything's straightened out."

For a heartbeat Leia looked as though she was considering it. Then she sighed and slumped down in the waiting room chair, folding her arms across her chest. "I'm sorry for my mood. Luke sounded concerned but politely ordered me not to join him just yet."

"Maybe we should buy you a strand of worry beads."

Leia laughed shortly. "Besides, there's a much better reason for seeing this through."

Han followed her nod to Allana, who was standing by the waiting room's tall windows gazing at Aurora Medical's spacious landing field. The *Falcon* was parked within sight, C-3PO watching over her, much to his discontent. Personal droids weren't permitted in the research building, where the Solos were scheduled to speak with Thorp.

"She's not back to her old self," Leia continued. "But at least she's back to being excited about our adventure."

"You don't think she's taking this 'adventure' a bit too seriously?"

Leia frowned. "Not in an unhealthy way. Why, you're not taking this seriously?"

"No, I am. I'm having a great time—well, except for Taris."

"I think the trip has brought the three of us closer."

A smile formed slowly on Han's face. "Back to better days."

"That was the idea, wasn't it?"

Sudden conversation in the corridor drew their attention to a smartly attired gray-haired woman who was approaching them with a determined stride, smiling broadly and extending her thin right hand before she even reached them.

"Princess Leia—or is it Chief of State Organa? I'm afraid I don't know how to refer to you. I'm Parlay Thorp."

"Leia will be fine."

"Leia, then," Thorp said, shaking hands and turning to Han. "Captain Solo. What a pleasure to meet you."

Han was surprised by the strength of her grip. "Dr. Thorp."

"And this must be Amelia."

Allana shook her hand, as well. "Look outside, there's the *Millennium Falcon*."

Thorp allowed herself to be led to the windows.

"My goodness. I've seen the ship countless times on the HoloNet, of course, but to see her in person after all these years . . ." She turned slightly to face Han and Leia. "What memories she stirs."

Han joined her at the window. "She was already called *Millennium Falcon* when you got her?"

Thorp nodded. "I couldn't come up with a name like that."

"Dax Doogun said something about her having been a medical ship."

"Yes. But even with her white hull spruced up and stenciled with symbols, the *Falcon* never really looked the part. Not with that dorsal-mounted cannon."

"The laser battery was already installed?"

Thorp nodded. "It didn't have the lower cannon."

"I was, uh, forced to make some upgrades."

"So I've heard. Otherwise she looks very much the way I remember her. I liked that she was decades old and still limber." She turned to Han again. "And I respect the fact that you haven't restored her. The dents and rust spots give her character—like age lines in a face. Not that you'll see many of those at Aurora," she added in a conspiratorial tone.

"We've noticed," Leia said.

Thorp sighed elaborately. "Yes, we specialize in restoring youth to the envelope and doing what we can to keep the contents in good working order. I like to say that our clients literally buy time for themselves. But even with organ and hormone replacement, we have yet to significantly extend the life spans of most species. For exorbitant sums of money, we can prolong life in humans by twenty-five, fifty, sometimes as much as seventy-five years. But the fact remains that, as a species, we are biologically programmed to decline early on, and that programming appears to be unalterable." She glanced at Allana. "Boring grown-up stuff, right?"

"Sort of," she said.

Thorp laughed. "Honesty can be so refreshing. In any

case, my area is research. I leave the actual hands-on rejuvenation procedures to Aurora's more-gifted profes-
sionals."

"Doogun mentioned that some of your research was
conducted in the Outer Rim."

"In the Tingel Arm, yes, and with the *Millennium Falcon* to thank for some of my discoveries."

A door slid open behind them, and a Ho'Din physician stepped into the room.

"I'm sorry for intruding—"

"You're hardly intruding, Dr. Sompa," Thorp was
quick to say. "Allow me to present Han Solo, Leia Organa Solo, and their daughter Amelia."

Sompa inclined his tressed head in a courteous bow.
"I'm charmed and humbled. I must say, however, that
I'm somewhat surprised to see you here. Frankly, both
of you look wonderful for your ages."

"Lial," Thorp started to say when Leia interrupted.

"You don't think my husband could use some . . .
restoration, Dr. Sompa?"

Sompa trained his eyes on Han. "Well, I suppose we
could do something with the chin and creases, as well as
take some of the lopsidedness out of the mouth. In other
respects Captain Solo appears to be very fit, if a few
pounds overweight."

"Hey, I'm wearing the same pants I've worn for thirty
years."

"He's not kidding about that," Leia said.

"Of course, it's what's inside that counts," Sompa
went on. "We would have to do scans—"

Allana's tittering burst forth as contagious laughter,
leaving the Ho'Din looking confused and possibly embarrassed.

"I'm sorry, Lial," Thorp said, wiping a tear from her
eye. "I'm afraid Princess Leia was having a bit of fun
with you. The Solos haven't come for a rejuvenation

consultation. They're tracing the history of Captain Solo's famous YT-Thirteen-hundred freighter, the *Millennium Falcon*." She turned and pointed out the window. "There—alongside the yacht. The mostly gray ship with the outrigger cockpit."

Sompa's confusion deepened.

"I owned the *Falcon* ten years before she came into Captain Solo's possession."

Sompa opened his mouth in understanding, then he moved to the window and spent several moments staring at the ship. "A YT-Thirteen-hundred, you say?"

"Made by Corellian Engineer—"

"What year?" Sompa said, turning to them abruptly. "What year was it manufactured?"

"I'm not certain of the exact year," Han said. "Probably a bit more than a hundred years ago."

Sompa looked at Thorp. "Who owned the ship prior to you, Parlay?"

"I was just about to tell the Solos the story of how I came to own her."

Sompa swung back to the window. "A ship like that . . . it's like a survivor from another era . . ."

"She's a survivor, all right," Han said. "Forty years ago you could find several dozen YT-Thirteen-hundreds on nearly every major world. Now they're classics."

"Han uses the terms *classic* and *relic* interchangeably," Leia said, taking Han's arm at the same time.

Sompa looked at Thorp again. "I would love to hear that story at some point, Parlay."

"Would you? I'm surprised, Lial."

"Yes, well, I'll leave you to your guests, then." He turned briefly to Han and Leia. "A pleasure. Enjoy your time at Aurora."

Thorp waited for Sompa to leave. "A very odd being. But brilliant and very dedicated."

"And in a rush," Han said.

"Normally, he is extraordinarily patient." Thorp shrugged. "Aurora's gardens are beautiful this time of year. Suppose I tell you my tale there?"

"I'll lead," Allana said and hurried through the door.

The university I attended required that once we received our medical degrees and had interned in medcenters, we spend three years bringing our skills to distant worlds. Many physicians opted to devote all three years to one world in particular, but I had other plans. Bolstered by university grants, contributions, and private donations, I founded Remote Sector Medical, which gradually attracted young physicians who might have had careers in archaeology, linguistics, or exploration had they not chosen medicine. A small fleet of aging starships took us on mercy missions to worlds in the Mid and Outer Rims, distributing medicines, administering inoculations and immunizations, and performing surgeries. We brought our expertise to planets ravaged by plagues and beset by natural catastrophes, and in the end there was scarcely a procedure we wouldn't undertake. It was during this period that I learned to pilot, and long before I completed my three years of compulsory service I realized that I would never be content with a residency in some state-of-the-art medcenter or in private practice on some wealthy world. In fact, I longed to be able to venture even deeper into the galactic arms, where many populations were in dire need of medical care as a result of being ignored by the Empire. Trade had fallen off, many formerly healthy economies were in ruins, and the Emperor had little to offer but lip service, while his Imperial forces focused on strengthening the Core.

Most of the worlds I yearned to visit were, for logistical and financial reasons, beyond the reach of Remote Sector Medical, but all that changed when I became the owner of the *Millennium Falcon*. The ship's military-grade hyperdrive put the entire galaxy within reach, and with donations continuing to pour in I was able to purchase a pair of aging medical assistant droids and outfit the ship with an array of diagnostic devices. As much as I had enjoyed my years as a volunteer, I loved being on my own and traveling when and where I saw fit. My peers from medical school jokingly refer to those years as my "fly-about period," and in some sense that's precisely what it was—a period of learning and self-awakening.

In terms of destinations, I allowed myself to be guided by what I heard or overheard in spaceports, cantinas, tapcafs, and the like—wherever professional spacers exchanged information or gossip. I admit to having taken a private delight in their mistaking me for a pirate, smuggler, or bounty hunter, based on nothing more than the rough-and-ready look of the *Falcon*, with her formidable-looking laser cannon—even though it wasn't capable of firing. If anyone had put me to the test they would have recognized instantly that as a pilot I was not up to the measure of the ship, and could do little more than get myself from place to place.

It was at some cantina on Roost that I learned about Hijado, which is way out the Hydian Way, halfway to Bonadan. An old spacer told me that if any world was going to be in need of relief aid, it was Hijado. Though he refused to say why, the reason became obvious the moment the *Falcon* reverted from hyperspace in the Hijado system and the sensors alerted me to a convoy of Imperial ships that was departing the planet. What I first took to be atmospheric storms turned out to be smoke billowing from dozens of northern hemisphere population centers. As I drew closer, the *Falcon*'s long-range scanners treated my eyes to the sight of squadrons of TIE fighters returning to their Star Destroyers on the completion of their strafing runs, and of small Hijadoan ships being obliterated on attempting to flee the destruction.

I had heard of recent attacks on the Imperial ship-yards at Ord Trasi or Bilbringi—I don't remember which—and my first thought was that the Imperials had discovered a Rebel Alliance base. But Hijado seemed too remote to host a base, and chatter on the comm suggested other reasons for the assault. The chatter was coming from medical frigates waiting for Imperial permission to approach Hijado. It was typical of the Imperial commanders to do this: permit relief ships access once the damage had been done.

Medical teams aboard the frigates updated me on the scope of the devastation and the general plan for providing aid. While the Imperials hadn't leveled Hijado, many cities were beyond help and many areas were going to remain hot for years to come. The rescue teams had been denied permission to evacuate survivors, and medical facilities located in the secondary targets were already mobilizing. Regardless, with power stations and tech centers annihilated, the native civilizations had been set back several hundred years. Worse, the Imperials were installing a base downside to discourage attempts by insurgents to come looking for converts and enlistees.

Once the frigates had been granted permission to insert into orbit, I took the *Falcon* down into the roiling atmosphere. I scanned for distress signals originating from remote targets but found none, and so relied on visual data and on the *Falcon* herself to guide me to a place where I might be of some use—since she evinced an atmospheric tendency to pull to starboard.

I spied an area that looked to have been a victim of collateral rather than deliberate damage and put down in a denuded patch of ground, in hot, teeming rain. All around me buildings and houses were engulfed in flames—the fires energized by whatever fuels the indigenous human population used. Everywhere I looked I saw bodies being pulled from raging torrents of water or cascades of thick mud. As I emerged from the ship, a human of perhaps forty standard years disengaged from a group of others in the process of collecting bodies and approached the ship.

"Thank you for responding to our distress call," he yelled over the driving rain in thickly accented Basic. When I told him that I hadn't received any distress signals, he said: "Through your ship, you mean." I confirmed it, but he only nodded. I was here, he told me, and that was what mattered. His name, he said, was Noneen.

I followed him into the rain, asking if he knew why the attack had been launched.

"The Imperials didn't explain," he said calmly.

It emerged, however, that the governor of the planetary sector was believed to have angered the Emperor, and Hijado was being made an example. It sounded all too familiar, and what with the number of dead surrounding me I must have allowed my despair to show.

But Noneen only said: "Don't mourn for us. There was no dying here; only going."

At the time I interpreted the words as merely poetic, little realizing the import they would take on in the coming weeks, months, and, ultimately, years.

In what amounted to a local week, I assisted in the retrieval of more than five hundred bodies, all of which were ritually burned in the remains of a place of worship. When not rooting about and helping haul corpses, my droids and I tended to wounds, burns, and broken bones in the small clinic the *Falcon* became. It took some time to set in, but gradually I realized that I had yet to encounter an elderly person among the injured or the dead, and I asked Noneen about it.

At first he didn't understand my question. Then he pointed to a woman perhaps a bit older than he was and said: "Magan has one hundred one stellar cycles." Then he pointed out a slightly older-looking man. "Sonnds has one hundred forty cycles."

Since I already knew that Hijado's year was roughly equivalent to Coruscant's, the ages Noneen quoted had to be wrong.

"How many cycles do you have?" he asked me. When I told him twenty-eight, he said that he would have thought I had many more.

Now, I don't know many young women who enjoy hearing that they look older—much older—than they actually are. But Noneen was right. Those of his people who were my chronological peers looked much younger. Still, I found it difficult to accept. Data on Hijado wasn't very extensive, but it was an established fact that the planet's human population had migrated from the Core several millennia earlier. So either Hijado's humans had evolved into longer-lived beings, or there was something about the now-ravaged planet that had granted them unusual longevity.

Within a month of my arrival Noneen and the others were already rebuilding their homes. If they had grieved for the dead, they had done so in private, for I had yet to see so much as a tear shed by anyone. Then one afternoon while I was collating the data I had compiled on the group's rapid ability to heal—physically and emotionally—Noneen and several others returned from a trek into the forest with a dozen or more huge vats of tree sap, all of which had been colored with fruit extracts, clay, and ground minerals. Without bothering to consult me, they were soon painting the Falcon with the saps, turning her from white to deep red, and replacing the medical symbols with enigmatic sigils. When they were done, the ship sported a snarling mouth and a row of fanged teeth, clenched fists at the tips of the mandibles, and flaming feathers covering her dorsal surface. The laser cannon had become a kind of fiery flower; the cockpit an angry eye.

When I finally asked Noneen for an explanation, he told me that the *Falcon* was being prepared.

"Prepared for what?" I asked.

His response was matter-of-fact: "Vengeance for those who went."

If he meant literal vengeance on Hijado's Imperial base, he had some news coming, and I provided it. "First of all," I told him, "I'm a healer, not a soldier."

"I am also a healer," he said. "What difference does that make?"

I told him that I dealt in saving lives, not sowing death.

"By avenging those who left," he said, "we will be saving lives."

I told him I wasn't a combat pilot, and that the droids weren't capable of executing more than basic maneuvers.

"But you can fly us over the Imperial base," he said.

I admitted I had enough skill for that, and then I lowered the boom. I told him that the laser cannon wasn't operational.

That seemed to stop him cold, but only for an instant. He said: "If it was constructed to be a weapon, then it will function as one."

My mind raced. I hadn't seen a single weapon among Noneen's people. Tools, of course, but no weapons, and certainly nothing that was going to power a dysfunctional laser cannon. So I asked myself, what was the worst that could come of my executing a fly-by over the Imperial base? The Imperials' scanners would show the *Falcon* to be harmless—even wearing the ferocious mask Noneen's group had applied. They would warn us to steer clear of the base, and that would be the end of it.

"If I agree to do this," I said, "will you permit me to live among you for a period of time?"

He assumed I had no home of my own, which was

true of course, but had nothing to do with my request. I told him I wanted to learn how it was that he and his people lived as long as they did.

"There is no technique," he said, surprising me. "We simply live as long as we wish to live."

I didn't reveal my suspicions that there was a lot more to it. I was still convinced that the secret was in the food or the water, or lurking in some endocrine gland Noneen had that I didn't. I did make it clear that I wanted permission to take blood and tissue samples—permission to *break the seal*, as Noneen would have said.

And he agreed to it.

The Imperial base was several hundred kilometers distant, close to many of Hijado's hardest-hit areas. Noneen stood in the cockpit behind me and one of the droids, while six others sat in a circle on the deck of the main hold. I had already observed one of these communal rituals, but neither then nor now was I able to determine the intent. Fifty kilometers out from the base, the *Falcon* let me know that the Imperials were scanning the ship, and shortly a voice barked through the comm, demanding to know who we were and where we were headed. By voice and telesponder I identified the *Falcon* as a medical ship and transmitted a bogus flight plan that would take us five kilometers north of the base. The comm went silent for a moment, then a different Imperial said: "Judging by the look of your ship, you've become a witch doctor."

"Just trying to blend in," I told him.

We were warned to maintain our heading, which was precisely what I planned to do. But Noneen said it was crucial that we fly closer to the base. Announcing that he was going *up top*, he hurried for the ladderwell that accessed the laser cannon turret, leaving me to come up with an excuse.

"My scanners indicate a storm along our heading," I

told the base, and requested permission to come about to a vector that would put us within three kilometers of the Imperials. Their response was just what I had expected.

"There is no storm," I was told. The *Falcon*'s scanners were in error. I was warned a second time to maintain my course, and advised that I would be shot from the sky if I didn't obey. Chiming from the instrument panel had already apprised me that the ship was in weapons lock, but I also knew that by disappointing Noneen I would ruin my chances of being allowed to remain among his people. So I did something I'd never done before: I gave the *Falcon* full throttle and flew straight for the base.

I still have no idea how I managed to evade the Imperial laser bolts that streaked for the ship, particularly because I had my eyes closed for a good part of the run. I think, though, our luck had everything to do with the *Falcon*'s astonishing speed and the Imperials' overconfidence.

After all, it was just an old freighter.

Before I knew it, we were fifty kilometers south of the base and Noneen had returned to the cockpit. I was so busy checking the threat screen for signs of pursuers that I scarcely heard him when he said that the mission had been successful, and that the base was gone.

I directed his attention to one of the scanners that showed the base to be exactly as and where it was when we left it, but he was adamant. The base was destroyed, and his people were avenged. If my way of looking at the world didn't restrict me to seeing in the moment, I would realize that the Imperials were gone.

I remember telling him that everything dies in time. And I remember him telling me that the base had left before its time.

On our return to the village, the *Falcon* was scrubbed clean of her mask, rubbed with oils enough to make a protocol droid envious, and adorned with flowers, inside and out. In small ceramic pots placed throughout the ship, sticks of fragrant incense burned. Though Noneen never said as much, I believe the ship became a kind of temple for his people. They would find the slightest excuses for visiting me—aches and pains, minor cuts and rashes—and they would submit without complaint to blood draws and scans performed by the medical droids.

My studies over the course of the next year turned up some remarkable findings. Noneen's people seemed to know beforehand when someone was about to die—though the term they used was *leave*. Noneen would sometimes say that this person or that was gone—even though I would be looking directly at the person, sometimes speaking with him or her. And sure enough, the person would die soon after, often without evidence of disease.

I asked him if his people had known before about the Imperial assault, and he said that they had. They saw the village gone.

Was this precognition the result of the Force? I wondered.

Noneen's answer was it might be.

Shortly into my second year of living among them, the entire village began to lapse into an uncharacteristically somber state. When I finally asked Noneen the reason, he told me that *I* was going. It was understood that I didn't realize I was going, and so everyone had kept it to themselves.

While I refused to believe it, I subjected myself nevertheless to every imaginable scan, all of which showed me to be in near-perfect health. Noneen, however, was insistent. I was going. But if I would allow a ritual to be performed on my behalf, it was possible that my leaving could be postponed for a time. I eagerly agreed to it, and when the ritual was completed Noneen told me that it had been partially successful.

Almost immediately I became terribly ill.

Had they done this to me? I asked myself. Was it a plan all along? Tests carried out by the droids eventually revealed that I had a congenital disease that had somehow gone unnoticed in almost thirty years of medical scans. By all rights I should have been dying, but I wasn't. Something was holding the disease in check. But for how long? I wondered.

I realized then that I was destined to remain with Noneen and his people for however long it would take to unravel the secret of their uncanny abilities. I became positively giddy with grandiose dreams. With all the progress the human species had made in the realms of science and technology, the secrets that would allow us to see into the future and perhaps extend our life spans had yet to be unlocked. And here I stood, poised to solve the mystery.

Save for one problem.

For months, I had been working up the nerve to ask Noneen how long he and his people would live, though I phrased the question differently. I said: "Are you here to stay?"

He gave his head a resigned shake. "We are going."

"When?" I pressed, my voice betraying my utter sense of loss.

"Soon. Long before you leave."

I doubled my efforts to learn everything I could about Noneen's people, but without success. And in the face of failure I'm afraid I morphed into more of a mad scientist than a medical practitioner.

Another year passed.

The *Millennium Falcon* had in large measure become part of the village landscape. But then one day the entire village turned out to clean the ship from stem to stern, removing the flowers and incense before coloring her with tree sap of the brightest hues I had ever seen them use. At least it wasn't war paint, I assured myself. Still, I found the sudden attention to be as worrisome as it was baffling.

By way of explanation, Noneen told me that the *Falcon* had disappeared.

"Gone like the Imperial base?" I asked him.

"Simply gone," he said. "Moved on."

There was nothing I could do. She had left.

Each morning for the next month I was amazed to find the *Falcon* resting on her landing gear, gaudy with paint but still there. I don't know what I expected to happen, but it wasn't until the Molpol Circus arrived on Hijado that I began to understand. Dax Doogun took one look at the ship and decided that he had to have her. And in fact the *Falcon* couldn't have looked more perfect for a circus. Dax's offer was generous beyond my wildest imaginings—more than enough to finance the medical and research center I dreamed of establishing on Hijado.

And how could I refuse, in any case, when the *Millennium Falcon* had already moved on?

"The research team I assembled remained on Hijado for ten years," Parlay Thorp said from one of the garden benches. "Long enough, I might add, to see the Imperial base destroyed—an event Noneen and his people took in stride, since to them it had been long gone."

"I take it you've put your discoveries to good use here at Aurora," Leia said.

Thorp smiled faintly. "How I wish. But the truth of the matter is that we never discovered the key to their precognitive abilities or their longevity. In an effort to find some link to other long-lived species—Hutts, Wookiees, Gen'Dai, and Falleen—we carried out exhaustive studies, but found none. We considered the possibility that Noneen's people were tuned in to the same sort of circadian rhythms to which many insectoid and saurian species respond, but the results were inconclusive. We thought that their health and longevity could be attributed to a naturally occurring form of bacta or bota, but found no evidence of that."

Thorp looked at Leia. "I never entirely let go of my belief that they had the Force."

Leia said nothing.

"After a group of Rebels destroyed the Imperial base, the Empire returned to make a further example of Hijado." Thorp glanced at Allana. "I . . . don't know what became of Noneen and his people."

"Maybe they were already gone," Allana said, climbing up into Leia's lap.

"Perhaps they were," Thorp said with a smile.

"And maybe they did have the Force."

"Well, who knows," Thorp said. "Perhaps someday we'll chance upon a sentient species that will provide us with the key to immortality. Until such time, there's little we can do but continue to rely on technology to extend our lives year by year." She brightened somewhat. "Doctor Sompa recently had a human patient emerge from a coma that lasted for more than sixty years. The exception to the rule, of course. Even with beings frozen in carbonite."

Han stirred uncomfortably in his chair. "Getting back to the *Falcon* . . ."

"Ah, yes. You're wondering how such a ship should find her way into the life of a young physician."

"Someone gave it to you!" Allana said.

Thorp's eyes widened and she laughed. "You're absolutely right, Amelia. Someone actually gave it to me. He said it was a donation."

"He," Han said, sitting forward.

Thorp turned to him. "At the time he refused to tell me his name, but I eventually found out. Someone had done a poor job of clearing the *Falcon*'s registry, which listed the owner as Quip Fargil. I've no idea where he ended up, but he was on Vaced when he gave me the ship. And I remember having the distinct impression that he was a soldier."

"An Imperial?" Han said, steeling himself for bad news.

Thorp shook her head. "He had the look of a Rebel."

"I'm telling you, Lestra, it's the same ship," Lial Sompa's 3-D image said from atop the holoprojector built into the hardwood floor of the mansion study on Epica.

Oxic's expression of incredulity didn't change. Muting the study's audio feed, he glanced at Koi Quire. "Any history of mental illness in Sompa's family?"

"None that I'm aware of. We should at least hear him out."

Oxic reenabled the audio pickups. "Lial, Corellian Engineering manufactured more than ten million YT-Thirteen-hundreds just in the first years of production."

"I'm aware of that," the Ho'Din said, showing some indignation. "But both Jadak's *Stellar Envoy* and Han Solo's *Millennium Falcon* came off the line at the same time. You don't find that the least bit significant?"

"I find it coincidental," Oxic said. "What's more, hasn't Solo had that particular YT forever?"

"No, he hasn't. He and his family are looking into the origins of the ship. That's why they visited Aurora—to ask Parlay Thorp if she knew who had owned it previously. Is it so hard to accept that Captain Jadak was one of the former owners?"

Oxic considered it briefly. "You're making a case that while Jadak has been searching for the ship forward in time, Han Solo has been searching into the past?"

Sompa shook his head tresses in exasperation. "Exactly."

"There is an appealing symmetry to it," Quire said.

"Here's another thing for you to consider, *counselor*," Sompa said. "Jadak was a professional swoop racer. Any *freighter* he piloted would have been a fast one, and the *Millennium Falcon* is known to be one of the fastest ships of its kind in the galaxy."

"Appealing and somewhat convincing," Quire said.

Oxic muted the audio once more. "Do we have a clue as to Jadak's present whereabouts?"

"Not a whiff of a clue. If he contacted Rej Taunt, he did so by comm."

"Have we checked incoming and outgoing communications?"

Quire laughed. "You can't be serious. Check Rej Taunt's communications?"

Oxic made a dismissive motion. "Forget I asked." Audio reactivated, he turned to the three-quarter holoimage of Sompa. "Was Dr. Thorp able to provide Solo with any useful information?"

"Of possible use. She was executing one of her mercy missions on Vaced when she was given the ship by a human named Quip Fargil."

"Vaced?" Oxic said, looking at Quire.

"Out past Bilbringi, I think." She frowned in thought. "I'll have to check."

"That, in any case, is where the Solos are headed," Sompa said.

"Thank you, Lial."

Oxic deactivated the holoprojector. Pressing the tips of his fingers together, he brought them to his lips. "How astronomical would the odds be?"

"That the *Stellar Envoy* and the *Millennium Falcon* are the same ship, or that Jadak and his partner are bound for Vaced?"

"Take your pick."

Quire shrugged. "If they are the same ship, then just about anything is possible."

"Let's suppose for the sake of argument that the ships are one and the same. If we could get our hands on the *Millennium Falcon* before Jadak does . . ."

Quire nodded. "Then Jadak would be forced to come to us to get what he needs from the ship."

He watched Quire closely. "At worst all we'll have done is steal the wrong ship. Or would that be a problem for you?"

She thought for a moment. "I've always thought of the *Falcon* as Han Solo's ship. But he happens to be married to the woman who in some sense rescued my species. Were it not for Leia Organa, my people might still be drifting among the stars in stasis or enslaved on some remote world."

Oxic narrowed his eyes. "If I knew your real name, I could compel you to help me."

Quire gave him a look he hadn't seen before. "That's not even funny, Lestra."

"I'm sorry. I'm simply trying to find a way to make this palatable." He blew out his breath. "I wasn't suggesting that you and I carry out the theft personally."

"That much was obvious. But that doesn't alter the fact that your employees simply aren't up to this, Lestra. Not against a former general and a Jedi Knight. Four of them couldn't handle Jadak, and the rest of us failed to keep even one Colicoid in custody."

"Perhaps it's more a matter of our being on hand to supervise them, Koi."

"On Vaced."

"Or nearby."

chapter twenty-five

"SOMETIMES I FORGET THAT PRIMITIVE PLACES LIKE this still exist," Leia said.

"I know what you mean, but I'm glad they do," Han said.

She looked at him askance. "You're starting to sound like Lando."

"Every once in a while Lando makes a good choice. Worlds like this make me wonder why we keep circling the Core when there are plenty of other ways to live."

They were meandering through the Vaced's principal spaceport settlement, which could have been the Mos Eisley of thirty years earlier, except that Vaced was savanna and forest as opposed to Tatooine's sand and more sand. Allana and C-3PO were several meters ahead of them, keeping count of the huge rodents that crossed their path. Structures on both sides of the unpaved street came in two varieties: preformed shells made of duraplast, and boxes banged together out of local woods.

Two days of exhaustive searching for Quip Fargil had yielded nothing. The HoloNet listed a human by that name, born on Denon about thirty-three years before the Battle of Yavin, but if Fargil was on Vaced no one seemed to know him or know of him, or they just weren't willing to say. If Parlay Thorp's hunch about him having been military was correct, then Fargil could have died during the Rebellion or in any of the bloody campaigns since.

"Why would someone give away a ship with a military-grade hyperdrive?" Leia asked for the third time that morning. "Even one with a discharged laser cannon."

"Out of respect for the relief work Thorp was doing?"

Leia nodded unconvincingly. "That sounds like someone who would join the Alliance. But still, a starship?"

"Okay, then maybe this someone had to get rid of the *Falcon* for some reason."

"Such as?"

"He bought it on time and couldn't keep up with the payments. Repossession neks were hounding him."

Leia looked around. "Does Vaced strike you as the sort of world a former Rebel would choose to retire to?"

"Looks more like a place you'd come to hide."

Leia pursed her lips and exhaled. "At least we know Fargil existed."

"Yeah, but remember that Thorp found the name in the *Falcon*'s registry, which could mean that Fargil was a previous owner, but not actually the guy who gave her the ship."

"Either way—"

"All I'm saying is that if it's come down to doing research, we don't have to do that here."

Han fell silent for a moment. "Would you want to live to be two hundred?"

"Only if you would," she said, taking his hand in hers.

Up ahead, Allana and C-3PO had turned around and were hurrying toward them.

"We have an idea," Allana said. "Tell them, Threepio."

The droid adjusted his stance. "Mistress Allana suggests that we make use of Vaced's local HoloNet to announce our interest in locating Quip Fargil. Assuming that he is somewhere onworld, he is certain to receive the message. And that way, our chances for success are greatly increased."

Han and Leia swapped smiles.

"Couldn't hurt," Han said.

"And it keeps us right here."

Jadak and Poste climbed off the aged Mobquet swoop they had rented at Vaced's poor excuse for a spaceport and stared down the dirt lane that allegedly led to Quip Fargil's cabin.

"Next time, you ride on top of the drive," Poste said, rubbing his rear.

Jadak grunted a laugh. "Not likely. I've seen how you pilot." He walked ten meters down the lane, inspecting broken branches on the tall shrubs that bordered it. "He owns a landspeeder."

"You think we would've had a hope of finding this guy if Zenn Bien hadn't remembered?"

"Not a hope."

They had been halfway out the door of The Kindest Cut when the Sullustan stylist had recalled that Quip Fargil had changed his name to Vec Minim, though she hadn't said why. The journey to Vaced had taken two days and all but cleaned Jadak out of what remained of Core Life's indemnity payment. Jadak had been cautious at the spaceport, on the watch for signs that they were being followed by Lestra Oxic's henchmen. Finding none, they had rented the swoop under Jadak's false identity and begun the search for Vec Minim.

Vaced wasn't an uncomfortable world; just one you wouldn't want to homestead on unless you had good cause. Covered with forest, relieved here and there by expanses of natural grassland. Indigenous wildlife had rule of the place. Settlers ran the gamut from humans to Gotals, most of whom were either subsistence farmers or shopkeepers. Visitors came to hunt, and were well served by a string of costly lodges accessible only by air-speeder. Jadak suspected that Quip Fargil wasn't the only local to have changed his name and reinvented himself.

He studied the dirt lane for a moment and returned to the swoop. "If this lead doesn't pan out, we're going to have to resort to finding work or stowing away on the next ship out of here."

Poste winced.

"Work won't kill you."

"Maybe not, but it could kill my spirit."

Jadak laughed and shook his head. "You figure we made a mistake coming here?"

"For what it's worth, yes. Look at it this way, even if the YT didn't end its days at Bilbringi, think how many times it could have changed hands since Zenn Bien stole it. Five? Ten? And like you say, we're almost tapped out."

"What's your plan, then?"

"We go back to Nar Shaddaa, pool our talents to earn some serious credits, and hire a slicer to work on finding out where the YT ended up."

Lestra Oxic was probably doing just that, Jadak thought. But unless the lawyer knew as much about the ship as he did, Oxic would need his help in locating the treasure. Maybe that's how it would have to play out. Still, Jadak wasn't ready to cash in just yet.

"Let me see that blaster of yours," he said.

Poste handed it over, and Jadak tucked it into the storage compartment that held their rucksacks. "I don't want you making Quip nervous."

They concealed the swoop in the thick foliage and

headed down the lane on foot. Just into the first curve they came upon a sign lettered in Basic.

" 'Intruders will be hunted down,' " Poste read, " 'and the wounded will be prosecuted.' " He looked at Jadak. "And you don't want me making Quip nervous?"

Jadak kept walking. In a hollow another quarter kilometer down the lane sat a small wooden structure with a landspeeder parked out front. "He's probably watching us already."

Poste gazed about him. "I don't see any cams."

"Macrobinoculars. Or maybe his eyes are still good. Raise your hands above—"

Two blaster bolts hissed over their heads, and a voice said: "Stay right where you are. The next stretch is mined, and unless you know the route, you're going to be whicci food."

"The local carrion birds," Jadak said, putting his hands in the air.

"And here I was hoping the local rodents would be picking our bones."

"Zenn Bien told us where to find you!" Jadak called out.

"Is he still selling weapons on Yaga Minor?"

"The Zenn Bien we know is a beautician on New Balosar."

A response was slow in arriving. "I've deactivated the mines. Come forward slowly and keep your hands where I can see them."

Jadak nodded, and they began to drop down into the hollow. A frail human male holding a blaster rifle almost as old as the swoop was waiting on the structure's front porch.

"Do we call you Vec or Quip?" Jadak asked.

"That entirely depends on why you're here."

"We want to talk to you about a certain YT-Thirteen-hundred freighter."

The old man added frown lines to the wrinkles that grooved his face. "Are you the ones who placed the HoloNet message?"

"Yeah, that's us," Poste said before Jadak could speak.

"What're you, writing a news story or something?"

"You got it," Poste went on. "For the *Coruscant Journal*."

The old man lowered the weapon. "Why'd you run the message for Quip Fargil, then?"

"We didn't, uh, want to blow your cover. Vec. For all we knew, you could've gone back to using your real name. Zenn Bien wasn't clear about everything."

Fargil snorted. "Even she doesn't know the full story."

He motioned them inside with a nod, Jadak giving Poste a brief look of bewilderment as they sat down on rickety chairs.

"Who told you how to find my cabin?" Fargil said, laying the rifle across his knobby knees.

"A Rodian at the spaceport," Jadak said.

Fargil nodded. "That'd be Nido. Good-for-nothing can't keep his trap shut." He studied Jadak for a moment. "I had no intentions of answering your message, but since you've managed to find me out . . ." He paused to laugh. "I mean, it's about time I told someone the truth. Most anybody'd care is probably long dead. But I am a bit perplexed. Did you arrive with the present owners?"

Poste swallowed hard. "The present owners of the ship?"

Fargil turned to him. "You mean you didn't even know they were here?"

Poste glanced at Jadak. "We had no idea."

Fargil slapped his knee in surprise. "That is amazing— amazing in the old way."

"So they're here," Jadak said carefully.

"A couple of friends of mine at the 'port comlinked me. Not that Nido character. And not that they know I have any connection. But just hearing about them being here made me sorry all over again about giving her away—even to a worthy cause like that Thorp woman was behind. I'm guessing you already know about her."

"Uh, we're still, you know, putting the pieces together."

"Dr. Parlay Thorp. Gorgeous young woman, and smart as a whip."

"We'll talk to her next," Jadak said.

Fargil stood up as abruptly as his legs would allow. "If I could interest you two in a drink, I've got a batch of potent homebrew waiting to be sampled."

"We're samplers from way back," Poste said. "Bring it on."

"Also got some eskrat stew if you're hungry."

"The local rodent," Jadak told Poste quietly, then he told Fargil: "My friend will have a double portion."

Fargil put the stew on the stove to heat and poured three glasses of thick yellow liquid from a metal container.

"I ferment it with spittle," he said, passing the glasses around.

Jadak took a gulp, finding it tolerable. "You were saying that the ship's owners are on Vaced."

"Strangest thing, isn't it, your being here and them being here at the same time?" Fargil shook his head in wonderment. "As sorry as I am to have given her away, I'm proud about all that she accomplished. Even if most of what she's done couldn't have been done without Han Solo's piloting skills."

Homebrew spewed from Poste's mouth and he began coughing without letup. Jadak rose and began slamming him on the back.

"Boy's apparently not tough enough for your brew, Quip."

Fargil pressed his lips together and nodded. "Happens to the best of them sometimes. Especially with the spittle-fermented variety."

Sluicing tears from his cheeks, Poste gaped at Fargil. "Han Solo is here? On Vaced? Right now?"

"Well, son, who else would be flying the *Millennium Falcon* if it wasn't Han Solo?" Fargil took a long pull from his glass, then sat back in his chair smiling broadly. "Gave her the name myself. But that's just part of the story."

Still trying to make sense of Poste's reaction, Jadak finished his drink in one gulp and handed the glass back to Fargil. "I think I'm going to need a refill first."

chapter twenty-six

"**Y**OU'RE TELLING ME YOU NEVER HEARD OF THE *Millennium Falcon*?" Poste said.

"I've been saying it for the past four hours." Jadak stroked his beard. "Maybe I read something about it when I was playing info catch-up at Aurora, but obviously it didn't stick."

Still half drunk on Fargil's homebrew, they were standing on the roof of a prefab building that overlooked the spaceport. In a roofless docking bay at the edge of the field, a modified YT-1300 freighter sat on her hardstand with starboard boarding ramp extended. Only moments earlier Han Solo, his wife, a young girl who was probably their ward rather than their child, and a golden protocol droid had boarded the ship.

"Let's start with the Galactic Civil War," Poste said.

Jadak held up his hands. "Save the refresher course for some other time—"

"No, no," Poste cut in, shaking his head, "you need to hear some of this right now before you land us in a very serious situation."

Jadak opened his mouth, then closed it. "Keep it short."

"Han Solo," Poste began, slurring his words, "Han Solo is . . . well, he's what you might call a certified hero. He's not only fought in every war since the Rebellion, he's played a major part in winning them. Understand? In *winning* them."

Jadak blew out his breath. "Okay. I'm impressed. What else?"

"His wife—that would be Princess Leia Organa of Alderaan, former Senator and Chief of State Organa, present-day *Jedi* Leia Organa Solo—is a hero of the same caliber. They're like a match made in the stars, and the point I'm trying to make is that we don't want to cross them. Under no circumstances do we want to cross them."

Poste was getting a bit shrill, and Jadak gestured for him to keep it down. "I appreciate your concerns for our safety—"

"No, I don't think you do. Not fully."

Jadak gritted his teeth. "You going to let me state my piece?"

Poste put his forefingers in his ears.

Jadak moved Poste's hands and forced him to sit on the roof's retaining wall.

"That ship, no matter what Rej Taunt or Quip Fargil or Han Solo calls her, is the *Stellar Envoy,* and no matter where she's been or what she's done in the past sixty-two years she's the key to our finding a treasure of unimaginable proportions. Now, if you're willing to walk away from that just because the present owners are two galactic heroes, you can do that and I'll take over from here. But after all the parsecs we've logged and with what we stand to gain, I think you've got to consider your decision carefully."

Poste stared at him. "Did I mention how good Solo is with a blaster? Did I mention how kriffing *lucky* he is? Did I mention that his wife carries a *lightsaber*? And knows how to use it?" He swung around to gaze at the *Falcon.* "Take another look. Maybe you're wrong about her being your ship. Maybe Parlay Thorp's broke down, and this is some other YT. A replacement."

Jadak turned. Though he wasn't about to admit as much to Poste, he did have his doubts. The *Falcon* wasn't just a modified YT-1300, she was a hybrid. More, she was closer to a warship than a freighter, boasting a thickly armored hull, outsized thruster ports, a pair of military-grade quad lasers, and a high-powered rectenna dish. The front mandibles were nothing like those of the *Stellar Envoy,* and the docking rings had been altered. Even the cockpit was slightly different.

And yet, despite the differences, every fiber of his being told him that the *Falcon* and the *Envoy* were one and the same ship, and just looking at the aged YT made him feel whole again.

"Here's what we're going to do," he said. "I'm going to answer the Solos' HoloNet message and arrange to meet with them. While I'm doing that, you're going to steal the ship and pilot it to Lesser Vaced. Then I'm going to get myself there, one way or another, and we're going to complete this treasure hunt."

Poste stared at him as if he hadn't heard or comprehended a word.

"I think you left out a few parts of the plan."

"What parts?"

"The part where I foil the *Falcon*'s anti-intrusion system, which the Solos most certainly will have enabled! The part where I pilot a starship to another planet! The part where I'm caught stealing a ship and sentenced to ten years in Carcel or some other kriffing prison!"

Jadak made a placating gesture. "Lesser Vaced is only a world away, and piloting a YT-Thirteen-hundred is child's play. It's no more difficult to pilot than that candy-colored airspeeder of yours."

"I don't take my airspeeder into outer space!"

Jadak's lips became a menacing thin line. "Are you going to calm down, or do I have to sedate you?"

Poste dropped his head into his hands and muttered at the roof. "Please tell me I'm hallucinating on Fargil's homebrew."

Jadak lifted Poste's head. "We passed a droid shop when we were casing the town. Do you remember it?"

"I remember."

"You're going to use the last of our credits to rent a slicer droid. I know there's one there, because I saw it through the window. The droid is going to help you overcome whatever security the Solos have installed in the *Falcon,* and the droid is going to link with the ship's droid brain and auto-guidance systems and pilot the ship to Lesser Vaced."

Poste regarded him openmouthed. "The droid is going to do all that."

Jadak nodded. "You just need to follow the droid's instructions."

"I just need to do what the droid tells me to do."

Jadak smiled. "See how easy it is."

"I'll just have a cup of tea," Leia told the Eatery's Twi'lek waitress. "Amelia, are you sure the frosty treat will be enough? You skipped lunch."

"I just want the treat."

"Is the nerf fresh or flash-frozen?" Han asked.

"Free-range. From a ranch south of here."

"Then bring me a double stacker with the special sauce."

Leia frowned as the waitress hurried off. "I thought you said you were cutting down on nerf."

"I am. That's why I only ordered a double."

"Can I have a bite if it's good?" Allana said.

Han threw Leia a covert wink. "Sure you can, sweetheart. We can even split it if you want."

That was one way of getting her to eat, Leia thought. Ever since they had heard from Quip Fargil, Allana—beside herself that her plan had succeeded—had scarcely stopped to breathe. It was Fargil who had suggested meeting at the Eatery, which was distant from the spaceport but advertised that its meals were home-cooked. As eager as C-3PO had been to join them, Han had asked him to remain aboard the *Falcon*.

A handsome, muscular man who looked decades younger than his seventy-six years, Fargil was sitting opposite Leia at the round table, tucking a napkin into the collar of his shirt. While he spoke in the archaic manner of some of the settlers they had met on Vaced, there was something almost sophisticated about him, and his hands were as soft as an executive's. His utility suit had come straight from one of the shops on Main Street; it was spotless—possibly right off the rack. Leia had noticed Han sit straighter in his chair when Fargil approached the table, and that Han was continuing to size him up at every opportunity.

"You know, we asked all over for you," Han said. "But no one had even heard of you."

"That's because you asked for Quip Fargil, and I haven't gone by that name in more than forty standard years. It was my name during the Rebellion."

"Parlay Thorp said she thought you might have been a member of the Alliance," Leia said.

"She was right—though a long way from where you served, Princess Leia. And maybe a couple of years earlier."

"Who was your commander?"

"Our group was based on Tuerto. We received orders from a lot of different people—Mon Mothma, even Garm Bel Iblis once—but I never met either of them."

"Mon Mothma," Leia said in surprise. "Then you might have had indirect dealings with my father."

Fargil hesitated for a moment. "Senator Bail Organa. No. But I knew of him, of course."

Leia smiled through a sudden feeling of distrust. For the briefest instant she sensed that Fargil was on the verge of saying *Anakin Skywalker*. But that couldn't be; Fargil would have been a teenager when Anakin became Darth Vader. How in any case would their paths have crossed? Still, there was more to Fargil's story than he was revealing, and Han had also picked up on it.

"I've got to say, Quip, you don't look a day over forty. What's the secret—something in Vaced's air or water?"

Fargil laughed to mask what seemed to be his embarrassment. "Simple genetics. My father's hair stayed blond until he was eighty years old."

"Lucky you, huh?"

"At looking young?" Fargil said, a slight edge in his voice. "Doesn't matter a whole lot to me."

"Is it true that you donated the *Falcon* to Parlay Thorp?" Leia said quickly.

Fargil nodded. "I gave her away."

"Was she already called the *Millennium Falcon* when you flew her?" Han asked.

"*Gone to Pieces*," Fargil said, then added: "That was her original name."

In the moment it took Han to comprehend it, Leia watched his face pale. "Are you saying—"

"I renamed her. Fast as a bat-falcon, resilient enough to last a millennium."

Han sat back as if he had just been sucker-punched and Allana said, "Wow a hundred times a hundred! Wait till I tell Threepio!"

"Our protocol droid," Leia said for Fargil's benefit.

Han ran his hand down over his mouth in an attempt to calm himself. It shouldn't have come as a shock, Leia thought, but she understood what he was going through.

It was one thing to have flown the ship, another to have named her.

"So who did you get her from?" Han said at last.

Fargil inhaled deeply. "Actually, I stole her from an Imperial impound facility in the Nilash system. Me and a Sullustan."

"Why was she in impound?"

"The Imps had confiscated the ship from a Nar Shaddaa crime boss."

Han's jaw became unhinged. "This is too much. Where did the crime boss get her?"

"Sorry, Solo," Fargil said, "but that's as far back as I can take you. Someone on the Smugglers' Moon might know."

"I spent a lot of years there," Han said.

"Oh, yeah? Me, too."

"I know that whole area like I know the back of my hand. Nal Hutta, Ylesia, Sriluur, Kessel . . . You name the world, I've been there."

"No kidding. Me, I took the *Falcon* to a lot of other places."

"Ever flown through the Maw?"

"That black-hole cluster? Sure. Oovo Four, too."

Han's nostrils flared. "I've raced swoops there."

"Swoops? I've raced swoops nearly everywhere."

"You ever fly the Hoth asteroid field?"

"No, not that one, but dozens of others."

"Ever hear of Lando's Folly?"

"Han," Leia cut in. "While I'm sure you two could spend several days comparing runs and whatnot, Amelia and I are more interested in knowing why Quip wound up donating the *Falcon* to Dr. Thorp."

"Was it because you loved her?" Allana asked while Han was simmering down.

"Loved who—Dr. Thorp?" Fargil said.

Allana nodded. "It was like a present."

Fargil wet his lips. "No, what happened was I fell in love with the ship, and that's why I had to give her away."

"The ship's proximity alarm system is activated," the slicer droid told Poste in a raspy voice that owed more to the shoddy quality of its vocoder than any intentional programming. "The system is linked to a Ground Buzzer anti-personnel blaster concealed in the dorsal bow. The alarm can be disabled, but there is a high probability that the protocol droid will contact its masters the moment the system is overridden."

Poste cursed under his breath. "How close can we get to the ship before the alarm is tripped?"

"The field extends to the perimeter of the landing bay. We can reduce our distance to the ship by one-point-three meters if necessary."

Resembling a primeval avian as much as it did a predatory reptile, the droid was held aloft by a small repulsorlift that dangled from a compact torso. Bulging, oval-shaped sensors atop the snout-like module that contained the slicing matrix might have been eyes, but in fact the droid's visual scanners and recorders were located beneath the tapered snout, where teeth might have been.

"What are our options?" Poste said.

"We need to interfere with communications to and from the landing bay."

"Go ahead and do that."

"The ability to interfere with communications is beyond my programming. We need a jamming device. A Locris D-Eighty field disruptor will suffice."

"Where am I supposed to get a jammer?"

"Master Druul has one in the shop. You will need to go there while I wait here."

"Go—can't we just have it delivered?"

"Certainly. Although I am obliged to point out that you will be affording Master Druul full knowledge of this operation. Normally he asks few questions of his customers, but in this instance his curiosity is likely to be aroused."

Poste cursed again. "How much is this jammer going to cost?"

"Absent current specials, the rental fee will be four hundred credits per local hour."

Poste puffed out his breath. "That'll wipe us out."

"Are we aborting the mission?"

"No, we're not aborting the mission. Find a place to hide yourself and I'll be back as quick as I can."

Hoofing it into town to save the few credits a speeder taxi would have cost, Poste hurried through the door of the droid shop, grateful to find the Gran—Druul—behind the counter.

"How is the droid working out?"

"Fine," Poste said. "But we—I need a jammer."

"Any particular model?"

"Locris D-Eighty."

"Just so happens I have one of those." Druul came out from behind the counter, his trio of stalked eyes scanning the shop. "Ah, there it is." He lifted the device from a shelf and carried it to the counter. "I charge an hourly rate of five hundred credits."

"I thought it was four hundred," Poste snapped.

The Gran appraised him. "Who told you that?"

"Your slicer droid."

"Kriffing droid," Druul said. "All right, it's yours for four hundred. One hour down, plus a deposit of four hundred. When will you be returning it?"

"Uh," Poste said while he was counting out the last of the credit bills, "not right away."

"I close at six local sharp. If you're not here by then, the price rolls over into the following day."

"Whatever," Poste said. Cradling the jammer in his arms, he raced out the door.

The slicer droid detected his arrival at the *Falcon*'s landing bay and drifted out from behind a stack of shipping containers. Breathless, Poste set the jammer on the ground.

"What now?"

"Simply follow my instructions," the droid said.

Poste muttered a curse.

Half an hour later, with the jammer already running low on battery power and Poste running low on patience, the hovering slicer droid issued a series of beeps and tones.

"It is now safe to enter the landing bay. I will override the proximity alarm as we approach the ship. On learning that communications are jammed, the protocol droid may attempt to raise the boarding ramp and lock it manually, so you will have to hurry."

"Nice to know I count for something," Poste said.

Side by side they circled around to the entrance to the bay. Poste took a breath and made straight for the boarding ramp, astern the cockpit. He hadn't covered a meter of duracrete when the *Falcon* loosed a blaring sound that ceased almost as abruptly as it began. Bounding up the ramp, he rushed into the YT's main hold, where he found the Solos' golden protocol droid bent over the engineering station's comlink and calling for Captain Solo.

"What!" The droid straightened and took a backward step. "Who are you? And what are you doing aboard the ship?"

"I'm borrowing it," Poste said.

"Borrowing it? We'll just see about that."

The protocol droid was stepping from the hold when the slicer droid drifted into the ring corridor, its pair of data-probe legs extended beneath it.

"Communications have been jammed, and I have disabled the manual release for the boarding ramp," the slicer droid announced. "In the event you are weighing the options of locking us inside the ship."

"A slicer droid?" C-3PO said. "What in heavens are you doing on Vaced?"

"That's none of your business."

"I've encountered your sort before," C-3PO said, mixing insult and defiance.

The slicer droid's snout turned toward Poste. "These protocol units tend to be garrulous and troublesome. I suggest you shut it off."

"Shut me off?" C-3PO said in sudden apprehension. "No, you mustn't do that."

But Poste was already moving in, one hand reaching for the switch behind C-3PO's head.

"You simply mustn't—"

"That's much better," the slicer droid said.

Poste nodded and glanced into the cockpit connector. "Follow me. I need you to talk to the ship's droid brain."

"It will be a pleasure, I'm sure."

Poste ducked through the cockpit hatch, lowering himself uneasily into the pilot's chair while he waited for the slicer droid to insert its probe into one of the cockpit's scomp link ports.

"I am interfaced with the brains."

"Brains?"

"The ship's systems are managed by three brains acting in accord."

"With their help, can you pilot this thing?"

The droid took a moment to respond. "The rental agreement you signed with Master Druul states explicitly that droids and other devices are, under all circumstances, to remain within fifty kilometers of Vaced Spaceport."

"Are you programmed to obey that condition?"

"No, I'm simply advising you that Master Druul will prosecute to the full extent of the law."

"I'll worry about that later. Can you pilot it or not?"

"What is our destination?"

"Lesser Vaced." Poste thought he saw the droid's visual scanner blink, but figured he had imagined it. "Yes or no?"

"Yes. I have limited experience in interplanetary travel, but this ship has a highly sophisticated autopilot system."

Poste grinned. Maybe Jadak was right and he'd be able to pull this off after all. "Any systems we need to override before starting the engines? Any anti-theft or anti-intrusion protocols? Any tracking devices or shut-down devices?"

"I'm searching . . ."

Poste swiveled the chair through a circle. *Han Solo's seat,* he thought. *Kark, Han Solo's ship. The famous* Millennium—

"There is a problem."

Poste planted his feet on the deck to bring the chair to a halt. "Huh?"

"With some effort on my part, the engines can be made to power up and the ship can be launched. However . . ."

"Yeah?"

"At the first attempt to employ the sublight engine or hyperdrive, the ship will automatically enter a default mode, during which it can only be made to return to the place from which it was launched. No amount of slicing or work-arounds can overcome this security feature, which relies on scans of the owner's retinas and palm-print identification by the instrument panel steering yoke."

It took a moment for Poste to realize that he was neither surprised nor disappointed. In fact, the slicer droid's pronouncement came as a relief. Nothing to do now but wait for Jadak's meeting with the Solos to wind up, then—

Sounds of some sort made him swivel the chair toward the cockpit hatch.

"Two beings have boarded the ship," the slicer droid said. "They are speaking Basic to each other in low tones."

Poste wasn't half out of the pilot's chair when a blaster poked through the hatch and the hulking human who was holding it all but wriggled into the cockpit, drawing himself up to his full height between the pair of rear seats.

"Stay right where you are, kid."

A Nautolan entered behind the human. "Well, if it isn't the hotshot from Nar Shaddaa," he said, showing filed teeth as he grinned. "The one who put a couple of bolts into the repulsorlift of our airspeeder."

"And he brought us a present," the human said, gesturing to the slicer droid.

Without lowering the blaster, the human turned slightly to his partner. "Cynner, take the kid into the main hold and secure him to something." He motioned with the weapon. "Up—and lay that toy blaster you're carrying on the seat."

Poste rose, thinking about how good he was getting at following instructions. Setting the blaster down, he squirmed past the human and stepped into the cockpit connector, where the Nautolan was waiting for him. He considered asking his captors who they worked for, but decided he was better off not knowing.

The protocol droid was just where he had left him, motionless at the intersection of the ring corridor and the main hold. The Nautolan shoved him gently in the direction of a hologame table that occupied the front part of the space. While the head-tailed goon looked around for something to use to bind him, Poste reached a decision of his own. The boarding ramp was still lowered. There would be no getting to it with both the Nautolan and the protocol droid standing where they were. But according to a sketch Jadak had made of how he imagined the interior of the *Millennium Falcon* was laid out, the corridor was circular, and he might be able to make it to the boarding ramp by coming around from the stern. It required trusting that the Nautolan wasn't familiar with the layout, and that he would chase him, but Poste saw no other way out.

He waited for Cynner's gaze to shift, then bolted for the port arc of the corridor.

"Remata, he's making a break for it!" Cynner called out.

But what mattered was that he was in pursuit.

Hearing the call, Remata barreled through the cockpit connector, nearly knocking the deactivated protocol droid off its feet as he entered the main hold. Listening for a moment, he said, "Idiot," and raced into the starboard-side ring corridor.

Poste banged his way to the stern of the ship, past the *Falcon*'s hyperdrive and the escape pod accessway, his eyes scanning the deck for the maintenance hatch Jadak had included in the sketch. He was three-quarters of the way around the corridor when he spotted it, opposite and just aft of the ship's small galley. Wedging his fingers into the section of grated decking, he lifted it clear and threw himself down the hatch, resetting the grating as best he could.

A moment later Cynner rounded the port bend, only to run straight into Remata, who had arrived from the opposite direction.

"Where is he?" Remata asked.

"He sure didn't come by me."

They searched the escape pod accessway.

Remata glanced up the port-side corridor. "Could he have ducked into one of the cabin spaces?"

"I'll check."

Cynner had no sooner set out than Remata spied the hatch's ill-fitted deck grating. Lifting it out, he turned his ear to the hatch.

"Cynner, he went belowdecks!" he yelled down the corridor. "There's another access in the main hold. Hurry!"

Poste stumbled through the *Falcon*'s unlighted cargo areas, tripping over tools, slamming into engine parts, and flattening toys that squeaked when he stepped on them. Above and behind he could hear muffled calls. Hands extended in front of him, he kept moving forward, feeling his way around bulkheads and obstacles impossible to identify. He reasoned that he had to be beneath the main hold when sudden light poured in from above and he caught a brief glance of the Nautolan, silhouetted against the ceiling illuminators.

"He just passed me!"

"I'll get him!"

Poste heard eager footsteps behind him, then the sound of Cynner landing on the deck of the central cargo area. Throwing caution to the wind, he propelled himself into the forward freight-loading room, which Han Solo had turned into a bunker housing an array of concussion missiles. Feeling along the slightly curved forward bulkhead, his hands found the opening to a maintenance burrow that provided access to the deflector shield generator, landing jets, and passive sensor antenna housed in the port mandible.

Poste pulled himself up and into the pitch-black tunnel, then began to worm his way forward over greasy components and through puddles of leaked lubricant to the mandible's top-side maintenance hatch, which he prayed wasn't secured from the outside.

The light of a glow stick danced around him.

"Any sign of him?" the human called.

"I don't see him. He could be anywhere. I'll try to find the lights."

"Don't bother. Let him rot down here."

"Good enough for me. I'm heading back up."

Bellying forward, Poste found the circular hatch and sprang it. Hauling himself out onto the forward tip of the mandible, he rolled to one side. Then with his fingers hooked around the right-angle edge, he dropped to the duracrete floor and squatted behind the forwardmost of the port-side hardstand disks.

Arriving in the cockpit, Cynner found his partner seated at the instrument console. "Fancy me, sitting in Han Solo's chair."

"I see the droid's gone."

"We don't need either of them." Swiveling to face front, Remata flicked the repulsorlift toggles and scanned the instruments. "Not all that different from the Two-thousand series."

"Should I check in?" Cynner said as he slid into the copilot's chair.

Remata nodded and threw a switch. "Secure your harness."

Comlink out, Cynner heard the boarding ramp retract. "We have the ship," he said into the comlink's speaker. "We're raising it now."

chapter twenty-seven

"WE WORKED FIRST LIGHT TO ABSOLUTE-DARK FOR two standard weeks retrofitting that hyperdrive," Jadak said, "the Verpine, the Jawas, and me. The days were so hot we were frying nogull eggs on the hull, and some nights it got so cold we'd wake to find our drinking water sheeted with ice. Took another two weeks to install the laser cannon. When we finished, though, the YT was sporting in the neighborhood of a Class One hyperdrive and a dorsal turret and battery. The Verpine, the Sullustan, and I piloted her through her first jumps to lightspeed, and let me tell you, we could hardly believe how fast she was. That's when I came up with the name, right after the initial series of test flights."

"She has a point-five now," Han said proudly, "thanks to an outlaw tech I knew in the Corporate Sector. After that was when I set the record for the Kessel Run. There's still nothing to compare to her. Even the hyperdrives of these new Mandalorian ships are only rated point-four."

"Ratings don't matter. A skilled pilot in a point-four could outfly an average pilot at the helm of a point-five."

"No way," Han said.

"I've seen it happen," Jadak said. "In sublight races, anyway."

"Well, sublight, sure. Now you're talking about something completely different."

Jadak worked his jaw. Each time he tried to stick to the script and relate the tale in Quip Fargil's vocal cadence, Solo would jump in with a question or a comment. His competitive nature would bring out Jadak's own and end up pulling him out of character. Already the story was as much Fargil's as Jadak's. And now that Solo's wife and daughter had stopped trying to rein Solo in, they were giving Jadak all their attention, and he could sense their suspicions mounting. But let them be suspicious. So long as Poste was succeeding.

"What was the plan for the *Falcon* at that point?" Leia asked.

"Back then one of our chief concerns was the number of Star Destroyers the Empire was turning out, so command came up with a plan to target one of the shipyards. Fondor, Ord Trasi, even Yaga Minor were considered as potential targets, but after all the analysis command decided that we had to go after the big one— Bilbringi." Grateful to be back on course, Jadak took a sip of caf and set his cup down. "Were you there during the Imperial years, Princess Leia?"

"Only once. But I couldn't have been more than nine at the time."

"Then you probably don't remember how tricky it was to insert into orbit there."

"Because of the asteroid fields," Han said.

Jadak nodded. "At the time, many of the asteroids were being mined for use in the shipyards, so Imperial forces were deployed not only in the shipyards but also close to many of the extraction operations. Even with prior authorization, it was difficult to navigate through the system because of all the checkpoints. So the notion of sneaking a hostile ship into Bilbringi wasn't even worth discussing."

Han smiled in sudden revelation. "Unless you had a ship with a powerful enough hyperdrive to microjump all the way in."

"You've done that?" Jadak said in genuine surprise.

"More times than I can remember."

Jadak refused to allow Solo to get to him. "Well, no militia members had done it. That's why I'm familiar with the Maw and all those asteroid fields we were talking about."

"Practice runs," Han said.

"Each and every one. You might say it was the beginning of my love affair with the ship. Experiencing what she was capable of. Extricating me from predicaments I'd gotten myself into. Exceeding expectations time and again. Like she was determined to outperform herself."

"Nothing's changed," Han said.

"But what were you supposed to do with the *Falcon* when you got there?" Allana asked. "To Bil . . ."

"Bilbringi," Leia completed. "What was the plan?"

"Destroy the shipyards to whatever extent possible."

Han frowned. "With a single laser cannon?"

Jadak laughed wryly. "The cannon was just for in-close defense. The *Falcon* herself was going to be the weapon."

"A bomb," Leia said suddenly.

Allana looked at her, then at Jadak. "You were going to blow the *Falcon* up?"

He nodded. "That was the idea. But even the best ideas don't always work out."

"What were you going to detonate?" Han asked.

Jadak turned to him. "A baradium fission device."

Leia sat back in shock. "Those were banned—even by the Empire. Alderaan led the cause."

"They were banned, all right. But we got our hands

on one without Senator Organa knowing. Besides, he was eventually persuaded to see that baradium was essential to our attempts to counter the weapons the Empire was developing." Jadak's gaze darted from Leia to Han and back again. "You two know this better than anyone."

"Was this before the Alliance started using ytterbium as a stabilizing agent?" Han said.

"Years before. This device wasn't just some supersized thermal detonator. It was a planet buster. And if it had been detonated at Bilbringi, the shipyards would have been out of commission for a decade."

Han shook his head in incredulity. "You were supposed to transport it aboard the *Falcon*?"

"That was the idea."

"Yeah, somebody's idea of a suicide mission."

"Not if things went right. Assuming I didn't annihilate myself on the way to Bilbringi or during any of the dozen or so microjumps I was going to have to execute to reach the shipyards, the plan called for me to ditch at five hundred thousand kilometers from the target."

Han shook his head. "That wouldn't have saved you. You'd still have been inside the blast sphere."

Jadak shrugged. "Like I said, that was the plan. No one was fool enough to guarantee that I'd survive." He paused for a moment. "Even when we put out the call for volunteers to transfer the device into the *Falcon,* we only ended up with two Duros. The rest of the group was made up of convicts who had been serving life sentences in Imperial prisons. Members of the insurgency broke them out in exchange for their help, and allowed them to go their own way after the device was safely aboard."

"Then it was up to you to follow through?" Leia said.

"Just me."

Allana stood up in the chair and leaned across the

table. "Couldn't you have programmed some droids to fly the *Falcon*?"

Jadak smiled lightly. "We didn't want to send droids to do a person's job."

Gently, Leia pulled Allana back into her chair. "What went wrong?"

Han put his arm around Leia's shoulders, but kept his eyes on Jadak. "I think I see where this is going."

"I'm sure you do."

"You'd already spent, what, a couple of months, almost a standard year, with the *Falcon*?"

"Ten months to be exact."

"And since you didn't want to increase the risk of the baradium detonating prematurely, you took a slow route to Bilbringi, to avoid long hyperspace jumps."

"Lots of time in realspace," Jadak said. "Weeks more. I lost thirty kilos sweating that some micrometeor impact was going to set the device off."

Han grinned knowingly. "You said you were already taken with the ship. How close did you even come to Bilbringi?"

"One jump shy," Jadak said. He cut his eyes to Leia. "But I swear to you, it wasn't cowardice. I wasn't thinking about the possibility of dying."

"I'm not sitting in judgment of you, Quip," Leia said.

"You just couldn't stand to see the *Falcon* destroyed," Han said.

Jadak lowered his head, just as Quip Fargil had done when he had recounted the story. "The thing was," he said, looking up, "a lot of good people had been counting on me. Bilbringi's destruction would have constituted a victory the insurgency sorely needed back then. And I sabotaged it—for a ship."

"You might not have made it," Allana said. "You could've exploded."

"She's right, Quip," Leia said.

"I told myself that over and over again when I was jettisoning the bomb. I might not have made it, anyway. And for a while I let myself be fooled into believing that. I even started dreaming about heading for the Outer Rim and setting up shop, just me and the *Falcon*. Vaced was supposed to have been the first stop, but it turned out to be the last. Not only couldn't I keep the ship, rebel agents were probably already looking to execute me for dereliction of duty—especially after an attempt was made to inflict damage at Bilbringi using a different YT-Thirteen-hundred and more-conventional explosives. The two pilots who died didn't get anywhere close to the planet before Imperials destroyed their ship.

"When I happened to run across Parlay Thorp and her crew of do-gooders, helping the sick, offering relief to folks the Empire had trampled underfoot, I realized I'd found a perfect future for the *Falcon*. So I just . . ."

"Gave her up," Han said.

Jadak nodded, playing his role to the hilt. He had his mouth open to say more when Poste burst into the restaurant, his face smeared with grease and his clothes stained with what looked like oil or lubricant of some kind.

"Hey . . . Quip," he said, breathless when he reached the table, "I bet you're surprised to see me—"

"Did you get those machines running?" Jadak said in a rush, his thoughts swirling.

Poste gestured to himself. "Uh, as you might guess by looking at me, I ran into a couple of problems."

Jadak turned to the Solos. "Mag, here, helps out at the ranch." He whirled to Poste. "I'm not sure I grasp why you decided to come *here*, Mag."

Poste looked at Han. "To tell Captain Solo that when I was coming past the spaceport, I saw the *Millennium Falcon* launch."

Han shot to his feet so quickly that his chair hit the floor. "What?"

"What?" Leia, Allana, and Jadak said at nearly the same instant.

"I'm certain it was the *Falcon*, Captain," Poste went on. "Launched straight from one of the landing bays."

Han was already halfway to the door. "Whoever took her won't get far!"

"He's right about that," Poste muttered to Jadak as Leia and Allana were hurrying off.

Han had asked local enforcement agents to meet him at the *Falcon*'s landing bay. By the time he, Leia, and Allana arrived at the spaceport, three agents were climbing out of an old landspeeder with a faulty repulsorlift, and the *Millennium Falcon* was just returning of her own volition from a short jaunt into Vaced's upper atmosphere. The human marshal—Climm—looked as if he spent most of his off hours bellied up to the Eatery's all-you-could-stomach buffet bar. His Bothan deputies were more interested in capturing comlink cam images of themselves with Han and the *Falcon* than anything else.

Pacing the bay's duracrete floor, Han was preparing to storm up the boarding ramp the moment it lowered when Marshal Climm ordered his two deputies to block the way.

"Your ship's a crime scene, Captain Solo. No one boards until evidence has been gathered and the scene cleared."

"I'll show you a crime scene," Han said, glowering at him.

Leia thought it prudent to intervene. Letting go of Allana's hand, she touched Han on the shoulder. "We do want to respect the local laws, don't we, sweetheart?"

Han scowled but acknowledged the sense of it.

It wasn't the first time the *Falcon* had gone missing

while Han was off on a treasure hunt. There'd been that time on Dellalt when he and Chewie had agreed to search for the *Queen of Ranroon,* the legendary treasure ship of Xim the Despot. But this was different; this time it was *personal.*

Settling onto her landing gear, the *Falcon* loosed a series of hydraulic hisses and mechanical clicks. The boarding ramp extended from beneath the starboard docking arm, and two large beings—a human and a Nautolan—descended, hands raised and looking downcast and embarrassed.

Climm and the deputies had their blasters out.

"You boys are under arrest," the marshal announced.

Han took a menacing step forward. "The *Falcon* had better be exactly as you found her. And how'd you get past our security system and droid, anyway?"

"Yeah. What'd you do to Threepio?" Allana barked.

"I've already advised my clients to remain silent," someone said from the entrance to the bay.

Looking over his shoulder, Han saw a well-dressed, abnormally tall human hurrying toward them. Accompanying him and toting an expensive-looking carry case was a woman of such ethereal beauty, Han did a double take.

"Counselor Oxic," Leia said in astonishment.

Oxic nodded his narrow head. "Princess Leia."

Han looked back and forth between them.

Leia gestured to the now-stun-cuffed ship thieves. "These two are your clients? You can't be serious."

"They have retained me as their lawyer."

Leia refused to buy it. "You traveled all the way here from Epica, or you just happened to be in the neighborhood?"

"In fact, I was wrapping up some business on Lesser

Vaced when they contacted me from the *Millennium Falcon*."

Again Leia gestured to the thieves. "You expect me to believe that these two can afford to retain the legal services of one of the most highly paid defense attorneys in the galaxy?"

Oxic lifted his shoulders in a shrug. "Looks can be deceiving." Indicating the woman, he added: "My personal assistant, Koi Quire. Koi, Princess Leia Organa Solo."

Leia's eyes lighted up in astonishment. "You're Firrerreo."

Koi Quire smiled and inclined her head in a bow. "I was aboard the sleeper ship you discovered so long ago. I'm honored to be able to thank you in person all these years later."

"Counselor," Climm said, "we're about to charge these boys with grand theft starship."

"Add breaking and entering," Han snapped. "This ship is practically our home."

"You've given up the conapt on Coruscant?" Oxic asked Leia.

"No. But—"

"Then I'm afraid you'll have a hard time making a case for breaking and entering. More important, my clients returned the ship to precisely where they found it."

"*They* didn't do that," Han shouted. "The *Falcon* did that."

"That may also prove difficult to establish," Oxic mused. "We are perhaps willing to admit to joyriding."

Han's jaw dropped. "They stole the ship!"

Oxic showed him a calm look. "You'll have to prove intent."

Han whirled to the thieves. "How did you get aboard?"

"I caution you to refrain from saying anything that may further incriminate you," Oxic said well over Han's head.

Leia was prepared to see smoke coil from Han's ears when Oxic turned to her.

"Princess Leia, may we confer in private for a moment?"

Leia nodded. "I won't be long," she told Allana, then stepped into the wake of Oxic's long strides. "This had better make sense, Lestra," she said, gazing up at him when they were out of earshot of the others.

He tweaked his smile so that it wouldn't seem quite so patronizing. "Princess Leia, I'm certain you don't want to spend any more time on Vaced than is absolutely necessary. If my clients take my advice and enter a plea of not guilty, you and Captain Solo and your young ward will be required to remain here for the arraignment, and be forced to return for the pretrial and trial, assuming the case should get that far. Furthermore, you will be obliged to reside in a hotel—assuming for the moment Vaced even has one—for however long it will take for this . . . law officer to complete his poking around in the *Falcon* on an ostensible search for forensic evidence."

Leia laughed shortly. "Nice to see you haven't lost your special touch, Lestra."

"I do what I must," Oxic said. "Of course, it's up to you to decide whether or not to press charges, though I suspect that the local judges are likely to grant my clients probation before judgment, even if the charge of ship theft holds. Out of respect for our long-standing acquaintanceship, I will try to convince my clients to plead guilty to joyriding and misuse of personal property, which will entitle you and Han to be reimbursed for the cost of fuel and the sheer aggravation of it all."

Leia narrowed her eyes. "Lestra, what are you doing here—really?"

"Nothing more than serving the needs of my clients."

"You can't be honest with me?"

"This is a legal matter, Princess. Attorney–client confidentiality must be observed."

Leia forced an exhale. "All right, Lestra, I'll put it to Han."

"What'd he say?" Han said, coming to an abrupt halt as she approached. "And who is he, anyway? How do you know him?"

"I'll explain later. Right now we've got a decision to make."

Allana stepped in to listen to Leia's summary, at the conclusion of which Han shouted, "This is a load of poodoo, counselor!"

"Han!" Leia said, putting her hands over Allana's ears, even while both of them were laughing.

"I'm sorry, Captain Solo," Oxic said. "It's not personal."

Han turned to the marshal. "Can we make ship theft stick or not?"

Climm took off his hat and scratched his head. "Maybe not in the long run. But the judge'll probably be willing to consider the charge as a way to keep you around. You see, he's kind of an admirer of yours."

"Great," Han said flatly. He shot the thieves his best glare, then turned to Oxic. "You win this one, counselor. But you'd better hope our situations aren't reversed someday."

"I'll be sure to keep that in mind, Captain."

Han cursed. "Joyriding." He gave his head a quick shake. "The sooner we're off this rock, the better."

chapter twenty-eight

"The Firrerreo's name is Koi Quire," Jadak explained as he and Poste watched from a landing bay adjacent to the *Falcon*'s. "She visited me at Aurora Medical, claiming to be an agent for Core Life Insurance. The tall guy she's with, that's Lestra Oxic. His holoimage was all over the head doctor's office at Aurora. He was also the lawyer representing the Colicoids back on Holess."

"And they're the ones who've been after you since Nar Shaddaa?"

"After me, and now after the *Falcon* because Oxic knows we need her to find the treasure."

Poste frowned. "How long have you known all this?"

"Only since Holess."

"And you didn't tell me because you didn't want to worry me."

Jadak clapped him on the back. "I've got only your best interests at heart." He paused, then said: "We have to get ourselves aboard the *Falcon*."

Poste gaped at him. "You're not thinking clearly. The protocol droid saw me."

"No one listens to droids." Jadak kept his eyes on the entrance to the *Falcon*'s landing bay. "If the Solos decide not to leave Vaced, we make another try for the ship. If they decide to launch now . . . well, just follow my lead."

"Right, because that's worked so well so far."

Vaced's primary had only dropped a degree or so when they saw everyone but the Solos file out. The deputies loaded the two would-be thieves into the clunky landspeeder and took off toward town. The rotund marshal rode with Oxic and Koi Quire in the rented speeder they had arrived in.

"Let's go," Jadak told Poste the moment the speeders were out of sight.

Han was inspecting the *Falcon*'s undercarriage when they entered the bay. Hearing them, he came out from under the starboard mandible with his blaster drawn.

"We just wanted to make sure everything turned out all right, Captain," Jadak said.

Han holstered the weapon. "Sure—if you call allowing a couple of ship thieves to get off with a charge of joyriding."

"Frontier injustice," Poste said.

"You're telling me. But to make a theft charge stick . . ." Han allowed his words to trail off. "Ah, frip."

"Anything we can do?" Jadak said.

Han shook his head. "I just can't believe those guys would try to make off with my ship."

"The *Falcon*'s as famous as you are. Word must have gotten around that she was here."

Han looked dubious. "It's not like somebody could sell her."

"Paint her, remove the cannons, install a new identity telesponder . . ."

Han grinned. "Yeah, but then she ain't the *Falcon*." He ran his eyes over the ship. "What's worse, they managed to sabotage my anti-intrusion safeguards."

Jadak watched him for a moment. "I'm guessing you'll

be headed for Nar Shaddaa to continue the search for past owners."

"Maybe," Han said in a distracted way. "I'm not sure. This little outing of ours has taken some pretty strange twists." He glanced at Jadak. "Why, what's on your mind, Fargil?"

"I know it's a lot to ask, but I'm wondering if you'd be willing to drop us at Toprawa."

Han waited for more.

"We need parts for some of the machines on the ranch," Jadak went on. "An order placed from here will take weeks to fill, and we can't afford to be shut down for that long."

"I know how that can be," Han said, rubbing his chin. "Toprawa, huh? Sure, why not? It's not so far out of our way. Consider it thanks for all the info you gave us." He looked at Poste. "And for telling me about seeing the *Falcon* launch."

"No problem, Captain."

"And thanks for cleaning up. You need time to throw some gear together?"

Jadak gestured to their rucksacks. "We've got everything we need."

"All right then." Han motioned to the boarding ramp. "Welcome aboard."

Han trailed them up the ramp and into the corridor, where Leia and Allana were standing alongside the still-deactivated protocol droid.

"We're giving Quip and Mag a ride to Toprawa," Han announced.

Leia tried to hide her surprise by turning to the droid.

"We didn't want to switch him back on till you were here," Allana said.

Han gave his head a theatrical shake. "Will you look at this? That's the last time we leave him alone with the ship." Reaching a hand behind the droid's head, he flipped the activation switch.

"What? Who are you? What are you doing on the ship?" C-3PO said. "Where am I? What happened?"

"You got yourself switched off is what happened," Han said. "Why didn't you comlink me when the security system went down?"

"I made every effort, Captain Solo. But someone— *yaaw!*"

Too late, Poste tried to conceal himself behind Jadak.

"Take it easy, Threepio, they're our passengers. You're a nervous wreck."

"But, Captain—"

"I know it's going to mean more work for you, but they're only aboard until Toprawa. Besides, we've all got jobs to do."

"But, Captain Solo—"

"Not another word, Threepio," Han said, raising his forefinger. "I mean it."

C-3PO straightened.

"Threepio, come and help us get the *Falcon* ready for launch," Allana said.

"Of course, mistress," he said shuffling off after Leia and Allana. "No one listens to me anyway."

Nudging Poste in the ribs as he stepped past him to take in the main hold, Jadak gasped in genuine wonder. "If I didn't know, I wouldn't even believe this is the same ship." He peeked into the ladderwell that led to the gun turrets and ran his hand over the console of the engineering station. "You've done a lot of amazing work since she was mine, Solo. You've even got a hologame table."

Han glanced around. "Most of the changes I made can't be seen, they have to be experienced. The dejarik board is actually the second one the *Falcon*'s had. The first was put in when she was part of a traveling circus."

Jadak laughed. "A circus?"

"Parlay Thorp sold her to the Molpol Circus and used the money to open a research center. You should contact her sometime. She's on the staff of the Aurora Medical Center."

Jadak gulped and found his voice. "Aurora?"

"The circus owner sold her to a gambler," Han continued, "who ended up losing her to . . . well, another gambler. Lando Calrissian."

"General Calrissian?" Poste said.

Han grinned. "Lando hasn't gone by that honorific in a lot of years. But, yeah, General Calrissian." He motioned to the hologame table's curved bench. "Make yourselves comfortable. I'm going to get her warmed up."

Poste waited for Han to disappear, then swung to Jadak. "I don't see the slicer droid anywhere," he said quietly.

"Maybe it left when Oxic's men were busy chasing you."

Poste looked around, even under the acceleration couch. "Maybe . . ."

"Listen to me," Jadak said. "After we launch you need to get Solo out of the cockpit so I can have some time alone in there."

"How am I supposed to do that?"

"Get him talking about the modifications he's made to the ship—the point-five hyperdrive, the turbolasers, anything that comes to mind. If I know Solo, he won't pass on an opportunity to show off."

"I hate it when someone sits in my chair," Han said as Leia came into the cockpit and strapped into the co-pilot's seat. "Except you, of course."

"Of course."

Han fiddled with the chair's control. "You know

when you have it perfectly adjusted for yourself, then someone goes and fools with it."

"Life can be hard," Leia said.

He frowned at her, and motioned with his chin to the instrument panel. "We good to lift?"

"We're good."

Han enabled the repulsors and eased the ship up and out of the landing bay, the spaceport shrinking below them. "Where's Allana?"

"Showing our passengers some of her favorite toys." Leia looked over her shoulder. "You trust them?"

Han glanced at her. "Obviously you don't."

Leia stared out the viewport for a moment, Vaced's blue sky darkening as the ship climbed and stars began to appear. "I can't get a fix on Mag, other than to say he seems like a fish out of water. But there's something not quite right about Quip."

"His story rang false?"

"Not at all. In fact, everything he said struck me as true—even when he mentioned Bail. I had a strong sense that he actually knew him."

"They were both there at the beginnings of the Alliance. They might have crossed paths or had dealings. He practically said as much."

"That's part of what I was feeling. But there was more to it. When he was telling us about falling in love with the *Falcon,* I felt the emotion behind his words. But when he began telling us about the mission to Bilbringi and his change of heart, I sensed that he was omitting some crucial detail."

"It didn't happen the way he said?"

"I can't be sure. I just didn't feel his remorse. He felt bad about what happened, but it was as if he had distanced himself from the events. Or that he was recounting someone else's version of the story."

"Distancing himself is understandable. It's been more

than fifty years. If I was telling someone about what I did on Ylesia way back when, it might come out sounding like I don't harbor regrets, but I do."

Leia sighed. "You're right. Maybe I'm being overly suspicious because of what happened on Taris."

"And now two strangers try to make off with the *Falcon*."

"What bothers me is Lestra Oxic's being on hand to speak for them," Leia said.

"I know I've heard the name."

Leia swiveled her chair toward him. "I've known him practically all my life. He represented many of the so-called loyalists in the years preceding the Clone Wars."

Han made his mouth a rictus. "You're kidding. He doesn't look half old enough. First Quip Fargil, now Lestra Oxic. What am I doing wrong?"

Leia laughed. "Lestra is one of the people who keep Aurora Medical in business—and not simply as a patron. He made occasional visits to Alderaan when I was growing up. He and Bail had many private talks. Bail respected Lestra because he continued to befriend and offer legal advice to Palpatine's enemies, despite the dangers that posed to his career and to his life. But for Lestra to represent two ship thieves on Vaced . . ."

"Maybe he's doing it for the public good?"

"That's as good an explanation as any. You know he was the lawyer for the Colicoids in that recent case."

"The lawyer who lost. So maybe he's taking work wherever he can find it."

Leia ridiculed the idea. "He's wealthy beyond even *your* wildest dreams. He's said to have one of the most extensive collections anywhere of Coruscant Republicana."

Han thought about it. "You don't think he hired those thieves to add the *Falcon* to his collection."

"I wouldn't put it past him."

Before Han could respond, someone said, "Permission to enter the cockpit, Captain."

Han saw Mag standing in the hatch and beckoned him in. "Take a seat."

A crescent of Vaced hung in the viewport, the world's small moon engulfed in shadow.

"Your ship is even more amazing than I'd heard," Poste said. "Quip told me a lot about it, but I guess I wasn't expecting a hundred-year-old vessel to look this good."

"A hundred and three," Han corrected. "Does Quip do a lot of bragging about having named her?"

"Quip? Never. Only a handful of folks on all of Vaced know him as Quip as opposed to Vec, and even those folks don't know he ever owned the *Falcon*. Besides, he feels too bad about what he did to tell anyone. He's still expecting some former member of the Rebel Alliance to come gunning for him. I was surprised when he agreed to meet with you."

"A story like Quip's, it gets bottled up. It has to come out sometime."

"Quip says the *Falcon* is running a point-five hyperdrive."

"It's a fact. With a Series Four-oh-one Isu-Sim generator."

"Incredible," Poste said. "What's the power source?"

"Quadex."

"What drives her sublight?"

"A pair of Giordyne SRB-four-twos—modified, of course."

"Deflector shields?"

"Torplex generator, with a Novaldex stasis for support."

Poste whistled in admiration. "If there's time, I'd really like you to show me around before you drop us at Toprawa."

"We can do it now," Han said. "As soon as we make the jump to lightspeed, I'll enable the autopilot." He swiveled away from the navicomputer to face Leia. "Unless you want to take the helm."

Leia shook her head. "I promised Amelia I'd help her prepare snacks."

"Don't go to any trouble on our behalf," Poste said.

Leia slid out of the harness. "No trouble. But we can't leave Threepio to do it all by himself."

Han studied the coordinates the Rubicon had provided. "All set. We'll start with the sublight engines."

Outside the viewport, the stars streaked.

chapter twenty-nine

JADAK HAD ENTERED INTO A DEJARIK MATCH WITH THE
hologame computer and was pretending to be en-
grossed in overseeing his bestiary of holocreatures when
first Leia, then Han and Poste left the cockpit for the
stern of the ship. Jadak waited until they disappeared
around the curve of the ring corridor, then paused the
game, rose from the table, and hurried through the connector to the cockpit. Planting himself in the pilot's
chair, he pivoted from side to side, then swung to face
the navicomputer.

For all the YT-1300 had changed over the decades,
the cockpit had undergone the fewest modifications
since the days the ship had been known as the *Stellar
Envoy*. Solo or someone before him had added an additional pair of chairs, and the instrument panel boasted a
bewildering array of retrofitted toggles and levers, re-
flecting the changes made to the stock propulsion, guidance, and sensor systems. Then there were the controls
for the quad lasers and Ground Buzzer repeater. Otherwise, the cockpit was much as Jadak remembered it, and
just sitting in the chair was enough to transport him
back in time. He half expected to turn and find Reeze
sitting in the copilot's chair, complaining about one
thing or another.

Jadak studied the navicomputer, which still retained

its original alloy faceplate with the name RUBICON in raised letters across the top. Spots of rust had formed around the bolts that fastened it to the bulkhead, but the keyboard was relatively new.

Jadak gazed at the raised letters. "Rubicon," he said softly.

Digging into his pocket, he pulled out a scrap of flimsi on which were scrawled some of his attempts at deciphering the mnemonic phrase Senator Des'sein had had him memorize.

He gazed again at the navicomputer, then studied the handwritten phrase. His forefinger moved across the flimsi.

"R . . . u . . . b . . . i . . . c . . ."

His heart began to race. He stared at the flimsi. "Restore," he said quietly. His finger moved over the letters. "R . . . e . . . s—" He stopped. "Reset? Reset . . . Rubicon . . ." He looked from the flimsi to the navicomputer and back again. "Reset Rubicon to . . ."

Some of the keyboard tabs were marked with numbers and letters. Had the mnemonic phrase been designed to remind the bearer to reset the Rubicon to the numbers represented by the nine letters that made up the final two words? If so, did the numbers represent time–space coordinates or was the numerical sequence itself a cipher?

In either case, he didn't expect the *Falcon* to respond, much less alter course—not while traveling through hyperspace. But it was possible that the navicomputer would furnish him with the name or the star map coordinates of the treasure world.

If at least that much happened, Jadak would have no further use for the *Falcon*. The Solos could drop him and Poste at Toprawa and be on their merry way to Nar Shaddaa or wherever else, and he and Poste could begin to figure out how to raise enough credits to finance an expedition to the treasure world.

Centering himself over the keyboard, Jadak hit the RESET button and used both his forefingers to enter the nine-digit code. The navicomputer chimed in response, but neither a name nor coordinates appeared in the display screen.

Instead he heard a pained cry issue from elsewhere in the ship.

Anyone observing Han as he whirled and high-stepped his way through the *Falcon*'s port ring corridor might have assumed that he was executing a rather sloppy interpretation of the Sacorrian Jig, which had enjoyed a brief revival in popularity on Corellia in the years after the Battle of Yavin. But in fact Han was attempting to yank from his trousers pocket the archaic transponder Allana had discovered weeks earlier, which was just now needling his upper thigh with a series of painful electric shocks.

Bouncing the device in his cupped hand when he finally managed to withdraw it, he was on the verge of smashing it underfoot when it suddenly calmed down.

By then Jadak had hurried from the cockpit and was standing in the center of the main hold when Han and Poste appeared from one side and Leia, Allana, and the protocol droid appeared from the other, none of them looking very happy.

"Kriffing thing went off in my pants!" Han shouted.

Leia gestured. "Maybe Mag or whatever his real name is can explain."

Jadak heard a sound he had thought he would never hear again—the *snap-hiss!* of a lightsaber being activated—and all at once he and Poste were being forced back toward the hologame table's arc of acceleration couch.

"Down," Leia said. "Both of you."

Poste sat, and Jadak followed suit.

"Last time I saw one of those it was dangling from the belt of Jedi Master J'oopi Shé," Jadak told Leia.

Her expression turned quizzical. "What?"

"What's going on?" Han said, glancing from Jadak to his wife.

"Tell him, Threepio."

C-3PO raised an arm and pointed to Poste. "Captain Solo, *he* was the one responsible for jamming communications and shutting me down. With the help of a nasty little slicer droid, I might add."

Han stared at Poste and Jadak. "You two are in league with those ship thieves?"

Jadak shook his head. "We're more like members of the opposing team."

Unholstering his blaster, Han stepped toward the table. Behind him, Leia deactivated the lightsaber and sat with Allana at the engineering station.

"What's your real name?" Han asked Poste.

"Flitcher Poste," he said quietly. "And I'm really sorry about—"

"And yours?" Han cut him off, glaring at Jadak.

"Tobb Jadak." Nodding toward Poste, he said: "He's only involved because I dragged him into this."

"Then you've got a lot of explaining to do."

Jadak exhaled through his nostrils and sat back in the couch. "Remember in the restaurant when I told you I had no idea who owned the *Falcon* before the Nar Shaddaa crime boss? I was lying." He tapped himself in the chest. "I piloted the ship before he had it."

Han's eyebrows formed a V. "When was that?"

"Well, about . . . seventy-two years ago. It was called the *Stellar Envoy* back then."

Han laughed. "What'd you fly it in, your diapers? There's no way you're that much older than me."

"Oh, I am, Solo. By a good twenty-five standard years."

Han stared at him. "That would put you close to a hundred."

Jadak nodded. "Don't I know it."

"Who is the Jedi you mentioned?" Leia asked suddenly.

"A Kadas'sa'Nikto of the old Order. Master Shé was present when I received my final orders regarding the *Stellar*—the *Falcon*."

Han looked at Leia. "Are you following this?"

Leia didn't answer him. "When and where was that?" she asked Jadak.

"The Senate Annex, the final month of the war. The year you were born, if I'm not mistaken."

Leia folded her arms. "You're not mistaken. But that isn't exactly classified information."

"Is any of this on the level, Jadak?" Han said.

"All of it."

"You're just a hundred-year-old pilot who's still in love with the *Falcon*, is that the idea?"

"I won't deny loving the ship, Solo. But the truth is, I don't want her. I want the secrets she's safeguarding."

Allana hurried from the engineering station before Leia could grab her. "What secrets?" she said, wide-eyed with anticipation.

Jadak looked from her to Han. "That transponder your dad's holding . . . I think it was installed on the *Falcon* by Master Shé just before I took off on what I thought was going to be the *Falcon*'s final mission."

"The *Jedi* sent you on this mission?" Leia said.

Jadak shook his head. "The outfit I worked for was known as the Republic Group."

"The covert loyalist organization?"

"The same, Princess Leia. I worked for them for ten years, carrying out all kinds of missions with this very ship. My orders on that day in the annex were to deliver it to an Antarian Ranger on Toprawa—a woman named Folee, who was going to look after the ship from that point on. The thing is, I never made it to Toprawa. Clone pilots pursued me off Coruscant and the ship took a hit from a Republic cruiser laser. My partner and I made a last-instant jump to Nar Shaddaa, but we reverted without the ability to maneuver." Jadak paused briefly. "We collided with a bulk cruiser. My partner died."

"I'm sorry to hear that, Jadak," Han said. "But I'm still waiting to hear where you've been for the past sixty or so years."

"In a coma," Jadak said evenly. "In a medcenter near Nar Shaddaa for the first couple of decades, and at Aurora Medical for the rest."

"We were just there," Allana said.

Jadak nodded. "Talking to Dr. Parlay Thorp, the way I figure it. But I don't think she has anything to do with this."

"To do with what?" Leia said.

"The game of hide-and-seek I've been playing with Lestra Oxic. He's the one who had me moved from Nar Shaddaa to Aurora, and he's had his underlings chasing me ever since I woke up. Those two joyriders back on Vaced? They belong to him. So does the doctor who supervised my rehabilitation—Dr. Sompa."

"We spoke with him," Leia said. "Parlay even mentioned you!"

Jadak mulled it over. "That explains how Oxic put two and two together about the *Stellar Envoy* and the *Falcon*." He looked up at Han. "Oxic knew I was searching for the ship. Once he made the connection, he figured on stealing the *Falcon*, knowing that I'd have no option but to turn myself over to him if I wanted a piece of the prize."

"I knew it!" Allana said. "There *is* a treasure!"

Han's eyes darted from Allana to Jadak. "Is she right?"

"The *Falcon* holds the key to locating a treasure that was described to me as 'sufficient to restore Republic honor to the galaxy.' "

Leia's brows furrowed. "Honor?"

"Credits?" Han said. "Aurodium? What kind of treasure?"

Jadak shook his head. "I don't know."

"How could the *Falcon* know where this treasure is cached?"

"The Republic Group set it up to know. They saw where things were headed with Palpatine and must have been preparing for a time when they could wrest power away from him. What they didn't foresee was how the Clone Wars would end, with the Jedi murdered and the Emperor all but untouchable."

Han holstered his blaster and began to pace. "Then this treasure could be a trove of weapons."

"Maybe," Jadak said, watching him. "Or a combination of weapons and precious metals."

"The Republic Group said *honor*," Leia chimed in, "not *strength*."

Han came to a halt and turned toward the hologame table. "How could Oxic have learned about it? Was he a member of the group?"

"I think I know," Leia said. "To the best of my knowledge he wasn't a member. But he was close friends with many of the beings who were. One of them may have told him about the cache."

Han considered it. "Why not just tell him where to find the treasure?"

"The location may have been a closely guarded secret," Leia went on. "Whoever told Oxic knew only that the *Falcon* was the key to finding it, and that Tobb Jadak was the last person known to have piloted it."

"Are we gonna go and find the treasure?" Allana asked.

Han steered a course around the question. "The first thing we have to do is check the ship for homing devices, just in case Oxic is thinking about following us. We won't be able to scan the hull until we revert to real-space, but we can run a scan of the interior." Han turned to C-3PO. "You know what to do."

"I'll begin at once, Captain Solo."

Han whirled to Poste. "Threepio said you had a slicer droid with you."

Poste gulped and nodded. "It was with me in the cockpit when Oxic's goons got the jump on me. It could have deboarded while they were busy chasing me through the ship."

"*Could have?* You mean to tell me it could still be aboard?"

"I'm just saying that I didn't see it leave," Poste said.

"Threepio!" Han shouted. "We have a revised priority!" As if only just remembering, he opened his left fist and glanced at the transponder. "Why did this thing suddenly go active?"

"Because I entered a code sequence into the navicomputer," Jadak said.

Han's eyes narrowed. "The transponder received the code, and tried to transmit."

"We need to put it back where we found it," Allana said, going to the bulkhead alongside the engineering station.

Leia looked at Han, waiting for him to speak.

"This is crazy," he said finally.

"It's not," Allana said. "It's just a treasure hunt."

*   *   *

"Nothing affixed to the hull," Han announced from the pilot's chair.

Leia and Allana were beside him, Jadak and Poste in the rear chairs. Outside the viewport the stars were visible once more, the *Falcon* drifting aimlessly among them.

Swiveling toward the ship's intercom, Han said, "Threepio, what's taking you so long?"

A note of distress punctuated the droid's voice as it issued through the cockpit enunciators. "I am working at all speed, Captain Solo. The cargo areas are free of tracking devices. I will sweep the rest of the *Falcon* from the stern forward."

"Fine. Just be quick about it."

Han muted the audio before C-3PO could respond. "Have to keep him on his toes," he said over his shoulder.

"Oxic's boys aren't stupid, just incompetent," Jadak said. "They'd expect you to scan for a homing device."

Han nodded. "Still, why take chances?"

"Captain Solo," C-3PO said a moment later, "I am receiving an anomalous signal originating from within the escape pod access."

"Could one of the pod trackers be enabled?" Leia said.

"Possibly." Han leaned toward the intercom. "Threepio, stay put. We're on our way."

The five of them filed out of the cockpit and wended their way into the *Falcon*'s rear hold. C-3PO was peering into the escape pod accessway, his photoreceptors glowing in the dimness.

"I believe—" he started to say when Han ducked into the space, sending the broad beam of a glow rod into the darkest areas. Twisting over, he craned his neck toward the ceiling and trained the light on a spot above the hatchway.

"All right, you," he said, "come down from there."

"What are you planning to do to me?" a raspy mechanical voice asked.

"That depends on what you tell me."

"I was only following orders."

"That's everybody's excuse. Now come out of there before I decide to use a disruptor on you."

No sooner did Han step back into the hold than the long-snouted slicer droid glided from the accessway, trembling as it hovered a meter off the deck.

Han slapped a data interface connector into C-3PO's hand. "He's all yours."

"Thank you, Captain Solo."

The slicer droid floated backward against the ring corridor bulkhead. "Hey, watch out with that thing, it has a probe on the end of it."

Locating the dataport beneath the slicer's snout, C-3PO inserted the probe and studied the tool's alphanumeric readout display. "He is harboring a homing device, Captain."

"As a precaution against theft, my master installs trackers in all rentals," the slicer said.

"How long has the tracker been transmitting?" Han said.

"Since the ship launched. It's not my fault."

Han nodded to C-3PO. "Go ahead."

C-3PO made an adjustment to the probe and deactivated it. Photoreceptors blinking out, the slicer droid drifted slowly to the deck, where it collapsed in a heap.

"Now can we put the transponder back?" Allana said while everyone was staring at the droid.

Leia had lost track of how many times Allana had asked the question. Putting her hand on Allana's shoulder, she looked at Han.

Han compressed his lips, then forced a laugh. "What could go wrong?"

"Can I do it—please?"

"Sure you can," Han said. "You're the one who found it."

"I'll probably have to reenter the navicomputer code," Jadak said.

Han nodded and prized the transponder from his pocket. "Leia, you have the helm while Amelia and I put this thing back where it belongs."

"Where do you want me?" Poste asked.

"I want you and Threepio to keep an eye on this droid."

The six of them split into three teams. Moments later, Han was in the main hold, watching Allana fit the transponder into its pocket in the bulkhead, the device's mimetic alloy making it seem to disappear.

"We're all set!" Han shouted.

In the cockpit, Leia watched Jadak reset the Rubicon navicomputer and enter a numerical code. Instantly time–space coordinates appeared on the display screen.

And the *Millennium Falcon* jumped into hyperspace.

"You've lost the signal," Lestra Oxic said.

The Gran rental agency owner, Druul, gestured dismissively. "They found the primary tracker—the obvious one. The redundant system is integrated into the slicer's carapace and will continue to function even if the droid is deactivated. The device uses the ship itself as an antenna."

The monitor in Druul's office beeped.

"What did I tell you," the Gran said.

Lestra looked at Koi Quire, who showed him a subtle nod of appreciation.

"Where is the ship?"

"In realspace, though nowhere in particular," Druul said, two of his three eyes scanning the monitor's star map. "Rimward of the Hydian, perhaps three-quarters of the way to Toprawa."

"What now?" Oxic said.

One of the Gran's stalked eyeballs fixed on him. "That's entirely up to you. You're the one paying."

"Patience, Lestra," Quire said. "We've come this far. Besides, Remata and Cynner are still being processed."

"Who's handling the bail arrangements?"

"We're using a local to supply the bond."

Oxic fell silent and began to pace. If things had gone according to plan, he would have had both the *Falcon* and Jadak in hand by now. Even so, they had caught a break, thanks to the slicer droid Poste had rented. That in itself had to be a sign that the treasure was destined to be his. As Koi had said, they had come this far—

"The ship has jumped back to lightspeed," Druul said suddenly.

Oxic hurried back to the monitor. "Where are they headed? Does it show a destination?"

Druul was doing input at the monitor. "It's showing coordinates. Give me a moment to see what they refer to." Alphanumeric text began to scroll on the display, and a series of star maps flashed onscreen and disappeared.

"The name!" Oxic said. "I need the name of the world!"

The Gran gave his full attention to the display, then turned to Oxic. "Tandun Three."

Oxic glanced at Quire, who shrugged. "I've never heard of it."

"It's unimportant," he said. "Quickly—to the ship."

With their organic technology—their tentacled war coordinators and gravity-generating dovin basals—the extragalactic Yuuzhan Vong had superseded every threat the galaxy had faced. But if the *Falcon* had discriminated between coralskippers and TIE fighters, she had kept the distinctions to herself and fought valiantly from the Outer Rim to the Core, taking on all challengers.

For a time following Chewbacca's horrible death on Sernpidal at the start of the invasion, Han had secretly wished that the *Falcon* would refuse to function. He knew that a ship was incapable of missing its pilot the way a pilot could miss his or her ship, and yet he wanted the *Falcon* to mourn the loss of the Wookiee's special touch, or at least to perform poorly without him. No one had put in more time working on the ship, and even when railing at it Chewbacca had a love for her that matched Han's. So when the *Falcon* failed to mirror Han's grief and despair, Han had given serious thought to retiring her from service.

With the *Falcon* stripped to the bone, Han had questioned if he could even set foot inside the YT without his first mate, let alone pilot her into action. And so the *Falcon* became a kind of ghost ship.

Then, in a complete reversal, Han had set out to

even the score with the Yuuzhan Vong. Driven by rage, he wanted the Falcon *to participate in exacting revenge. And in the midst of his one-man campaign he found that although he had lost his closest friend, Leia was there to fill not only Chewbacca's outsized copilot's chair but the empty space the Wookiee had left in Han's heart.*

But in the same way that the Yuuzhan Vong had left vestiges of themselves and their exotic savagery on Coruscant and a host of other worlds, the war itself had opened wounds that were long in healing, leaving scars that refused to fade. Chewbacca was one of those; Anakin, the Solos' youngest son who had seemed destined to live forever, another.

Years later Jacen's death had reawakened all the anguish.

Jacen, who in a real sense had come closest to under-standing the Yuuzhan Vong and had looked to the Force for a peaceful resolution to the war. Only to fall . . . to die and merge with the Force rather than disappear into it. Or was he, as Han sometimes liked to believe, merely exiled, as the Yuuzhan Vong had been to the sentient world of Zonama Sekot, and advancing toward redemption?

chapter thirty

"WAS SWOOP RACING PART OF QUIP FARGIL'S PAST or yours?" Han said.

"That was some of me creeping into Fargil's story. I raced on all the major circuits before the war—the Clone Wars."

"Same for me—before the Galactic Civil War."

Jadak showed him an appraising look. "Guess we have more in common than we know, Solo."

"Or like to admit."

Glimpsing the smile in Han's eyes, Jadak laughed and Han joined him. The *Millennium Falcon* had returned to hyperspace, and the two of them were seated side by side in the cockpit. Han's chair was swiveled to face the hatch, and he had his booted feet propped on one of the high-backed rear chairs, ankles crossed.

"You mind a personal question?" Han asked.

"I'll let you know."

"Those years you were in a coma . . . I'm guessing that a lot of your family members and friends died."

"All of them."

Han took his feet off the chair and sat up. When he spoke, his voice was lowered, almost conspiratorial. "This quest of ours, into the *Falcon*'s history, it started out something like a game. I've always wanted to know who had piloted her before Lando Calrissian won her at

Bespin, but it's not something I ever figured I'd be doing with Leia and Amelia, and it's turned out to be a lot more than I expected, which is saying a mouthful. 'Course, I don't know why I ever expected things to go smoothly."

Jadak sniffed. "Sorry about what Poste and I contributed."

"Forget it. But I'm curious. You wake up after sixtysomething years and the first thing you do is go chasing after your ship."

"Like I told you, I was looking for the ship only because of what I thought it might lead me to."

"This supposed treasure trove."

Jadak swallowed what he had intended to say. "What, that's not enough? You married a princess. But I'm sure you were madly in love."

Han's eyes narrowed in anger, then relaxed. "As long as we're being honest with each other, the idea of being wealthy did appeal to me—for about a standard day."

"What changed your mind?"

"I started caring about the people I accidentally got thrown in with."

"The Rebel Alliance," Jadak said. He swung to face Han. "Well, then that's another thing we have in common. You'd think a few decades in a coma would make you forget, but it didn't. I woke up feeling exactly as I had the day Reeze and I collided with the Corellian cruiser—that I had a mission to discharge. That the *Stellar Envoy* had to be delivered as planned." He gave his head a rueful shake. "I still haven't been able to shake that feeling."

"Getting to Tandun Three will allow you to do that?"

"I sure the frip hope so."

"Suppose we don't find this treasure. What then?"

"At least I tried to deliver the ship."

The navicomputer chimed. Han glanced at it and pivoted the chair to face the instrument panel. "Reversion coming up."

Jadak raised his gaze to the viewport in expectation. Following a moment of wake rotation, the stars firmed up and a crescent of planet hung in the middle distance. Han changed vectors, bringing the *Falcon* around so that they could approach Tandun III with starlight at their backs.

"Let's see what the long-range scanners tell us," he said.

Jadak watched Han's expression change as he studied the readouts. Then Han shouted: "Threepio! Get in here!"

"Coming, Captain Solo," C-3PO said.

The sound of the droid's footfalls issued from the connector, and a moment later he was ducking into the cockpit, trailed by Leia, Allana, and Poste.

"What was it you told us about Tandun Three?" Han said.

C-3PO cocked his head to one side. "I said that initial surveys were conducted approximately twelve thousand two hundred fifty years ago, under the supervision of a Dr. Beramsh, whose expedition departed from Ord Mantell. Tandun Three was described as a youthful planet in a young star system, lush and well suited to humans and humanoid oxygen breathers, with close to standard gravity and studded with the ruins of ancient population centers Dr. Beramsh posited as having been constructed by the Rakata. For no particular reason, save perhaps for its distance from the Hydian Way, Tandun Three was never settled, though there are some indications that a second survey was conducted during Finis Valorum's second term as Chancellor of the Republic."

Han scowled and jabbed his forefinger against the scanner display. "Yeah, well, take a look at these readings and tell me if you'd call Tandun Three a 'youthful' planet."

C-3PO squeezed between Han and Jadak to study the readouts.

"Oh, my," he said.

"Oh, my, is right," Han said.

"What is it, Han?" Leia asked over C-3PO's shoulder. "Let's hear Threepio's revised description."

The droid turned to Leia. "The scanners reveal extensive areas of volcanic and tectonic activity. While still breathable, the atmosphere is high in carbon dioxide, methane, and sulfur. Surface temperatures have rendered landmasses in the northern hemisphere unsuitable for all but the most extremophilic of sentient species. In short, the planet is in the grips of catastrophic forces that are likely to destroy it."

"Are there any signs of life?" Leia asked.

"Intact forests in the southern hemisphere are showing abundant life," Han said. "But I'd argue that any sentient life we find down there can't be called intelligent." He shook his head. "Whatever may have been here then is probably buried under lava or volcanic ash." Then, catching sight of Allana's expression, he added: "But we'll take a closer look, just to be sure."

With Tandun III in full starlight, Han slewed the *Falcon* away from the churning sky of the planet's northern hemisphere. Dropping the ship into a cloudless patch near the southern pole, he adjusted the scanners to feed video to the instrument panel display. Static crazed the screen before the images stabilized.

"Oh, no," Han said, as if someone had let the air out of him.

Peering over his shoulder, Leia put her hand in front of her mouth. "Oh, Han."

Poste went up on his toes in an effort to see the display screen, and Jadak leaned to his left to have a look.

"I've never seen vegetation quite like that," he said.

"That's because you slept through it," Han said out of the corner of his mouth. His forefinger hopped about the screen. "See that cliff face that looks like the bow of a starship? That stuff's called yorik coral. And those trees that look like they've been dipped in blood? Those are called s'teeni. All this forest? This is tampasi. That bird—that bird right there, that's a whatchamacallit—a scherkil hla."

Jadak lifted an eyebrow. "You want to translate that into Basic?"

"There are no translations," Leia said, one arm around Allana's shoulders in a protective embrace. "Those are Yuuzhan Vong words."

Poste whistled. "Parts of Nal Hutta looked like this for a long time."

"The entire place has been Vongformed," Han said. "The Vong did it to a bunch of worlds, even Coruscant."

Jadak nodded. "I remember reading about that."

Han glanced at Leia. "You think there's a yammosk down there? You don't think there'd be a yammosk down there . . ."

"A Yuuzhan Vong war coordinator," Leia said for Jadak's benefit. "A creature that oversees the transformation."

"Even if there is," Han said, "it's fighting a losing battle. The planet's about to come apart."

Leia heard Allana sigh in disappointment. "I'm afraid the treasure is beyond our reach, sweetheart."

"If there was a treasure," Han said. Then, at Leia's nudge, he added: "I mean, by now the treasure's probably been engulfed by the Vong's biots."

"Chin up," Leia told Allana. "We found the hiding place. We just can't collect the treasure chest."

"They always do on *Castle Creep*," she said.

Jadak gazed out the viewport. "The Republic Group must have asked for help from the Antarian Rangers in setting up a kind of depot here. A storehouse of some sort."

"Whatever was here is long gone now."

One hand gripped on the yoke, Han was about to climb higher into Tandun III's tortured atmosphere when he stopped.

"What?" Jadak said quickly.

"We're getting a signal." Han's free hand made adjustments to the comm controls. "Very faint."

"A distress beacon?"

Han shook his head. "Just a beacon."

Jadak studied the comm screen. "It's transmitting on a covert frequency used by the Republic Group." He shot Han a look. "Whatever's down there has recognized the ship."

"No one could possibly be alive," Leia said.

"No one would have to be," Jadak said. "The installation could still be operational."

Leia looked from Han to Jadak and back again. "Are you two suggesting we go down there and find out?"

"Of course not," Jadak said. Then he glanced at Han. "Are we?"

Han considered it. "I'm not saying we are, but if we were, we'd be doing it for Amelia." He looked at Leia. "We owe it to her to at least check things out, don't we?"

"Yes!" Allana said.

Han centered himself at the controls. "Everybody strap in. This is going to be a rough entry."

Han leaned into the yoke and eased the throttle forward. The *Falcon* lowered her nose and dived deeper into the atmosphere, cutting through icy clouds, then dark embankments as the ship homed in on the beacon.

Powerful winds began to buffet the ship, and forked lightning split the sky to all sides. Han feathered the controls, as if encouraging the *Falcon* to pursue her own course through the chaos. In response, the YT veered and planed before leveling out over the tops of exotic trees, whose zigzagging branches seemed to reach out for her. In the distance, volcanoes belched fire and thick smoke into the already-sulfurous air and scoured the carpeted ground with rivers of bubbling lava. Hailstones and sheets of blowing rain sizzled against the *Falcon*'s nose and evaporated long before reaching the super-heated ground. From obstructed vents in the molten hill-sides flew boulders the size of small houses. Still closing on the beacon, the ship powered through gusts of vol-canic ash one moment, glowing cinders the next. In the west, Tandun III's primary hung like a blind eye.

"Now that's what I call seat-of-the-pants flying, Solo," Jadak said, just short of shouting. Having surren-dered the copilot's chair to Leia, he was in the naviga-tor's seat, lending what assistance he could. Allana, Poste, and C-3PO had returned to the main hold.

"Couldn't let you think my reputation was all hype," Han said over his shoulder.

"I know better now." Jadak glanced at the display. "The topographic sensors can't make sense of the ground cover."

"We shouldn't have deleted those old programs," Leia said.

"This isn't your first brush with a Vongformed world?" Jadak asked into Han's ear.

"We took on Coruscant," Han said, indicating Leia with a nod of his chin. "Flew the *Falcon* right into the old Senate building, in fact."

"Ship must have felt like she was returning home," Jadak said.

Han had his mouth open to reply when the comm

emitted a steady tone of recognition. Jadak checked the displays again, then extended his arm between Han and Leia, pointing to a forested rise in the distance.

"Signal's coming from that mesa."

Han studied the readouts in silence. "That might not be a mesa," he said at last. "Remember what Threepio said about ancient ruins? I think we're looking at one."

"Like the Massassi temples on Yavin Four," Leia said.

"Yavin," Jadak said. "Where the Emperor's weapon was destroyed, right?"

Han grinned. "The first weapon. You slept through that one, too."

"Guess I missed all the fun."

"Not this time."

Han overflew the mound, then banked through a broad return, bleeding velocity as the *Falcon* made a second approach. Beneath its thorned mantle, the structure could be seen as a four-faced, flat-topped pyramid surmounting a massive circular base. Surrounding it were dozens of smaller mounds, equally overgrown and apparently part of the ruin complex.

Han throttled the engines back and engaged the repulsorlifts, allowing the YT to hover directly above the structure. "The signal is coming from somewhere inside."

Jadak leaned toward the viewport. "There could be a landing grid under all that cover. Probably an old turbolift type."

"That's what I'm thinking," Han said. "Only one way to find out."

Han used the positioning jets to maneuver the *Falcon* off to one side of the structure, then lowered the ship until her belly was just about even with the flat summit.

"Solo, if you're thinking about using the quad laser—"

Han cut him off with a derisive snort. "I'm not planning on razing the place." His hand flicked switches on the console. "One of the first things I did when I got the *Falcon* was install a retractable blaster in the bow. It's gotten us out of a lot of tight fixes."

Han brought a targeting reticle onscreen and began triggering the weapon, each defoliating bolt revealing a narrow swath of the aged platform beneath the impenetrable tangle of thorn trees. A tedious procedure, the clearing took longer than expected, but in the end the BlasTech Ax-108 had bared a platform slightly larger than the ship itself. Han raised the *Falcon* and positioned it directly above the exposed area. Thousands of reddish-brown beetles were scurrying across the denuded platform as if in a daze.

"Now what?" he asked. "Magic words?"

Jadak tightened his lips. "Maybe we need to set her down."

"Worth a go."

His hand steady on the repulsorlift control, Han began to lower the ship a meter at a time. Fighting gusts of cinder-laden wind, the *Falcon* was fifteen meters from the platform when Leia shouted: "Stop!"

Schematics flashed on the display screen. "We're being scanned by some kind of authenticator," she said.

"It's trying to confirm that she's the *Stellar Envoy,*" Jadak said.

Han blew out his breath. "Then we're out of luck. Just since I've owned her, the registry transponder has been changed more times than I can count."

Leia's eyes were still fixed on the displays. "The authenticator isn't interrogating the transponder. It's trying to establish a physical match between the ship and the platform."

"A template," Han said. "We could set down, but the turbolift won't take us inside until the authenticator tells it to."

"Then why isn't it doing that?" Leia said. "The *Falcon* and the *Stellar Envoy* are the same ship."

"Key's the same," Han mused. "Maybe the lock's been changed."

"But they're not the same ships," Jadak said a moment later. "The *Envoy* was rebuilt with parts taken from an old YT-Thirteen-hundred-pea."

"And she's a couple hundred kilograms lighter," Han said. "But none of that should matter. The pea had an almost identical profile. The differences were all on the inside—cabin space instead of cargo space."

"*Almost* identical."

"I'm not about to start chopping pieces off her." Han pivoted the chair toward the hatch. "Threepio!"

"Coming, Captain Solo!"

By the time the droid had clattered into the cockpit, Han had called up side-by-side schematics of the *Falcon* and a vintage YT-1300p.

"What's wrong with this picture?" When C-3PO made his confusion evident, Han said: "The landing platform is only going to respond to a stock YT-Thirteen-hundred. How's the *Falcon* different?"

C-3PO fixed his photoreceptors on the schematics and responded almost immediately. "The escape pods, Captain Solo."

Han, Leia, and Jadak scrutinized the schematics.

"Can't be," Han said.

"The way they are positioned, the *Millennium Falcon*'s number one and number four escape pods exceed the YT-Thirteen-hundred template by three-point-two centimeters at each side. The difference is quite obvious, Captain Solo."

"He's right," Jadak said.

"Don't encourage him," Han muttered. But he managed to muster a grin when he looked at C-3PO. "Go below and use the manual override to drop the number one and number four pods. Activate their locators, in case there's time to retrieve them before we leave."

"Yes, Captain."

"Go with him, Poste."

"Brother, the duties I pull."

"That droid's a wonder," Jadak said when the two had hurried off.

"Keep it under your hat, but I don't know what I'd do without him."

Han maneuvered the *Falcon* to the rear edge of the cleared area in the hope that the escape pods would land short of the thorn trees. When two telltales on the console flashed, showing that the pods had been jettisoned, he took the ship forward and hovered directly over the center of the landing zone.

Below them an array of illuminators, configured to match the outline of the ship, came to brilliant life.

"We've been recognized!" Leia said.

But Han kept the *Falcon* right where she was.

"This facility's been sitting here for at least sixty years—twenty of them buried under Yuuzhan Vong foliage. We don't know what shape the lift is in." He glanced at Leia. "I want everyone out of the *Falcon* while I set her down."

chapter thirty-one

BY THE TIME THEY HURRIED DOWN THE BOARDING RAMP, the wind had picked up and the air was loud with the strident keening of sentinel beetles and the rumble of distant volcanic eruptions and thunder. Cinder, ash, and swollen drops of rain swirled around them as they ducked their heads and scampered to the edge of the platform. Thousands of noxious-smelling dweebit beetles ran riot at the edge of the barbed vegetation, and sparkbees swarmed overhead.

Buffeted by the gales but held in place by corrective bursts from the attitude jets, the *Falcon* descended into the illuminated outline. Racing around to the leading edge of the platform, Jadak placed himself in view of the cockpit and began semaphoring his arms to direct Han down.

Concern rose in Leia like a tide. She had limitless faith in Han's ability to pilot the ship to a safe landing, but conditions were rapidly deteriorating. The structure itself was trembling beneath her.

"Threepio!" When the droid turned to her, she gestured to what looked to be a safer spot at the extreme edge of the platform. "Take Amelia over there!"

The wind made off with C-3PO's response, but he obeyed, taking Allana by the hand and leading her away.

The *Falcon* was just five meters from touching down when the port braking jets flared out and that side of the ship crashed down onto the platform. From inside the structure came the sound of aged machinery grinding into service. Massive parts slid into place, cogs engaged, and the turbolift began to descend into the structure, taking with it the suddenly lopsided ship and everyone outside it. The *Falcon*'s repulsorlifts were still holding the starboard side of the ship aloft, a few meters above the deck of the turbolift, when all at once the lift tipped violently to the opposite side.

Leia was sliding toward the edge when she felt someone grasp her outstretched arm. Looking up, she saw Poste, flat on his back, with one hand clasped on an illuminator and the other vised around her wrist. At the same instant Leia heard Allana scream and twisted her head around in time to see the girl and C-3PO plummet over the edge of the tipped turbolift and land in foliage that had fastened itself to the pyramid's interior walls.

"Grandma!" Allana shouted.

Giving herself over to the Force, Leia scrambled to a squatting position. Still anchored by Poste's hand, she gazed down over the edge of the deck. C-3PO, who had fallen backward into the vegetation, had managed to find handholds among the branches. By landing on top of him Allana had missed being impaled on the thorns, but her grip on him was tenuous.

Scattered illuminators shone through the foliage, but their light wasn't strong enough to penetrate the gloom beneath the turbolift. The floor could be hundreds of meters below.

"Link your arms around Threepio's neck!" Leia said. "Threepio, don't let her fall! Just hold on! I'm coming for you."

But even as she said it she knew she couldn't reach them. Strength in the Force didn't confer superhuman abilities; those had to be earned through practice, and the distance to Allana was simply more than she could leap with any surety. She experienced the same lack of faith in herself that she had experienced at Coruscant three years back, when she had tried to hold the *Falcon* together during a difficult landing.

Her blood ran cold.

Had they come this far only to lose another member of their family?

Han's hands flew across the instrument console with the accuracy of a concert keyboardist. Functioning intermittently, the *Falcon*'s front left repulsorlifts had lifted the mandible from the tilted turbolift, so that the ship was now hovering almost parallel to it. But touching down was out of the question, since the *Falcon* could very well slide right over the edge.

Concealed behind vegetation that had crept into the structure, banks of illuminators affixed to the interior walls had winked on, adding to the luminosity provided by the *Falcon*'s running lights and floodlamps. Even so, Han couldn't see more than twenty meters in front of him. A moment earlier, Leia, Allana, C-3PO, and Poste had been visible off to port, but they were now out of view, and Han was worried that they had been knocked off their feet the way Jadak had. Where he had been flapping his arms like a man intent on flying, he was currently spread-eagled on the slanted deck, only his fingertips and bent toes keeping him in place.

Judging by the manner in which the lift had tipped, Han suspected that it had been designed to do so for some reason, which meant that the shaft that moved the device was probably snugged into a full-tilt joint beneath the deck. He considered his options, but only briefly. If he was wrong, the starboard undercarriage of the *Falcon* was about to take a pounding. But if he was correct, he could put things right.

He took a steadying breath. Then, fine-tuning the repulsorlift controls, he allowed the ship to come down hard on the starboard landing gear. Struck, the platform instantly leveled out, but when it did the *Falcon*'s drooping mandible was walloped in turn, knocking out the already crippled maneuvering jets.

Again, the ship slammed down onto her port side, and the turbolift deck tipped in the same direction.

Jadak had just gotten to his feet when the *Falcon*'s port mandible began to drop. Prepared for just such an eventuality, he raced for the ship and used the tilting motion of the lift to propel him up onto the blunt nose of the forward viewport, where he hung as if the cockpit had rammed into his midsection.

Han's expression was an amalgam of amazement, anger, and admiration.

"Can you release the mandible access hatch from the cockpit?" Jadak yelled with one cheek smooshed against the transparisteel.

Han all but crawled across the instrument panel to hear him better.

"Say again!"

"Spring the access hatch! I'll try to fix the jets!"

Han nodded, maneuvered back into the pilot's chair, and flipped a couple of switches mounted to the rear bulkhead. Jadak waited for Han's thumbs-up before dropping back to the tilted turbolift and allowing himself to slide beneath the belly of the ship. Arresting his motion at the forward landing gear, he clambered up onto the mandible, picked his way to the unlocked hatch, and disappeared inside.

Leia and Poste hadn't even tried to stand up, but they had taken advantage of the deck's brief fling with evenness to scramble to the illuminators that outlined the YT's saucer-shaped body. Leia had a perfect vantage on

Allana and C-3PO, who was now supporting the girl with one arm.

Deep in the Force, Leia fed stamina to Poste and strength to Allana and support to Han, whose fear for Leia and Allana's safety was eroding his ability to stabilize the ship. Like Leia, he was desperate to keep Allana from harm. But buried deep under his anguish he was thinking of *Jacen*.

Calling to Jacen for help.

For the first time, Leia realized the full depths of Han's pain and grief. And she seized on the source of Han's turmoil.

"Child, listen to me," she shouted to Allana. "Your father understood the beings who transformed this world. Long before you were born we were at war with them, but your father was a force for peace, and his powers were unmatched by those of any other Jedi. He wanted you to grow up in a galaxy free of war. He wanted to protect you at all costs. I want you to reach deep into yourself and find him. As painful as it is, you need to find your father. Stretch out with your feelings. Use the Force!"

Han tried to keep himself from worrying about Leia and Allana, but it was no use. Where only moments earlier his every action was a stroke of piloting genius, his hands were now fumbling with the repulsorlift and maneuvering jet controls. Another drop like the last one could send the *Falcon* over the edge, and probably take everyone with her.

Jadak was still inside the port mandible's maintenance nacelle, but whatever repair work he was doing had yet to show any effect.

Leia . . . Allana . . . Jacen . . .

And that was all it took.

Jadak's improvisation had borne results Han was unprepared for. The faulty pressors and jets came back on-line with enough vigor to seesaw the *Falcon*'s starboard side down against the turbolift deck. The deck dropped, as well, so far and so forcefully that it tipped past level, nearly launching Jadak from the maintenance nacelle. Recovering from his oversight, Han rocked the ship to port, sending Jadak back into the mandible and at the same time succeeding in leveling the turbolift. Quickly then, Han set the *Falcon* down squarely on the now-horizontal deck, which resumed a smooth descent into the interior of the pyramid.

Leaning as far as he could into the viewport, Han watched Jadak clamber out of the maintenance access hatch and pick his way to the tip of the mandible. Hooking his hands around the floodlamp bracket, he lowered himself over the edge and dropped to the deck.

Han scanned the area in front of the ship for Leia, Allana, C-3PO, or Poste, but saw no sign of them.

Clinging to separate illuminators, Leia and Poste found themselves rescued from a plunge into the abyss by a sudden lurching of the lift deck that came close to catapulting them clear over the seesawing *Falcon*. The deck had leveled out and was beginning to move steadily downward. But now Allana and C-3PO, still entwined in the spiked vegetation, were suddenly *above* the ship.

Racing to the edge of the turbolift, Leia stretched her arms toward Allana.

But it was Jacen she saw; not with her eyes, but in her mind's eye. Jacen, living on in his daughter. Leia's heart swelled, and tears streamed from her eyes.

Drooping away from the structure's inner wall, the exotic foliage seemed to reach out for her and for the *Falcon*. At the same time, Allana and C-3PO extricated themselves from the thorns and all but walked through the air to the front area of the deck, carried there by the

Force. Leia raced for her granddaughter and gathered her up in her arms.

Allana's voice was tiny and tentative when she spoke. "I shouldn't have been able to do that, right?"

"Wrong," Leia said, wiping tears from her cheeks. "You were born to do that."

With Poste, Jadak, and C-3PO in tow, Leia and Allana were just rounding the starboard mandible when Han came barreling down the boarding ramp, eyes wide and mouth ajar in apprehension. On seeing them, his entire expression changed. He rushed forward to hug them, and they remained in an embrace for the rest of the time it took the turbolift to descend.

Additional illuminators had flared, filling the air with electrical static and bathing the cavernous landing bay in eerie light. The keening of sentinel beetles was distant, but sparkbees bombinated overhead and the barbed undergrowth that had infiltrated the structure was crawling with larval insects and newts the color of arterial blood. Worse, the ancient floor was shaking in concert with Tandun III itself.

Already formulating an escape plan, Han gazed up at the opening in the roof. "We can't stay down there. This whole place could collapse."

"Just a quick look around," Jadak said.

Allana stopped gnawing at her fingernails long enough to give Han a fervent nod.

Stepping from the lift, the six of them headed for a corbeled archway that marked the entrance to an even more brightly lighted chamber. Last in line, C-3PO slowed his pace, cocking his head to one side, as if in response to something his audio pickups had monitored, then hastening to catch up with the others.

*   *   *

"I recognize this," Leia said loudly enough to be heard over the thunderclaps reverberating in the vast chamber. "It was the emblem of the Republic."

Hung on brackets affixed to the ancient block wall, the gleaming three-meter-tall by three-meter-wide emblem was an eight-rayed stellar symbol, centered in a circle whose circumference was made up of dashed lines. Other than a stack of empty storage crates, it was the only thing in the room.

Leia reached out to caress the luminous metal. "An emblem identical to this hung in the Hall of Justice on Alderaan—up until Palpatine's declaration—"

"But this is not that one," a voice said from behind them.

Han had his blaster out even before he completed his turn; Leia, her lightsaber, its shimmering blade raised in front of her. Approaching them were Lestra Oxic and his assistant Koi Quire, surrounded by a quartet of armed bodyguards, two of whom were the ship thieves from Vaced.

"Lestra!" Leia said. "You tracked us."

"Actually, my dear, it was the owner of the rental shop on Vaced. He has already reported the theft of his slicer droid to the authorities."

"So you're here to see whether we want a lawyer," Jadak said.

Oxic motioned for his henchmen to holster their blasters, then inclined his head to Jadak. "A pleasure to finally meet you, Captain, after all these years."

"Don't expect me to say the same."

Oxic's eyebrows arched. "No. Well, perhaps you'll change your mind once you know the full story."

Jadak looked at Koi Quire. "What happened, insurance game didn't pay enough?"

"Lovely to see you again, as well," Quire said, smiling lightly. "Does your offer to show me around still stand?"

"It might."

Leia deactivated her lightsaber and hooked it to her belt. "Let's see if you can change all our minds, Lestra."

Oxic grinned and gestured to the emblem. "You're gazing on a piece of history that hasn't been seen for eighty standard years. Princess Leia was correct in recognizing this as the emblem of the Republic, but this one"—he stepped toward it, raising his hand reverently to touch it—"this one once adorned the podium of the Senate Rotunda. Cast of pure aurodium, orichalum, and Coruscanthium, and detailed with half a dozen equally precious metals and alloys, it was known as the Insignia of Unity. But seven years into the reign of then–Supreme Chancellor Palpatine, it was stolen from the Senate during a much-needed renovation of the Rotunda and replaced with a counterfeit."

Oxic cast a glance at Jadak. "Stolen, Captain Jadak, by members of the Republic Group, which had it shipped here for safe storage until such time as it would be needed to—"

"Restore Republic honor to the galaxy."

Oxic grinned broadly. "Precisely, Captain. A symbol meant to rouse and reawaken those who had allowed themselves to fall under the sway of the Emperor." He paused briefly. "Well, we all know that even the healthiest of seedlings don't always bear fruit. The replacement emblem was discovered to be a counterfeit during restoration work occasioned by General Grievous's attack on Coruscant. No attempt was ever launched to uncover the original. The Emperor didn't care, and most of the Senate was beyond caring by that point. But collectors of Republicana art and sculpture have been combing the galaxy for it ever since." He swung back to face it. "And here it is at last."

Oxic fell silent while a powerful tremor shook the room. Han holstered his blaster, but pulled Leia and Allana close to him.

"I've been chasing it for almost fifty years," he said, almost as if to himself. "It's the reason you weren't left to flatline in the Nar Shaddaa facility to which you were medevaced after your collision there, Captain Jadak." He glanced over his shoulder. "You're certainly entitled to a finder's fee for leading me here. But let us face facts: you never knew precisely what you were chasing—whether it was riches beyond your imaginings or simply a dream—and, more important, the *Millennium Falcon* turns out to have been the real key to unlocking this particular treasure chest.

"Therefore, I lay claim to it. I've known from the start what I was pursuing. And my expenditures in time, energy, and credits far exceed the sum total the rest of you have contributed."

From his jacket pocket, Oxic drew a small cylindrical probe. Applying the tester's bulbous scanner to the most accessible part of the emblem, he studied the readout. "Its worth in precious metals is of little import," he said. "It is the piece itself, soon to be the prize in my collection. To the envy of all who have sought it—"

Eyes riveted to the tool's small display screen, he cut himself off. "This can't be right," he said in a shaky voice. More roughly, he pressed the scanner to another section of the emblem. "This can't be right!" His hands were trembling now, and the motion had nothing to do with Tandun III's quakes, which were increasing in both duration and severity.

"This can't be right!" Oxic slashed at the emblem, as if the tester had become a knife, then staggered backward with his hands pressed to his head, Koi Quire and the Nautolan ship thief hurrying in to prevent him from keeling over onto the floor.

Without looking at Leia, Han said, "Did I ever tell you about the time Chewbacca and I were in the treasure vaults of—"

"Xim the Despot," she completed. "On Dellalt. I'm saving that little tale for chapter seven of my book."

He frowned at her. "Book?"

"*The Crook, the Wook, and Me.* Volume two of my memoirs."

Han's jaw dropped a little more. "Who's a crook?"

Throwing the tester to the floor, Oxic shucked out of the Nautolan's grip and stood to his full and impressive height. "It's a fake! A counterfeit!" Shuffling to the wall, he supported himself with one arm and began to sob. "Not even worth the metals it was forged from!"

The floor shook again, more violently.

Oxic composed himself and swung around to face Koi Quire, his red-rimmed eyes ablaze. "Obviously the Republic Group never realized that they had spirited a fake from the Rotunda. That suggests that the authentic old Republic emblem had to have disappeared earlier—perhaps at the earliest phase of the Rotunda's renovation." He locked eyes with Quire. "The name of the construction firm hired to oversee the renovation!"

"Naffiff Brothers," she said.

Oxic balled his fists. "Sils Naffiff, yes . . . now wealthy beyond all expectation. He could have fabricated the counterfeit even before the renovation commenced!" His eyes found Jadak. "Or might the actual emblem have been stolen by the person to whom you were to deliver the *Stellar Envoy*?"

"An Antarian Ranger," Jadak said.

"Yes, yes, I wouldn't put it past one of those people to plunder a treasure!"

"You'd be better off figuring this out somewhere else, counselor," Han said.

The strongest quake yet shook the room, knocking Oxic and Quire off their feet and vibrating the emblem's brackets loose from the wall. Jadak was just helping

Quire up when the emblem tipped to the floor and smashed to countless pieces.

"A just fate!" Oxic said in disgust, then whirled on Jadak and Poste. "What would you two say to throwing in with us to continue the search? I'll pay you well. And Jadak—what else is there for you?"

Jadak glanced at Quire, who smiled. "I'm in," he said.

"Me, too," Poste said.

"I want to go," Allana started to say, when Leia interrupted.

"Don't you even think about it, kiddo. I'm afraid you're stuck with us."

The lot of them raced into the landing bay, where the light had taken on a different quality. Han looked up to see a horde of Yuuzhan Vong gricha attempting to seal the lift shaft.

"The *Falcon* will never fit through that," Oxic said. "There's room in my yacht for all of you, Captain Solo."

Han glanced at the sleek yacht that had followed the *Falcon* in, then leveled a look at Oxic. "Leave her here?"

"Has it occurred to you that the *Falcon* is meant to be entombed here? The ship's final mission executed? Its destiny fulfilled?"

Han's silence was momentary. "She'll fulfill her destiny when I say so!"

Oxic nodded in respect. "Suit yourselves. Princess Leia, Amelia, See-Threepio . . . I hope we meet again under more favorable circumstances."

Han extended his hand to Jadak. "Your rucksacks are aboard the *Falcon*."

"I figure we can make do without them."

"Stay out of trouble, Captain," Han said.

"You, too, Captain."

"And grow up, will ya," Han said as Jadak and Poste were heading for Oxic's ship. "Start acting your age."

"I'll give it a try on one condition."

"What's that?"

"You agree to take good care of my ship."

The Solos bolted up the *Falcon*'s boarding ramp, exhorting C-3PO to pick up the pace. Han skidded to a halt in the ring corridor and swung to Leia. "You and Threepio are going to have to raise her. Hot-scramble!"

Her eyes searched his face.

"I'll be up top. She's not sporting quad lasers for nothing."

Leia took her lower lip between her teeth and nodded.

"I know," Han said as C-3PO entered the corridor. "It's going to be tight. Rotate her around a hundred eighty degrees and bring her nose up. I'll do the rest. Got it, Threepio?"

"Got it, Captain Solo."

Han smiled. "And make sure nothing happens to her."

"Not a scratch," Leia said as Han ducked into the ladderwell.

Leia had the repulsorlifts quick-started by the time Han harnessed into the high-backed chair and clamped his hands on the twin firing grips. Outside, the walls of the structure were heaving and pieces of the landing platform roof were piling up on the *Falcon*'s hull. Before too long the entire roof would come down, and the ship would be buried. Han watched Oxic's snazzy yacht perform an exacting rotation and ascend through the narrowed opening.

"Raising ship," Leia told Han through the earpiece of his intercom rig.

Levitating from the turbolift deck, the *Falcon* turned and trimmed. The bow-maneuvering jets fired, the mandibles came up, and Han was waiting.

The quads chugged and a hail of crimson bolts made short work of the gricha's roofing efforts.

"Now, Leia!"

Great tangles of vegetation peeled from the walls and huge stones plummeted, ricocheting off the ship's armor plate. Wearing a beard of Yuuzhan Vong thorn tree, the *Falcon* shot up and out of the ancient structure, then rose into the crazed sky on a pillar of blinding energy.

Oxic's yacht was veering to starboard to avoid a flight of airborne boulders when the *Falcon* overtook it and raced for space at top speed. By then Han had dashed into the cockpit and strapped into the navigator's chair alongside Allana. Caught in Tandun III's death throes, the *Falcon* bucked like a marble in a juice blender.

"Your chair, Captain Solo," C-3PO said, rising.

Han clapped him on the shoulder. "Stay put, Goldenrod. You deserve to ride in the front for a change."

"Are we gonna escape?" Allana asked, without evident apprehension.

" 'Course we are," Han said, mussing her hair. "Just like on that HoloNet show."

Impassive stars winked into existence, losing their dazzle the higher the *Falcon* climbed. When they had attained a safe distance from the planet, Leia banked through a broad turn that left them facing Tandun III, cracked like an egg about to release a creature made of pure fire.

Then in unsettling silence, the planet simply came undone, flaring like a star for a fleeting moment before hurling massive chunks of itself into the void. Of what almost seemed its own volition, the *Falcon* reared up as the shock wave whirled out into the night.

A telltale light flashed on the instrument panel, and Leia glanced at the displays.

"Port landing jets and repulsors are out."

Standing up, Han pounded his fist against the control panel above Allana's head, and the telltale light blinked out.

"Back online," Leia said, directing a smile over her shoulder.

Han sighed. "I'm gonna have to get that landing jet fixed."

chapter thirty-two

"THIS LEVER CONTROLS THE ENGINES THE *FALCON* uses to travel through realspace," Han said. "This one takes the ship into hyperspace, after the navicomputer here figures out when it's safe for the ship to jump to lightspeed."

"And these?" Allana asked, pointing to a pair of trackball controllers just left of the central display monitor.

"Hopefully, you'll never have to touch those. They control the laser cannons."

It was just the two of them in the cockpit, Han in the pilot's chair and Allana seated on his knee. Leia was in the main hold trying to reach Luke on the comm and C-3PO was crating up the slicer droid for shipment back to Vaced. Free to pursue her own course, the *Falcon* was purring through interstellar space.

"Can I steer?"

Han stood her at the yoke. "Go ahead."

Allana experimented with the instruments. "Can I make it go faster?"

"Can you reach the throttle?"

She stretched out her right hand and made a sound of effort. "Got it."

"Wow! Not so fast," Han laughed, thankful he had the inertial compensator dialed to full.

Surrendering the yoke, she climbed into the copilot's chair.

"I think you're going to be a terrific pilot," Han told her.

"Like Aunt Jaina?"

"Just like Aunt Jaina."

Allana inclined her head to one side. "Is she going to marry Jag?"

Han smiled. "I don't know. We'll have to ask her when we see her."

"Did your grandpa teach you how to pilot a starship?"

"No." Han gave his head a pensive shake. "I didn't know my grandfather."

"We could go look for him."

He laughed. "I think I've had my fill of quests for the time being."

"Why?"

"You're full of questions," Han said, pivoting to face her. "But I've got one for you. Do you want to visit your mom? We're not too far from the Hapes Consortium right now. A quick hyperspace jump and we're there."

Allana smiled. "I want to see my mother." She looked up at Han. "And if Mom says it's okay, I want to stay with you and Grandma some more."

"You're sure?"

Allana nodded. "Sure."

"You know it's not always going to be a treasure hunt. Sometimes Grandma and I just sit around doing nothing."

"I can do that," she assured him. "Anyway, how do you know another adventure won't happen?"

Han had his mouth open to respond when Leia entered the cockpit, C-3PO a step behind her. Her look told him that she had big news.

"What?"

"The GA government is planning to file criminal charges against Luke."

"Charges? What's he done this time?"

Leia's gaze shifted briefly and deliberately to Allana. "Dereliction of duty."

Han nodded slowly. So Daala's government had decided to blame Luke for having allowed Jacen to slip to the dark side. *Will it never end?*

"How are the Jedi taking it?" he asked.

"Not too seriously."

"Maybe they're right. Daala could be doing this because she *has* to, not because she wants to."

Leia gave her head a quick shake. "He's going to need our help, Han."

Han snorted. "Of course he is."

Allana swung to C-3PO. "Threepio, we're going to help rescue Master Luke!"

"Oh, dear. Not again."

Han and Leia laughed.

"Everyone strap in," Han said. "You never know what kind of ride we're in for."

The *Millennium Falcon* responded to his call for power with an enthusiastic leap. Tasked with heading for Coruscant and raring to go, the old but venerable YT-1300 gathered her strength for the jump to lightspeed, then streaked into hyperspace and vanished from sight.

Read on for an excerpt from
Star Wars: Darth Bane: Dynasty of Evil
by Drew Karpyshyn

Published by Del Rey

". . . adhering to the rules established through the procedures outlined in the preceding, as well as all subsequent, articles. Our sixth demand stipulates that a body of . . ."

Medd Tandar rubbed a long-fingered hand across the pronounced frontal ridge of his tall, conical cranium, hoping to massage away the looming headache that had been building over the last twenty minutes.

Gelba, the being he had come to the planet of Doan to negotiate with, paused in the reading of her petition to ask, "Something wrong, Master Jedi?"

"I am not a Master," the Cerean reminded the self-appointed leader of the rebels. "I am only a Jedi Knight." With a sigh he dropped his hand. After a moment's pause he forced himself to add, "I'm fine. Please continue."

With a curt nod, Gelba resumed with her seemingly endless list of ultimatums. "Our sixth demand stipulates that a body of elected representatives from the mining caste be given absolute jurisdiction over the following eleven matters: One, the determination of wages in accordance with galactic standards. Two, the establishment of a weekly standard of hours any given employee can be ordered to work. Three, an approved list of safety apparel to be provided by . . ."

The short, muscular human woman droned on, her voice echoing strangely off the irregular walls of the underground cave. The other miners in attendance—three human men and two women crowding close to Gelba— were seemingly transfixed by her words. Medd couldn't help but think that, should their tools ever fail, the miners could simply use their leader's voice to cut through the stone.

Officially, Medd was here to try to end the violence between the rebels and the royal family. Like all Cereans, he possessed a binary brain structure, allowing him to simultaneously process both sides of a conflict. Theoretically, this made him an ideal candidate to mediate and resolve complex political situations such as the one that had developed on this small mining world. In practice, however, he was discovering that playing the part of a diplomat was far more trying than he had first imagined.

Located on the Outer Rim, Doan was an ugly, brown ball of rock. More than 80 percent of the planetary landmass had been converted into massive strip-mining operations. Even from space, the disfigurement of the world was immediately apparent. Furrows five kilometers wide and hundreds of kilometers long crisscrossed the torn landscape like indelible scars. Great quarries hewn from the bedrock descended hundreds of meters deep, irreparable pockmarks on the face of the planet.

From within the smog-filled atmosphere, the ceaseless activity of the gigantic machines was visible. Excavation equipment scurried back and forth like oversized insects, digging and churning up the dirt. Towering drilling rigs stood on mechanical legs, tunneling to previously unplumbed depths. Gigantic hovering freighters cast shadows that blotted out the pale sun as they waited patiently for their cavernous cargo holds to be filled with dirt, dust, and pulverized stone.

Scattered across the planet were a handful of five-kilometer-tall columns of irregular, dark brown stone several hundred meters in diameter. They jutted up from the ravaged landscape like fingers reaching for the sky. The flat plateaus atop these natural pillars were covered by assemblages of mansions, castles, and palaces overlooking the environmental wreckage below.

The rare mineral deposits and rampant mining on Doan had turned the small planet into a very wealthy world. That wealth, however, was concentrated almost exclusively in the hands of the nobility, who dwelled in the exclusive estates that towered above the rest of the planet. Most of the populace was made up of Doan society's lower castes, beings condemned to spend their lives engaged in constant physical labor or employed in menial service positions with no chance of advancement.

These were the beings Gelba represented. Unlike the elite, they made their homes down on the planet's surface in tiny makeshift huts surrounded by the open pits and furrows, or in small caverns tunneled down into the rocky ground. Medd had been given a small taste of their life the instant he stepped from the climate-controlled confines of his shuttle. A wall of oppressive heat thrown up from the barren, sun-scorched ground had enveloped him. He'd quickly wrapped a swatch of cloth around his head, covering his nose and mouth to guard against the swirling clouds of dust that threatened to choke the air from his lungs.

The man Gelba had sent to greet him also had his face covered, making communication all the more difficult amid the rumbling of the mining machines. Fortunately, there was no need to speak as his guide led him across the facility: the Jedi had simply gawked at the sheer scope of the environmental damage.

They had continued in silence until reaching a small, rough-hewn tunnel. Medd had to crouch to avoid scraping his head on the jagged ceiling. The tunnel went for several hundred meters, sloping gently downward until it emerged in a large natural chamber lit by glow lamps.

Tool marks scored the walls and floor. The cavern had been stripped of any valuable mineral deposits long before; all that remained were dozens of irregular rock formations rising up from the uneven floor, some less than a meter high, others stretching up to the ceiling a full ten meters above. They might have been beautiful had they not all been the exact same shade of dull brown that dominated Doan's surface.

The makeshift rebel headquarters was unfurnished, but the high ceiling allowed the Cerean to finally stand up straight. More important, the underground chamber offered some small refuge from the heat, dust, and noise of the surface, enabling them all to remove the muffling cloth covering their faces. Given the shrillness of Gelba's voice, Medd was debating if this was entirely a good thing.

"Our next demand is the immediate abolition of the royal family, and the surrender of all its estates to the elected representatives specified in item three of section five, subsection C. Furthermore, fines and penalties shall be levied against—"

"Please stop," Medd said, holding up a hand. Mercifully, Gelba honored his request. "As I explained to you before, the Jedi Council can do nothing to grant your demands. I am not here to eliminate the royal family. I am only here to offer my services as a mediator in the negotiations between your group and the Doan nobility."

"They refuse to negotiate with us!" one of the miners shouted.

"Can you blame them?" Medd countered. "You killed the crown prince."

"That was a mistake," Gelba said. "We didn't mean to destroy his airspeeder. We only wanted to force it into an emergency landing. We were trying to capture him alive."

"Your intentions are irrelevant now," Medd told her, keeping his voice calm and even. "By killing the heir to the throne, you brought the wrath of the royal family down on you."

"Are you defending their actions?" Gelba demanded. "They hunt my people like animals! They imprison us without trial! They torture us for information, and execute us if we resist! Now even the Jedi turn a blind eye to our suffering. You're no better than the Galactic Senate!"

Medd understood the miners' frustration. Doan had been a member of the Republic for centuries, but there had been no serious efforts by the Republic Senate or any governing body to address the injustices of their societal structure. Comprising millions of member worlds, each with its own unique traditions and systems of government, the Republic had adopted a policy of noninterference except in the most extreme cases.

Officially, idealists condemned the lack of a democratic government on Doan. But historically, the population had always been granted the basic necessities of life: food, shelter, freedom from slavery, and even legal recourse in cases where a noble abused the privileges of rank. While the rich on Doan undoubtedly exploited the poor, there were many other worlds where the situation was much, much worse.

However, the reluctance of the Senate to become involved had not stopped the efforts of those who sought to change the status quo. Over the last decade, a movement demanding political and social equality had sprung up among the lower castes. Naturally, there was resistance from the nobility, and recently the tension had escalated into violence, culminating in the assassination of the Doan crown prince nearly three standard months earlier.

In response, the king had declared a state of martial law. Since then, there had been a steady stream of troubling reports supporting Gelba's accusations. Yet galactic sympathy for the rebels was slow to build. Many in the Senate saw them as terrorists, and as much as Medd sympathized with their plight, he was unable to act without Senate authority.

The Jedi were legally bound by galactic law to remain neutral in all civil wars and internal power struggles, unless the violence threatened to spread to other Republic worlds. All the experts agreed that there was little chance of that happening.

"What is being done to your people is wrong," Medd agreed, choosing his words carefully. "I will do what I can to convince the king to stop his persecution of your people. But I cannot promise anything."

"Then why are you here?" Gelba demanded.

Medd hesitated. In the end, he decided that straight-forward truth was the only recourse. "A few weeks ago one of your teams dug up a small tomb."

"Doan is covered with old tombs," Gelba replied. "Centuries ago we used to bury our dead . . . back before the nobility decided they would dig up the whole planet."

"There was a small cache of artifacts inside the tomb," Medd continued. "An amulet. A ring. Some old parchment scrolls."

"Anything we dig up belongs to us!" one of the miners shouted angrily.

"It's one of our oldest laws," Gelba confirmed. "Even the royal family knows better than to try and violate it."

"My Master believes those artifacts may be touched by the dark side," Medd said. "I must bring them back to our Temple on Coruscant for safekeeping."

Gelba glared at him with narrowed eyes, but didn't speak.

"We will pay you, of course," Medd added.

"You Jedi portray yourselves as guardians," Gelba said. "Champions of the weak and downtrodden. But you care more about a handful of gold trinkets than you do about the lives of men and women who are suffering."

"I will try to help you," Medd promised. "I will speak to the king on your behalf. But first I must have those—"

He stopped abruptly, the echo of his words still hanging in the cavern. *Something's wrong.* There was a sudden sickness in the pit of his stomach, a sense of impending danger.

"What?" Gelba demanded. "What is it?"

A disturbance in the Force, Medd thought, his hand dropping to the lightsaber on his belt. "Somebody's coming."

"Impossible. The sentries at the tunnel outside would have—ungh!"

Gelba's words were cut off by the unmistakable sound of a blaster's retort. She staggered back and fell to the ground, a smoking hole in her chest. With cries of alarm the other miners scattered, scrambling for cover behind the rock formations that filled the cavern. Two of them didn't make it, felled by deadly accurate shots that took them right between the shoulder blades.

Medd held his ground, igniting his lightsaber and peering into the shadows that lined the walls of the cave. Unable to pierce the darkness with his eyes, he opened himself to the Force—and staggered back as if he had been punched in the stomach.

Normally, the Force washed over him like a warm bath of white light, strengthening him, centering him. This time, however, it struck him like a frozen fist in the gut.

Another blaster bolt whistled by his ear. Dropping to his knees, Medd crawled to cover behind the nearest rock formation, bewildered and confused. As a Jedi, he had trained his entire life to transform himself into a servant of the Force. He had learned to let the light side flow through him, empowering him, enhancing his physical senses, guiding his thoughts and actions. Now the very source of his power had seemingly betrayed him.

He could hear blaster bolts ricocheting throughout

the chamber as the miners returned fire against their unseen opponent, but he shut out the sounds of battle. He
didn't understand what had happened to him; he only
knew he had to find some way to fight it.

Panting, the Jedi silently recited the first lines of the
Jedi Code, struggling to regain his composure. *There is
no emotion; there is peace.* The mantra of his Order allowed him to bring his breathing under control. A few
seconds later he felt composed enough to reach out carefully to try to touch the Force once more.

Instead of peace and serenity, he felt only anger and
hatred. Instinctively, his mind recoiled, and Medd realized what had happened. Somehow the power he was
drawing on had been tainted by the dark side, corrupted
and poisoned.

He still couldn't explain it, but now he at least knew
how to try to resist the effects. Blocking out his fear, the
Jedi allowed the Force to flow through him once more in
the faintest, guarded trickle. As he did so, he focused his
mind on cleansing it of the impurities that had overwhelmed his senses. Slowly, he felt the power of the light
side washing over him . . . though it was far less than
what he was used to.

Stepping out from behind the rocks, he called out in a
loud voice, "Show yourself!"

A blaster bolt ripped from the darkness toward him.
At the last second he deflected it with his lightsaber,
sending it off harmlessly into the corner—a technique he
had mastered years ago while still a Padawan.

Too close, he thought to himself. *You're slow, hesi-
tant. Trust in the Force.*

The power of the Force enveloped him, but something about it still felt wrong. Its strength flickered and
ebbed, like a static-filled transmission. Something—or
someone—was disrupting his ability to focus. A dark
veil had fallen across his consciousness, interfering with

his ability to draw upon the Force. For a Jedi there was nothing more terrifying, but Medd had no intention of retreating.

"Leave the miners alone," he called out, his voice betraying none of the uncertainty he felt. "Show yourself and face me!"

From the far corner of the room a young Iktotchi woman stepped forth, holding a blaster pistol in each hand. She was clad in a simple black cloak, but she had thrown her hood back to reveal the downward-curving horns that protruded from the sides of her head and tapered to a sharp point just above her shoulders. Her reddish skin was accentuated by black tattoos on her chin—four sharp, thin lines extending like fangs from her lower lip.

"The miners are dead," she told him. There was something cruel in her voice, as if she was taunting him with the knowledge.

Gingerly using the Force to extend his awareness, Medd realized it was true. As if peering through an obscuring haze, he could just manage to see the bodies of the miners strewn about the chamber, each branded by a lethal shot to the head or chest. In the few seconds it had taken him to collect himself, she had slain them all.

"You're an assassin," he surmised. "Sent by the royal family to kill the rebel leaders."

She tilted her head in acknowledgment, and opened her mouth as if she was about to speak. Then, without warning, she fired another round of blaster bolts at him.

The ruse nearly worked. With the Force flowing through him he should have sensed her deception long before she acted, but whatever power was obscuring his ability to touch the light side had left him vulnerable.

Instead of trying to deflect the bolts a second time, Medd threw himself to the side, landing hard on the ground.

You're as clumsy as a youngling, he chided himself as he scrambled back to his feet.

Unwilling to expose himself to another barrage, he thrust out his free hand, palm facing out. Using the Force, he yanked the weapons from his enemy's grasp. The effort sent a searing bolt of pain through the entire length of his head, causing him to wince and take a half step back. But the blasters sailed through the air and landed harmlessly on the ground beside him.

To his surprise, the assassin seemed unconcerned. Could she sense his fear and uncertainty? The Iktochi were known to have limited precognitive abilities; it was said they could use the Force to see glimpses of the future. Some even claimed they were telepathic. Was it possible that she was somehow using her abilities to disrupt his connection to the Force?

"If you surrender, I will promise you a fair trial," Medd told her, trying to project an image of absolute confidence and self-assurance.

She smiled at him, revealing sharp, pointed teeth. "There will be no trial."

The Iktochi threw herself into a back handspring, her robe fluttering as she flipped out of view behind the cover of a thick stone outcropping. At the same instant, one of the blasters at Medd's feet beeped sharply.

The Jedi had thought he had disarmed his foe, but instead he had fallen into her well-laid trap. He had just enough time to register that the power cell had been set to overload before it detonated. With his last thought he tried to call upon the Force to shield him from the blast, but he was unable to pierce the debilitating fog that clouded his mind. He felt nothing but fear, anger, and hatred.

As the explosion ended his life, Medd finally understood the true horror of the dark side.

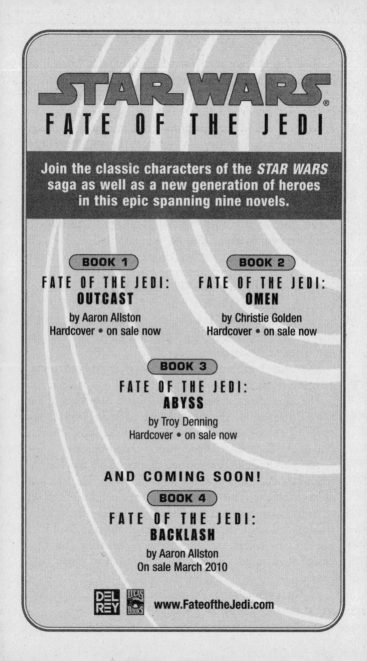